IMMORTAL

Krishna Udayasankar is the author of the bestselling Aryavarta Chronicles series (*Govinda*, *Kaurava* and *Kurukshetra*), and *3* – a novel based on the founding myth of Singapore. She is also the author of *Objects of Affection*, a full-length collection of prose-poems and the co-editor of *Body Boundaries: The Etiquette Anthology of Women's Writing*. Her short fiction and poetry feature in many print and online anthologies.

Krishna holds an undergraduate degree in law and a PhD in strategic management. She lives in Singapore with her family, which includes three bookish canine-children, Boozo, Zana and Maya, who are sometimes to be found at her laptop, trying to make her writing better.

IMMORTAL

KRISHNA UDAYASANKAR

First published in 2016 by Hachette India
(Registered name: Hachette Book Publishing India Pvt. Ltd)
An Hachette UK company
www.hachetteindia.com

1

Copyright © 2016 Krishna Udayasankar

Krishna Udayasankar asserts the moral right to be identified
as the author of this work.

Author photo on cover by Alvin Pang

All rights reserved. No part of the publication may be reproduced, stored
in a retrieval system (including but not limited to computers, disks, external
drives, electronic or digital devices, e-readers, websites), or transmitted
in any form or by any means (including but not limited to cyclostyling,
photocopying, docutech or other reprographic reproductions, mechanical,
recording, electronic, digital versions) without the prior written permission
of the publisher, nor be otherwise circulated in any form of binding or cover
other than that in which it is published and without a similar condition being
imposed on the subsequent purchaser.

This is a work of fiction. Any resemblance to real persons, living or dead, or
actual events or locales is purely coincidental.

ISBN 978-93-5195-008-0

Hachette Book Publishing India Pvt. Ltd
4th/5th Floors, Corporate Centre,
Plot No. 94, Sector 44, Gurgaon 122003, India

Typeset in Bembo Std 11.5/15.7
by InoSoft Systems Noida

Printed and bound in India by Manipal Technologies Ltd, Manipal

For
J, my rock, without whom I would never have found my long-lost words;
P, who once saw a man in a bookstore;
and
A, because no one should ever have to hide what you hid.

Not non-existence nor existence was then,
There was no realm of air, no sky beyond. What
Dimensions held it and where? To what purpose?
Was there water, unfathomable water?

Death was not then, nor was there deathlessness, nor
Cognition of night and day. That One then was,
The breathless, breathing without air by its own
Nature, self-sustaining; There was no other.

Darkness there was, concealed within its darkness.
A causeless dissolution, a formless void,
Lightless water. The One took sentience, from that
Contemplation, all Creation came to be.

At first, arose in the One the Desire
to be — This was the primeval seed-thought. That
thus are tied existence and inexistence
Those seers inquiring with heart's reason do know.

Transverse radiance filled all there was; what then
Was above and what was below? From seed-thought
Then was potential, that was existence,
Forces of causality and consequence.

Who truly knows and who can declare why the
World was created and what caused Creation?
The gods themselves came after that beginning,
Who then knows why all becoming came to be?

That One, the primordial being, whether
Sustaining all there is or not, that
Pervasive presiding principle, perhaps
That verily knows or perhaps that knows not.

Ṛg Veda 10:129

Three kilometres south of Lake Titicaca, Bolivia

The skull grinned.

It did not, the man knew, *truly* grin, for he had no faith in the local lore that the moonlit ruins were haunted: by old gods, as some said, or by new ghosts. He was nevertheless glad to encourage the tales, for they kept inquisitive residents at bay. As for tourists – between the nearby wonders of Lake Titicaca and the prehistoric city of Tiwanaku, complete with tales of human sacrifice, no one cared for the unimpressive heaps of rubble that had once formed a lesser settlement of the pre-Incan empire.

Like Tiwanaku, these ruins were significantly subterranean, the underground tunnels and hollows a perfect hideout from which the *pandillero* – gangster – could run his death-dealing operations in drugs, arms and antiquities; his small part of a multi-billion dollar empire. Strangers such as the person to whom the shining skull had once belonged, who were unfortunate enough to blunder their way in here, became without exception part of the non-attractions of the area.

The man kicked the skull aside as he walked ahead. It shattered against the ancient stone wall, shards of bone mingling with the wood and sawdust debris of used crates.

No loss, he concluded, for it would soon be replaced. Yet another ill-fated adventurer had wandered where he ought not to have. He turned to the ubiquitous armed bodyguard. 'Are you sure about this?'

'Absolutely, *jefe*,' the bodyguard replied. 'We slit his skin and threw him into the old tunnel for the rats to eat alive, like we always do. Didn't think twice about it. But…' He stopped and shrugged his shoulders for lack of words. Then, switching on the powerful torch he carried, he began to lead his employer down a narrow flight of stairs.

The stench of slowly decomposing flesh and maggot-waste stung the men the moment they entered the narrow confines of the stairway. Even the hardened bodyguard, who made his way into the stone bowels of the ruins many times a week, screwed up his nose. The *pandillero*, however, showed no such weakness. He moved ahead, resolute, till they stood in front of a new, nevertheless rotted wooden door. The bodyguard opened the door, revealing a space that first appeared to be a room but was actually a large tunnel that no one had cared to explore to its full reaches. The immediate space was also the obvious source of the inhuman odour: A mass of flesh in the rough shape of a man wiggled in lifeless animation as the rats that had burrowed their way into the cadaver reacted to the sudden presence of light.

The bodyguard reached instinctively for his gun as a rodent crept out of the corpse's mouth and ran towards the open door, but his chief saved him the trouble, stamping down on the creature with quick reflexes. 'Who is this?' he asked, gesturing to the rat-feast before them.

'The *tombo* you asked us to deal with,' the bodyguard replied. With a cold chuckle he added, 'No one will miss an honest cop. It was when we came to dump him in here, three days ago, that we chanced upon the other man...still alive. His wounds had already healed, and...and...I know it sounds impossible, *jefe*, but he had killed many rats, and the rest wouldn't go near him. And he was just sitting there, like a lazy fisherman by the lake... We pulled him out and brought him back upstairs, beat the crap out of him... But he still won't talk, won't tell us how he survived.'

The gangster took a last glance at the horrors within and gestured to his crony. The bodyguard closed the door and made his way up the stairs, leading them out.

'Where is the man now?'

The bodyguard said, 'He is here, *jefe*. We have him under guard. Some of the others wanted to put bullets through his head, but I thought we should tell you...'

'Good for you, *churro*. If what you say is true, someone like that is worth more alive than dead. But I think you're a fool to come to me with such ridiculous tales!'

The chastised bodyguard hung his head and walked on in silence, but only until his awe overcame him. He blurted out, 'Yesterday, we broke his legs, shattered his kneecaps; he should never be able to stand again, but...'

But...

The *pandillero* stopped in his tracks, stunned crony alongside, at the sight that greeted him.

The prisoner stood naked against a wall, his arms splayed wide, every inch of his moonlit body taut, tense muscle. A thick iron chain ran from the tight manacle-like cuffs on his wrists through a ring set overhead in the stone. Scars were all that showed where he had been slashed at with a knife so that his blood would attract the rats, but many new gashes made up for the healed ones, evidence of the torture the man had recently undergone. His bare feet were a bloody mess, for all but one of his toenails had been pried out. His powerful thighs bore the mark of the soldiers' heavy boots; and his chest and even his genitals showed evidence of brutality. Dirt crusted his lips, and blood from a cut on his forehead had congealed on the strong brows that framed closed eyes. Despite it all, the man stood firm, fingers wrapped around the chains that secured him, as though he were holding the iron aloft.

Two burly men, soldiers in the *pandillero*'s private army, were on guard at the site. One of them came forward to hand over a bundle to his leader. 'His clothes, *jefe*. Nothing unusual. His passport and cell phone are there too.'

The mobster looked to his bodyguard, who handed over a small, unassuming stone statuette that had been appropriated from the prisoner before he had been given over to the rats. He then reached out for the prisoner's passport and flipped it open, reminding himself of his captive's name. 'Professor Bharadvaj,' he began. 'Your reputation as a treasure-hunter precedes you. I was assured that you would, without doubt, lead me to the famed lost idol of Viracocha, and it was proved right. But I was not informed that you were a man of other…talents.'

The prisoner slowly opened his eyes. They gleamed; a flash of gold fused into the brown in what could have been a trick of the moonlight. The soldiers shuffled, inexplicably uncomfortable. Then he spoke, his voice deep and calm, 'I am a historian, *jefe*, not a treasure-hunter. But you didn't come here to discuss the difference.'

'You're an interesting man, Professor. Indestructible? Is that the right word for you? Something tells me you, with your splendid abilities, would be worth a lot more than this relic here... I might be persuaded to make a deal of some sort. What do you think?'

'I think,' the prisoner growled, 'that you've made a huge mistake.'

'*Cojudo*! What do you mean, you asshole?'

'The only reason I haven't walked out of here already was because I want the statue back. You see, unlike you, I'm a man of honour and when I say I'll do a job, I deliver. It would have been most inconvenient to have to search half of Bolivia for you, and it was way easier to make you bring it to me, as you just have. You should know better than to believe in tales of indestructible men...*cojudo*.'

One of the soldiers laughed and made a disparaging comment in his native tongue. The chief guffawed and then addressed the prisoner. 'Do you know what he said? He said you speak too much for a man in shackles.'

In response, the prisoner looked straight into the *pandillero*'s eyes. Letting go of the chains, he tightened his left hand into a fist and smashed it into the old stone behind him, once, twice, three times till the metacarpus – the bones of his knuckles and palms - shattered, collapsing within the skin in otherworldly formlessness. His body shuddered and his chest heaved as his breath caught against the excruciating pain that followed, but the man seemed to make little of his discomfort and waited, letting it pass. He glanced down, considering his hand and its manacle. Then he smashed again at the stone, this time doubling over and grunting through clenched teeth as the bones of his wrist and upper forearm took the impact.

Standing up straight, the man took a deep breath and pulled his deformed hand through the manacle around his wrist till his left arm hung at his side. Free of the counter-weight, the chain that had secured him to the wall rustled musically through the stone rings till his right arm, still in the grasp of its metal cuff, also hung at his side. Satisfied at the outcome, the man allowed himself a brief, cold smile.

The chief and his soldiers watched, open-mouthed. '*Madre de Dios!*' one of the men hissed. He swung forward his M90 semi-automatic gun and racked the slide, the action prompting the other men to do the same. But it was too late.

The prisoner darted forward, deflecting the nearest gunman's weapon with a right forearm block. In the same move, he drove the point of his elbow into the man's throat, the action bringing instant death. Using the dead soldier in front of him as a shield, the prisoner advanced on the others, pressing the soldier's lifeless finger down on the trigger. Bullets riddled the limp corpse, spurts of blood drenching the prisoner. The noise of gunfire rang off the stone, ebbing only when the prisoner shot down the chief's bodyguard and then emptied the clip into the second soldier. That left the chief, and his gun, now also empty. The prisoner pushed aside his human shield and readied to face his adversary.

The chief was not a man to be cowed; his fearsome reputation was justifiably earned. He charged at the unarmed prisoner, swinging his empty rifle into the man's face. The prisoner caught the blow head-on and went flying back to land on the ground. Making good on the opportunity, the chief moved in to drive the butt of his weapon into the prisoner's stomach, drawing from him a guttural yell. At that, the chief grunted in satisfaction, but it came a little too soon.

As the next blow descended, the prisoner caught the butt of the rifle with a single hand. Opposing the chief's weight with brute force, he thrust the gun upwards till the muzzle bored into the other man's gut, pushing him back. Springing to his feet, the prisoner tackled the *pandillero*, pinning him against the wall he had been bound to moments ago. Then he grabbed the chains that still hung from the manacle on his right wrist, wound the links around the chief's neck and drew tight.

The chief strained against the pressure, clawed at the air in a desperate attempt to breathe. His face contorted, fear coursing through his being, he rasped, '*Que*...what...are you?' And then he went limp.

The prisoner kept the pressure up for a good five minutes, waiting for the subtle pulse at the chief's neck to ebb before letting the man fall to the ground. He moved swiftly, retrieving first the key to the manacles from the bodyguard's person, then his belongings from where the chief had let them fall. Tucking his clothes under his mangled left arm, he used the recovered cell phone to dial a memorized number. 'Come get me, Manohar,' he said into the phone before hanging up and sliding out the SIM card. He broke the SIM into two with his teeth and slipped both pieces into the pocket of his shirt along with the phone, all to be disposed of later. He pulled on his clothes and his boots, grunting as he failed to tie his shoelaces as neatly as he would have liked with just one hand. After a couple of attempts, he gave up the effort with a wholesome laugh; the sound echoing through the ruins. All the while, the chief stared at him with wide, lifeless eyes and a slack-jawed grin.

The prisoner walked over to the cadaver. What ought to have been a mundane historical expedition had turned into a bloodbath, the very kind of carnage that he had managed to avoid for years. In moments, everything had changed. He had known it was bound to happen.

It is time.

He pushed the intuition aside, setting his mind to more immediate concerns. After all that gunfire, he had little chance of a quiet escape or an easy journey to the predetermined extraction point by the lake. More of the chief's henchmen were likely to come storming in at any second, and he would have to deal with them the only way he could. In any case, he could not risk leaving a single man alive to tell the story – his story. The story of the man who would not die.

1

Varanasi, India.

'Jellyfish.'

'Jellyfish?' Hariprasad Namdeo, known to all of Kashi as Baba Shivdas, took cognizance of my statement with the utmost gravity by reaching for the remote and switching off the interminable noon-time mega-serial that was playing out on the television behind me. The glycerine-teared heroine in her chiffon finery flickered satisfyingly out of existence.

'There exist,' I continued, 'insenescent jellyfish, creatures that are biologically immortal, blessed to live forever unless ripped apart by predators or killed by disease, as some of them are.'

Hari twirled a strand of his long and immaculate white beard as he spoke. 'And these jellyfish are relevant to this discussion because…?'

'Because when these immortal jellyfish are faced with a crisis, they regress into an immature state and subsequently regrow into a new adult organism – the old jellyfish's configuration changes, but not the essence of its being.'

'The way you've changed multiple identities to protect your real one for nearly four thousand years?'

The statement lacked all value in terms of effecting shock by the simple reason of being the truth; my truth. I said, matter-of-fact, 'Precisely. Like them, I do not die, and like them I too must change state. My current alter has lasted me more than half a century, but a self-declared academic is of no use to me any more. The Professor's good name comes up a little too often in the dubious circles of the global antiquities black market for him to remain effective or discreet enough as an alias. Just yesterday, a would-be client got in touch, claiming that she'd heard of me from the job I did a year ago at Chirala.'

In his typical laid-back fashion, Hari ignored the premise and resorted to reminiscing about inessentials. His eyes twinkled at the mention of the small town in Andhra Pradesh where I'd located a complete set of Pallava dynasty copperplates from the fifth century buried in a crypt, and he had charmed the heiress who'd engaged me to recover them. Both their dalliance and my project had been covert, and that someone had picked up our trail from there proved the point that I was trying to make.

I said, emphatic, 'When an identity outlasts its utility, Hari, it is time.'

Hari sighed, an almost-wail accompanying the exaggerated exhalation, and baited me with all the authority of being the only living man I called my friend. 'Aah. And here I thought you were being existential. Who are you? What are you doing here? What does everything mean? But no, I see yours is a different problem. A jellyfish problem.'

I studied him, not without some warmth. If one met Hari at this very moment they would, quite justly, mistake him for a senior corporate executive or a respectable businessman about to set out on his morning walk. His pristine white kurta perfectly matched the shade of his well-styled hair and beard, and his oval nails shone from the weekly attentions of a personal manicurist. His physique, however, defied all attempts at maintenance and, despite what he assured me was a strict diet, Hari's well-rounded belly remained as it had been since the day I'd first met him. That, along with commensurately chubby cheeks and a kind face, gave him an avuncular air that was well-suited to his occupation: A professional mendicant, Hari in his role as Baba Shivdas was an avant-garde lifestyle guru to the more experimental seekers of spirituality. The occupation had proved lucrative, regardless of which Hari remained an unpretentious, if irreverent, man content to spend his afternoons in his hotel room-like apartment, smoking a ganja-filled chillum and watching the eternal battles of mothers-in-law and daughters-in-law play out on cable TV. The latter habit, particularly, served to give him stellar insight into the human psyche – a talent that he put to good use.

With me, however, he was always blunt. 'Utility is overrated, especially the utility of human existence.'

'Utility, my friend, is nothing but karma – and karma is much more than the seventies' hippie-grunge synonym for destiny that your adoring disciples throw around as a catch-all phrase to explain why everything is the way it is. Karma is knowing that reason and choice, not destiny, explain our world. We worship the sacred with our actions, for all actions are sacrifice. And when a rational person sees that, when he has to then live with the consequences of his choices, he is much more discerning about his actions.'

'As you have been?'

The question wasn't meant as a counter or as inquiry. Hari was aware — as were probably a billion other people — of the legend of an undefeated scholar-king who, for his exceptionally bloody part in the Great War, had been condemned by a god to roam the earth in restless agony till the apocalyptic end of the age. But Hari also knew what none of those billion people did — it was a secret I kept well and at all costs — that only part of the story was true: the fantastical part about a mortal turned into a man who could not die. The other part, about my seemingly endless life being the result of a god's curse — that was rumour.

My condition was born of something far worse, something that had defined my purpose, my karma, from the day I'd become immortal. Every persona I'd assumed, every role I had played, had been towards fulfilling that purpose — a fact that Hari did not fully comprehend. He believed that I sought to set the record straight, redeem my name and honour. Like much else about me, this too was only partly true.

There are heavier, darker burdens to bear than immortality.

That was something that neither the myth-loving masses nor Hari had the least clue about. I intended to keep it that way.

'Yes,' I finally answered the pending question. 'If Professor Bharadvaj cannot help me find what I'm looking for, then it is time I became someone who could. In fact, I may have waited too long already.'

'Aah, yes. Rule number one, wasn't it?' Hari remained flippant. It was his way of goading me to reveal more.

I didn't oblige. Instead, I took out a pack of cigarettes from my pocket. Lighting one, I threw the pack across the room to Hari. He caught it with a perceptive smirk, teased a stick out and lit up. Sitting back, he took a deep drag and said, 'You know what? I think you like being Professor Bharadvaj. I think it gives you hope. Some day, the Professor might buy a house, complete with satin-finish distemper and housing loan installments. Someday he might fall in love, marry, have children… From what you've told me, he's been the closest you've had to a normal life, Asva. Surely, you don't have to give him up?'

I laughed, dismissing the suggestion. 'Hope? I've given up the certainty of death. Here and now, if you were to put a bullet through my brain, what might become of me? My body seems incapable of dying by any means whatsoever, but what of my mind? What if I was left a vegetable, a voice trapped inside my head for the rest of eternity? I've had to make my peace with that possibility, Hari. Hope is of little consequence. To a man like me, hope, life, normalcy…these are just illusions.'

'And what of all those clients out there who need the Professor? What of the lady from Chirala and her mystery?'

'They'll manage. I'm not the only historian on earth. In fact,' I added with a sneer, 'I'm not really a historian at all.' Standing up, I reached over to drop the butt of my spent cigarette into the ashtray next to Hari. 'I don't even know why we're having this conversation. My mind is made up.' I held up a white envelope, which I then balanced on top of the large wall-mounted LED TV.

'In that case,' Hari said, 'this circular discussion was redundant.' He studied me in silence, coming to terms with what I was going to do. His sad smile was the sole admission of farewell as he said, 'Pass me my chillum on your way out, will you? It's on the shelf behind you.'

I did as he instructed and then, with a nod, I turned to go.

Stepping out of the smoke-filled den, I found myself in a corridor that was as hazy as the room in which I had been. Bodies spilled out from a nearby hall and into the passageway, evidently the aftermath of the previous night's party: An indiscriminate mix of gender and nationality united in the common search for *moksha* – salvation – by means of a chillum or two, preferably an acid-laced shot of vodka. That was the thing about Kashi – in formal parlance, Varanasi. Throughout its long history as the oldest inhabited city in India, in the world even, it had a way of sanctifying all things, the profane, the despicable and even the frightful. Death was a way of life here, displayed in all its glory alongside the frail human quest for salvation necessitated by the compulsion of human birth. It was here that I had begun my journey as Professor Bharadvaj and now, after more than half a century of being, by modern reckoning, forty-seven years old, it was here that this journey would end.

I weaved my way through the ever-teeming mass of the living and the dead that filled the city, relishing the mindful wandering. By the time I turned towards my eventual destination – one of Kashi's numerous burning ghats – it was late in the afternoon. Soon, the bright glow of the many funeral pyres came into view and, behind them, the muddy blue-green of the unbounded Ganga. My pace quickened.

A thin, tired-looking priest, dressed in a threadbare dhoti and a moth-eaten towel that served as an upper garment, came up to me near the ten-foot-high log piles that framed the approach to Manikarnika Ghat, offering, for a pitiful sum, to perform the all-important rites of final passage for seven generations of my ancestors. I refused him, but with a hundred rupees. He accepted the money without much protest and shuffled away. I made a mental note to find the priest tomorrow, when I would come back as a nameless kinsman to perform the last rites for Professor Bharadvaj.

The sickly-sweet odour of corpses descended around me like a shroud. Cadavers waited their turn in neat rows, some alone and unclaimed, others surrounded by grieving relatives, the heat, the acrid taste of smoke and the smell of charred flesh. Manikarnika Ghat alone was host to over a third of the three hundred or so cremations that took place in Kashi every day.

I walked down the perpetually wet steps to the river's edge. Taking off my shirt and my shoes, I handed them to a beggar nearby. He promptly scampered away, lest I changed my mind and reclaimed the items. Amused, I turned to the river before me, feeling lighter, as though it weren't clothing that I'd cast off but gnarled, scabby skin. A gentle breeze began to play. A few metres away, a pack of hungry dogs on the riverbank lunged at a partly burnt cadaver stuck in a green and orange eddy of banana leaves and half-withered garlands of marigold, even as the dead man's family watched in horror. I thought to intervene, to chase away the would-be scavengers, but then decided to let both species be. This was their karma. Mine was to keep searching, till I found what I was looking for.

The Ganga, it was said, washed away all sins. I would let her take my hotel keys, my wallet and ID cards, my mobile phone and even the sacred thread I wore, let Professor Bharadvaj vanish without a trace, merge into the pure spirit and rank offal that was the river, leaving behind nothing that held meaning for anyone. And then I would make a fresh start.

The water lapped at my toes, inviting, loving. A stray bloom of marigold tickled playfully at my ankles. I took off the Professor's signature wireframe glasses and threw them into the water. With a deep breath, I brought mind and heart together in living meditation till the hum of life around me became a nothingness into which I could disappear – and slowly turned into awareness that a naked, ash-smeared ascetic who stood nearby in penance over a burning corpse was scowling at me. I met his ire with cold challenge. He shrugged, and his glance swept downwards. I realized that he was trying to direct my attention to the loud jangling that emanated indisputably from the pocket of my trousers. My cellphone, always on silent mode, was vibrating against the metal of my hotel room key.

I knew better than to be irritated by the ironic interruption, yet I swore under my breath as I fumbled for the offending instrument. Six missed calls since morning. I picked up as a matter of compunction. 'Yeah?'

'Boss, Manohar here.'

Manohar. Professor Bharadvaj's assistant. *My* assistant, I admitted. I had not bid goodbye to him and I did not plan to, though right then I did feel the urge to say something he would later recall as having held ulterior finality, if not fondness.

But Manohar spoke first. 'I've been trying to reach you since morning. About the client who got in touch yesterday. The background check turned out fine. She's a historian herself, specialization in ancient languages and comparative linguistics; has a foreign degree and all that. Anonymous investors backing her. The money is mainly in untraceable offshore accounts – nothing new in our business. But…'

'Forget it, Manohar.'

'Boss…'

'Let it go,' I said, intending, for my part, to do exactly that.

'Professor, we can't. You have to meet this client. I think she…that is…you know, she…'

It was not so much the dramatic effect of what he said next or the irony of it. It was the fact that it was an amazing coincidence, given what I had just been about to do. Manohar, I knew, did not believe in coincidences; neither did I.

A brief lull followed as the evening breeze faltered, then died. All was still, and then a ripple floated across the water as a cool wind rose, less gentle than the preceding breeze but also less fickle. Around me, a host of temple bells began to ring as my beloved Kashi came alive against the dimming sunlight. Crowds were gathering further down the river, at the Dashashwamedh Ghat. Soon the river would be speckled with hundreds of small wick lamps, and resounding chants would fill the air as the famed Ganga-aarti began. Manohar waited on the phone, silent, patient.

I turned away from the water, resisting anticipation. A part of me wished that I hadn't given away my shoes and my shirt. 'All right. Set up a meeting. I'll get to Delhi in a couple of days.'

'Done.' Manohar's voice became perceptibly more cheerful at my answer. 'You want me to meet you at the station?'

'No. I'll get in on my own. Let me know when the meeting is.'

'Cool. *Chalo* then…'

'Hmm.' I hung up the phone, shaking my head at the facile mix of languages that made for 'Hinglish'. As with the many other things I'd adapted to, I used it on occasion but not with ease. Perhaps, no matter what name or identity I went by, there was a part of me I could never be free of. I would always be an anachronism, a man from a distant age placed in today's world. Perhaps I clung to such trivial irritations in a bid to prove my detachment and refute the possibility that, as Hari had pointed out, I liked being Professor Bharadvaj after all. Perhaps I did like it enough to want to forget who

I really was. But I couldn't. Four thousand years of searching and not finding, and yet I went on. Karma. *We worship the sacred with our actions, for all actions are sacrifice.*

Holding on to that reflection, I plunged into the river for a quick douse and a prayer, a careful eye on the wallet, keys and mobile phone that I'd left on a nearby step. Then, shirtless and shoeless, wet trousers clinging to my legs, I made my way back to my hotel.

2

Memory inevitably reared its head as the train chugged into New Delhi railway station. But I wasn't a man to react to the past, especially not the past that had irrevocably defined my present. The stories survived, kept alive in bedtime tales and television serials, in religious discourse and, sometimes, at the edges of history. Men and women who had ruled alongside me were not just remembered, but some were even revered as divine. My own recollections could never compare. It was, in fact, an effort to hold on to them in the face of such overwhelming, mostly sincere, belief.

Had I been on the winning side, no doubt my tale would have been told differently and many parents would, these thousands of years later, have named their children after me. This very city that I now stood in had once been Indraprastha, the heart of a vast and prosperous empire. When the empire had been won over by another and the former ruler exiled, the newfound conqueror had not dared to claim the city. Instead, I had lived here as Regent, for I'd been the only man with the skill and the strength to defend the city if ever the exiled emperor and his mighty allies tried to take it back by force.

That was the kind of warrior I'd been: *Asvatthama, the undefeated.*

And now?

My teacher, my father – he was still held in esteem, monumentalized on the spit-stained signage of a metro station somewhere on the way between Delhi and Gurgaon. I, however, was the spit on the signboard, the stain on my noble father's reputation. I'd never been able to please him while he'd lived. Death might have ensured I kept the fame I'd earned as a scholar and commander of men but, even so, I doubted it would have improved his estimation of me. The life I'd led since was only likely to add to my infamy. Then and now, I was a man dangerously out of place anywhere and everywhere, a wanderer, even in a city I'd called home.

Two men fell in beside me as I walked out of the railway station, mistaking me for a tourist – a taxi-driver quoting the best rates for sightseeing in Delhi and a pimp offering women, boys, drugs, booze, and all permutations thereof. I stopped and turned. It took just a glance for the two men to hasten away, their eyes revealing the fear that their minds did not discern. No one else noticed a thing, and the swarm of humanity parted around me like water against a stone, and moved on.

I plunged into the tight, noisy crowd and made my way down the unimaginatively named Main Bazaar Road before veering off into one of the alleyways that led to the glamorously notorious part of Paharganj – its brothel district. The streets were narrower here and the buildings were clustered so close that they allowed in little sunlight, even on such a bright afternoon. Lampless lightbulbs hung from the façade of most of the buildings, their multicoloured spectrum an indication of what might be available within. It was a different world from the one merely three streets away, but it was also a far cry from the rich, boudoir-red decadence eulogized by Bollywood. A faint smell of ganja wafted through the air, reminding me of Kashi — but for the irritating thump of bhangra-techno from one of the many dance bars that remained open any time of day or night. More pimps walked alongside, rattling out offers under their breath, and then dropped behind as I showed no interest. A jasmine-loaded woman called out to me from one of the decrepit low-rises that lined both sides of the alley. I waved to her, but kept walking.

An intersection lay ahead, marking the end of the red-light area. Policemen, thugs and pimps mingled with customers at a roadside teashop strategically overlooking the junction. Beyond, the roads were more crowded and better lit. A young couple, both foreigners carrying huge backpacks, peered tentatively at me as they tried to shrug off the crowd of street children hailing them in various foreign languages, promising them the best and cheapest hotels in Delhi. I ignored them, as I did the apprehensive yuppie wondering whether his Audi, or some such, was safe where he had parked it while he wandered about in search of the darker attractions of the inner alleys. Sooner or later, touts would see both categories of seekers to their destinations.

As traffic came to a haphazard stop at the signal, I crossed the road and headed for one of the larger buildings, an 'office complex' as it proclaimed itself to be. Cars filled the open lot in front of the complex, but the building was deserted. My car – now practically Manohar's, since he was the one who drove it – was also parked in the lot. As always, he'd washed and polished the old Maruti Esteem to a shine – a feat in Delhi's dusty summers. Me, I preferred a motorcycle any day. I liked to feel the wind in my face, the sense of the world falling behind in blurred insignificance. But a car had its advantages, and I used my copy of the old-fashioned mechanical key to open the trunk and throw in my backpack. Then I made my way into the building.

As I stepped into the lift, I caught a glimpse of myself in the patch of steel that lay under the peeling paint on its walls and found myself smiling. To look into a mirror was possibly the most private thing I did. Sometimes I was reassured by what I saw. Brown eyes that were mostly inscrutable but could quickly flash golden with anger, the air of cold arrogance that went well with my polished, restrained manner – these were things that would not, could not, change.

Beyond that, I saw a stranger; an exceptionally tall man with grey-black hair that was cut short and combed neatly into place. His rimless spectacles left no marks on the bridge of his nose, suggesting that the frames were titanium and the wearer was reasonably well-off. The blue cotton shirt he wore was neither expensive nor new, but it was well-ironed and tucked into a pair of impeccably tailored pants that claimed to remain wrinkle-free in defiance of all activity, the resultant luxury brand label hidden under a simple leather belt. On his left arm was a near-antique stainless steel HMT watch, its age evidenced by the new, shinier links that had been added to the original metal strap to make it fit around his broad wrist.

I looked away from the image and down at myself, noticing, not for the first time, that the tastes Professor Bharadvaj indulged in were not too far from my own. At once, I dismissed the admission as a futile and inefficient sentiment, but my smile too was gone. No loss; I'd never been one to show emotion.

I got off on the top floor, stepping into a carpeted, air-conditioned world that was in stark contrast to the general air of disrepair that marked the rest of the building. The doors on this floor were numbered, but otherwise indistinct. A variety of operators that required discretion – for social or legal reasons – had their offices here. Those who had no business on the premises did not dare venture beyond the paan-stained ground floor, and those who did, enduring the stench of urine that hovered around the lift, knew well that an expensive reprieve awaited them at their destination.

I walked my way down to the end of the corridor without meeting a soul. The door to my office had been left ajar and the lights were on.

'Morning, Manohar.' I greeted the sturdy-looking man behind a wooden desk in the far corner of the space. He was the only person in the large, rectangular room, though it was furnished to serve also as a reception and waiting area.

Manohar glanced up from the newspaper he had been reading with an honest, boyish grin that made him appear younger than his thirty-three years. 'Hey, Boss! How was

Kashi?' he said, drawing out his vowels in an unintended American accent, the residual effect of years of study overseas. He would, I knew, be horrified and possibly ashamed if someone pointed that out to him.

'Good. Smoky as always. Hari says hello.' I didn't wait for a response, nor did I give him a chance to raise the matter that had sucked me back from the edge of blissful disappearance. I walked through to the small inner office that was mine and shut the door behind me.

Like the room outside, my office held a dark rubberwood desk and a comfortable chair. The laptop on the desk was on and running, more for effect than utility. Both Manohar and I used the machines in the office for nothing more than playing card games or reading the news off the web, leaving the computers clean and disposable. The real stuff – the hours of research, details of bank accounts, travel plans and clients' contact information – was kept on iPads purchased on Manohar's recommendation, devices that could be easily carried or destroyed.

I made a note of the time – a few minutes short of four in the afternoon – as the *azaan* began to sound from a nearby mosque. I sat down at the desk and began a game of Solitaire.

The knock at the outer entrance was punctual. I heard the indistinct rise and fall of polite conversation as Manohar let our prospective client into the office, then the tell-tale silent pause as she presumably took in the décor – or the lack of it. For that matter, the lack of any kind of paraphernalia that one associated with an academic, howsoever eccentric. No degrees on the walls, no proud display of published texts or journals, no untidy pile of exam scripts waiting to be marked; only starkness that gave away much about me – that I taught nowhere, wrote nothing and met with no one.

A second knock, this one at my door, and then it opened.

I stood up as Manohar led in a woman whom I placed at thirty-five or so. Dark brown hair with strands of flaxen sat well on her pale skin, hinting at a mixed parentage. She wasn't too tall, but her build was athletic – a hard-earned result, I surmised, taking in the strong, toned muscles of her calves below the hem of her formal skirt. She wore a matching blazer over a fuss-free white shirt but had personalized the otherwise regulation look with an elegant pair of cufflinks. Her make-up consisted, as far as I could tell, of nothing more than a dash of brown lipstick, the sparing application of which showed confidence rather than indifference, for she had applied the colour evenly and outlined it with a firm hand. In all, she was attractive, to me all the more so for the adventure that possibly lay ahead. Manohar shot me a silent glance, as though saying, *I told you so.*

'Professor Bharadvaj.' She came up to take my hand in a firm shake. Without waiting for me to reply, she went on, 'Since I hear you're a man of few words, I'll get straight to the point.'

I managed a polite twist of the lips and gestured at one of the chairs facing the desk. She took it with a word of thanks, smoothing her skirt into place as she sat. Manohar took his customary position, leaning casually against a wall as though his presence was of little consequence. He would not miss the least move our visitor made.

'My name is Maya Jervois,' she began. 'I'm here on behalf of certain collectors who prefer to remain unnamed. We hope, Professor, that you might be able to help us find a certain historical artefact that I'd mentioned earlier to Mr Manohar …'

The clichéd beginning made me suspicious. If Manohar was right, she was more than an uninformed intermediary. I decided to rankle her a bit to find out. 'Let me save us time here, Ms Jervois. First of all, I'm expensive. Second, I don't like digging through rubble without good reason. I'm not, and I say this for a reason, I'm not your Indiana Jones variety of tomb-raiding, whip-snapping adventure hero. If you're looking for someone to crawl up and down trenches dressed in khakis, then you're in the wrong office.'

Manohar echoed my derision with a snigger and it was not just for effect. We'd seen too many nouveau riche collectors and their lackeys to care about our customer service skills. Erratic financial markets had made for overnight billionaires and instant insolvents both, and I, personally, was tired of being asked to deal in centuries-old statues and carvings that were going at half-price like used household items at a moving sale.

Maya Jervois kept her eyes on me as she opened her handbag, took out a cheque and placed it on the table. Without a word, she leaned back in her chair.

I picked up the cheque, inspected it front and reverse, then put it back on the table. 'Okay, so your clients are rich as hell. That doesn't impress me, Ms Jervois.'

'Maya. Please, call me Maya. And I think you might find my proposition worth considering, Professor. You've heard, no doubt, of Nagarjuna – the legendary alchemist credited with having discovered the key to transmutation – what he called the Vajra, though the generic tags of elixir stone and philosopher's stone are more familiar to…'

Disappointment stirred in me, but turned at once into ire. I willed myself to maintain a practiced expressionlessness and was only partly successful, giving in to a stiffness that was imperceptible and a frown that wasn't. The melodramatic situation, complete with anticlimax, was as laughable as it was revolting. Manohar had undoubtedly let his personal sentiments get in the way of business. If it weren't for the singular fact of who I was, he'd have laughed Maya Jervois out the door the moment she opened her mouth, as would have every decent historian on the planet. Instead, he had suggested we meet with her, to which I had agreed, for Manohar had said the only words that could have disrupted my intended tryst with the river at Kashi.

'She knows.'

I supposed he'd come to that conclusion from her ridiculous submission, but disgusted as I was with the turn of events I didn't want to look at him for confirmation or denial. Letting snideness take the edge off my temporary rancour, I said, 'I specialize in history, Ms Jervois. The Harry Potter section is further down the corridor.'

'I'm sure I'm in the right place, Professor. I hardly need to explain to you the importance of symbols and myths recurring across cultures. The quest for a single source of transmutative power, of immortality, is well-documented in Vedic scriptures.'

I resisted the urge to roll my eyes. Few notions were as persistent and futile as the search for eternal life, a fact I had personal and indisputable evidence of. In itself, the proposition wasn't fantastical. All things changed. Liquids evaporated; gases precipitated. Iron rusted and cells decomposed. Seeds germinated and grew into trees and a mass of flesh and blood could evolve into a foetus and be born as a living creature made up of numerous cells. Replication and renewal were essential to growth and healing, without which no living creature could survive. But everything had its boundaries, for boundaries ensured natural balance. Immortality was in fundamental violation of such a balance.

None of that was material I cared to present to Ms Maya Jervois and so, without skipping a beat, I said, 'Immortality... That's down one floor, right next to the door that says "Vampires, werewolves and other things that refuse to bloody die."'

'With all due respect, Professor...'

'With greater respect, Ms Jervois, there is no scientific basis to a substance that turns base metal into gold and offers other entertaining conjurations. Ergo, like many mythical objects, *it does not exist*. As for tales of such elixirs across cultures – it is established that nations that engage in trade and social exchange end up sharing their narratives and lores, even more so when conquest and annexation lead to social integration. Merging superstition and belief is an essential factor in creating a stable society, a way of blending together the conquering and vanquished cultures. I guess you missed that particular lecture back at wherever it was that you...'

'Oxford, sir,' she cut in. 'And as familiar as I am with all these theories of historical integration, I also know that when the seed idea is common across cultures but the surrounding legend or tale is different, it does imply some degree of independence and reliability...'

I raised an unimpressed eyebrow. 'Tell you what. Write it up. Submit it to the *Historical Review* or the *Asian History Quarterly*. I'm sure you'll rack up many citations, one way or another.'

To her credit, she took no offence. But it didn't look like she was about to give up either. 'Professor...'

I stood up. 'Goodbye, Ms Jervois.'

'Wait...' She moved to the edge of her chair.

'Thank you for your interest in us.'

'The Vajra exists, Professor. It's more than legend.'

'Then I wish you luck in finding it.'

'I already have.'

I responded to the statement in the only reasonable way I could. I laughed.

3

Life, in its infinite wisdom, had taught me to laugh heartily, but never for too long. I settled down and let Maya Jervois's offended silence fill the air while I collected my thoughts.

As a pupil, I'd been instructed never to ignore the duality of all things – for that was where most solutions to perplexing problems lay. In less abstract terms, it meant that all things had boundaries; for every form there was anti-form. Death was the boundary of life; the two always went together. Science agreed.

Old age and demise in living beings was determined by the number of times a cell could replicate itself without compromising the integrity of its chromosomal structure, a constant known as the Hayflick Limit. Embryonic stem cells – cells that were undefined in function but had the ability to evolve to form more specific types of tissues, such as muscle or bone – could, however, renew themselves in perpetuity. This possibly explained the 'immortality' of some kinds of amoebae and even jellyfish, but it did not apply to anything higher up on the evolutionary chain. And with good reason. Creatures composed entirely of such biologically 'immortal' cells would be nothing more than lumps of matter or tumours, capable of only one thing: constant and perpetual growth. Multicellular beings – humans or otherwise – were much more complex than that and the price they paid for it was their assured mortality. It was here that the cutting edge of genetics had hit a stumbling block.

Throughout the ages, when physics, biology and chemistry had failed to provide solutions, even the most astute of scientific minds had turned to alchemy, including one of the greatest contributors to science as we knew it: Sir Isaac Newton. When Newton had died in 1727, his estate had declared over 300 of his documents 'unfit to be published'. These went to his niece Catherine, the Viscountess of Lymington, of the house of the Earls of Portsmouth. Passed down from generation to generation, the Portsmouth Collection, as it then came to be called, saw public light only two hundred years later, in 1946, and it caused all hell to break loose. Over a third of the Collection, it was found, was devoted to the study of alchemy, containing as many esoteric references to dragons, tridents and lions as it did to bonafide chemical processes such as distillation and calcination.

The Portsmouth documents served to rekindle scholarly interest in the subject, and Newton's involvement sanctified and admitted into record what historians had long suspected – that alchemy was an ancient and well-established discipline that could be traced back from medieval Europe, through ancient Greece and Arabia, to India. Nevertheless, all efforts to apply the results had, in Newton's time and since, been in vain.

I had concluded as much for myself, having wilfully suffered the scratchy wigs and horrendous frock coats in fashion at the time to obtain a membership to the Royal Society in London and befriend the lauded scientist, in order to be able to observe his work closely. After that attempt had failed to yield results, I had, quite ruthlessly, used the occasion of his passing to make my acquaintance with Catherine – a woman as irresistible for her intellect as she was for her appearance – and thus get access to the Portsmouth papers. It was not the first time that I'd applied my skills, political or otherwise, in search of answers.

It would also not be the last, because what I'd found in the papers had left me disappointed. For all his sketches of dragons and pipettes, Newton had done little more than what many who came before him had – he had insisted that transmutation was possible, but nothing in his records gave any clue about *how* it could be made to happen. In the matter of alchemy, even Isaac Newton had left humanity no wiser than before. Sobered by that reflection, I turned to look at Manohar.

He took the opportunity to break the impasse. 'Professor? A word?' Mumbling polite excuses at our client, he eased me out of the room and into the relative privacy of a corner of the outer office.

Before I could begin to berate him for his actions, he said, 'There are two possibilities here, Professor, both of which cannot be dismissed. Either she's come to you with this ludicrous story because she knows more than she should about you, which is my sense of the situation, or...'

'Or?'

'Or she might be right.'

For that statement and all that had come before it, I let him have it. 'You're out of your bloody mind, Manohar. How could you take her seriously? You've absolutely wasted your time and mine.'

'But…'

'There is no such thing as an elixir stone. It doesn't exist. Don't tell me that you were stupid enough to believe…'

'Boss…'

'And if *she* is such a blithering idiot that she can't cook up something more plausible to cover up an ulterior motive, then I couldn't give a damn what she knows or suspects about me. She's hardly a concern!'

To Manohar's credit, he stood his ground. 'Are you sure, boss? I mean, about this Vajra? Are you absolutely sure? I mean… We know what we know…'

Manohar had never liked putting our secret into words. I'd always had to do it for him. This time, however, I was amazed that I had to do it at all. I shifted, intending at some level to dismissively wave him off and storm out of the office, but then abandoned the idea. Manohar was an intelligent man and he considered me his mentor. Despite my recent plan to disappear without telling him, or maybe because of it, I felt I owed him answers, even if it meant sharing more than I would have preferred to.

I said, 'Do you think this is the first time some historian or chemist or random knucklehead has claimed to find this legendary stone? Haven't hundreds of other people looked over the years? Haven't *I* looked? All those years of wandering, all those personas I've assumed... Did you never wonder why I've spent my life as I have, instead of just disappearing into the Himalayas? I've travelled the world for centuries, thrown myself into the thick of conflict and upheaval, followed the rise and fall of civilizations... Surely, as a historian, you can see why?'

He nodded, a little subdued for not having taken it into account.

I continued, 'Nearly every megalomaniac in history aspired to a long, if not eternal, reign. This search is not new. But it is futile. Every attempt I've made to find out what made me biologically ageless, to discover how I became this way, has ended in failure... I'm an anomaly, Manohar, a statistical exception, whereas alchemical immortality implies method; it implies science. One of the two is a fallacy.'

Manohar forced a nod of acknowledgement, though he would have been well within his rights to ask me why I'd continued to search for something I didn't think I could find. Clearly, he was embarrassed at being reminded of the details he was already privy to. 'So,' he said, 'that leaves the first possibility. Someone suspects you of... Well, like you often say, a coincidence as big as this is no coincidence at all. But...who?'

There was only one way to find out.

I turned away and, storming back into the inner office, perfunctorily declared, 'Let's see it, Ms Jervois.'

'No, Professor. I'm not so stupid as to have brought it with me before I could be sure of what I was getting into.

I've hidden it in a public place. We go there, get a civilized drink, and you hear me out fully. And then I show you what I've discovered.'

I couldn't tell whether she was being cautious or difficult, but her insistence was entertaining. At any rate, it made sense to take her up on the invitation. It was either that, or drinking by myself at some loud, bright dhaba, cursing Manohar all the while. 'All right,' I said. 'If I'm going to listen to bullshit, I could do it with some alcohol in me.'

Maya Jervois's choice of watering hole disappointed on two counts: not only did it involve driving through Delhi's infamous peak-hour traffic, making for a strained, silent hour and-a-half in the closed confines of the Maruti, it was also indecently expensive, even by the city's absurd standards – a feature that bothered my ego more than it did my wallet. On the flip side, it meant that the place was not crowded, particularly where we sat, on the first floor. The décor – a desperate attempt to channel retro-chic through dark velvet upholstery and dim lighting – was far from sophisticated and gave the place the look of a majestic conqueror mellowed by loss. I found it strangely appealing and decided the restaurant was worth visiting again on the rare occasion when Manohar insisted I celebrate his birthday or some other such event with him.

I took my seat at a table for four by a large window. Maya Jervois sat directly across from me. Manohar slid into the chair next to hers and buried his head in the menu. If he was at all bothered by our rather blunt strategy of walking headlong into possible danger, he didn't show it.

Manohar was a private man, with neither family nor friends, and in the eight-odd years that I'd been acquainted with him, he had built no lasting relationships but wasn't above an occasional affair. He had no qualms putting his statuesque looks to unscrupulous use claiming, in his defence, that people who assumed he lacked brains as a result of his appearance deserved no better. I agreed wholeheartedly, for he was one of the smartest men I'd ever met. He'd taken to the disclosure of who – or what – I was with consummate ease and without judgement or superstition. But then, he too was a man with a secret, though no one should have had to hide what Manohar hid.

'Sir?' The hovering waiter inquired.

'Lagavulin. No ice,' I answered.

'I didn't figure you to be a whisky person,' Maya Jervois said, reminding me of her presence.

'The Professor here loves his single malt,' Manohar declared with perceptible approval. 'He has a beer or two sometimes, but that's never out of choice.'

'And you, Manohar? You ordered whisky too, didn't you?'

'Yes, but I hardly have the Professor's acquired taste for it. I'm a simple Royal Challenge kind of guy…'

'You're hardly simple, Manohar,' I said, joining in the banter. 'You just like to pretend you are. There's much more to him than meets the eye, Ms Jervois. Did you know he holds a PhD from Harvard's Sanskrit department?'

She appeared to be suitably impressed. 'That's nice. I knew a researcher there. His name is...'

As I'd hoped, she and Manohar fell into conversation, leaving me effectively alone. I looked out the window, taking in the picturesque view of the Qutb Minar – believed to be named after the king who had begun its construction in 1193, Qutb-ud-din Aibak, but in fact so called after another man who lived at the same time, the Sufi saint Qutbuddin Bakhtiar Kaki. I'd met neither man, but felt some affinity to the monument in my own way. I'd counted the saint's teacher and mentor, Moinuddin Chishti, a friend, for our paths had crossed in the 1160s at Bukhara, now a city in modern-day Uzbekistan.

Chishti had then been a young renunciate, and I a warrior in the service of Saladin, the founder of the Ayyubid Sultanate, fighting not only to help him take the Holy City of Jerusalem but to also defend it from Richard the Lionheart's forces during the Third Crusade. Neither of their religions had been mine, but the war had. *Whatever you have is transient; whatever is with God is everlasting*, Chishti had quoted from the Quran when I'd told him what I was looking for. It had been part advice, part well-merited warning, for the battle for Jerusalem had been bitter. I'd fought against men who were driven by their deepest convictions and alongside those who'd held equally strong beliefs. But I'd fought only for myself.

'Let me know when you're ready to discuss things, Professor,' a voice dispelled my memories.

It was as good a time as any. 'I'm ready, Ms Jervois.'

Maya Jervois cleared her throat and began to speak as if she were making a presentation at some conference. 'The written history of an alchemical tradition in India begins around the turn of the era, in the first century CE, with the scholar-sage Nagarjuna – a man recognized more for his contribution to the rise of Mahayana Buddhism than as a typical scholar of the post-Vedic period. What we know of his life, in fact, comes mainly from Tibetan Buddhist accounts. He was born somewhere in western India and had his laboratory at Srisailam, in modern-day Andhra Pradesh. Some say that he converted to Buddhism and developed his own school of thought, which amalgamated Buddhist teaching with Vedic principles. His precepts, I've read, are comparable to Sartre's modern philosophies. He's also named as a student of Agnivesh, a scholar mentioned in the Mahabharata.'

She paused as our drinks arrived. I downed my whisky in a single gulp, motioned for a refill and leant back into the plush cushions, closing my eyes and enjoying the warmth of the liquor spreading through me. Soon, I heard the waiter set down a glass in front of me. 'Thank you,' I said, and he scurried off. I took an unhurried sip of my second drink. 'Continue.'

She kept her hands on her lap in a show of self-possession but her voice betrayed her excitement. 'I'm sure you're familiar enough with Nagarjuna and know that his work as a philosopher-scientist was subsequently recorded in Dhanvantari's treatise on Ayurveda. Nagarjuna's exploits also reached the ears of Hiuen Tsang, and he's mentioned in Al-Biruni's comprehensive accounts of Indian society – not as a scholar or sage, but as a pioneering alchemist. The basis of Nagarjuna's claim to fame was what he called the Vajra – an object made of the transmutative substance central to alchemy that could not only turn any metal to gold but also prolong human life. The story goes that when a famine swept Magadha, he used the Vajra to help the huge community at Nalanda University survive. Some say that Nagarjuna himself lived for over 500 years. But the most interesting part of his story is his death.

'Nagarjuna was a subject of the Salivahana kings. Either due to greed, or for political reasons that may well have been justified, Prince Sindhu of the Salivahana decided that both the alchemist and his source of power – the transmutative object – had to be destroyed. Nagarjuna obliged, breaking the Vajra into three bits and hiding the fragments at different locations. He then submitted himself to execution. Till today, there's nothing to tell us where these three pieces are, except for Nagarjuna's cryptic response to the Prince's final query.'

'My life is alchemy. I go now to the Blissful Lands but I shall return to this very body,' I quoted. 'A statement that says much for Nagarjuna's passion for his work, but gives no information on these hypothetical fragments and does even less to support his scientific credence. I'm waiting to see where you take me with this literature review of yours, Ms Jervois. And, for what it's worth, I'd remind you that the same Dhanvantari, whose professional reference Nagarjuna so relies upon, has written of his own attempts at transmutation. Specifically of his utter failure at it.'

'Surely, you don't think that one man's failure is cause enough to entirely dismiss the possibility that this substance can catalyse chemical change? Isn't that sheer dogma, Professor?'

I didn't return her compliment, as I could have, by pointing to her own stubbornness. Instead, crossing my arms, I looked at her and asked, in all sincerity, 'Ms Jervois, if you can make these tenuous connections hold, and I shall for a moment assume you can, don't you see this could pretty much make your career for you? Why are you out here trying to hire us instead of filing for academic grants and hiring research assistants? Or getting yourself a lucrative book deal and exploding this truth on the world, as the phrase goes. Why aren't you doing any of that?'

She held my gaze with confidence. Her brown eyes, I assumed, were a gift from her Indian parent; her mother, if I was to apply the common, somewhat chauvinistic, rule of thinking she'd taken her father's name. Or I could be further chauvinistic and assume it was her married name. I dismissed the frivolous line of enquiry, but as the silence continued I began taking in the youthful glow of her face, the stubborn conviction in the strength of her ideas. She was, I had to admit, a very attractive woman, in more ways than one. Despite my initial impatience and reluctance, the conversation had not been that bad, or the evening a complete waste. In fact, if we…

'No one would believe me.'

'I'm sorry?' I instinctively responded, though her words had sunk in through my reverie.

'You asked me why I don't make my career out of this or write a book and all of that. It's because no one would believe me.'

The best-kept secrets are the ones hidden in plain sight. My grandfather used to say that all the time.

She continued, 'I can't prove anything using established evidence or published research papers. We *are* in the realm of rumour and conjecture, of treasure-hunting. And that is why I have come to *you*, Professor. Personally, I find it hard to accept that a man who can find the Chirala plates, a man who has shown that copper-smelting and fine metallurgy existed in India about a thousand years before conventional texts say it did, is going to throw precedent and probabilities at me.'

'You have a penchant for alliteration, did you know?' I responded.

'Professor, please. I'm not here to make small talk. I've taken everything you've said at face value. Can't you extend me the same professional courtesy?'

'Ms Jervois, it's out of courtesy that I'm telling you exactly what I think. What ifs don't make for scientific theory. As refreshing as I find your conjecture, and I mean it, I told you right at the outset that I'm not your heroic treasure-hunter. You've got to give me more than this... If it were as straightforward as what you're proposing, this Vajra of yours would've already been located a hundred times over.'

'I believe you're quoting the alchemist Geber. Or rather, Jabir ibn Hayyan. ...*they say this science hath been so long sought by wise men, that if it were possible in any way, they would a thousand times, before now, have been masters of it.'*

I was impressed, but not enough to concede the argument. 'Quoting the dead doesn't change anything, Ms Jervois. Nagarjuna has been well studied by both Western and Indian historians, and this alleged secret article has already spawned many a dubious bestseller. There's nothing new in all this.'

Maya Jervois smiled. 'You can't find what you don't look for, Professor. Much is still hidden behind old myths.'

I chuckled, and in the pause that followed turned to Manohar. He nodded at her handbag. My regard for the argumentative Ms Jervois went up one more notch. I said, 'Whatever it is that you discovered…you haven't hidden it here or anywhere else. It's been in your purse all along, hasn't it?'

She glanced at Manohar and then back at me. 'So that explains his reticence. You play Dr Brains with your talk, while Mr Handsome here acts as your silent sidekick but observes everything. Nice. You two make a good team.'

I didn't respond, but drained what was left of my whisky. The attentive waiter stepped up, ready to repeat my order, but I dismissed him with a wave of my hand and waited, an eye on Maya Jervois in unstated question. She reached slowly into her purse. The action might have been meant to tease, but I chose to read it with indulgence. She was entitled to her smugness, and I let her enjoy it with the cultivated patience of a man who knew that in the larger context of the universe few things were truly worth getting excited about.

Taking out a small, transparent, sealed canister, she placed it on the table before us. Inside the container was a blue-black pebble, smooth and rounded on one side, while its other surface was dull and even. Reddish-green flecks and silver striations formed delicate patterns within its glowing depths. Whatever it was, it certainly had a quiet magnificence.

'What the – ' Manohar exclaimed. He threw both his hands up in disbelief and then let his palms slam softly on to the table as he leaned forward. 'You're kidding me, right? You're fucking kidding me!'

'I'm not,' Maya Jervois declared, triumphant. 'This is it. This is one of the three pieces of Nagarjuna's broken Vajra. Now, will you two help me find the others?'

I gestured to the waiter, silently ordering another drink.

4

Five awkward minutes and a large shot of whisky later, I stood staring into the mirror in the exceptionally clean men's room of the restaurant. Staring but not seeing.

It's not possible. It's simply not possible. There is no such thing as a transmutative substance.

I knew this with the utmost confidence from what I was and *who* I was, or had once been, for I too came from a long line of scientists, though few remembered us as such: Then and now, much of our technology was seen as magic. For our part, we had accepted the reputation without complaint, for it gave us an edge where we needed it most – in warfare. Whereas our metals had made for splendid armaments, it was our chemical discoveries that had wreaked the most havoc and found their place in legend as astra-weapons.

I'd laughed at the sight of armies of fear-maddened men swinging and hacking at each other in drug-induced panic when the Brahmastra was unleashed, primal paranoia turning dearest friends and trusted brothers into blood-curdling demons of their darkest dreams. By the time the soldiers finished gutting their own, there'd be little left for their opponents to do. There was no antidote to that ultimate hallucinogen, no counter-weapon that could save the person it affected. All one could do was learn to fight off its effects, face the demons inside of them. Few had a reputation for success, as did I. Yet, I did not for once believe that mine was the more fortunate fate.

In spite of our prowess with chemicals, my fellow scholar-warriors and I had regarded transmutation as a vain pursuit long since abandoned by our forebears, and no one wasted any time on it, not even under cover of scripture or ritualism. I was sure of this for a reason – once I'd been… transformed…friend and enemy alike had viewed me with revulsion, and that was to be expected. But the contempt that my kin – the greatest scientific minds of the time – had shown had astounded me.

It took me a while to understand that their reaction stemmed from the fact that their science couldn't explain my transformation and their politics wouldn't let them take responsibility for it. They viewed *their* failure as *my* fault. I was disowned and declared a loathsome aberration, and immortality was explained as my punishment for my so-called crimes during the Great War, for that alone gave them the authority to assert that what had happened could never happen again. And so, as everything changed in the aftermath of the war, alchemy was set aside and forgotten.

For my part, I had left the land of my birth soon after my transformation, driven from it by the loathing and fear of those closest to me. But the world was a small place for a man who had as much time to spare as I did, and news from the east was never out of my reach. When I spent time as a soldier for hire, news came to me as rumours and conjectures in the darkness of drinking houses. During my sojourns as a scholar, I found information in the form of reports from more discerning travellers. But it was in the service of those who sought power that I received word, often whispered and paid for with bloodletting, that the quest for immortality continued in the land I'd called home.

By the time the expanding Mauryan Empire reached its zenith, alchemy had indisputably regained its pre-eminence in India, this time with stronger and deeper roots in religion and the mutual influence of Greco-Egyptian traditions and, later, Chinese and Tibetan practice. From this first and oldest wave of globalization, a legend was born and it had a name: the Vajra.

Modus tollens, I reminded myself, a form in logic known as 'denying the consequent'. If Nagarjuna's alchemical prowess had no basis in fact, then it logically followed that the Vajra too would be a baseless construct. But the absence of evidence was not the same as the evidence of absence. Even if one were to admit that the Vajra was in fact a real object, as Maya Jervois had assumed from the fragment in her possession, it did not imply that the rest of the mythos had any factual basis.

So where did that leave me? *Trapped in a cycle without end.* I splashed some water on my face, forcing the implications of that thought into the background. Then, smoothing my hair back, I left the washroom.

Back at the table, I found Manohar and our potential client in hushed conversation. They fell quiet as they saw me. 'Do you want to get some food, Professor?' Maya Jervois asked as I sat down.

'I'm not hungry. You guys go ahead.'

The two of them began to flip through the menu. I gazed out the window again, taking in the artful play of light and shadow around the Qutb Minar. I heard Manohar order some pizza and it arrived shortly, sufficient for the three of us should I choose to change my mind. There was the scrape of a plate against wood and an inviting aroma as a slice was politely pushed towards me, but most of my attention was elsewhere, having moved on from the times of Qutb-ud-din Aibak.

After Saladin's passing, following again the trail of power, I'd thrown myself into the heart of another storm, this time in the form of the unprecedented rise of the Mongol empire of Genghis Khan. Like many conquerors before and after him, Genghis too sought the ultimate hedonistic prize of an unending life – first from the mystical Hashshasin and their supposedly undying leader Hasan-i-Sabah, and then from the Taoist monk Qiu Changchun, who was said to be in possession of a stone that could confer eternal life. But Genghis had died, as had they all.

Whatever you have is transient... Chisthi's words had been prophetic and pragmatic, for those who had sought the secret of eternal life had found nothing but bloody death. The quest, it seemed, would always be the devil's own.

The admission pushed the scene unfolding before me into place. 'Something's wrong,' I said, without turning away from the window, as disparate observations came together to form a picture.

Maya Jervois began to speak, but Manohar shushed her quiet. I peered past their reflected images, at the black Land Cruiser that was making its deliberate circuit around the area for the third time. At first pass, it had seemed merely one more vehicle on the road searching for a place to park. But the 'For Registration' tag that temporarily did away with the necessity of a licence plate was uncommon enough to merit further scrutiny, at which point it became obvious that the Land Cruiser was neither letting its passengers out nor picking anyone up. It allowed other cars to beat it to a parking spot when one became available; not once had its driver lowered the tinted glass window to hurl out the mandatory abuse of a disgruntled Delhi driver.

'Professor?' Manohar interrupted.

I glanced up, in time to see a man's reflection in the window as he drew his gun. I was instantly on my feet, my hand reaching for the pizza platter. With a flick of my wrist, I sent the heavy wooden plate whizzing through the air like a discus to strike the gunman in the chest. He staggered back, and the weapon went off, firing into the air as he fell to his knees. The three of us ducked low, Maya Jervois grabbing the canister from the table and tucking it into a pocket of her jacket.

A scream sounded from the other side of the restaurant, and a terrified waiter started yelling. I looked around, grateful that the only other patrons in the place had been seated away from us, in a corner. They had, quite sensibly, crawled under their table.

Two more men burst into the restaurant, their hands moving to their holsters. The first man too was back on his feet. Leaving him to Manohar, I threw myself at our new assailants, bringing them down to the ground before pulling at a nearby tablecloth and throwing it over their heads in comic but effective distraction. It bought us only a few seconds, but that was enough. Maya Jervois picked up a chair and swung it against the nearby window, shattering the glass. 'This way,' she said, clambering out on to the foot-wide outer ledge.

Manohar was next. He stopped halfway out the window to take out his wallet and throw some money on to the table. I expected it wouldn't nearly be enough to cover the damage.

I was the last one out; our escape had taken merely seconds. But it wasn't over yet.

We ran along the window ledge till the point where it met the low wall of a landing area between two flights of stairs. I clambered across the wall to find the stairs inexplicably empty. I dawdled; Maya Jervois gave me a rough shove and set off down the steps at a run, Manohar right behind her. With a glance back in the direction of the restaurant, I followed.

We made our way to the parking area to find the Land Cruiser waiting at one end, its lights off but the engine running.

'Where did we park?' Maya Jervois asked in a breathless whisper.

'There,' I pointed. 'That's where we parked. They've taken out the nearest street lights.'

'Fuck!' she cursed. 'They're waiting for us to try and get to the car so that they can run us over!'

Manohar was grim. 'That's the backup plan. They probably have someone lying in ambush. That's why no one from the restaurant has come after us.'

I had no doubt he was right. I said, 'I'll bring the car. Meet me on the main road, it should be crowded enough to be safe.'

'But...' Maya Jervois began to protest.

I ignored her and took the keys from Manohar. 'Go.'

'Professor...' she persisted. Manohar grabbed her by the arm and led her away.

I waited till they were less than a stone's throw from the main road before creeping towards our vehicle. I kept behind the line of parked cars, glad after all that the street lamp was out.

It was tough to spot the men waiting in the shadows, their stealth evidently cultivated through years of training. But once they came into sight, it was easy to deduce from their build and bearing that they were ex-soldiers, perhaps even mercenaries. Such hired muscle was expensive and in stark contrast to the men who had attacked us in the restaurant, and I briefly entertained the theory that more than one group might be after us before dismissing it as hubris.

There were two of them, each waiting fifty metres from our car, on opposite sides so as to cover possible directions of approach. That was an advantage: I needed to deal with them only one at a time. The problem was that they were both in line of sight of each other and that gave me about twenty seconds to bring down the first man before the second would be on me. I decided that there was no point trying to be surreptitious.

I began walking directly towards the first man, lighting up a cigarette as I neared him. The click and the resultant glow of flame drew the men's attention towards me, but I continued to walk on and they turned away, checking with the caution I expected of them that nothing else had slipped their notice in those few seconds. The second man turned back my way just as I drew up with the first. He began to shout, but before his fellow thug could comprehend the warning I landed a blow on the back of his neck, hitting a bunch of nerves that fed into the spine. He crumpled to the ground. He would remain that way for a good ten minutes. The other man was already running towards me. I jumped on to the hood of the nearest car, a Mercedes, and used it to launch myself at him. He was ready for me and punched me as I landed on him, our combined efforts throwing us on the tarmac. The thug, quite literally, had the upper hand, and was about to lay a punch on my head when I brought my leg up to strike him in the groin. He crumpled; I turned us both over. Holding him down with one knee, I applied a choke-hold long enough to see him into unconsciousness.

That left the Land Cruiser.

Keeping low, I made my way to my car, opened the door to the driver's side with the key and slid in behind the wheel without shutting the door. Getting the car out without a chase was nothing more than a matter of patience. The parking lot served a whole cluster of buildings, most of them eateries and watering holes, and someone had to be leaving soon.

Sure enough, within a few minutes, the loud banter of sated merrymakers came ringing through the night. In all statistical likelihood, they'd parked nearby – those who had started their evening earlier would've had the choice of parking spaces closest to the building. I listened, feeling more confident as the footsteps and conversation drew closer. A car beeped unlocked less than ten metres away. A shuffle of feet, an exchange of goodbyes, and the door shut with a slam.

I was ready. The moment my unintentionally helpful neighbour started up her vehicle, so did I, the sound of my action lost in the obviousness of hers. As her headlights came on, I swung out of the parking spot at full speed, zipping past the still-idling car towards the exit. Even if the thugs in the Land Cruiser sighted me, the other car would be between us. It was enough to give me a head start. I suspected that the Land Cruiser wouldn't bother with a chase.

Manohar and our client were waiting for me outside the exit to the parking lot, in the messy, crowded proximity of a paan shop. They piled into the car with obvious relief, Manohar beside me and Maya Jervois in the rear. We pulled away and blended into the flow of peak-hour traffic, Manohar glancing back every thirty seconds.

'What do we do now?' Maya Jervois asked, too calm for my liking.

I studied her in the rear-view mirror, before replying, 'We go back to the office.'

'Paharganj?'

'Yes.'

'But, what if…'

'They know? I'm sure they do. I think they followed us from there.'

'Then why the hell are we going back?'

'It's called centralization, Ms Jervois,' I said. 'We need to throw them off our tail and, trust me, it's near-impossible to do that without leaving clues. But we can minimize how much we give away by concentrating all our activity in one area before breaking clean.'

'So we leave the car back at your office, because they'll come looking there anyway?'

'Yes.'

She let out a low whistle of appreciation and made a comment about the two of us deserving our reputation as the best in the trade. I overlooked the statement, as did Manohar. Shaking her head, Maya Jervois settled back to peer out at the city lights. She remained that way till we reached our destination.

5

The main road leading to the office building was bright and noisy, but as soon as we turned on to the service road and entered the parking lot, the noise faded.

'You two wait here,' Manohar said as we got out of the car. 'I'll go upstairs and check things out.'

Maya Jervois snapped, 'No! Are you mad?'

'We need to…' Manohar began.

I disregarded the bickering and walked into the building. The two of them stopped their argument and followed. We rode the lift up to the top floor without incident. The moment we stepped out into the corridor, we realized that whoever was after us had already been there.

The door to the office was wide open and the lights were on. I paused, listening for any sign of the intruders. Convinced that they were no longer there, we entered. Inside, the office was a wreck. There had been nothing for the intruders to take, so they had settled for breaking the desks and shattering the computers to pieces. A useful clue. Whoever these guys were, they were unsophisticated hunters.

'We'd better go,' Manohar cautioned. 'They might be lurking around in the building.'

He was right. But there was something I had to do first.

Without warning, I grabbed Maya Jervois by her wrist, spun her around and slammed her against the nearest wall. Gripping her other hand, I pinned her down with her back to the concrete and leaned in close. She cried out, more in alarm than in distress, and resisted, the muscles of her arms tautening with hidden strength. A whiff of perfume, earthy and floral, veiled me and a few strands of her hair fell loose to brush against my cheek, making me abruptly aware of our proximity.

Manohar was taken aback, though he knew well that I was an equal-opportunities offender in matters of so-called chivalry. 'Professor!' he chided, despite himself. I ignored him. The highest respect one could show to any individual was to hold them responsible for their actions. And that was exactly what I was doing.

'If you please, who were those men, Ms Jervois?' I asked her, pointedly polite.

'I don't know,' she hissed. 'Let go of me!'

I clucked my tongue in admonishment. 'Come now, Ms Jervois. You were telling me earlier about professional courtesy…?'

She stopped resisting as I tightened my hold on her wrists, but her eyes widened with well-merited fear. 'All right,' she gave in. 'But first, please, let go of me…'

I did and took a step back.

A swift move of her hand, and it held a new-generation .45 calibre Glock. I wasn't at all surprised. The way she'd constantly sat forward, the fact that she'd kept her jacket on all through the evening and, finally, the tell-tale clunk when I'd thrown her against the wall had all pointed to a gun, either tucked into the band of her skirt or worn in a waist-holster.

'I like your conversation style, Ms Jervois,' I taunted.

'A lot like yours, isn't it, Professor?'

Manohar sighed, as though he were bored. 'Professor, please…'

'He's right. This isn't the time or place for platitudes.' Maya Jervois rubbed her left wrist against the material of her skirt as she spoke, and I wondered if her skin bruised easily. Her wrists had felt small in my hands, and I'd been rough. But then, I wasn't the one holding the gun. Our client was hardier than she chose to let on.

With measured coolness, I said, 'I asked you a straight question, Ms Jervois. Give me an answer, and we'll all be on our way.'

She tried to hide behind anger. 'Bloody scum. That's who they were. How the hell should I know? Some stupid rich kid's hired goons, I imagine. The world is full of jerks who want to play tomb-raider.'

'Like your employers?'

She eyed me with nervous innocence. It lasted for an instant, and then her brusque manner was back. 'Are you in, Professor? Do I have your word that you'll help me?'

The demand made me recognize that the situation was more complicated than I'd initially expected. There was another player in the game, someone whose allegiance and intent I couldn't as yet fathom. Maya Jervois, for her part, continued to keep information from us, but she did seem to believe in the existence of the Vajra. And then I had my own unstated motives that hovered between suspicion and intuition.

I said, 'I got shot at for sitting next to you, Ms Jervois. I got shot at, even when I didn't and still don't have a clue what it is you want of us. *And* I'm standing here while you hold a gun to my head. Yes, I'd think I'm in. Or did you want that in writing, on a letterhead?'

She shot me a look of pure disbelief. 'Crazy!' she muttered under her breath, looking at Manohar for some sort of affirmation. He glowered back. With a shake of her head, she turned to me again and declared, 'I work for a government agency, Professor. A high-level special-ops division.'

'A government agent?' Manohar scoffed. 'You mean, like a spy? You're kidding me! This is way too corny to be real!'

'No. It's true.'

'No way! What do you think I am, stupid?'

A hint of desperation entered her voice. 'You must believe me. I know it's corny, but that doesn't make it untrue. This isn't the first time governments have treated history as a matter of national interest, even national security.' She risked an embarrassed grin at me. 'I found it ironic, Professor, when one of the first things you said to me was that you weren't Indiana Jones… You know, like in the first movie, with the Nazis searching for the Holy Grail and all…'

I groaned loudly at that statement. Hollywood yarns had irreversibly glamourized both history and historians, and though it meant that I probably got paid more than I deserved, such stereotypes often got in the way of being professional.

'And those men?' I asked.

She shrugged. 'I'm sorry. I had a feeling I was being followed, but…'

'Bitch!' Manohar hissed. I raised an eyebrow at his uncharacteristic reaction, but Maya Jervois was far more demonstrative.

'How dare you…' She whirled around to point the gun at him but, reconsidering, immediately swung it my way again.

'Manohar, calm down,' I interrupted. 'You too, Ms Jervois.'

They complied, but continued to glare at each other. I let them wallow in their self-indulgent animosity and went over to the debris of my desk.

'What the…?' Maya Jervois reacted to my sudden movement by snapping back the safety catch on her gun.

I held up a calming hand that didn't really explain anything and rifled through the mess on the floor to come up with a more or less intact pack of cigarettes. Drawing one out, I lit it, uncaring of our air-conditioned confines.

She waved away the smoke with her left hand, the gun steady in her right. 'These things kill you, you know.'

I didn't bother dwelling on the obvious paradox. Instead, I said, 'Are they more of a hazard than what you're looking for, Ms Jervois? You and your friends back at the National Defence Research Organization – that's where you're from, isn't it? The NDRO? You think this thing, this Vajra or whatever you want to call it, has potential as a weapon, don't you? What are you expecting? Magnetic resonance? Explosive ability? Some sort of nerve chemical?'

She opened and shut her mouth, in an ineffective bid to respond. I waved her quiet anyway and said, 'Put the gun away. Manohar, we have work to do. We need to take a good look at that trinket Ms Jervois has been flashing at us. It's high time we figured out what we're getting into.'

'But...' Maya Jervois persisted.

I said, 'There are two ways to stalk a quarry. We can go after it, track it, and hope our aggression prevails over its survival instinct. Or...'

'Or?'

'We wait, we prepare, and once we're ready, we present ourselves as the prey and make our target come to us.'

6

'Where...?' Maya Jervois began, looking around the dark, deserted street with its empty plots of land.

Manohar did not answer her and set about unloading our luggage – two large bags of field equipment and my haversack, all retrieved from our car before leaving Paharganj. I paid off the taxi-driver, uncaring of the dubious looks he threw my way as he wondered what sort of fetish I had in mind with my companions in this out-of-the-way place at this hour. I watched till the headlights of the taxi merged with the tiny dots of light that marked the highway in the distance.

'My place is down this way,' I said and began to walk down the lightless street with familiarity.

'Damn!' Maya Jervois stubbed her toe on a large stone and pulled out her mobile phone to use as a torch.

Manohar explained, 'There aren't any electricity lines here. The government hasn't yet got around to it.'

'Then how...?'

'The Professor has a generator...'

'Oh.'

I led the way towards the two-storey building that I currently called home. It had a total of three apartments, all of which I'd leased out through a shell corporation that I used for such niggling purposes. From the outside, the structure looked like one of the many unoccupied bad investments that dotted the outskirts of Delhi, where people had bought land with much hope but few had been stupid enough to build homes.

We let ourselves in through a small door set into the high metal-sheet gate that afforded a poor view of the building inside. The place lacked the other Delhi institution that spoke of inhabitation and respectability – the omnipresent watchman. I switched on the generator as we passed through the ground-level parking lot towards a small lobby area that housed a staircase and a lift, bringing on a dust-covered light bulb that hung from a corner of the garage.

'Careful,' Manohar cautioned as we went up the stairs in the semi-darkness. For all the earlier resentment he had shown, he was now at complete ease with our client and our case. I knew this was simply because I'd committed us to both.

The loud hum of the generator followed us up, but was shut out once we entered the single apartment on the first floor. Minor inconveniences aside, when I did stay in the apartment I appreciated the privacy and solitude it provided. In fact, there were days when I wouldn't use the generator at all, preferring the light of a candle or two and the sounds of the night. The highway was too far-off for the noise of traffic, and frogs and crickets often set up in full force. On occasion, I'd even been rewarded with the rustle of a padded tread – the sound of a predator afoot. All other creatures would then fall silent, letting the wandering leopard, as I suspected he was, rule the night.

As for human company, in all the years that I'd rented this particular apartment, no one but Manohar and the exact count of one electrician and an enumerator from the Census Authority had ever stepped into it. Having Maya Jervois visit my Zen-sparse living room wasn't the most optimal arrangement; it made me want to get out of the way in my own house. I settled for standing with my arms crossed against my chest, my back against an unadorned wall. Manohar perceived my discomfort. He took over the role of the good host, sparing me the trouble of playing nice. 'Can I get either of you some coffee?' he asked, as he dropped the bags he'd been carrying and made his way into the kitchen.

'No.'

'Me neither,' Maya Jervois added, too quickly. Then she asked me, 'Your family…er…I do hope we aren't inconveniencing them in any way? I mean…'

I was terse. 'No, we aren't.'

'Oh.'

It was small consolation to see that it bothered her more to be here than it did me to have her. Apparently, no amount of secret-agent training could help deal with socially awkward situations. I continued to watch her as she walked around the room, taking in the over-stuffed bookshelves. She surveyed the piles of everything from comics and fiction to books on pop-economics and positively beamed as she came to stand in front of a genuine first-edition Oscar Wilde, which occupied a place of honour on a shelf of its own. She opened her mouth, and I sensed she wanted to ask how I had got my hands on such a collector's item. But she said nothing, possibly assuming instead that 'Consulting Historian' was a lucrative occupation. As for the book, it had been a relatively recent purchase, a memento of one just like it that had been given to me personally by the playwright himself. A most cherished gift, for the many days of conversation on human nature that had accompanied it and for the fact that in the aftermath of his reprehensible trial, Wilde had lived only a short while, mostly in penury and disgrace. My then persona, and consequently my ownership of the book, had been just as short-lived. Nothing I ever possessed, absolutely nothing, was indispensable, partly so as to maintain the integrity of my alter-identities and partly to ensure that I never forgot the inevitability of impermanence. Detachment was essential to staying sane.

I watched Maya Jervois flip through the volume, stopping to read a line here and there. She treated the book with respect, and I wondered what her tastes in literature extended to. Done browsing, she shut the book with a hard snap – a seemingly irresponsible act but one that was said to extend the life of a book's spine. Then she tapped a finger on the faded gilt lettering and let out a sigh before putting the book back in its place.

This time, I pre-empted conversation by saying, 'The washroom's over there, if you want to…' I pointed to one of the three doors that led off from the living area.

'Thanks,' she replied, but continued to stand around.

'What do you want to do, Professor?' Manohar asked, as he came out of the kitchen with a steaming cup of coffee and settled himself in one of the two low, single-seater sofas in the room.

Maya Jervois cleared her throat and said, 'I don't know how to convince you, Professor…'

'Don't try to convince me, Ms Jervois. Tell me what you know.'

She paused, but then appeared to reach a decision. 'Okay,' she began, sitting down on the other sofa. 'A few months ago, we received the first reports from a survey based on a new method of geo-exploration. The satellite feeds suggested traces of mercury ore – primary ore to be precise. I won't go into the science behind how we density-map the earth's crust and all of that, but suffice to say we were astounded by what we discovered.'

I didn't react, though I could appreciate her enthusiasm. Mercury had long been held as the magical element in alchemy, all the more so since it was not known to be found naturally in India. But as far as modern science was concerned, it was a common enough commodity. As a result, contemporary scholars supposed that early scientists had imported mercury from the Greeks or possibly from China, just as we did in current times.

'That *is* a find,' Manohar interjected. 'The consensus is that there are no primary ores of mercury in India.'

'Correct!' Maya Jervois said. 'Of course, the mercury we located isn't easily extractable, and the first reaction was to dismiss it as a computer glitch. When that didn't make the problem go away, the next step was to treat it as an uneventful discovery. In this day and age, finding elemental mercury may excite a few geologists, but it hardly has larger implications unless it turns out to be commercially viable. The fact that this report landed up on my desk was nothing but serendipity. And that's where the whole thing started. Can you guess where the mercury ore was recovered from?'

Serendipity wasn't something I had much faith in, and I was in no mood to humour Maya Jervois in her games. Historical accounts traced the location of Nagarjuna's laboratory to Srisailam in Andhra Pradesh, a fact she had mentioned earlier. Subsequent sources also identified Srisailam as home to a line of alchemists or *siddha*s and the temple-town became the centre of the cult of Shiva Siddheshwara, the lord of the *siddha*s. Around the twelfth century, however, the *siddha*s faded away into mystical oblivion, leaving behind the mammoth Siddeshwara temple, which stood to date.

'Srisailam?' I ventured, though I was certain of the answer.

She was impressed. 'Yes! We – NDRO – went in to verify the mineral deposits, and it was completely by accident that we came upon a series of subterranean passages in the vicinity of the temple. We shut the whole operation down at once, because…'

I interrupted her by holding out my hand.

She stood up, reached into her jacket and took out the canister she had shown us earlier. She passed the vial to me with reverence. I took it from her with a lot less finesse and yanked out the stopper. She started and made to protest, but it was too late. I had the vial open and the fragment out.

The stone looked bigger on my palm than it had inside the vial. I ran my fingers over it, taking in the smoothness of its polished surface. The piece was about three inches in length and would have been about the same in width, if it had been whole and not a fragment. The final product would most likely be in the shape of a disc. I turned my scrutiny to the unpolished side.

On the reverse, as I liked to think of it, were indentations – dots and lines set in an intricate pattern, the partial arrangement again suggesting that the final motif would have the broad outline of a series of concentric circles. The design was stunning in its complexity, as though someone had injected liquid silver into the stone to form a miniature three-dimensional filigree sculpture within.

The third side was the most interesting, particularly in its patterned unevenness: small square protrusions and indentations, like a miniaturized city skyline or the early equivalent of a Lego block or jigsaw piece, except of course that it had been made with the precision of a modern laser-cut key, the purpose then explaining the unconventional shape of the stone. It was part of a set of three, which would fit together as one. Nagarjuna, I had to admit, with growing respect for the man, had been as wily a fox as any. He hadn't actually broken the Vajra, just pried it apart. A much more believable explanation than suggesting he'd destroyed what he'd worked all his life to create.

All the while, Manohar stared at the piece in my hand. 'That fragment...' he said, 'what is it? Did you have it analysed?'

'We did,' Maya Jervois replied. 'Only preliminary density analysis, mind you. The fragment is made of volcanic rock, but as with all sedimentary stone, other ingredients have been bound in. Mercury and sulphur, and also a variety of salts. By isotope-dating, we know the age of the matrix rocks around it, but that doesn't mean much, and because this isn't a natural fossil, carbon-dating the fragment itself wouldn't have worked. The indentations on the back – well, I can only imagine what kind of technology they must have had in those days, to make such precise markings. I've examined it under a scope, and each one of those dots is a perfectly concave etching.'

'If you say so,' Manohar said, taking the fragment from me to put it through his own inspections, including holding it up to the light. There wasn't, he reported, anything to see, beyond the natural striations and the minute particles of suspended debris. But as his fingers ran over the pattern of indentations, his face lit up in pleasant wonder. I could tell that, like me, he was beginning to take our client and her trinket more seriously, though neither of us believed that it had any transmutative properties. He gave the fragment another careful look before returning it to her. She slid the piece into the vial, which she tucked back into her pocket.

'And you said you want us to find the other two fragments?' he asked her.

'Yes. In all these years, we've had no starting point, no means of even engaging with the issue. Now that we have hard evidence to show it really existed, the search for the Vajra can start all over again!' Her point made, Maya Jervois sat back, now seeming a little more at ease.

'What do you think, Manohar?' I asked.

All he said was, 'I'll start reading.'

I left Manohar poring over the contents of our mini electronic library on his iPad and, picking up my haversack, slipped away into the relative privacy of my bedroom. Finally alone, I closed my eyes, focusing inwards. A few seconds were all I needed to feel as fresh as a well-napped baby. I contemplated a quick shower but then decided it could wait till later. For the moment, I simply wanted to get moving and be rid of our client's presence. I took out a few clothes from my cupboard and folded them up. Then I emptied my haversack of dirty laundry from Kashi and packed it with fresh items before stepping back into the living room.

'Do you need anything, Manohar?' I asked.

He didn't look up from his reading, but jabbed his thumb towards one of the equipment bags to indicate he had already packed a few of his things into it.

'I'll need to get some stuff,' Maya Jervois cut in. 'I always have a bag ready at the local office. It won't take me more than a couple of minutes to pick it up...'

'You're not coming with us, Ms Jervois,' I declared.

'*What?* Why not?'

'For one, it's not safe. Second, I have no clue where we're going, but we'll have to move soon before someone comes after us again. Third, because I work on *my* terms and they are what I say they are. Here...' I handed her a slip of paper. 'That's my account number and other bank details. Please arrange to wire in fifty thousand towards our expenses, asap.'

'Rupees?'

I snorted, disdainful. 'Dollars, Ms Jervois. US dollars. Leave me your number too. I'll be in touch.'

'I'll arrange for the money, but the other condition – that's not happening, Professor. I'm going with you.'

'No way.'

'Yes, I am.' Her tone was as adamant as her words ridiculous. 'It's a deal-breaker, Professor. You can call this off and walk away if you don't like it. But if you're taking this up, I'm coming with you.'

'No, you're not. Don't make me get nasty.'

'Professor...'

'With all due respect, Professor; I've hired you to work for me...'

'Professor...?'

'I work for no one, Ms Jervois. But if you insist on putting it that way, you did hire me to work *for* you and not *with* you. And if you want me to deliver results, I can't have you getting in the way...'

'I'm the one with the gun...'

'And I'm the one with any clue as to what's going on, so...'

'PROFESSOR!'

My attention slowly shifted to Manohar.

'You'll want to see this...'

Maya Jervois jumped up from her seat. 'What is it?'

In response, Manohar flipped the screen of his iPad towards us. I didn't have to hear the voiceover to see that the news coverage was happening from Paharganj; in fact, from the parking lot in front of our office. The camera zoomed in on the buzz of activity around the burning wreckage of what had once been a black Maruti Esteem.

'The bomb exploded hardly minutes after we left. If we'd taken the car, instead of ditching it there...' Manohar left the implications hanging in the air between us.

I swore silently in my native Sanskrit and out loud in English, and then favoured our egregious client with a scowl. 'Where's your office?'

'Mathura Road.'

'Right. Let's go.'

'But...how?'

'Motorbikes. Downstairs in the car park. Ride with Manohar.'

7

An old, rust-stained rolling shutter sectioned off the furthest end of the ground-floor garage. I pushed it up to reveal a huddle of shapes under a stained tarpaulin that even the most desperate of scavengers would find repulsive. Walking into the garage-within-the-garage, I switched on a second, more powerful light. Maya Jervois raised an arm up against the brightness, using her other hand to cover her nose against the inevitable eddies of dust as I drew back the canvas to reveal my treasure.

Her reaction quickly turned to one of admiration. 'Oh wow!'

I briefly relished the unstated compliment.

Bikes were to me now as horses had been in the past – each one different in temperament and ability, but all equally spectacular in their beauty. The collection of metallic steeds that I'd built up over the last few years was a relatively modest one, more for reasons of discretion than affordability. Two India-made Royal Enfields – one a 500cc Bullet and the other a 350cc Thunderbird; a 650cc Kawasaki Ninja – a less flashy street variation of its mighty racetrack-only cousin and custom fitted to my height; a BMW GTL that had seen me to many a distant corner of the country; and, finally, my complete concession to vanity, for I could never ride it without drawing attention – a late model of the 1300cc Suzuki Hayabusa.

'Wow!' Maya Jervois repeated and looked from me to the bikes and then back at me. Manohar stood a polite distance away from the machines, his arms crossed in a posture that I recognized as one of restrained anticipation. Our arrangement over the car notwithstanding, he knew better than to touch one of my bikes without explicit invitation.

'Can you ride, Ms Jervois?' I asked.

'Yes,' she said and extended her hand as though she meant to stroke the grey-white Hayabusa as she might a prize stallion. Then, as an embarrassed self-awareness prevailed, she stepped back. Her face clouded over as I pulled the tarpaulin back over the Hayabusa, the GT and the Ninja.

Despite her confirmation that she could ride a bike, I passed the keys to the 500cc Bullet to Manohar. Then I strapped my backpack as well as the two duffel bags with our equipment on to the 350cc, lifted it off the centre stand and slipped into the seat. Ignoring the electronic starter, I kicked the machine to life. The solemn throb of the engine filled the air, and a strong beam of light cut through the garage, lighting up the dust swirls. Manohar switched off the generator and threw a quick look around the place before swinging on to the Bullet. He followed my lead in firing up the bike the old-fashioned way and then flashed his trademark wide grin at me.

I chuckled and said, 'Mathura Road, then. I'll meet you guys near the water treatment plant and from there we'll go on together.'

'What about you…?' Maya Jervois asked suspiciously as she climbed on behind Manohar and adjusted the over-large helmet I had given her.

I grinned and then, slipping on my own helmet, gunned the Thunderbird into action.

Behind me, I heard Manohar say, 'We can't keep up. He rides like a bloody maniac. He'll… Oh damn, we need to close the gate. Maya, hop off, will you, and…'

I heard no more as the distance between us grew, and the wind began whistling past. For the next forty minutes, I left all concerns of the Vajra and pretty much everything else behind.

As expected, I reached Mathura Road first. Stopping at a small shack on the main road, I bought a bottle of mineral water and waited. Soon, Manohar drove by without halting. I got back on to my bike and followed him. We headed south for some time and then turned right into an industrial enclave alongside the railway track. Manohar brought his bike to a stop in front of a small, stand-alone office building. I did likewise.

'I'll be quick,' Maya Jervois said as she got off the bike.

'Leave your gun in there,' I told her.

She smirked. 'Afraid of me, Professor?'

'We're flying. And *not* private,' I curtly replied.

Her cheer didn't fade as she made her way towards the building.

The watchman stood up with a salute and a 'Namaste, Memsaab' and opened the gate to let her in.

I nudged Manohar. 'Go with her. Don't let her out of your sight.'

'But...'

'She's NDRO all right, and not some harmless desk agent. But no government department has the kind of money she's ready to throw around. She's already sold out to a private investor, and we need to find out who it is.'

Manohar set off at a jog catching up with Maya Jervois and making small talk as he fell in alongside. The two of them disappeared into the building.

'Sirji...?' The guard gave me a tentative look, deliberating whether he ought to continue holding the gate open.

I shook my head and took out my pack of cigarettes by way of explanation. I offered him a stick.

'*Nahin,* sir,' he declined, though visibly pleased and tempted.

'It's okay, have one,' I urged.

He took a cigarette from the proffered pack, but instead of lighting up tucked it away into his pocket for a peaceful smoke later, I presumed. I began pacing around, getting a look at the surroundings.

'All software company, sir. This import-export business,' the guard proudly informed me.

'Hmm...' I cast about up and down the brightly lit street. It was mostly quiet, but the muted hum of music and wisps of conversation here and there hinted at a fair number of late-night employees around, as could be expected in call centres. This had been a strange, and thus eminently suitable, place to situate an office of the NDRO – ostensibly one more of the many insipid think-tanks that provided employment to India's burgeoning research and civil service personnel – back in the times when it had been an industrial area full of factories and workshops. Nowadays, the organization probably derived secrecy by blending right in.

My first encounter with NDRO had been incidental. Sometime around 1955, in the early days of being Professor Bharadvaj, I'd been one of a large group of bored historians who were led on a privileged tour of an Archaelogical Survey of India research facility. Although the exhibits and finds shared with us had been exciting, I'd been more curious about the challan-pink paper tags and chalk scrawls that identified innocent historical finds as the property of the NDRO. Discreet enquiries had directed me to a colonial-style red brick building in Calcutta, its cobwebbed ceilings and dusty shelves portraying an endearing harmlessness. In its basements, however, I discovered the most modern burnished-steel facilities and state-of-the-art weaponry that would have put the MI6 to shame.

Knowledge was power – no one knew that better than I did. And all knowledge that could be power, whether of a political, social, economic or even psychological kind, was of interest to the NDRO. Their involvement in the situation at hand added to the bona fides of the assignment – there was something to be uncovered at the end of this trail, whether it truly was Nagarjuna's Vajra or not.

That settled, I turned my mind to the second of our problems, the one I hadn't given much regard to as yet: our pursuers.

The gunman in the restaurant had not fired his weapon even once. The car bomb too had apparently been mistimed or, more likely, very well-timed – and that was most telling. The ease of our escape from both situations suggested that the men had meant to frighten us and spur us to action, but had not intended to kill. While the obvious inference was a trap set by the charming Maya Jervois or her employers, her insistence that she had nothing to do with it couldn't be dismissed – adding to the intrigue. The patent competence of the men in the parking lot, as well as the nature of the car bomb, made me admit that our adversaries ought not to be underestimated, not till we knew who they were. Of course, it could well be that I was over-reacting, and that our pursuers were, as Maya Jervois had said, no more than some rich kid's hired goons. But I hadn't avoided testing the limits of my immortality all these years by being reckless or lacking instinct.

'Sirji...?' the guard's voice sounded again.

I looked up to see him point at my hand. Only then did I notice that I'd let my cigarette burn out. I threw away the butt and smiled my reassurance at the guard before lighting up another one and returning to my reflections, this time directing my focus to the matter of what we would do next.

Assuming that this Vajra did exist, where would we begin? The new information that had been thrown into play was the discovery of mercury ore in Andhra Pradesh.

And what would this discovery mean to an alchemist?

It was the first thing I'd learnt when I'd set out from home thousands of years ago to eventually end up at the Akkadian city of Uruk on the Euphrates river in modern-day Iraq. A bustling trade centre, Uruk had been established in the fourth millennium BCE, rising to become the high-walled city of enduring fame over two thousand years later under the Sumerian king, Gilgamesh. Gilgamesh, the tale went, had been so distraught at the death of his dear friend Enkidu, that he had set out to find the secret to eternal life – a transmutative substance, which he recovered from the depths of the sea but then lost due to the intervention of the gods.

The story was familiar in its structure as a moral caution against arrogance and pride, which was what most Mesopotamians had taken it for. They regarded the idea of living forever as distasteful and believed alchemy was impossible. Their sentiments were often expressed with a vehemence that had been reminiscent of that of my own kin, forcing the alchemists amongst them to preserve their knowledge in subtle ways that still endured – in this case, through astronomy. The association of planets to metals that the Sumerians had charted was still in current use, though often without knowledge of its origins.

Which could mean....

'Professor!' Manohar and Maya Jervois were hurrying towards me. She had traded in her business suit for a pair of dark cotton trousers and a short kurta. Her hair was tied back in a ponytail that emphasized the contours of her face in a becoming way.

'I'm ready,' she declared. 'I told you I wouldn't be long.'

'Well done,' I replied, not without a touch of sarcasm.

She missed it, and instead asked, 'So, where do we go?'

I had my answer. 'Mumbai.'

The indefatigable Ms Jervois was clearly about to ask why, but Manohar shook his head in a clear signal that now was not the time for questions. 'All right,' he began planning. 'We need to get to the airport. There's a whole slew of flights around six in the morning.'

'You two leave right away. Take the Thunderbird, so you can keep all the bags with you. Head for Hazrat Nizammudin, but don't approach it directly – go around the Nizamuddin *baoli* and then head to the railway station. Leave the bike in the public parking area and take a cab to the Taj Palace on Mansingh Road. Hang around the coffee shop there for a couple of hours. Stay in plain view. From there, book a cab through the hotel's front desk for the airport. Buy tickets on the first flight there is to Mumbai at the counter out front and wait for me.

'And you?' Maya Jervois could no longer hold her questions.

'I'll be watching you, all the time. I'll make sure no one's following and then head for the airport myself.'

Manohar nodded and swung into the saddle of the Thunderbird. He gave me a sad smile as he started it, knowing that there was no telling whether or not we'd get the bikes back once this was over. Oblivious to our silent exchange, Maya Jervois got on behind him, her backpack swinging from one shoulder.

'Are you okay?' I asked, as she struggled to slip her leg between the large duffel bag and the frame of the bike, onto the leg rest. Without waiting for an answer, I crouched down next to the machine, to adjust the strapped-on bag. I caught a whiff of cheap carbolic soap and realized I was barely inches away from her left arm as it hung at her side. She seemed to think she was in my way for she muttered a 'sorry' and moved her hand, bringing it to to rest lightly on her thigh. Her fingers were thin and elegant, and her nails had been trimmed short.

Practical for a field agent.

The note served as a distraction from the sudden mental image of her hands on my bare skin. I laughed soundlessly at my own foible, finished tinkering with the bag and straightened up.

'Thank you, Professor,' she said. 'Take care. Don't get into any trouble without us.' Despite all the deceit and lies that stood between us, her expression was one of genuine concern. I couldn't help but find it pleasing.

'I won't. See you both in a few hours.'

The Thunderbird sped off. I lingered for a few seconds before taking out another cigarette and lighting up. The guard had vanished. I wondered if he'd been trained to stay out of earshot when his employers engaged in conversation. More likely he'd wandered off to take a piss.

Alone, in the dark, I let my mind drift to Maya Jervois's lovely eyes, the thick, luxuriant lashes, her lips, full and inviting as they spoke their caution. How tempting it was to read so much more into those words, to pretend that it was the woman who had me hooked and not a sweeter seduction.

Stubbing out the cigarette, I swung on to the Bullet and started it up, revving it a couple of times to ensure that anyone watching knew I was leaving. Maintaining a moderate pace, I followed the route Maya Jervois and Manohar would have taken, waiting till they came within sight. Then, letting the throttle out to maximum, I sped past them and vanished into the night.

8

The rest of the night passed without event. We were no longer being followed. Though reassuring, this development didn't make complete sense till I got to the airport and chanced upon Manohar standing around alone, sipping steaming hot coffee from a disposable cup.

'Where's Ms Jervois?' I asked.

'Washroom,' he replied, jerking his head towards her backpack, which lay on the ground, right next to the other bags.

I paused, taken aback by my own stupidity. *Carbolic soap.* I asked Manohar, 'When you guys went into her office to get her stuff, you didn't leave her on her own, did you?

Manohar looked shocked. 'She said she had to change, boss. Obviously I couldn't... I'm sorry, but...?'

'It's all right,' I reassured him, feeling nonetheless irritated. Maya Jervois must have used the opportunity to call the goons off, thinking I didn't need further prodding. But why go to the trouble of a double game, and one that was so obvious that it seemed juvenile? Either our client was a bigger fool than I'd estimated, or she wasn't quite the blithering idiot, after all. Clearing my throat, I said, 'I'm going to get some coffee. You want one more?'

'*Haan*, please,' Manohar replied.

I walked towards the vending machine I'd seen on my way in. By the time I'd got our coffees, Maya Jervois was back. 'Hey, Professor!' she greeted me as I walked back to join them. She leaned in conspiratorially to ask, 'Well? Are they behind us?'

I was tempted to meet her misplaced sense of humour with sarcasm, but before I could do so Manohar spoke.

'No,' he said. 'We weren't followed. He wouldn't have come here if we were. He'd have called and had us move again and again till we lost our tail. He doesn't like to look over his shoulder all the time.'

I smiled into my coffee as I drained what was left of it, then threw the cup away. 'Shall we?' I didn't wait for an answer but began leading the way towards the departure terminal. Manohar caught up, passing me the security-mandated copy of a printout of my ticket.

The airport was abuzz, given the early hour. Fortunately, the check-in counter for our flight did not have the customary long queue. I slid my ticket across the counter-top to the prim executive on the other side.

'Good morning. Travelling together?'

Maya Jervois was right behind me, far too close for me to deny her as my companion for the journey. 'Yes,' I said. 'Three of us.' I passed over their tickets as well.

Manohar and I had our own unspoken travel arrangement. On our way out from Delhi, we checked in individually and sat wherever the system assigned us. When we came back, though, we checked in together and sat next to each other. Most importantly, we did it this way unthinkingly. Which was why, I reminded myself, one never took a client along on a project. The principle was quickly reaffirmed. Just as we'd been issued our boarding passes, Maya Jervois asked, 'What's your first name?'

'I'm sorry?'

'Your first name? You know, your boarding pass says P. Bharadvaj. What does the P. stand for?'

'Professor.'

'Come on!'

I didn't reply, but turned back to the airline executive to thank her before moving away from the counter. It bothered me that the cold professionalism that I'd respected about Maya Jervois less than twenty-four hours ago had already dissolved into such assumed familiarity. What irked me more was the realization that I would actually be pleased if this was a calculated move, a guise she had assumed to throw me off guard. The contrary would simply disappoint me.

I maintained a taciturn reserve right through the security-check process and all the way up to the aircraft itself. Only when we were at our assigned seats did I open my mouth again.

'Window or aisle?' I offered, gesturing to the twin seats on my left.

'Window,' she replied. 'In any case, I assume you gentlemen would both prefer aisle seats, right? You're not exactly short....'

Manohar looked pleased at that. He wasn't, as she had noted, a short man by any standards, and spent way more time at the gym than I cared to. And I…I was a good head-and-a-half taller. It was all the more useful to look down upon people from. Making a wry comment about how height could come in handy, I placed our cabin bags in the overhead compartment. By that time Manohar had settled himself into the third of our seats, across the aisle. He grinned, inviting me to protest. I declined to play at his game. With a meaningful pat on his shoulder, I lowered myself down into the empty seat, next to Maya Jervois.

The usual medley of shuffles and clicks filled the air as passengers tugged at seatbelts and fastened them. Crew announcements, droned safety instructions, the distant boom of huge engines and the high-pitched rush of take off all became a familiar blur of background noise. Shortly after, the smells took over: The standard whiff of the garam-masala-coated monosodium glutamate stuff that passed for food and the sharp, acrid aroma of over-heated coffee.

Meal over, I glanced at my watch. Less than an hour to land. Across the aisle, Manohar was reading on his iPad.

'Do you need anything, Professor?' he asked me, looking up.

I shook my head and gestured to the newspaper I'd just folded up. Our recently exploded car had made for a small story on an inside page. Given the sorry state of affairs in the country, a casualty-free bomb blast in New Delhi was a non-event. A day or two of press, a week or so of the police on high alert and then everyone's interest would turn to the next incident. No doubt there would be an investigation of the blow-up, but there was little for me to be worried about. The people I leased the office from would handle things. The unbelievably high rent I paid them wasn't exactly for the décor, nor had I chosen the place for its companionable neighbours — most other occupants of the building ran far shadier operations than I did.

It was little wonder then that I'd always felt right at home, for I had absolutely no pretensions to being a *good* man. I wasn't one. Good and evil, legitimate and shady were relative concepts that I had little patience with. Fact. Reason. Truth. These were the only virtues that made any sense and the reason behind why I never had, and never would, speak a lie.

Such commitment to honesty could have been a troublesome limitation for a man who wished to keep his identity a secret, but just as truth had always been a way of life for me, so had politics. Never did I say: 'My name is...' for then the only appellation that could follow would be my own. Always, it was, 'You may call me Athanasios', or 'I am known to friends as Javed', and all the names had meant 'Asvatthama'. As the world had changed, so had its morals. I, however, chose to remain the man I'd been. The immutability, the sense of defiance, was a heady feeling.

I settled contentedly into my seat and in the process banged my elbow into Maya Jervois's. I mumbled an instinctive apology without looking at her, hoping that her silence would persist, as it had thus far. But my luck and her patience had both run out.

'Look,' she began, 'I hate to sound rude, but...'

'You want to know where we're going and why,' I said, resigning myself to conversation.

'Yes.'

I turned towards her, uncrossing and recrossing my long legs with some difficulty in the cramped space. 'What are we looking for?'

'Fragments of the Vajra, obviously,' she declared with a shrug.

'Put it differently...'

'Pieces of a gemstone, pieces that were dismantled but can fit back together to form a whole?'

'Well defined. Now, you turned up one piece at Srisailam. Do we even know why Nagarjuna placed it there? Or where he may have left the other fragments?'

She shrugged again, unimpressed. 'I don't know. But others must have, right? So what we need to do is to follow up on the last so-called sighting of the Vajra and...'

'No,' I cut in. 'What you're suggesting is what historians have done all along. And they haven't been very successful, have they? Let me do the job you've hired me for, Ms Jervois. What can you tell me about alchemy?'

'Not much,' she admitted. 'Just the basics I picked up from historical texts. All matter is made up of two types of elements: Base and chemical. Base elements are the building bricks of alchemy. Aristotle talked about four: earth, fire, water and air. In the Eastern world – Japan, India and China, that is – there have always been five; the Chinese count wood and metal as elements, whereas we have space and air on the list, and Japan has air and spirit. Fire, water and earth are common to all three. As for chemical elements, Indian texts place it at twelve key elements, mostly metals, as do many other cultures. Mercury, however, is common to most alchemical traditions... Yeah, that's about it.' She sank back into her seat, her head resting sideways on the small pillow as she watched me with anticipation.

'And where does the Vajra fit into all this?' I asked.

'It links to the longstanding theory that there is a secret alchemical combination, a process or substance that can transmute metals and, by extension, confer eternal life. The Vajra is the key to that secret.'

'Would it surprise you, Ms Jervois, to hear that it's no secret at all?'

Her lips parted in prelude to an exclamation but then she pulled herself together into what she supposed was a neutral expression. I smiled, enjoying the dramatic effect my declaration had, then pulled out a ubiquitous black pen from my pocket. I began to draw on a corner of the newspaper, as I spoke. 'The formula for a transmutative substance is given by many sources, including the Vedas, the Upanishads and the Ayurvedic texts. All of these tell us in no uncertain terms that the elixir is made of three ingredients: Rasa, sometimes also called soma, is mercury, and represents the essence or seed of the cosmic creator; Agni is sulphur, the fiery life-blood of creation; and Vayu – that is, air or life-breath – signifies arsenic. Alternately, the three are described as Moon, Fire and Wind. Combine them, and there you have your transmutative substance.'

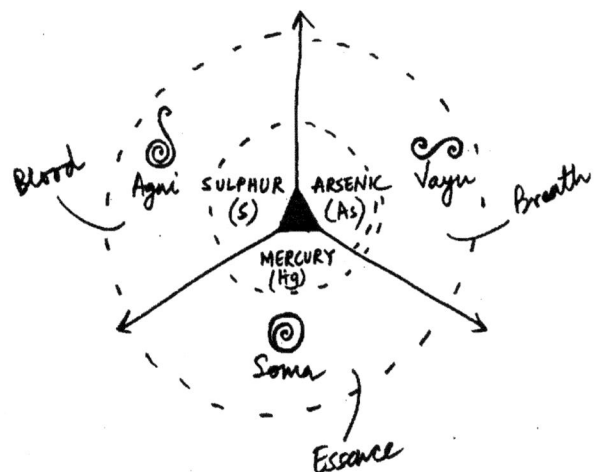

Maya Jervois studied the diagram with due attention before bursting out, 'But that's...'

'Bullshit? Indeed. Hence my reluctance to believe even in the remote possibility that such an object exists.'

She gave me a perceptive look. 'You're here. You must believe some part of it.'

Across the aisle, Manohar had put away his reading and was eyeing me keenly. I continued to address Maya Jervois. 'I don't work on faith. I work on logic. The absence of mercury deposits in India has led scientists and historians alike to conclude all along that it was just an allegorical reference to a more esoteric concept – the seed of the cosmic creator. Likewise with the other two ingredients; the microcosmic, physical world was seen as a symbol of the macrocosmic or spiritual. What you've unearthed opens the door on another possibility altogether. The metaphor may well go the other way round.'

'You mean you use the ethereal as a metaphor for actual physical things?'

'Not me, Ms Jervois; a wiser and better man than I. Nagarjuna himself. I suspect that somewhere in this mix of fact and metaphors, hidden within the benign discussions of medicine and the sensational eroto-mysticism of "tantra", the ancient seers and scientists have chronicled their dealings with the Vajra in much more detail than we think.'

'But why hide it in metaphor?'

'Why did Galileo and Da Vinci hide their theories and findings?'

'You think Nagarjuna faced persecution? That's...'

'Ridiculous?' I finished for her. 'Nagarjuna lived at a time when Shiva and Vishnu were at loggerheads for a position as the god of choice, and the seeds of Buddhism had been sown. As seen in all cultures at some point or the other, both politics and science were subsumed by religious doctrine and creativity was relegated to the custody of esoteric practices. The fear of persecution was bound to become an actuality. No responsible scientist could overlook the possibility that his or her discovery was likely to be politicized. Come on, the story goes that Nagarjuna allowed himself to be beheaded at the behest of Prince Salivahana...'

Maya Jervois mulled over what I'd said. 'So, in order to find the Vajra, we need to decipher the metaphor — to see what these other allegorical ingredients might be in real terms? But how?'

'That's the second step. If we're going to assume that there is a physical basis to the Vajra, we must, by corollary, assume that there is a basis to the legends associated with it. Especially since it fits rather neatly that the Vajra was taken apart into three pieces, there are three main ingredients, three lines of metaphors... The recurrence of the number three is consistent and thematic, too much so to discount it.'

'So we follow the legend trail? But you said that...'

'I know what I said, and I'll tell you again: There's no point picking up the thread from the last reference and running with it, because it is invariably a repetition – with or without distortion – of something from an older source. That's how myths are born.'

'What do you propose?'

'That we begin, not with the most recent, but with the oldest reference we can find. The very basis of what later became legend.'

She was unconvinced. 'How can we know what the oldest reference is?'

'Any reference to the first Indian alchemist is, in relative terms, the oldest.'

'Nagarjuna? But we can't even be too sure of him, given that there are at least three alchemists by that name. And then we also have the Nath-Siddha cult, of whom much is written and said but with no context. How...?'

'There are many, many things we don't know, Ms Jervois, but we always know where the story begins. Everything starts with the gods. The first and foremost of alchemists is none other than Shiva himself.'

The seatbelt signs pinged to life, and we lapsed into silence as the plane began its descent.

9

The transit through Mumbai was uneventful and, on my part, largely silent. Maya Jervois and Manohar insisted on carrying on a conversation from their seats in the waiting lounge on either side of me, while I sat semi-recumbent, legs stretched out, arms crossed over my chest and eyes closed. I could easily go without sleep for a long time, but the posture kept our inquisitive companion from probing me further. Besides, from what I could hear, Manohar was doing an excellent job of fielding her questions.

'It's your basic mythos for the waxing and waning of the moon,' Manohar was saying. 'The story goes that Soma, the moon, progressively lost his effulgence because of a curse. He prayed to Shiva, who could do nothing to stem the loss but did ensure that the process also took place in reverse – a gradual gain in Soma's effulgence. The Taittriya Samhita provides what is, by far, the clearest alchemical account, though with the caveat that it merely records events of the past – history within history, if you like. It talks about how Shiva restores the moon's potency through a soma sacrifice – soma here denoting not only the connection to the moon, but also to rasa, the seed-essence that's a part of our triad of alchemical ingredients. The son that is begot as a result of this restored effulgence is none other than Buddh, the Indian name for…'

'The planet Mercury,' Maya Jervois completed, making the same connection that I had last night, courtesy the Sumerians.

'Exactly,' Manohar confirmed. 'And so begins the legend of Shiva as Siddheshwara or Adi-nath, the first of the alchemists. Srisailam's temple holds a similar link. Shiva is known there as Mallikarjuna; "mallika" being fragrant jasmine – so you see the Vayu or wind element link coming in there. But our interest is not so obscure. What we're going to do is to try and find the physical basis of this metaphor. "Microcosmic" is the word the Professor would use. The myth itself would be mesocosmic.'

'And the macrocosmic? Is there a philosophical explanation for this?'

'There's a philosophical explanation for everything. The first scientists didn't see the gods as the limit or ultimate meaning of all creation. The gods were manifested. There also is an unmanifested part of creation that lies beyond what is perceived as existence. This particular story of the moon and his rasa would link back to the Primordial Creator and the Sacrifice of Creation.'

'You sound like your boss, when you say that.'

'Yeah, I suppose I do. I mean, that's kind of his take on the subject. But I don't have his amorphous view of the gods and Creation.'

Maya Jervois's voice held scepticism. 'Are you a religious man, Manohar? More inclined to a structured view of divinity?'

'No. On the contrary, I'm an atheist. I use that word to particularly distinguish myself from the Professor. He doesn't dispute the existence of a Creator, but firmly holds that it does not provide ground enough to suspend investigation into such an entity's existence. He doesn't believe in belief, if you know what I mean. I, on the other hand...I believe that there is no God. Don't know how to explain it, *yaar*,' he finished.

Maya Jervois began rocking in her seat, making the whole row of chairs wobble. I kept my feet firmly on the floor and refused to let the movement disturb me. 'So,' she said, 'how does this tie in with Rajkot? And we *are* going to Rajkot, aren't we? I saw you checking out the flight timings.'

It was Manohar's turn to be impressed. 'Yes, we're going to Rajkot. As for why... Here, check this out. You can read ITRANS notations of Sanskrit, right? Read this. It's the Samhita that I was telling you about.'

The smell of her hair, fresh and earthy, came at me as she leant across my seat to take Manohar's iPad from him and faded away as she settled back to read what he was showing her.

'Somnath?'

'Yes. The Somnath temple. The place where the legend of alchemy begins and, by coincidence or otherwise, also the place where the alchemist Nagarjuna was born. We take a cab from Rajkot to Veraval, the nearest town.'

'And then? What about the final piece of the Vajra; where will we find that?'

'No idea. Zooming in on Somnath was the easy part. But it's a beginning. That mercury was one hell of a find, Maya. Look what it's started off...'

'Luck. Or destiny.'

There are no such things as serendipity or destiny, I noted, but said nothing.

Manohar made my point for me. 'The Professor doesn't believe in that sort of stuff. Nor do I, just as I don't believe in things like magic and snap-your-fingers changing iron to gold, and all that. What we call magic is what we don't have the science to explain as yet. And just because science can't understand immortality, it doesn't mean it's otherworldly or some such.'

It was so like Manohar to say that. His acceptance had always been a contrast to my insistence on rationality, but he had a calm way about him that had made me come to respect his views over the years we'd been working together.

Maya Jervois's thinking seemed to run along similar lines, for she asked Manohar, 'Where... How... How long have you been working for him?'

With *him, not* for *him*, I silently corrected.

'I met the Professor on a dig in Egypt,' Manohar replied. 'You've heard of the Lepsius Pyramid II? The Abu Rawash cluster? It's also called the Djedefre Pyramid, after the pharoah who commissioned it.'

'Wasn't this the one that was in the news some years ago? I think it was a big find – one of the few pyramids that hadn't been looted because no one knew how to get to the burial chamber at its centre? I don't recall reading of anything coming out of there, certainly not a sarcophagus. One theory was that Djedefre had left the pyramid empty, so there was nothing to find.'

I suspected that Manohar had smiled, for Maya Jervois bristled, 'What?'

'Hey, chill!' he replied. 'It's nice to chat with a fellow historian – other than the Professor, that is. Only we would say sarcophagus and not mummy. Most people don't know the difference! Anyway, getting back to Lepsius II: you're partly right. Nothing much *officially* came out of it. After about two years of explorations, the project was closed down.'

'Why?'

'Too many people died. Lepsius II was one hell of a *kameena*, with traps that haven't even been imagined by Hollywood, let alone Egyptologists. Of course, once they shut it down, that's when the real search began – by the well-financed private historians, with their mercenary armies and high-tech gadgets. You won't believe the stuff that finally did come out of there, Maya. All of it ended up on the black market.'

'And you were with one of these private teams?'

'Yes. It's not as bad as it sounds. I admit, there's some hired muscle who're pretty dubious characters, but mostly its a bunch of academics who reckon that the only way to ever find anything is to work for private collectors, given their research grant would get them a return economy ticket to Cairo, nothing more. But to go on…it was the day we broke through into the chamber that overlay the burial vault. All around me, people were fidgety and nervous…even afraid. The last trick wall standing in our way comes down, and about eighty-odd people – three different exploration teams racing each other to the find, mind you – storm into the chamber. It's like a *mela*, total mob frenzy. And then, Professor Bharadvaj saunters in, hands in his pockets, looking around as though he were some lazy tourist admiring the scenery along the Nile…'

I resisted the temptation to correct him. I hadn't exactly sauntered in. But, yes, my patient methods had been far more effective than the misplaced enthusiasm of the other teams, and it was I who had managed to open up the burial vault and the sarcophagus inside…only to find a rigged mummy that had tried to choke the hell out of me. The Egyptians were smart, I'd hand them that. I'd lived amongst them for many years, but their tricks and skills never ceased to astound me. Be that as it may, Djedefre had died and his pyramid built around the time I was born so I'd had no personal knowledge of the monarch or his commission.

Meanwhile, Manohar continued, '…and then the Professor picks up the Was sceptre and says, "If this fucker hadn't been dead already, I swear I would've killed him!"'

Maya Jervois's laugh rang out warm and unabashed in the vast airport lounge. 'I can't imagine him cursing like that,' she said.

'Like a sailor! On fewer occasions, though,' Manohar clarified.

'And then he asked you to work for him, and you agreed, right?'

'Eventually...' Manohar was evasive.

At the end of it all, we'd found ourselves in the same bar in Cairo, drinking alone, he for his reasons, I for mine. Conversation had struck up, a rare occurrence with me. Rarer still, I'd acted on sentiment – he'd reminded me of an old friend – and offered him a job, regretting the act at once. To my relief, he had declined, his logic indisputable. If he came to work with me, he'd argued, it would suggest we'd been conspiring all along. After all, he pointed out, he'd been the only other person inside the burial vault when I'd worked out how to open the sarcophagus without getting throttled by a mechanical skeleton. I'd been taken aback at his refusal, enough to ask him if a man in his position, a man in it for the money, cared about reputation. His answer had made up my mind. There was, he'd said, such a thing as integrity.

The next morning, I'd flown out of Cairo, but not before leaving behind a nondescript parcel for Manohar, along with a piece of paper that had my phone number on it. He'd called three months later and turned up one week after that.

I emerged from my self-absorption in time to hear him say, with a snap of his fingers, 'And just like that, he gives up Djedefre's sceptre. I mean, this guy risked breaking every bone in his body to get his hands on it and then he gives it away.'

'Yes, but you made your choices too. That sort of a find would have pretty much made your career, either in the consulting line or in academia. For you to give that straightforward kind of job up...'

'I don't know if I gave anything up, but if I did, it's been worth it. Can you imagine the things I've learnt over the years from the Professor? He's taught me more than I could have ever dreamed of learning, no matter where else I was and what else I did. You've seen how he does it all the time? The interrogation, the way he forces you to think, the way he takes you through, step by step.'

'True,' Maya Jervois admitted. Lowering her voice to a whisper, she added. 'Your boss elevates history to a fine art.'

'Not art, Ms Jervois,' I said, without opening my eyes. 'It's a science. A systematic science.'

'You're awake!'

'Well, it's impossible to sleep with you two around. I give up a bloody good sceptre and look what I get in return for my troubles.'

She laughed again and threw herself back in her seat. This time, I could identify the smell in her hair: a heady swirl of shikakai against the soft, creamy smell of sodium laureth sulphate. I glanced at her through half-open lids, taking in for the first time the soft-looking skin of her neck and the small silver hoops she wore in her ears. It made for frivolous but pleasant imagination till Manohar laid a hand on my shoulder and told me it was time for our next flight.

10

By the time we reached Rajkot, my general disposition had markedly improved. Manohar often joked that I was happiest in the midst of old, inanimate objects, from long-dead inhabitants of sarcophagi to never-alive ruins. He was right, though I refused to concede it. As for why the past fascinated me so… It was simple. It rationalized my present.

There was, after all, only a single piece of evidence to affirm that I was who I said I was: In my mind I knew it to be true. But what assurance did I have that I was not deranged? The truth was so incredulous that it would be irresponsible to dismiss the possibility that I was just some schizophrenic convinced he was the Asvatthama of myth. Or, for better or worse, I could well have been a man or a woman in a coma trapped inside my own deluded brain. Were my constant age and appearance evidence of such an incredulous truth or could these also be a product of my make-believe? I found this endless process of deduction quite entertaining.

'You look happy…' Maya Jervois commented.

'I am.'

To my wonder, she left it at that. It occurred to me that the less aloof I acted, the less she displayed what I had come to think of as her near-juvenile side. Was it a defensive reaction on her part, I wondered. The result of having had an indifferent parent? Or the relic of a bad relationship? Did I really care?

Would it be so bad if I did? *It would*, I reminded myself. For me, it was a matter of survival.

Living long had made for many experiences, each instance turning into anamnesis as present became past. But time, I'd been taught by my philosopher mother, was more than a linear unit to be marked only by its passage. It could be relative, it could be cyclical or it could tend to infinity, casting human existence as something that didn't simply begin at birth and end with death but instead was a miniaturized reflection of a force immeasurable on any dimension, including time itself. There was no room in such a life for nostalgia or regret, just as there was no fear of the future or attachment to the past. Without the context of time, all events were merely facts, and memories were made only of information, details one had simply come to know. To a methodical mind, knowledge was hardly a burden.

It was emotion that complicated matters; emotions reduced a rational being into a Pavlovian animal driven by the memory – and thus, expectation – of joy and loss. I'd been trained to never feel in excess under any circumstances and, where the choice presented itself, to not feel at all. For that the credit lay with my father, a man who'd held practice in higher esteem than philosophy. He had considered such traits essential to my evolution into a consummate warrior. I couldn't tell whether it was his karma or mine that those lessons had proved effective, but I knew that my mother's postulates had undoubtedly made the prospect of an eternal future, and the infinite past that lay ahead, bearable.

As for Maya Jervois, it was useful to know what made her tick and it was entertaining to be in her company. Any assessment beyond that was unneccessary.

A blast of warm air enveloped us as we left the air-conditioned airport building and stepped into the shimmering heat that enveloped Rajkot city.

'We're booked in at the Safar Resort,' Manohar said. 'Someone from the hotel should be here to pick us up.'

No sooner had he said the words than we spotted a white-capped chauffeur standing in front of an old but clean white Toyota Qualis. He held a sheet of white paper that proclaimed, in typical title-first-name fashion: 'Dr Manohar, New Delhi.'

Manohar made his way towards the man, who snapped to attention. 'Namaste, sir. Welcome to Gujarat.'

'Thank you,' Manohar said. He handed over his bag to the waiting driver and made to help Maya Jervois with hers.

'My dear, chivalrous Manohar! Not once have you taken this old man's bag so readily and with such concern!' I teased.

Manohar was taken aback, but only for a moment. He grinned and, overlooking Maya Jervois's protests, took her bag and placed it in the Qualis.

She raised an eyebrow at me and said, 'That's because you're hardly an old man, you know. You look fit enough to give a twenty-year-old a run for his money!'

I took the compliment without protest, noticing that ever since the exchange at the airport over my name she avoided addressing me as 'Professor'.

We bundled into the waiting vehicle, glad of the air-conditioning inside, and soon we were out of Rajkot city and on a highway.

'How did you find this hotel?' Maya Jervois asked.

'Tripadvisor.com,' Manohar proclaimed. 'According to the reviews, it has clean bathrooms, a decent restaurant and a good view of the sea; in that order of priority.'

'Not to mention it's barely two kilometres from the Somnath temple,' I added.

'Did you know,' she began, 'there's an old novel by Wilkie Collins called *The Moonstone*? Apparently, there used to be a diamond on the forehead of the idol at Somnath. The story is a murder mystery about some chaps who take the gem to England and all that.'

Manohar was curious. 'Really?'

'You don't think the story has any basis, do you?'

Before I could reply, the driver interrupted. 'Madam, you want to buy moonstone? I can take you to a good shop, no problem. All types of gemstones, very cheap. Gujarat famous for gems and for cutting. Best diamond cutting in world.'

'Err, no, thank you.'

'Very good quality, madam,' he persisted. 'Also available other stones. I can take you to very good jyotish as well.'

'Sorry, I don't believe in astrology.'

Dismissed, the crestfallen driver fixed his gaze on the road.

Manohar glanced over his shoulder at us, a bemused look on his face.

'Well?' Maya Jervois demanded.

'Hmm?'

'The story. Any basis?'

'Moonstones come from Sri Lanka,' I replied, toying with her.

'Try again,' she riposted.

I leaned over to tap the driver on his shoulder. '*Bhai*, what can you tell us about the Somnath temple?'

The man was immediately in his element. 'Sir, Somnath is very holy place. One of twelve jyothirdhams, fire-temples of Shivji. This particular temple very, very old. Story is, first building by Moon-god. Moon-god has many wife, but one favourite wife. So his father-in-law curse him that he will fade. But Moon-god worship Shivji, and Shivji give him blessing that every time he fades he will grow again. That is why we have phases of the moon. So place where Moon-god prayed to Shivji become Somnath. Next temple here built by Raavan, and when that destroy Bhagwan Shri Krishna build temple here. That also destroy. Then Gujarat king build in red sandstone, but destroy by invasion of Ghazni Mahmud. One more king by name Bhima build again but was destroy by Allaudin Khilji. Many more times destroy till demolish by Aurangzeb and convert to mosque. After independence from British, Honourable Deputy Prime Minister of India Sardar Vallabhbhai Patel shift mosque to new site nearby and reconstruct the Somnath temple. Sir, you want tour guide to see around temple? Also see Pandav *gufa*, cave?' he finished.

'We'll let you know,' I replied. 'But that was very informative!' The driver turned his attention back to the road, satisfied that we weren't philistines after all.

Maya Jervois shrugged. 'I don't get it. What're you trying to say here? Somnath's iconoclastic history has been a subject of academic debate for so long. The most prominent of historians have been through the whole story and taken it apart in god-knows how many ways! On the one hand it's been held up as an example of how Muslim invaders of old decimated Hindu shrines and, on the other, of how political forces ushered in a Hindutva uprising in the post-colonial era. Add to that the strong British colonial interest in Somnath, probably because of the rich mines in the region or the supposed wealth hidden inside it.'

'And do you know what is hidden inside it, Ms Jervois?'

She faltered. 'No. I don't know.'

'Nothing.'

'Nothing?'

'Absolutely nothing. The Somnath temple is hardly sixty years old. You heard what the driver said. It was consecrated sometime in the 1950s.'

'What about the old temple?'

'The few ruins that were left are in a museum. It's not the edifice that makes Somnath sacred, it's the place. The new temple is built exactly on the same spot at which the ruins of the older temple stood. One can safely assume that the older temple too was built on the ruins of the one before it, and so on...'

'You mean the temples built by the Moon-god and Raavan, and all that?'

Manohar said, 'Have you heard of a text called the *Rasendra Mangala*?'

'Of course. Matsyendra's work. *In Praise of Alchemy*, I believe, is how you'd translate it.'

'Yes. In that and in Vaghabhatta's text, as well as many Tibetan Buddhist works, you have a list of alchemists – a lineage of the masters, if I can call it that. Nagarjuna himself is fifth on that list. The list begins with Adi-natha; the first master. We talked about this, remember – Shiva himself as the first of the alchemists? Any bets on whose name is second in line?'

Maya Jervois smiled. 'I feel such a fool sometimes, around you both. You make it all look so easy... Is the second alchemist in the list Soma?'

Manohar nodded. 'Chandra, to be precise. But that's another name for Soma, the Moon. The third is Lankesa – Lord of Lanka, or Raavan. In fourth position we have Suraseni, a Yadava king. Then comes our dear friend Nagarjuna. Of course, we could forget the deductive approach and go with popular lore instead. Many believe that the original idol of Somnath, the one worshipped by Soma himself, is still there, somewhere underground.'

'You mean, a vault?' she asked. 'Like the ones at the Padmanabhaswamy temple in Kerala?'

'Exactly. But it's probably just a yarn.'

'Probably,' I added, with a wide grin. Manohar was right. I did enjoy doing this, after all.

The conversation ebbed, and in the lull that followed, Maya Jervois fell asleep. I did a discreet check in the rear-view mirror to make sure that the driver hadn't followed suit, before throwing my arms up and out in a stretch and resettling myself in my seat. Before I knew it, we were at Veraval.

We entered the city from the north and drove alongside the coast, the sea on our right and a large ship-building yard on our left. I rolled down the windows to let the evening sea breeze in and, after some hesitation, laid a hand on Maya Jervois's shoulder.

'We're here,' I said. She opened her eyes and looked up at me, her gaze dreamy. 'We're here,' I repeated. 'You might want to look outside; it's a nice evening.'

She immediately sat up and, taking a small camera out of her bag, began snapping pictures of the magnificent streaks of red that nature had brushed across the sky. A towering silhouette rose in the distance and drew closer. 'Is that…?' she asked.

'That's the new temple, yes. It's quite a building, modern though it may be.'

'It's pretty close to the sea. Of course, it wouldn't have been that way when the first temple was built there: Sea levels along the Indian coast have been rising at about one-and-a-half millimetres a year…'

I nodded absently, but said nothing. My mind drifted to

another city, a huge, magnificent capital built on a gigantic rock, surrounded by the sea on all sides. It had existed not too far away from where we presently were. In fact, Veraval itself had once been named as Prabhasa – the infamous place where the Yadava rulers of old had destroyed themselves through civil war.

Manohar, however, ran with the premise. 'So, assuming the original temple was built circa 500 BCE…'

'Why 500 BCE?' Maya Jervois interrupted.

'There's sparse evidence to show widespread temple-based worship of gods before then. Both the Indus and the pre-Vedic civilizations were all about nature worship, even when they built the rare structure, like at Kashi or Mathura. They hadn't yet started housing more omnipotent gods in temples or surrounding them with scripture and ritual. Of course, if you want to be picky, astrologers claim that on the basis of the Puranas they can date the first temple here at Somnath to the Treta Yuga, making it over seven million years old. That's not an estimate I'm comfortable with.'

'Fair enough,' she accepted.

'So, what was I saying?' Manohar continued. '*Haan*, assuming the temple was built around two thousand years ago and taking your statistics of one-point-five millimetres, we're looking at a rise of two to three metres in sea level. Two metres of vertical rise could inundate huge areas of coastal land, particularly here along the western coast. I don't have the exact information, but I do know that historians and geologists agree that the Kutch and Kathiawar peninsulas were in fact, a larger land mass. Much of it has been submerged over the years.'

'Which also means,' Maya Jervois added her own calculations, 'the original Somnath temple would have stood around a kilometre or two away from the coastline. Of course, now there appears to be a sea-wall around the whole temple complex. It is picturesque though, the sea washing up right against it like that.'

The three of us stared out the window. The driver thoughtfully slowed down as we drove past the temple and then picked up speed again.

'Where's the hotel?' Manohar asked him.

'Sir, two minutes. Before the road to Gir Forest.'

We arrived within the promised two minutes. Cheered by the driver's punctuality as much as his general eagerness, I gave him a large tip. Hardly had I done so than I saw what a strategic mistake it had been – he'd probably haunt us till we checked out, offering to take us shopping or find us a tour guide.

'The place is packed,' Manohar informed us once he'd checked us in. 'Peak season, I believe. The new moon is a couple of days away.'

I frowned, thinking of the inevitable crowds in and around the area. On impulse, I handed my bag to Manohar. 'Take this upstairs for me, will you? I think I'll take a stroll down to the temple and get my bearings a bit.'

Leaving him and Maya Jervois to their devices, I made my way out of the hotel. I crossed the wide main road in front of the building and walked down a slope to find myself right on the beach. The air was cool, and a gentle sea breeze added to the pleasantness of the evening. To the north, about two kilometres away, the colossal tower of the Somnath temple dominated the entire city. I began walking in its direction.

The closer I got to the temple, the more crowded it was. Tourists, or rather pilgrims who'd finished with the devotional duties of the day, sought secular distraction. Children played in the sand; some watched enviously as others took rides on colourfully decked ponies. Families sat around munching on cheap snacks sold by hawkers. Here and there, a couple of peddlers tried to sell postcards and plastic souvenirs.

I was one of the few solitary wanderers on the strip. Nearby, a forlorn-looking homeless man sat staring out at the waves. Another lone wanderer, a dapper man stood with his hands stuck deep in his trouser pockets, gazing up at the towering façade of the temple with pride. I studied this young Indian-and-proud-of-it type with mild curiosity. He must have felt me staring, for he met my gaze and nodded in polite greeting. I returned the silent salutation and moved on. It seemed absurd to think that a mundane place such as this could hold anything secret. There was a reassuringly commonplace air about it, like a park or a shopping mall. Bustle and activity and beneath that, nothing at all.

The beach narrowed as it ran past the high wall that formed the outer perimeter of the temple complex. At high tide, the waves would lap against the wall, even as the temple tower stood defiant, hardly fifteen metres above the water's edge. A temple built and destroyed so many times that it had become a symbol in its own right, and a contentious one at that. Riches, Al-Biruni's description of which had allegedly driven Mahmud of Ghazni to invade this land. And, of course, tales that spoke of the amazing resurrection of the moon's power and the underground crypt in which this change had taken place.

Assuming this underground crypt existed, how could I find it? *Correction. How would Professor Bharadvaj find it?*

I was a man of motley careers, most of them incidental to the character I'd assumed in pursuit of my professed goal. Professor Bharadvaj had been one of the few exceptions to the rule, a conscious choice of career that had led to the persona, rather than the other way round, the result of a rather prosaic conversation with a bullock-cart driver.

A citizen of a five-day-old Republic of India in 1950, I'd been making my way towards New Delhi from a village in Haryana, where I'd settled all loose ends of my brief and partly selfish involvement with the freedom movement and the nation-building that had followed. Having hitched a ride on said gentleman's bullock cart – a vehicle that trundled along at an excruciatingly slow pace – there had been no escape from small talk. He'd asked me what I did for a living and I'd told him, truthful as always, that I was unemployed. He then asked me, in his rustic but undeniably perceptive way, what my craft was, adding that jobs could come and go but one's knowledge and craft was a gift from the gods. I'd hesitated, having answered similar questions in the past with a reference to what I'd fought for, whom I'd fought for, or the indisputable fact that my trade was fighting. But something in his mild demeanour and his hope-filled eyes had made me want to speak of peace.

'So, what can you do? What do you know?' the man had persisted.

I'd said, as a confession, 'I know the past.'

Two weeks later on the riverbanks of Kashi, Professor Bharadvaj, the historian, had come into existence.

I'd been exceptionally good at the calling, not only because I had lived through history but also because I understood how people thought, how such thought had evolved over the years, and how things had changed as the world had changed. And the key to finding that which even history had lost sight of lay buried, not in time but in that process of change.

Letting my mind remove the people, the construction, all the trappings of modernity around me, I saw the place as an idea, a map, a project on some ancient architect's canvas. How would he have built this city? What had he built it for? What did he want to hide and what did he want to preserve?

Five kilometres away to the north, right along the beach, were three Shivalinga idols set in a perfectly straight line and visible only when the tide was low: They were all that remained of what had once been many. I drew an imaginary line of idols along the same axis, letting it run south, past the Somnath temple and where I stood. It would, I knew, run without touching land all the way to the Antarctic.

My mind's eye shifted again to the temple as I extended the East-West latitude it lay on to intersect my imagined meridian of submerged Shivalingas. Then I turned eastward, trying to find a point on the same axis, at about the same distance from the temple as the line of Shivalingas. The result was gratifying. My axis cut the banks of the river Hiren at the very place where there stood a small cave temple with the spiral mark of Anantasesha, the king of snakes.

Many believed that this was where Balarama, elder brother of the avatar Krishna, had passed from his mortal existence in the form of a snake. Few recognized the emblem for what it truly was: the symbol of rising inner energy, the ultimate totem of the alchemist. Anantasesha's energy was both the key to eternity and the final destroyer of the world at the end of every age.

I smiled. Veraval stood before me as it had moments ago. But I saw it as the microcosm, the model of the universe that every temple-complex, even whole cities aspired to be. I saw the lines my mind had drawn – a series of mandalas or squares that I could superimpose as a plan for things that no longer had form but existed nonetheless and always would.

Now it was just a matter of getting in.

11

'Here?' Maya Jervois was incredulous.

'Shh!' Manohar warned, looking around to make sure we were alone.

I placed a calming hand on his shoulder. 'Relax, Manohar. No one expects anyone to be here. What is this, Tirupati? There's not even a gold pin to steal!'

'All the more reason why we'd get into trouble for skulking around at one in the morning.'

'I don't get it,' Maya Jervois said, this time in a whisper. 'What are we doing here?' She looked at the distant but unmistakeable silhouette of the Somanth temple against the blue-black night sky, as though wondering why we weren't there instead.

Manohar turned to her in mild alarm. 'Don't tell me you want to hear the whole thing all over again!'

By the time I'd got back from my walk around Somnath, Maya Jervois had been asleep. Manohar and I began discussing our options and making plans right away. At about midnight, we'd woken her up and explained my theory to her. She'd sounded convinced then, but I wondered if I'd mistaken her sleepy acquiescence for logical acceptance. Now, wide awake and alert from our nocturnal walk, followed by the acrobatic feat of climbing over the boundary wall, she sounded sceptical.

She took a deep breath and let it out. 'When you said "cave", this certainly wasn't what I expected.'

Indeed. We stood next to a board that categorically identified the location as the 'cave temple' – a small site that was under the auspices of the main Somnath temple. Despite the nomenclature, there was neither cave nor rock in sight, only a small concrete structure, complete with the dark pinkish-cream paint that was characteristic of the region's modern temple architecture. An expanse of open space, part lawn and part concrete, bordered the building. Pathways connected the structure to an office building on one side and to the riverside promenade and the open gazebo beside it on the other. That was where the footprints of a man I'd once known were captured on a marble pedestal and worshipped. I smiled in the dark as I imagined exactly what the 'avatar' in question would have said about the adulation that posterity had showered on him.

'Could you hold this, please?' Manohar thrust a flashlight into my hands as he bent over the lock. He had it open in seconds. Maya Jervois was about to step inside, when he grabbed her arm.

'What the...?' she began.

He pointed to her shoes. 'This is a temple, no matter what our purpose for being here may be.'

She glared at him, then at me. I took off my shoes but left my socks on. With a sigh, she did the same. We entered.

'Shut the door,' I instructed, glad that the building had no windows or openings for the light to give us away on the odd chance that some random temple official or guard happened to pass by.

The room we were in was barely three metres long and just as wide. It was also absolutely empty, a fact emphasized by the polished pink granite that covered the floor and the walls. A small door was set into the opposite wall, leading possibly to an antechamber or hallway. Maya Jervois opened this second door with enthusiasm. She gave a start and took a step backwards.

'Nicely done,' I said, crouching down by the narrow doorway to flash the torch down into what presumably was a pit of blackness. The floor of this second room – a rock grotto – was set a few metres lower than the one we stood on, and steps made of the same pink granite used in the outer room led down into it. Etched into the wall of this grotto and covered with saffron paste was the spiral symbol of Anantasesha, the serpent with seven heads. A small pedestal that served to hold a lamp and some other items of worship completed the contents of the room.

'What next?'

'Let me take a closer look. Wait here.'

I stepped into the grotto and systematically pored over every inch of the rough walls. The original stone ceiling was low, just about level with the floor of the outer room. Whatever rock or mountain the cave might have once been a part of had since been broken away.

Unless...

I dropped down on my knees at a corner and flashed my torch along the joints. 'See how the wall and the floor meet at a perfect angle?' I said. 'Nature can't do that. The elements tend to round, not chisel. This is a stonemason's work. This wasn't a natural cave, it was part of a larger structure. And I'm willing to bet that this was the eastern entrance to what we're looking for.'

Standing back up, I turned my attention to the carved symbol set into the wall and then to the pedestal before it. Following the worn-out designs carved on to the block all the way to the floor, I happened upon a further incongruity. 'And this isn't a pedestal, at least it wasn't originally one. This was a pillar,' I declared.

Maya Jervois was shining her flashlight all around the room. 'But where's the entrance? Or is it that the entrance survives and the building itself is gone?'

Manohar said, 'Can't be. What we're looking for is underground.'

'How come the Archaeological Survey has never studied all this? I mean, if we excavate down there…'

I said, 'If you excavate down here, you'll be lynched. Somnath has always been a sensitive and controversial monument. Remember the outcry, some years ago, when that historian proposed an alternate theory to the destruction of the earlier temples? This is a communal hotbed. No one in their right mind would dare dig up Somnath – or for that matter half the Indian countryside. Seriously, there's no shortage of groups we might offend across the religious spectrum. That's why unscrupulous men such as Manohar and I get rich, and a nice woman like you is here in the middle of the night with us, instead of resting at some five-star resort in Diu with a full excavation team at your beck and call.'

Manohar chuckled. 'I don't know if we qualify as unscrupulous, Professor,' he remarked.

'No?'

'I would say just irreverent.'

'Says the man who made me take off my shoes,' Maya Jervois quipped, as she carefully walked down the steps, into the grotto. Sliding her torch out from the waistband of her pants, she examined the etching with interest.

'Well, Ms Jervois, what next?' I teased.

'Beats me!' she confessed. 'Honestly? I don't think I've ever been tomb-raiding like this. I'm more a desk-job kind of person.'

I did toy with the thought of passing a snide comment about the kind of desk job a historian could do at the NDRO, but let her lie stand, saying instead, 'Tomb-raiding is easy. There's always some button to push, some lever to manoeuvre, and everything opens up into huge underground chambers with statues of Kali and Bhairav and all that.'

'All we have here is this.' She pointed to the etching, suddenly serious. 'This doesn't add up. What does a Vishnu symbol have to do with Shiva?'

'Shiva wears a snake,' Manohar said. 'Round his neck. It's a mark that he is the ultimate yogi, with complete control over mind and energy, passion and desire. Coiled snakes such as this one represent the potential of that energy.'

'And the seven heads?'

'That can mean many things. The seven chakra points along which energy rises. The seven sons of Brahma with whom all creation began.'

'The seven netherworlds, the manifested realm of Rudra himself,' I added. 'Atala, Vitala, Sutala, Rasatala, Talatala, Mahatala, Patala.'

I reached out to touch the figure carved on the wall. Maya Jervois gasped, expectant. Feeling captivated myself, I ran my hand over the shape, feeling the contours of its seven heads, tracing the never-ending spiral of its body right down to the centre.

'Well?' she asked.

'Nothing.'

'Have you been here before?'

'Never.' *Not as Professor Bharadvaj, nor as anyone else. Not even when it had thrived as the matchless city-state of the Yadava tribes during the time of the Great War.*

'Then what on earth made you think…?'

'Logic. You know the old Sherlock Holmes dialogue, I'm sure.'

'Yes, yes; when the impossible is eliminated or some such…'

'"Some such" won't work here, Ms Jervois. "Some such" is the stuff movies and books are made of. Not life.'

'Then?'

'Science. We need science. Manohar, pass down the bag, will you?' Manohar held out the black duffel bag that had accompanied us all the way from Delhi. I reached out to take the bag, saying, 'Got it. Let go.'

He did, and I felt the full weight of the equipment on my hands. Maya Jervois came forward to help but I shook my head and crouched down to place the bag on the ground. Opening it, I began hauling out ostensibly innocent tubes, clamps and a small motorized contraption.

'What's that?' she asked, as I began assembling the apparatus.

'It's called a vacuum lifter. This gadget here has the power to lift two tonnes.'

'Whoa!'

Manohar said, 'You should see the industrial version – lifts hundreds of tonnes. This baby is a lightweight, battery-powered army-specification thing. Borderline illegal...'

'So you're trying to get through the floor. But how do you know there is a way through?'

I pointed to the patterns of saffron on the floor, left behind from the daily ritual cleansing and anointing of the Sesha symbol. Stains had collected in what could have been a natural crevice in the rock, except that they formed far too neat a line. Aligning the vacuum lifter with the line, I fixed the suction plate in place.

'Will this work?' Maya Jervois looked doubtful.

'The stone itself won't be more than half a tonne or so, at the most. The lifter should do the trick. But it's going to make some noise...'

As she stuffed her fingers in her ears in jest, I powered the vacuum lifter on. Hardly a few moments of high-pitched whining and then the slab gave, faster and easier than I'd expected. The suction plate yanked it clean out of the floor to throw it loose. I'd calibrated the machine for a higher load – expecting the stone to have been cemented in over time – and the excess suction had caused a recoil in the light metal frame of the lifter. The smell of burning rubber filled the air; the machine let out a wheeze and listed to one side, making the suspended block swing wildly to and fro in the narrow space.

'Watch out!' I grabbed Maya Jervois and rolled out of the way, right over the opening in the ancient floor. The lifter moved again under its own momentum, and the stone altered its arc to come directly at us. Before we could react, a cracking noise filled the air – one of the machine legs had given way. The heavy slab was jerked back as the unstable lifter tilted. Like some geo-mechanical wild creature set to pounce, stone slab and lifter both hovered over us, threatening to crush us at any moment.

'Jump!' I heard Manohar shout. 'Jump, Professor! Jump!'

Maya Jervois reacted first, tucking her knees to her chest to roll neatly under the suspended block, her arm held out to me. 'Come on!'

I complied, grabbing hold with one hand as I used the other to push us both into the breach.

And then we were falling. So was the stone above us. Just as I drew in my trailing arm, the slab resettled into its rightful place and shut out the world above with a thundering crash. The flashlight slipped out of my hand, struck rock and went off. I tried to grab on to something, anything, but I was plunging down an incline... No, not smooth like an incline but also steep... A flight of stairs. This was meant to be a way in and down.

Finally, the stairs came to an end, and I to a stop. Pain shot through the entire right side of my body. I blinked rapidly, trying to adjust my vision to the darkness, but it made no difference. A yelp sounded through the blackness.

'Maya?' I called out, using her first name despite myself.

'I'm here. I'm okay...I think. Hang on.' A strong, steady beam of light came on, and I made out a crouching form not too far away. I got to my feet and went over to her.

'I'm okay,' she repeated. 'A few bruises, that's all. Lucky I hung on to my torch, eh?'

'All right, I'm impressed,' I said. 'Give me that.' I took the torch from her and shone it over her in a wave. She had a couple of visible bruises on her face and arms and probably more where I couldn't see them, but she appeared otherwise unhurt.

'What happened?' she asked.

'Stairs. We fell down a flight of stairs. I should have expected the slab to give easily – it was designed to open and shut, like a trap door.' I shone the beam around us and exclaimed: 'Frigging hell, we came through *that*?' It was hard to believe that neither of us had broken any bones or had our heads bashed in. Hewn into the rock, the stairs were each about half-a-metre high and ran all the way up to the ceiling, about twenty metres overhead. Beyond that, there was no indication of the trapdoor through which we had fallen, nor did there appear to be a way to trigger the mechanism from the inside. I took out my cell phone and checked for a signal, though I didn't expect to get one.

'What do we do now?'

I hesitated, unsure. Manohar and I had our emergency protocols, but most of them involved waiting for me to figure my way out of trouble. After all, it wasn't as if the delay was going to kill me. With Ms Jervois...Maya...involved, I wasn't quite sure of what Manohar would do, or what he'd think I'd want him to do. And then there remained the matter of our pursuers, rather, Maya's accomplices. Sooner or later, they would surely apply themselves to the matter of getting her out of there.

All things considered, I said, 'Manohar will figure something out...' I stopped short and shone the flashlight on the ground at my feet. It was smooth and well worn. Around us, the walls had, in places, the irregular touch of nature's creation but were largely symmetrical. We were in a tunnel that was roughly five metres in width and twice that in height.

'Is this...?'

'Yes,' I said. 'We're inside.'

12

Maya and I exchanged looks in the semi-darkness.

'It wouldn't hurt...' she noted. 'I mean, it's another four hours to first light...'

I weighed the options. It was judicious to try to find another way out. If that failed, we could always come back here and wait for Manohar to help us. I nodded. She stood up, and we began walking, cautious at first and then with more confidence. The smell of bats, the expected inhabitants, was strong, but the creatures were clearly out on their nocturnal hunt.

'There's water on the floor,' Maya said.

'A small stream from somewhere? This passage must open out to some place, if there are bats living here.'

'Yeah... Hang on. Are those bones?' Maya grabbed my arm to steady the beam of light, shining it on a cluster of white shards.

I bent down to pick up one of the pieces and examined the marrowless insides. 'Yup.'

'Could be animal bones,' she said.

'Hmm.' I didn't refute her suggestion, though I was pretty sure she knew, as I did, that the remains were human. In a way, it gave more credence to our search. It was, after all, unlikely that no one had ever come here in search of some historical legacy or the other. And it was downright ridiculous to think that no one had ever died in search of the Vajra. But I couldn't explain why the shards of bone lay as they did, as though they'd been pushed or swept together by someone or something. I kept my ominous observations to myself, and we moved ahead.

Around us, the passage narrowed in width and height. The walls took on a smoother look, and the puddles of water coalesced into a small stream that gurgled across the floor of the tunnel within an indented channel, leaving hardly any room on either side for us to walk on.

Roughly two kilometres from where we had started, we hit a T-junction. 'Well?' I said, looking left and right.

'Remember what you told me about mandalas – the square-on-square maze-type plans used in olden times?'

'Hmm?'

'This might be a maze that we have to walk through to get to the building. What we've done is walk from the outer square, towards the inner one. To get inside, though, we'd have to turn right or left. That is, we'd have to walk north or south, before we get a chance to go east again, see what I mean?'

'I do. But I'm also sceptical. A mandala doesn't have to be square-on-square – the old texts on architecture talk about more than sixteen different temple layouts, square and rectangular being the most generic. However, there are other elements fundamental to the symbolic representation of the cosmos that are not negotiable. For example, your typical mandala architect would've considered it imperative to have a doorway here – towards the east. That it's blocked makes me wonder.'

'It might have been blocked later. Centuries is a long time, you know.'

Indeed.

Maya took my reticence for indecision and persisted. 'Look, the water channel also runs both ways. It must go somewhere!'

'All right.'

'North or south?'

'North.'

We turned right and continued walking. I kept looking at my watch, concerned that we might lose track of time in the darkness. I was about to call a halt when the tunnel cut at a perfect ninety degrees, to our left. A kilometre along this new bearing, and the passage changed course again.

Maya was elated. 'See? There's your mandala.'

I didn't say anything but I wasn't convinced. No self-respecting ancient architect would've blocked off both the eastern and the northern gateways.

'Hey, I need some light here!' Maya was already well into the side passage.

I followed.

The passageway narrowed further. We could hardly stand side by side without stepping into the water channel at our feet. The ceiling too was lower; any more and I would graze my head.

'I hope you're not claustrophobic?' Maya asked, solicitous.

I shook my head to say no. My father had made sure that I'd overcome that and many other fears by the effective method of making me face them. In this particular case, he'd shut me inside a lightless vault deep inside the royal prisons for three days. The challenge had not been to survive thirst or starvation; the body could do without food or water for a good length of time. This had been a test of reason and nerve. Alone in the darkness, one's mind became the enemy. The imagination created demons that didn't exist, ratified fears that were irrational and brought out the worst in one's self. Courage, I'd learnt that day, came not from faith, love or other such sentiments, but from unswerving logic.

When I'd finally been released from that dungeon, a bit shaken and highly dehydrated, my father had shown me the marks, the desperate scratches left on its walls by the men who'd died in there. But before that had happened, he explained, they'd gone mad – every man, without exception. My stomach had churned and I'd coughed up bile, imagining what each one must have gone through. I'd endured it too, but had been kept sane solely by my ignorance – a strength that had since been replaced by the resilience that came of the knowledge that my father had been genuinely happy with me, but it was a happiness for which he'd been willing to risk *my* life and *my* mind.

My tone belied the muddle of anger and confidence that the memory stirred, and I said, cheerful, 'Go on, Maya. I'm right behind you.'

Maya took a few steps, trying to straddle the water channel. She soon gave up and stepped into the water with an expectant grimace.

'Slimy?'

'No,' she replied. 'Though I am kind of pissed off that Manohar took our shoes.'

The wet trek was short. We'd splashed our way through for less than ten minutes when the tunnel veered to our left and, a few metres later, opened up into an underground chamber.

'Well, I'll be…' Maya exclaimed, as she stepped out of the tunnel and into the vault. I knew exactly how she felt. To stand in a place so ancient and yet undiscovered, to realize what had endured through the ages even as one wondered how much of the past was irrecoverably lost…

Leaving Maya to take in the experience, I began to examine the room we were in. It was perfectly proportioned, and the ceiling was higher here than in the tunnel, but low enough for me to touch. Our companion, the water channel in the floor, bifurcated and ran parallel to the walls in a smaller quadrangle, pooling ultimately into a receptacle about a square metre. A similar channel entered through another tunnel right opposite where we stood, completing the symmetry. Within the pool, the water churned and swirled, the opposing currents from the two inward conduits setting up a small eddy. By the light of the torch, the water looked like molten silver.

I took a step back to run my hand over the wall near the doorway, searching for some mark, some indentation in the stone that would help me identify the way we'd come, but there wasn't any. Trusting in the virtues of being systematic, I kept a count of my steps in each direction as I walked around the room, Maya at my side.

'What is this place?' she whispered. 'Where are we?'

'Don't you know by now? We're right under the Somnath temple. Think of how we got here and the distance we've covered. Consider the shape of this room, the way the corridor turned... These two doorways would be aligned on an east-west median. This is the original inner sanctum of the *old* temple, the *garbha griha*.'

'But...it's empty. Where's the idol? The idol is supposed to be here, right? And what about the doorways? If this is an inner sanctum, then shouldn't the opening be set differently?'

'I don't know, Maya. This place is like...well, a temple and yet not quite. No doorways, no inscriptions, nothing. This is a man-made structure but it's not any historical building that we know of. It's neither epic age nor medieval, and certainly not more recent.'

Something older?

Or something different. Not a temple. Not quite.

Maya came upon the answer first, though she did not grasp its full significance. 'It could be because we were talking about Egypt earlier in the day,' she began, 'but this place reminds me of the Valley of the Kings.' She added, as she might for a layperson's benefit, 'You know, where they shot *The Mummy Returns*.'

It took some effort, but I showed no reaction. I did not

wish to dignify her statement with a response, mostly because I was astounded that I'd missed what she'd so easily caught. As though affirming my lapse, the image in my mind flashed as a reflection on the pool of silver water: I saw myself as I'd once been, a familiar, friendly figure at my side. He leaned in to whisper to me; his dulcet voice rang soundlessly through the room.

'As above, so below, as within, so without, as the universe, so the soul...'

The famous words of Hermes Trismegistus.

Mentioned on record for the first time around the first century CE by Plutarch, Hermes Trismegistus – or Hermes, the thrice-great master – was renowned in fable as the founding father of alchemy and had since been appropriated as symbol or saint by many a mysterious group, the Freemasons included. Modern historians, however, were aware that Hermes had, in fact, been the Greek name for the Egyptian god Thoth, who, in no less a feat of fantasy, had brought the slain Osiris back to life. Beyond that, nothing pointed to a more accurate determination of who this Hermes might have been. Except, when I'd first met the man in question, he had traced his name on the sandy banks of the Nile, spelling it out phonetically in old Greek, for my ease. The letters had come together to form the Greek word 'Thoth' but in the language of Egypt, the word had been pronounced 'Djehuty'.

The name of Djehuty was equally well-known in history, though it seemed he had little to do with Greece or alchemy. He'd been an architect and had designed the first mortuary-temple – a structure different from the pyramid-tombs of previous rulers – for Pharaoh Hatshepsut of Egypt sometime around 1600 BCE. While modern archaeologists continued to debate the true use for such a structure, I knew that it had been a workshop, the place where Hermes-Djehuty had set new frontiers in metallurgy and raised ancient Egypt to the pinnacle of its glory. He had discovered a means to extract the purest gold from dull ore using mercury through a process of large-scale amalgamation. And for that he had built inside his temple huge extraction chambers, tanks that held the enormous amounts of water necessary for the process and were emptied and replenished constantly through an elaborate network of aqueducts – all of which had lain underground.

The ghost of Djehuty placed his hand on my shoulder in a reassuring way. And then, it disappeared, leaving behind a stone chamber and silver-like water.

In the mental speechlessness that followed, I understood. 'Vadhava...' I said.

Maya started. 'What?'

I gestured to the pool before us. 'You wanted to see what it was that the Moon-god worshipped, Ms Jervois. This is it. Vadhava is the liquid force that stems from Shiva's third eye, the original life-blood of alchemy.'

13

Maya gaped at me, incredulous. 'The life-blood? This? You're messing with me! This is just water. Not fire. *Water!*'

'So you'd say. But an alchemist deals not with the way things are, but with the potential of things – what they can be. And seawater is the biggest natural sink for organic sulphur which, in turn, is an essential component of protein molecules – the building blocks of life.'

I walked to the shallow pool and bent down to scoop some shimmering water into my palm and sipped it for taste.

Maya came to kneel next to me and dipped her hand into the pool. 'But what does Vadhava have to do with this?' she asked. 'Isn't that the name of a horse?'

'There's more to it. Most ancient cultures have some sort of creation and destruction myth. The Upanishads tell of Vaishvanara, the soul-fire that spews from the mouth of the primordial equine creature, as the force of creation. Vadhava, on the other hand, is the cataclysm that will surge from an under-sea volcano known as Vadhava-mukha to annihilate all life on earth. In fact, some scholars believe it's a reference to Krakatoa. But here's the beauty – or the irony, if you will.

Since all energy forms – even destructive ones – are part of the universe's creative potential, the name Vadhava is also used for the life-force inherent in the sea – whether it is the atoms that became the first living creatures or the latent conductivity of salt water. It's also described as the energy that causes the waters of the oceans to rise and to precipitate as dew, rain and snow. If that isn't an ancient theory of condensation, I don't what is. As for this mechanism right here – I suspect it is an old means of coagulation: A technology that can be used to extract pure silver from seawater using mercury as an amalgam; except in modern times, we've never been able to do it on an efficient scale. Of course, I don't need to tell you that condensation and coagulation are both part of the seven alchemical processes, as is amalgamation...'

I dipped my fingers into the water again, with reverence. 'Seawater,' I said again. 'All life began in the sea. And it all ends with the rising of the oceans. The power of creation and destruction. And this is a temple to that power.'

'A pagan temple? In India?'

I took her ignorance to heart. 'Paganism is a Western concept and not the only culture of nature-worship,' I pointed out, scowling. 'Just because they got famous doesn't mean you confuse all forms of elemental worship with Paganism. You know about layers, in archaeology?'

Maya made a *isn't-it-obvious* kind of gesture and said, 'Of course! New settlements tend to be built on top of old ones. Sometimes conquerors built their new capitals on the ruins of cities that they'd destroyed, often because it wasn't easy to find viable sites from security, economic and even geographical perspectives. Sometimes it's symbolic, like what Manohar said about this temple.'

'So the deeper we go, the older the civilization?'

'In a way, yes. I mean, even Dwarka is hypothesized to be six chronologically distinct settlements built on the same foundation. The Dwarka of the epics is just one of them, and not the oldest either. Are you saying...?'

'I am, yes. I do think this is a temple, perhaps the oldest kind of temple that we know of so far. But I also think it was meant to be more. It was meant to be a laboratory. Whether our old alchemists harnessed the power of the sea or merely borrowed it as an allegory from earlier communities who worshipped the feature of nature that was closest to them, I can't really say. But...'

Placing the flashlight to one side, I eased myself into the pool till the water was level with my shoulders. I took off my glasses and placed them by the side of the pool, noting their position to serve as a direction marker once I came out of the water. Then I dived.

A sliver of light glimmered in the distance, its glow turning the water into molten silver. But the gleam was deceptive, as were the dimensions of the pool. What had appeared a small square structure from above actually opened out into a larger subterranean body. I resisted the temptation to look around and made straight for the glimmer of light, but it was difficult to judge its distance, for the water went on, endless, and the sliver seemed to come no nearer than before. I considered heading back to the surface – and a breath of air. But just as my lungs began to protest, the sliver floated forward, within arm's length and then…disappeared.

It didn't take me long to discern what had happened. The water was creating an optical illusion of some sort, for the gleam now appeared diagonally opposite to its previous location. I fought the pain gathering in my lungs and swam towards it, but I had a feeling that this wasn't going to work either. Again, the glow of light faded as I neared it and reappeared some distance away.

'What happened?' Maya asked the moment I surfaced, gasping for air. I didn't bother to answer the question, trite as it was. She frowned, displeased, but didn't persist.

I set my mind to the problem before me. I had no doubt that the gleaming sliver was the Vajra fragment we'd come in search of, but I didn't see how to negotiate the visual trick to get my hands on it. Determination alone could never suffice to solve a puzzle of the mind, I knew. One had to understand the puzzle…

Hermes Trismegistus used to say that in order to comprehend something one had to accept it as it existed – that is to say, the only way to comprehend immortality was to believe it possible. When I had confessed my incomprehension even in the face of actual deathlessness, he'd laughed and said there was a difference: I was aware of immortality as a fact, but I did not accept it as a premise.

As above, so below…

Maya was staring intently at me, still frowning. Ignoring her, I drew a deep breath and dived again, making for the gleam where it appeared. As before, it vanished once I drew close, leaving only darkness ahead while a sliver of light flashed some distance away. Undeterred, I reached out for the darkness, claiming instead of searching, using touch rather than sight. My fingers found what I sought. I used a fingernail to pry it loose from the groove that housed it. All around me, the water lost its silver effulgence. Closing my fist tight, I made my way back to the surface.

Maya was waiting; her eyes uncertain, yet conveying a grudging respect. I climbed out of the pool, retrieved my glasses and turned to her. A black and silver fragment, its shape a mirror image of the piece from Srisailam, lay on my palm.

Maya Jervois looked as though the fragment was the last thing she'd hoped to see.

I laughed at her reaction, 'You didn't expect this, did you? That we'd just saunter in, take a swim and pick up some shiny trinket and be done with the whole thing? I don't blame you. In fact, I find it hard to believe that it was so easy to get into a place that's remained undiscovered for so long.'

It's getting out that's going to be the tough part.

The caveat persisted. My attention was drawn once more to the omnipresent channel of water.

Subterranean reservoirs. Salt water.

Instinct immediately pounced on me. Reason, its slower cousin, followed. 'We need to go,' I declared.

'Yeah...' Maya replied under her breath, eyes fixed on the fragment as though she were in a trance.

I snapped at her. '*Now*, Maya!' In a placating tone I added,

'We'll figure out the connections later. For now, we'd best be getting back. Do you have one more of those vials?'

In response, she took a deep breath, as though summoning her wits about her. Reaching into one of the many pockets of her cargo pants, she drew out an empty tube and handed it to me.

I slid the fragment into the vial, pushed the stopper in tight and then thrust the container deep into the front pocket of my trousers, checking again to make sure it wouldn't inadvertently fall out. 'Done. Let's go.'

Maya got to her feet and moved towards the entranceway. She'd hardly walked a few steps, when she stopped.

'What happened?' I asked.

'We know we can't get out that way. Why don't we follow the passage further and see where it leads? It either has to double back to where we began, or we just might find another way out of this place.'

'We'll come back tomorrow night. Find the right way to work the trapdoor and also bring some rope and more torches. For now, let's focus on getting out.'

She gave me an angry frown. 'After coming this far, after *this*...' she waved to the pool of water, 'you want to go back? Just like that? You said this was a laboratory... Who knows what else we might find in here!'

'We've got what we came for. Don't be greedy.'

'Greedy? You... Never mind! Shouldn't expect more from a maverick like you, I suppose.'

'Maya, listen...'

But she didn't. Turning around again, she stomped her way out of the room, sloshing through the small stream as she went. I waited, torch in hand, hoping that a few seconds alone in the darkness would make her come back. Then, with a groan of resignation, I followed.

14

The very first junction we reached had me regretting my decision. The passageway opened up to our right and not to the left, as it ought to have if it were leading us back to the entrance. Maya threw me a tentative look. I paid her no heed, but turned right and kept walking. The water in the channel now splashed against my legs with a strong, distinct current as it headed past us towards the inner sanctum we'd been in. 'Professor...?' Maya ventured, calling me that for the first time in a while. 'Where...why isn't this...? I mean, shouldn't we have turned left by now?'

'We should have,' I replied. 'But we haven't. And that means...'

'This isn't a mandala. The symmetry is incomplete.'

'Well done, Ms Jervois.'

That Maya didn't react to my sarcasm was a sign of how preoccupied she was.

Despite the apparent asymmetry, the exit was where I'd expected it to be, though it wasn't quite what I'd anticipated. The tunnel ran into an undisputable dead end, except for a chute leading up through the ceiling of the rock. This one was different from the passage we'd fallen through, for it was more of a tunnel than an opening, much smaller, and there were no stairs leading up to it.

Maya beamed, triumphant. 'Look! We can go up this way. Careful though, it's wet. This is where all that water is coming in from.'

'And how do you propose we get up there?' I asked, but Maya was already feeling the walls for some purchase that would help her clamber up.

'There's a ledge here, sort of,' she announced. 'Barely wide enough to grip. Hang on, flash the torch again. Wait, there's one... No, there are many more up there. It's like a ladder cut into the stone. Ow! Damn, it's slippery. The water's pretty cold too.' She shook her hand, splattering me in the face with a few drops and then stepped lithely back down. 'You're right, we should head back...'

'Climb!' I ordered.

'What...?'

'Maya, the tide is coming in and it's going to flow right into this tunnel. Can't you hear it?'

She looked down, noticing for the first time that the water had risen past her knees.

Calmly, I repeated, 'Climb. We don't have the time to go all the way back. Climb!'

Filled with a new urgency, Maya complied. Water seeped down along all sides of the chute. I held the torch in my mouth and, trying my best to keep it away from the flow, scrambled up behind her.

'I'm at the top,' she called out. 'The water's less here; I

don't know how, but... Anyway, watch your head.' Then she disappeared from view. I followed her up the rocky shaft and threw myself over the side and out of the chute.

The noise of the sea was overwhelming. We were inside a small cave; waves crashed loudly at the narrow slit that passed for its mouth. Water surged in by the moment, some of it pouring down the hole in the floor which we'd just climbed through, the rest pooling at the back of the cave, where we lay sprawled. 'Where are we?' Maya asked. 'What the hell is this place?'

'We're at the mouth of the river, southwest of the temple,' I shouted, trying to make myself heard above the noise. 'There's a low cliff that runs along the coast there; it cuts the beach off from the river's mouth. This cave must be set into the cliff-face.'

Maya looked at me, as though I'd just described some dull monument. Her voice eerily calm, she said, 'We're going to die here, aren't we?'

The irony of her words rankled me. She had that certainty. I, however, could only imagine what it might be to drown but not die. My lungs would fill with water, and I'd lose buoyancy and begin to sink. The lack of oxygen would also mess up my brain cells. I wouldn't be able to swim but I'd stay alive, long enough for the fish to start on me, eating, picking at my flesh. More than a couple of days, and the water would make my skin rot while it was still on me. I wouldn't be able to smell it, but I wasn't sure if I'd be able see it. No, probably not. In any case, my body would also begin to heal itself, sending me into an endless spiral of decay and renewal.

At some point, as I was dragged in deeper, water pressure would make my eyeballs pop out of their sockets.

The horror was tempting. Surely, a part of me reasoned, at some point, it would end? How could a man live beyond such destruction? My body might never break but my mind could, because it wouldn't be just about the torment in that moment, but also the despair that it could not, *would not* end. I would only heal, over and over, for as long as there was suffering to be endured. The grim prospect served to strengthen my resolve.

'Can you swim?' I asked Maya.

'Yes.'

'That's good enough. We should be fine.'

'Professor, the current is too strong. As soon as we hit the water, we'll get dashed against the rocks.'

'We'll be fine.'

'Are you out of your bloody mind? We're going to die. Can't you see...?'

I tucked the torch under my arm and cupped her face in my hands. 'Look at me, Maya.'

She obeyed despite her fear, her discipline reminding me yet again that she couldn't be just a desk agent. Yet, the same fear showed that she had no expectation of rescue, which meant she was acting alone, and the goons on our trail hadn't been hers after all. For the first time, I wondered if Maya Jervois had, in fact, been telling the truth all along.

Dismissing the doubt, I said, 'Listen to me. You see the opening down there? It's about two metres below our position. That means by the time this cave fills up with water, the tide outside will already be past the height of the mouth. If we swim out then, we'll remain below the surface flow, the actual pull of the waves. We can swim clear of the rocks and then head to the surface.'

Maya gave a single, tentative nod.

'Okay,' I went on. 'But here's the tough part. We'll have to do this in the dark. This torch is going to short-circuit the moment the water hits it.'

She nodded again.

'Another thing. No matter what, remember this: It takes a full ten minutes to drown.'

'And only two to lose consciousness, after which you're as good as gone anyway,' Maya said. She forced a wan smile on her face. 'Don't throw statistical significance and margin of error at me, Professor.'

I scowled and then realized it must've made me look angry, because Maya's smile faded. I didn't care. 'Fine,' I said. 'Two minutes. But you'll stay alive for ten and we will get out by then, Maya; so hang in there.' I took her hand in a tight grip.

Maya looked down at our entwined fingers and then up again at me. 'Do you have any family?' she asked.

'No.'

'I have a grandmother,' she went on. 'She's my mom's mom. I grew up overseas for the most part but from the day I came back here, to India, she took me in and was there for me.'

I didn't reply.

'She lives in Bangalore. And she makes gulab jamuns that are to die for...' I wanted to make some wisecrack but could think of nothing to say.

The water had reached my waist. It wouldn't take long for it to rise to neck-level and then over our heads. I took off my glasses and tucked them into a pocket.

A surge of water, and the torch flickered. In spite of our predicament, or perhaps because of it, I found myself thinking that Maya looked all the more alluring in the gloom. And then the light was gone.

'Now!'

Together, we plunged into the darkness.

I let go of the torch and used my left hand to feel my way across the floor of the cave, past the shaft we'd climbed out of and right to the mouth of the cave. The tide pushed against us, but we managed to time our strokes to resist the current and then to let it suck us forward till, with less trouble than I'd expected, we were out of there. I made to rise up through the water right away, but my shoulder hit the rough, mossy rock of an underwater shelf that stood between us and the surface. This wasn't going to be that easy, after all.

At once, my mind jumped to the most logical and efficient plan possible. It was quite simple: *Let Maya drown.*

There was no doubt that I had a better chance of getting out of the situation well and whole on my own. Besides, I no longer had any reason to keep her alive, now that I thought she was working alone. There was no enemy for her to lead me to, and with her dead I could just deal with the situation to my convenience. As for our pursuers – they weren't interested in me, only in Maya and her Vajra fragment…

The Vajra.

What if she were carrying her piece on her? How would I find it again?

But I don't need to find it again…do I?

I didn't. But…

The whole reasoning had barely taken a few nanoseconds, but Maya was already shaking my arm. In response, I tightened my hold on her hand and pulled her closer. Then, I used my feet to push against the rock and thrust us forward through the water.

We kept moving into the viscous darkness, the resistance of the water the only evidence that we moved at all. I saw no light, heard no sound, felt no sensation beyond weariness, heaviness and the urge to sink. I didn't know if we were headed away from or back towards the underwater cave. Maya held firm, part crawling, part swimming, her trust in me propelling her on. Her faith became mine, and I summoned the will to keep moving.

A surge of adrenaline shot through me as I felt the underwater shelf end. I imagined that the darkness around us faded a little, though that wasn't possible in the absence of sunlight. The surface was, I estimated, a good fifteen metres above us. I signalled to Maya by tapping her shoulder and then, together, we kicked hard. We had hardly risen a couple of metres through the water when I realized we'd made a big mistake. The underwater shelf had served as a wave-breaker. Deprived of its protection, we had moved right into the clutches of a raging torrent, caused possibly by an approaching storm.

The rough sea threw us around like pieces of driftwood. Maya lost her hold on me and flailed about as I tried to push us up the last few metres, to break the surface and get some air. But the churning tide caught me again. My head threatened to explode as I bumped it against something hard. Seawater burned at my throat and within my chest as I unwittingly swallowed gulp after great gulp. With the last bit of strength left in me, I reached out and, feeling for Maya, grabbed her arm. My other hand tried to hang on to whatever it was I'd banged into.

I couldn't.

It was too rounded, too smooth, too even.

Rudra, be my strength.

I pushed hard against the smooth stone, using the counter-force created to rise vertically through the water, against the currents. The moment I surfaced, a sharp spray stung my face. I didn't care. All I knew was that I could breathe again. A moment to gather my strength, then I hauled Maya up till her head was out of the water. Her chest heaved as air rushed into her lungs, and she began to cough. But she was alive and, as yet, completely conscious.

'Here, hold on to this. Hold tight.' I turned her towards the rock that had saved us. She clung to it, her breath coming in gasps.

The first flashes of lightning rent the sky, and I caught a glimpse of the shore. It would have been a tough yet possible swim during fair weather, but now... It came to me again that I had a better chance on my own, but I dismissed it quickly, reminding myself of what I'd just decided and why. For the present, I wanted Maya alive.

'Maya,' I whispered in her ear, 'I need one last burst of courage from you, my dear.'

It took her a few moments but she said, her voice hoarse, 'Let's do it.'

'Use your legs, that's enough,' I told her. Wrapping my arm tight around her waist, I pushed off into the water and towards the shore. I didn't look, I didn't think, I just moved forward stroke after stroke.

The water did what it would. I let it.

Don't look. Don't think. Keep going.

It took me a while to comprehend that I was walking, stumbling rather. My feet had made ground. Dry shore was a good hundred metres away but the water was shallower here, and we weren't swimming anymore. Maya cried out – I guessed she had stepped on something sharp – and her knees buckled, sending her under. I stopped and, with a grunt of effort, lifted her clear of the water, hoisted her over one shoulder and carried her across the last stretch. By the time we were on the sand, I feared I was going to drop her. And I did.

Maya hit the ground without complaint and immediately began to throw up. She gagged over and over as her traumatized lungs and throat cramped. At length, she stopped heaving and lay on her back, a vacant look on her face.

'It burns,' she whispered. 'Water. It burns, like fire. You were right, Professor…you were right all along.'

I could have found irony in the statement, but it would have been wasted on me. Instead, I drew much-needed amusement from it.

Laughing softly, I dropped to my knees next to Maya. She watched, first with suspicion, then with contagious laughter of her own for the sheer joy of being alive. At length, we quietened down, and I lay back on the sand, relishing its roughness against the skin of my palms.

'Well, Ms Jervois,' I said, 'let's just say I've been in this business for a long, long time.'

15

I didn't have dreams. I didn't need to. My memories were crystal clear; they could neither hide in my subconscious nor surface only under cover of sleep. What I was in – or was it within me – was more of a dazed reverie that wouldn't let go. I could feel the evening sun on my face, hear the sounds of life and people around me. But I couldn't move, not till the vision was done with me. And so I watched in suspended animation, resurrecting every emotion, feeling every sensation I'd once felt, except that it was impossibly enmeshed in the present. It was, I knew, the bitter aftertaste of long-forgotten sentiments. The rational thing to do with such transient, and thus inconsequential, states of mind was not to react or resist, but to endure.

The heat from the yagna's fire pierced my skin as I sat before it, near-naked and bloody, my mind filled with rage, desperation and the arrogance of victory. I and two other warriors were all that was left of a massive army, the largest force in the entire land. Two-and-a-half million soldiers routed to nothing. We'd lost, almost. But not completely, not yet. I was alive, and while the blood of my ancestors flowed in me, I owed it to them to fight on.

Images of the past within the past filled my sight.

My father had died in my arms, his adamantine body reduced to a mass of mangled flesh. His right arm had been severed at the shoulder, his legs flapped useless from a broken spine, arrows lacerated his chest and blood poured from the many wounds. The blood of the man who was both my father and teacher. *My* blood. It had covered me, coated me and filled my awareness just as it had the day I'd emerged from my mother's womb. My father had died with his eyes open. They'd held disappointment, as though he knew that I wouldn't, couldn't, do what the least of men ought to do for honour, for duty, for loyalty and ties of blood: Seek vengeance. His eyes had held shame.

The warmth of the fire had cocooned me, fed me. I'd prayed with all my heart and soul to Rudra, invoked by the yagna's flames, for strength to kill. I'd prayed to be able to set aside all compassion, all vestiges of humanity within and become an instrument – no, a butcher, a killing machine.

I had.

I'd become the ideal killer, one who could not be killed.

I'd slaughtered them that night, in the hundreds. I'd burnt men alive, jeered as they screamed. I'd slit their throats with slow precision, delighting as they writhed and flailed. In the end, I was amazed that I hadn't got down on my hands and knees and gorged on their warm flesh. Perhaps, if the sun had risen just seconds later that day, I'd have done that too.

'*Mmmm. Delicious.*'

Maya's voice cut in on the images in my head, blending, merging, till the mirage changed. I was a young man, barely out of my teens and filled with the headiness of youth, the power of my warrior's body, as I made love to a girl for the first time.

The next morning my father had used the flat of his sword to beat me black and blue in front of all his other students. Over and over, he'd said the same thing: *How can you control your mind, command the immense power that is yours, if you can't even keep your hands off some good-for-nothing wench?* I was, after all, a brahmachari – a word that now meant a celibate, but had then meant much more. *Brahma-achari* – a man who could control his every desire and passion, remain centred inwards in complete self-awareness. A man to whom breathing in and out was an act of oneness with a greater sentience, and even sex held spirituality. Nothing was wanton, nothing was impulsive. Unlike what I'd done.

I felt myself twitch as the blows fell on me in my dream, every one of them hard and humiliating. The same night, I'd gone back to that girl, letting her run her hands over my bruised body. She'd cried, moved by what I'd endured for her. She'd made promises of togetherness as I'd taken her.

And then I'd never seen her again.

I hadn't gone back for her; I had gone back simply to spite my father.

'It's awesome! I think I'll order one more. Do you want anything, Professor?'

'I think he's asleep, Maya.'

Maya. Illusion. The voice of illusion asking me if I wanted anything. Was that Reason that replied that I was asleep? No, it was just Manohar. Handsome, brave Manohar. I'd killed so many boys like him in a flash. I'd tasted their blood as it splashed on my face; it had been sweeter, purer than that of the old, decrepit hacks who'd been celebrated kings before I'd lopped off their heads. My mind spiralled deeper into a bizarre mix of images. Manohar, many Manohars, in an ultra-modern swimming pool, titanium-white lights overhead refracting to form small lightning-bolt reflections against blue ceramic tiles, but the water was not water, it was sparkling red blood. Maya standing over me as I lay wounded on a battlefield. She too made promises of togetherness, before I took her in my arms and jumped into a dark sea that opened up right under our feet. Our descent was long, but I savoured every second of it, feeling her bare skin against mine as I pressed her close, very close. Desire set us ablaze, the flames grew till we were but burning cinders in the roaring embrace of a yagna fire, like the one I had been seated next to. The smell of ghee and camphor and burning flesh filled the air. Maya melted away as the flames began to sear at my skin. I wouldn't scream. I couldn't scream; I wasn't allowed to.

I'd made a promise to die. Death was sacrifice and it was good.

That promise had made me the myth I was, of which this much was true: I'd offered my life as sacrifice to Rudra, and in return, he had made me unstoppable for that one last night of the Great War.

But the deal that then played out was not at its agreed price. No stories were told of the next day's dawn, of how I found myself alive, irreparably alive, the horrors I'd unleashed indelibly branded on my mind. No tales bore evidence of the next hours, of the questions I'd asked and the answers I'd been denied, till finally I'd been disowned and cast out by my own family and left an empty shell with neither kin to love, nor liege to serve, nor deity to worship.

Legend said I was damned to wander the earth as a slime-oozing, disease-stricken creature; a sentient being in undead, spectral form. Reality, however, was far less gruesome, and the gods far more fickle than they were made out to be. And yet I did not count myself amongst the damned, for the damned lost their souls to the devil. I was immortal. I had lost my soul to human betrayal.

'No, Manohar, I don't think he's asleep. Are you, Professor? Professor...?'

Wake up!

I stirred, reaching habitually for my glasses before remembering they'd broken during my underwater adventure and had been my last spare pair. In any case, I really didn't need them to see. A golden haze bloomed before my eyes and then the world came into focus.

'Well, well, well. Good morning once again, Professor,' Maya said. She was sipping an exotic-looking cocktail, looking quite the tourist in a dark blue tank top and a pair of shorts. The late afternoon sun teased out the flaxen strands in her hair, which she had left loose to hang over her right shoulder. A tattoo peeked out from under her top, an inch or so below her left collarbone, but I couldn't make out what it was.

Drawing in a deep, nourishing breath, I propped myself up on my elbows. Manohar leaned forward from where he stood in the clear swimming pool to rest his arms on the edge. 'Good afternoon is more like it. Nice snooze, boss?'

I reached for the bottle of beer next to me. It was still cold. I'd fallen into my surreal sleep for hardly a quarter of an hour. I took a long swig of my beer, while Manohar briefly ducked underwater in a bid to fight the heat.

'The water's nice. You should get in,' he recommended as he came up again, sleeking back his hair.

I hadn't the least desire to get wet and supposed the same for Maya. The two of us sat on lounge-chairs next to the pool where she took in the sun with all the stereotypical enjoyment expected of her part-Caucasian ancestry. For my part, I didn't mind it either, but I wasn't at all the kind to lie around in a pair of swimming trunks. My trousers were of a lighter shade and one button on my shirt was undone for the sun, but that was it.

'Forget the pool. You absolutely need to try this, Professor.' Maya held up her drink. 'That beer looks boring.'

'Only till the sun goes down a bit, Ms Jervois. It's too warm for whisky.'

'You sound like a total *bewada*, a real drunkard,' Manohar pitched in.

I raised my bottle to that.

When Maya and I had dragged ourselves off the beach at Somnath and made our way back to the hotel, we'd found a frantic, near-apoplectic Manohar waiting for us. Without a word, he had led us to his room and got busy settling us in there. I'd taken one step inside and burst out laughing. Despite his anxiety, Manohar had remembered to bring our shoes back from where we'd left them, at the entrance to the temple.

Fussing over us with towels and hot coffee, Manohar had explained how he'd been torn between calling for help, which would mean blowing the lid on us, and waiting. I suspected, though, that what had really torn him apart was knowing that there would have been trouble of a very different sort if we'd been discovered inside many days later, Maya dead, me alive. I was glad of his choice, but I'd had no decent way of telling him that. I'd settled for ordering him around, asking him to get a pack of cigarettes and a bottle of whisky through room service. He'd given me a pitiful look and reminded me that we were in Gujarat – a prohibition state – and then offered to step out and buy me a bootlegged bottle. I'd refused on principle, though not without regret. That's when Maya had suggested from her soggy corner on the sofa that we get the hell out of there. I couldn't have agreed more.

Manohar had arranged for a car, while Maya and I had gone to our rooms to pack and change. I'd thrown away my wet clothes, savoured the luxury of a quick but hot shower and been downstairs in the lobby in fifteen minutes to find Maya, as well as a taxi, waiting. We'd left Veraval as the sun rose, heading southwards for the island city of Diu. Manohar had made a couple of phone calls from the car, and by the time we arrived in Diu, about two hours later, rooms were waiting for us at the Azzaro – the sole five-star resort on the small island. Now, three beers over brunch, a few hours of sleep and one more shower later, I felt fine. Maya too appeared none the worse for our ordeal.

The moment of companionable ease appeared to be what Manohar had been waiting for. He cleared his throat and asked me the question he'd been holding back all along. 'So, what happened?'

I glanced at Maya, who was assiduously studying her drink. Clearing my throat, I sat up, swinging my legs off and down on either side of the lounger. I recounted, in precise detail, all that had happened since Maya and I had fallen down the trapdoor. An impassive Manohar listened to it all. His voice was strained as he said, 'I tried to come in after you, to open that damned thing. I couldn't. I just couldn't. I waited till dawn, in case you somehow got back. And then I left, before someone saw me there. I...I'm sorry.'

'I'm the one who ought to apologize,' Maya began in a small voice. 'You kept saying we should come back later to explore further, Professor. I didn't listen, I'm sorry.'

I looked from one forlorn face to the other before saying, 'And I'm very sorry that I don't have anything smart-assed to say right now, but can we please stop this? Enough!'

'It's not that easy, Professor,' Maya said. 'I was rude in there. Way too rude and way out of line. I might have disagreed with you, but it wasn't reason enough to speak to you that way.'

'Maya, Manohar knows this already, but since he seems to have forgotten it, I shall say it this once: We can't work together effectively if we're going to keep owing each other or holding things against each other. Let it go. I know beyond doubt that Manohar would've clawed his way in with his fingernails to get us out if he could have. I also know that you had no clue that the sea would flood into that damned tunnel like the wrath of some pissed-off Greek god. I didn't expect that to happen either. And, for what it's worth, looking for the tunnel was my idea; I take as much responsibility for what happened as you. So can we just stop with the self-blame and apologizing?'

Manohar asked Maya, 'What did you call him?'

'A maverick...'

I said, 'Manohar, please tell her that it's hardly an insult. I've been called far worse...'

'That's true,' Manohar mused. 'I recall some of the things my old team used to say about him...'

'Your old team?' Maya was curious. I'd normally have insisted that Manohar not tell this particular story, but right then I was glad of the distraction.

'Uh huh. They used to call him a cheapskate because he worked alone.'

'And is he? A cheapskate, that is?'

'Will you pay for my beer if I confess to being one?' I riposted.

Manohar, however, had taken her question to heart. 'Do you know, Maya, right from the very first job we've been on together, he's never had me on a salary? We split what we make down the middle.'

'Enough,' I said.

Manohar shot me a look of mock disappointment, but obliged.

If I'd been at all given to emotion, I'd have viewed Manohar with something akin to affection. As it stood, everything Professor Bharadvaj owned had been made out to him in a deed, though he didn't know it. If I'd gone ahead as planned at Kashi, then one month later Hari would have opened the envelope I'd left with him and passed the documents inside it to Manohar. It was why I'd gone to see Hari in the first place.

The prospect of leaving it all behind came to me again – an urge, a need that carried with it a weariness that felt new but really was old, very old. I couldn't tell whose fatigue it was, the Professor's or mine. I dismissed the notion and turned back to the duo, business-like. 'Right. Next steps.'

Maya sat up and reached out to lay a hand over mine. 'Do you know what the next step is, Professor?'

'We need to find the third piece of the Vajra. I think we should...'

'Not today. Manohar and I, we both trust you and you know it. Whatever it is, tell us tomorrow and we'll do exactly as you say. But for what's left of today, I don't want to talk about any of this. We got what we wanted, and I'm just happy to be alive. I'm also too tired to think. Please, is it such a bad thing to relax for just a day?'

She finished with a coy look. I wanted to make a joke about how she didn't have to seduce me just to get me to shut up, but decided that it would needlessly embarrass her. 'All right,' I said, like some tolerant tutor who had agreed to postpone an inevitable lesson. 'Both of you take it easy then.'

I added, addressing Manohar, 'You should get out and party tonight. There's a nightclub in this hotel, I think. It reminds me of Goa...'

Manohar grinned at that statement. Much as I preferred he have his one-night stands on the road so that they could never come back to bite us, for once I was willing to make an exception. Life was far too long to leave room for regret.

16

'Hah!'

I let the barbell fall to the ground as my body reached its temporary limit and my mind paused to gather itself. Muscles cramped and nerves pinched, sending a surge of discomfort through my limbs. My breath sounded loud and ragged in the air-conditioned silence of the empty hotel gym. Wiping my face on the already-wet sleeve of my sweat-soaked T-shirt, I mentally counted down my fifteen seconds of rest. Then, reaching down, I set the barbell back into position, loaded it up to twice my body weight and prepared to continue.

Maya's injunction to relax notwithstanding, the matter of our next move weighed on my mind. For centuries, philosophers had believed that the fundamental questions of existence and creation were common to all civilizations, and there were obvious similarities between the Vedic Hiranya garbha and the golden egg from which Ra came into being, our Pralaya and the Sumerians' flood, Hades and Yama, Enki and Agni. But to see these beliefs converge in practice as science, in the form of the alchemical laboratory under Somnath had given rise to unfamiliar emotions: Confusion and doubt. I wondered, not for the first time but certainly with more vigour than I'd previously shown, whether the fault was mine that I hadn't found what I had been searching for over millennia.

The need to silence such thoughts and dismiss my protesting ego had led me into an intensive workout, the kind that would drain the body and focus the mind till they were in balance.

Hermes-Djehuty, whose posthumous assistance had helped me find the second Vajra fragment, had used that word frequently. *Balance.* To him, I hadn't been a freak or an aberration. I was, as he put it, the 'ultimate potential' – what every human being would be, could be, if the elements were in perfect balance. It had sounded like a load of crap then and it was no different now.

As for the concept of balance, it had been an oft-repeated theme throughout alchemy. Some said it was the balance of substances, particularly mercury and sulphur, which was the key to transmutation; others claimed it was the balance of elements – fire and water, wind and earth. But it was the work of Abu Musa Jabir ibn Hayyan, whom Maya had spoken of when we'd first met, which had given alchemy – from the Arabic *al-kimiya* – the status of a science in modern terms. Jabir had believed that the formless meaning of things could be quantified and, thus, balance achieved.

He had explained it to me in detail when we'd met sometime during the middle of the eighth century CE in Kufa, Iraq, saying, in conclusion, that the key to my transformation lay in the meaning of who I was. Certain that he knew nothing about me, I'd responded with scorn, using pretty much the same words I'd said to Maya – that if it were as easy as that, the key to transmutation would have already been found a hundred times over. He'd laughed and promised me that one day, when he left his legacy for the world to see, he'd remember me and immortalize me in words. I'd kept the irony to myself. It had gone well with a familiar – and inevitable – sense of failure.

I let the barbell fall to the floor again, stamping down on the bar to stop the bumper plates from bouncing up despite their weight. Just then, the door to the gym opened and two men bustled in, making loud conversation about the stock market. I left as quickly as I could and headed towards the beach. Beyond the people nursing cocktails around candlelit bar tables set on the sand, a signboard pointed through some trees to a nature trail even as it cautioned guests not to use the pathway after dark. Spurning the advice, I set off down the path at a run, needing to leave behind the sensory overload and find solace in being alone.

The darkness was soothing, as was the steady rhythm of feet thudding against leafy, wet ground. Sounds of the night played in an unorchestrated symphony all around me, and the clean, crisp air filled me with renewed vigour. I picked up speed, trusting instinct to guide me over the uneven terrain as I let myself go with abandon. As the runner's high kicked in, my mind fell silent, beaten into submission. Though I didn't have the clarity I'd wanted, I felt blissfully blank and that would suffice for the moment.

The feeling endured, time became irrelevant, and I returned to mindfulness only as the lights of the resort came into view. I used the last of my energy to run towards and into the building. My arms and legs trembled as I walked the last few metres to my room, my sides cramped and I had to pull off my wet, clingy T-shirt and wipe my hands on it before I could insert the room key in its lock.

'Hey, Professor!' I heard a voice call out.

I turned to see Maya emerge from a room a few doors away. Before I could respond, she had walked down the corridor to mine. I unlocked my door and stepped inside. She followed, closing it behind her.

'I had this idea,' she said, oblivious to my exhaustion. 'I just had to run it by you. I was thinking of where to go next...'

I tried to summon my wits to focus on what she had to say. 'Hmm?'

'You know what you had told me about the triad of ingredients that lead to transmutation – mercury, sulphur, arsenic; moon, fire and air? We found mercury at Srisailam, a place connected in alchemical tradition not to the moon, but to air – and thus arsenic. At Somnath, the allegorical reference was to the moon. But instead of finding mercury there, we found a connection to sulphur, through seawater. Do you see what's happening? The clues are jumbled, but in a systematic way.'

'Okay...?'

'Technically, we now need to look for the third element, arsenic, which would generally link to life-breath or air. But, if we follow the logic of the jumble instead, we should look for a place where the allegorical reference is to fire. Also, like Srisailam and Somnath, I'm pretty sure it's a Shiva temple. You did say, didn't you, that he was the original alchemist...'

I exhaled hard, finally making Maya aware that I stood within reaching distance, dripping sweat and dressed in nothing more than a pair of running shorts and my sneakers. If she was uncomfortable with it, she didn't let on. I, for one, wasn't going to pretend to be bashful. 'All right,' I said, wiping my face and arms with my T-shirt before throwing the garment aside. 'The premise is logical. So where do we start?'

'Well,' she said, her eyes fixed on mine, 'taking a microcosmic approach, as you call it, if we focus on essence, blood and breath as elements in themselves, *without* the reference to mercury, sulphur and arsenic, where else do you see these three substances?'

I kept quiet and waited for her to answer her own question. After a few moments, she gave up on me and exclaimed, 'Tantra! Breath is the force that drives the mingling of essence and blood — the male and the female. But when that happens, the force that is created as a result is symbolized as fire. So you see — breath and fire. We need to find a tantric temple; not surprising given that, at the end of the day, Shiva is a phallic god.'

Her final analysis disappointed me, and I let it show. 'Do you know what tantra means, Maya? Or do you, like everyone else, think it's just a term for mystical eroticism? I've told you before; I'm not in the bestseller business.'

She didn't back down. 'What does tantra imply then, Professor? I certainly didn't figure you for such a prude that you'd overlook this obvious connection, the indisputable meaning in the layers of alchemy, one that we can't afford to disregard if...'

My voice cut into her tirade, cold as steel. 'Tantra,' I said, 'is much more than you think. The very root word *tan* means the human body, the warp and weft of the cosmic weave. Tantra comes from that; it's about living, breathing sacrifice, a mirror to the act of cosmic conception when the Primordial Creator destroyed himself to create all of existence. Sex is only a part of it, Maya. It's again a mirror, this time to the combination of spirit and matter to create the manifested world. But at the end of it all, everything in the scriptures, the metaphysical and mystical practices, are all means to liberation and enlightenment.'

'How would you know?' she shot back. 'You speak of scripture and liberation and enlightenment as if it's the prerogative of every man and woman in the world. But you and your kind have used religion and scripture as a yoke for generations.'

'My kind? And what kind is that, exactly?'

Maya seemed to engage in some sort of inner battle with herself. As one side won over the other, she thrust her chin out and said the words with undisguised contempt. 'You're a Brahmin, aren't you?'

The statement irked me, though I'd no clue why she'd said what she had. On another day, at another time, I might have behaved differently. But right then, I was too tired and far too raw with forgotten emotions, to care. I stepped forward, forcing her to retreat till she was up against the wall. She didn't fear me, but nevertheless flinched at the intrusive proximity as I placed one hand on the wall behind her, hemming her in. With the other, I yanked at my *yagnopavitham*, the sacred thread that ran across my bare chest. 'Brilliant observation, Ms Jervois. I suppose *this* gave it away, even before my name did.'

She grimaced, disgusted. 'You're the same, you lot. You're all the same!'

I returned her fiery gaze with practised neutrality. Then I dropped my arms and stepped back. In the same icy tone as before, I said, 'Thank you for your suggestions on how to go forward with this, Maya. As much as your theory sounds promising, it leads us nowhere. A Google search would've told you that. There are far too many parables and places associated with your ideas for us to even try using them as a starting point. No shocker there – Shiva is, as you so astutely pointed out, a phallic symbol, though many of *my kind*, as you call us, would prefer to see him as a form of the Creator. Now, if you'll excuse me, I just finished a workout and need to get cleaned up.'

Maya shifted, as though she were about to do something, but then seemed to think better of it. With one last glare, she stormed out of the room.

I waited till she was gone and let out a sigh. Her response, replete with judgement and scorn, was why I'd assumed and discarded identities through aeons. I had seen that look before, seen the loathing and repugnance, and sometimes fear, in others' eyes. And the mere possibility of having to face any kind of judgement again was enough to make me believe that I had been right to hide the truth of my identity all along.

Sighing again, I leaned over the built-in dresser that ran the length of the small corridor, looking into the mirror. An image watched me; unyielding, unforgiving. I felt the overwhelming urge to wear the glasses I neither had nor needed, and hide behind the personality that a pair of cotton pants and a neatly tucked-in shirt could give me. But no assumed identity would ever fill the void. Perhaps, I admitted, Maya had been justified in her disgust, after all.

Once, every Arya woman and man had worn the *yagnopavitham*. It wasn't a sign of caste, but of honour. Warriors and artisans, priests and kings, had all worn the thread as an acknowledgement of adulthood, of belonging to a way of life. But now? Norms and beliefs had been systematically altered to create an inequitable power structure, the *yagnopavitham* had turned into a whip that controlled the convoluted system of class and caste, a system that struck at the heart of everything that I'd once believed in and stood for. My thread, the most enduring symbol of my origin, had become a symbol of oppression.

I carried it as a sign of contrition, a reminder of the things I'd done to protect the man I could never again be. Like my thread, he was just a symbol, for his world was long gone. My 'meaning', as Jabir would've called it, was long gone.

As I stared at myself, at the thread that made and unmade me, I saw the answer to our present puzzle right in front of me.

My life is alchemy.

Nagarjuna. Born at Somnath, died at Srisailam. But he had been an Arya.

Like me, he was twice-born. And that had given him meaning.

17

The trill of angstsy dialogue from a faraway television invaded my sleep. I was fully awake at once. Groaning in frustration, I reached out for the bedside lamp and then my watch. One a.m. I cursed the poor, sleepless sucker watching mind-numbing serials at such an hour, that too at a beachside holiday resort. Settling down against the pillows, I tried to go back to sleep, but in vain. In the end, I threw aside my covers and slipped out of bed.

I headed towards the small balcony, picking up my cigarettes and lighter on the way. Out in the cool air of the night, I lit up with relish. It was the first cigarette I'd had over the past day – at last, my chest and throat had stopped burning enough for me to want a smoke. I savoured the mix of night, solitude and tobacco…till the shrill sounds from the damned television invaded these surrounds too. Growling expletives, I looked around, trying to identify the room that housed this uncharitable guest.

Light filtered out through open curtains, three rooms away, and by its glow I could see a man on the balcony. Maya's balcony. I would've dismissed her nocturnal visitor as being none of my business if a second shadow had not peered out, as though summoning the first man in. Stubbing out the cigarette, I threw on a shirt over the shorts I'd slept in and made my way over.

I knocked on the door. No answer, but I could hear voices inside. Throwing aside all restraint that stemmed from decency, I tried the door. It opened.

I heard the soft thump of a silencer gun firing and, simultaneously, Maya's muffled screams from behind the gag over her mouth. The crack of wood followed, as I ducked and the bullet nicked the door frame.

In the split second between the events, I saw the two men. The first, whose outline I'd seen earlier on the balcony, was one of the two hired guns from the restaurant parking lot in Delhi. He stood towering over Maya, who lay heaped awkwardly on the floor. The second man was thinner and wore a black scarf as a mask around the lower half of his face. I immediately hurled myself at the leaner man, who was nearer. He went down with a look of disbelief but soon recovered. Though he was strong for his size, he didn't waste his force on fighting me. Instead, he tried to slide out of my grasp. I pinned him down and yanked off his mask to reveal a familiar face. This time, the surprise was mine. He was none other than the young man I'd exchanged silent nods with on the beach at Somnath.

I raised my arm to land a punch when I heard Maya's muffled shout again. The first man now had his gun trained on her. With his other hand he waved me away. The message was clear. I let go of my opponent and stood up, noticing as I did that the gunman sported a cut lip and winced as he moved his left arm. Clearly, Maya had held her own against him before his weapon had forced her into submission. As it now would me.

'Step back!' the gunman ordered. I obeyed. He turned to his companion, who was picking himself off the floor with an infuriating confidence. 'Let's go.'

The young fellow complied, making his way out on to the balcony. The gunman joined him, keeping his weapon trained on us all along. He closed the part-wooden-part-glass door from the outside and jammed a chair under the handle to block it shut before he and his companion swung over the low balcony. I threw myself at the door, but the few seconds it took me to get it open were all they needed. By the time I was outside, they were gone, vanishing into the shadowy shrubbery that surrounded the low-rise building.

My first instinct was to jump over the balcony railing and chase them, but Maya let out another incoherent shout. Not ungrudgingly, I gave up all intention of pursuit and went over to her. She lay curled up in a corner next to the bed, her hands tied behind her back with her own dupatta. The awkward rag in her mouth was a bra. I crouched down next to her and pulled out the gag. She began coughing and panting.

'Here, drink this.' I passed her a half-filled glass of water, which she refused.

'That shit-head drank from it!' she complained, in a hoarse voice.

I said nothing but picked up a fresh bottle of mineral water, opened it and held it to her mouth. She gratefully took a few gulps.

'What happened?' I asked, undoing her hands.

'I don't know,' she said, her voice uneven. 'I was asleep, and then I woke up and these guys were standing over me.' She took another gulp of water, and her voice grew stronger. 'I tried... For a few moments, he didn't know what had hit him, but... I wanted to shout, but he stuffed *that* in my mouth.' She motioned with disgust to the lacy apparel I'd thrown aside. 'Then he pinned me down and...I...I thought he was going to...'

I didn't probe further. Her room was a mess, more for the way it had been tossed than for any actual damage. Her bag lay empty on the ground, its contents scattered all over the bed. Cupboards and drawers had been pulled open. I said, 'Did they take anything?'

Maya maintained a stolid silence. I pushed back the hair that swept over the left side of her face. An ugly, purple bruise was spreading across her cheek.

'You didn't get this fighting for a window seat on a public bus, Maya.'

She winced as I ran my fingers over her bruise. 'The fragment from Srisailam. I'm sorry...'

I ignored the apology and went to rummage through the mini-fridge for some ice. I bundled up a few cubes of ice in a hand towel from the bathroom and handed it to Maya.

She placed it over the bruise on her cheek, hissing at the sting.

'I'll help you tidy up the room, and then you'd better get some sleep. Tomorrow's a long day.'

'Don't bother, I'll manage.' Maya tried hard to sound nonchalant. She attempted to get up, her hand going to her ribs. It didn't take a genius to see she was hurt there as well.

As if needing to explain, she went on, 'He was strong. The second guy, with the mask... He looked thinner, I know, but he threw me down on to the floor and, for what it's worth, I *am* a brown-belt. The other guy was a pig. He slapped me and kicked me and then... I...' Her shoulders drooped.

I fought back my immediate instincts, first to hold her close and tell her that she was safe and second to find the bastards who had done this and break their necks. Doubt and suspicion of many kinds followed, driven by the conviction that Maya was very much a woman capable of taking care of herself. Eventually, I said, 'Maya, I can't help you or protect you unless you tell me the whole story. Those men came after *you*; they came after *your* fragment of the Vajra. How do they even know about it? Are you really NDRO?'

Her eyes took on a glassy stare as they met mine. 'I am from NDRO, Professor. Was, at least. I swear to you I don't know who those men are, but I presume that they know about me and the Vajra from a colleague of mine...my supervisor, actually. It was his idea to bury our findings in some non-report and sell out to private investors. I refused. Call me patriotic or naïve or whatever you want but...'

She descended into a fit of coughing. I passed her the bottle of water once more.

She emptied it in one go and went on. 'I knew there was no point trying to escalate the matter to our superiors. It was far too suspicious, not to mention the fact that the scientific evidence was gone. That's when I decided to take the fragment and go under the radar. I headed to Delhi and managed to contact Manohar, thinking the best thing to do was throw in with you. Why do you think I insisted on coming along with you, Professor?'

'Anyone else at the NDRO know about this?'

'No. Just my supervisor. His name is Dr Sushant Kumar, if you want to verify my story. The money I gave you was from my share of…the pay-off. Frankly,' she added, 'I didn't really believe the whole story till I spoke to Manohar. Somehow, the way he reacted made me think there was more to the Vajra than I'd realized. And by the time I met you, I knew I was being followed. I was afraid that if I were anything less than totally enthusiastic, you wouldn't take the job, and where would that leave me? All I wanted was to be safe…'

I studied Maya, trying to get a read on her. I didn't trust her; I couldn't trust her. But I also couldn't deny that her words had a ring of truth to them.

'All right.' I stood up.

'Where are you going?' she asked, suddenly sounding vulnerable.

'I need to take a look around, Maya, find out what I can about those two. You try and get some sleep. I'll take your room key and check in on you later, okay?'

'But…'

'Maya, if those guys had wanted to kill you, they'd have

done so already. They're gone and won't be coming back. You'll be fine, won't you.' It was a statement, not a question.

Maya glowered at me for a moment, then drew her shoulders back and sat up straight. 'Yes.'

'I have my mobile with me. Call if you need anything.'

'I will.'

I studied her briefly, but she was already gazing absently into space. Making sure that the balcony doors were closed and the curtains drawn, I left her room, locking the door behind me. Out in the corridor I walked towards Manohar's room, calling him on his mobile phone as I did. I was right in front of his door when he picked up.

'Hello?' His voice sounded distant but not from having been woken up. I cursed under my breath as it dawned on me that he had a visitor in his room.

'Manohar, I'm sorry. Can you step out, please? Bring your torch.'

'No probs, boss. Is everything okay?'

'Yeah, things are fine. I could just use you for a few minutes...'

'I'll be right there.'

A few seconds later the door opened and Manohar came out, his hair tousled and his faded Harvard T-shirt crumpled. 'Hey,' he whispered by way of greeting.

'I'm sorry. My timing sucks, eh?' I apologized.

'That's okay. I told him I have a horrible slave driver for a boss. He felt pretty sorry for me, I think. He'll make it up to me once I go back...' he added, with a wink.

I smiled, then became solemn. 'Two guys broke into

Maya's room. She's fine, but they took the vial she had – the piece from Srisailam.'

Manohar let out a low whistle. 'What about the Somnath piece?' he asked.

I took the second vial out of my pocket. I knew better than to lock it away where I couldn't get to it in a hurry. Besides, I trusted myself more than I did a mechanical safe.

'That's good,' he remarked.

'Maybe. Maybe not. They should have known that we recovered it. My guess is they were still looking for it amongst Maya's things when I interrupted them. Anyway...I just wanted to make sure things were fine with you – figured it was best you heard at once what happened.'

'Of course. Is there anything I can do...? I mean... Maya, how is she?' He glanced down the corridor, towards her door.

'She's fine. Pretty shaken up, some bruises. She took a punch to her face, but doesn't look like anything's broken.'

Manohar hesitated, and I could tell he was deliberating whether to go see her. For whatever reason, he opted against it. 'You're heading out? That's why you wanted the torch?'

'Yes. I plan to scout around outside.'

'I'll come with you.'

Together, we walked down the stairs and made our way to the rear of the building.

'Door showed no signs of forced entry,' I said. 'Either they had a key, or they came in through the balcony. In any case, that's the way they went out.'

Manohar surveyed the setting. 'Getting up to the balcony is no big deal. They could've easily clambered up there.'

'Hmm...' The light in Maya's room was on, and behind the thin curtain I could make out her shadowy shape still huddled on the floor.

'Professor, over here!' Manohar shone his flashlight on a small shrub nearby. A black cotton hoodie and a black scarf lay bundled up under the greenery. 'Labels and tags have been ripped out,' he said, examining the garments. 'This guy was a pro.'

'You're right... Manohar, call Kamal-bhai in the morning. Ask him where's the nearest point he can get a couple of guns to us. I want smart ones, with silencers. Those guys are bound to come back for the second fragment. I want to be ready.'

'Okay.'

'See if he can lend us a car as well. I also need you to run a check on a Dr Sushant Kumar. NDRO.'

'And that is?'

'Maya's ex-boss,' I explained, adding what Maya had told me about him.

'Done.' He added, with sudden vehemence, 'Poor Maya! I don't know what the goddamned point of all this is!'

I considered him for a moment, framing my question so as to elicit more than one answer. 'Do you truly think it's pointless?'

If Manohar picked up on my ulterior motive, he didn't show it. He replied, 'I don't think the Vajra exists as such, Professor. I think it's a figment. And we can find many ways to connect the dots, to come up with theories for where to look and we'll keep finding stuff simply because there's so little we know about all this. But that doesn't mean anything. As for those goons… I don't think they have any clue about you. Nor do I think that Maya is in it with them – she could've died at Somnath, why would they have stood by without helping her if she'd been one of them? This is just another historical artefact to those cowboys, something to make money off. You were right; this won't lead anywhere. I'm sorry I…'

'No, it's all right. You did what you did in good faith.' I didn't add that the very fact our pursuers had come to retrieve the Vajra fragments *after* we'd recovered the Somnath piece was enough to determine that they'd known, far better than we had, where it had been hidden and how difficult it would be to get in…or out of there. I also didn't mention that his sudden change of heart, his newfound scepticism, was hardly unexpected or that it served to spur me on in a way that no show of enthusiasm could have.

'What do you want me to do with these?' Manohar held up the hoodie and scarf.

I pointed to the garbage bin nearby. The last thing I wanted was for Maya to step out on her balcony in the morning and be confronted with a reminder of the night's events. Manohar bundled the garments up tight and threw them into the bin. With one last look around, we began walking back to our rooms.

'Anything else, Professor?' he asked, as we reached his door.

'Nothing. Get some sleep,' I told him, adding, 'since you won't be getting much of anything else…'

'Oh, I'll get lucky yet. You should've come along too, to the club, you know…'

'And stood up some pretty lady, just as you have your date? Goodnight.'

I heard him shut the door as I walked off. I slowed down as I passed Maya's door, but kept going till I was back in my room. I began taking off my shirt with every intention of getting into bed. And then, swearing loudly, I picked up my cigarettes and lighter, checked to see if my balcony door was shut and stepped back out into the corridor.

I knocked at Maya's door and, without waiting for a response, let myself in with the key. She was as I'd left her, on the floor, hugging her knees to her chest. I wasted no time on words and cleared some space on the bed by pushing all the stuff strewn on it to one side. Then I went to her and pulled her to her feet. 'Come on, get up. Let's get you into bed.'

She didn't say a word but slid in between the sheets and curled up again. I said, 'I'm going to switch this light off, okay? I'll leave that table lamp on, so it won't be dark. And I'm going to be right outside, on the balcony.' In response, Maya turned away, to lie on her side.

I waited till her breathing turned even with sleep before raiding her mini-bar and making my way out to the balcony. With a tired grunt, I settled myself in a chair and put my feet up on the railing. Many images came at me, from the evening's assailants to old, faceless ghosts. Dismissing them all,

I took a good, long swig from a miniature bottle of Johnnie Walker and lit up the first of what I was certain would be many cigarettes between then and first light. As I leaned back in my chair, it struck me that it had been seven hours since I had solved Nagarjuna's puzzle; that I knew where the third fragment of the Vajra was hidden. But after what had just happened, it wasn't all that important. I was hunting a different animal now and my prey was closer than it had been before. I smiled to myself and blew a ring of smoke into the night.

18

At some point during the night I sought refuge from the horde of mosquitoes on the balcony by moving back inside. For lack of options, I lay down on the roughly carpeted floor between the bed and the door to the balcony.

I didn't stir till my mobile phone rang, buzzing uncomfortably in the pocket of my shorts. 'Hmm?' I growled into it.

'Professor, where are you?'

'Manohar. What time is it?' The query was rhetorical; I glanced at my watch. It was 9.54 a.m.

'It's about ten. Did I wake you up? Where are you? I've been knocking at your door…'

'I'm in Maya's room. Hang on, I'll just be out.'

I hung up and stretched myself out with a yawn, banging against a small coffee table in the process. The sound of that, coupled with the resultant curses, woke Maya up.

She looked about her in a confused way. The soreness in her side as well as the general disarray of the room must have brought back the night's events, and she shrunk into the pillows.

'Good morning,' I ventured cheerily.

Instead of returning the greeting, Maya asked, 'Is that where you slept all night?'

'Part of it, yeah. I was outside, but the mosquitoes got to me.'

'You could've taken one of the pillows.' She gestured to the many piled on her bed.

'I was fine, don't worry. How're you feeling? You ready to get up?'

Maya didn't budge from under the sheets. I took the hint. Getting to my feet, I said, 'I'm going back to my room to freshen up. Why don't you get ready and meet me there in about half an hour? I'll order breakfast through room service...'

'Sounds good,' she managed to say.

I left the room. Manohar was right outside, looking well rested and fresh.

'You're up early,' I remarked, glancing down at my rather dishevelled self. I ran a hand across my cheek, feeling in desperate need of a shave.

'I was making enquiries about that guy at NDRO.'

'And?'

Manohar shrugged, indicating the obvious. 'How is she? Maya?' he asked, as I opened the door to my room and let us in.

'Better.'

'Does she need a doctor?'

'I don't think so. I've asked her to come here for breakfast. We'll order room service. She's in no position to be seen around in the restaurant, not with that bruise of hers. Anyway, I'll check for concussion then.'

'Okay. I've spoken to Kamal-bhai. He had a fellow in Daman who could arrange things.'

'Hmm?'

'The car's outside. I said we didn't want a driver. Also, it comes with accessories.' The last was a reference to the guns I'd wanted.

I was impressed and I let it show. 'Well done, Manohar! I don't know what I would have done without you!'

Manohar waved off the compliment, though he was positively beaming. 'Shall I order room service then?'

'Yes, please.' I headed off for a bath. By the time I came out, breakfast had arrived. A little later, so did Maya.

'Hey! Feeling better?' I asked her.

'Much better,' she replied.

'That's good. Here, let me take a look.' Using the torch, I checked her eyes for signs of concussion or, worse, ruptured blood vessels. She obliged without a fuss.

'Your eyes are clear. But we should get you to a doctor for a check-up.'

'I'm fine, Professor; honest. Trust me, I'm not the kind to play martyr when it comes to things such as this. I really am okay, other than a few bruises to my body…and my ego too.'

'Prove it,' I said.

'Prove it? You want me to run around the resort or…?'

'I mean, tuck in. Nothing says you're all right like your

appetite. You eat a good breakfast, and I'll agree that you're fine.'

Maya sat down, wincing as she did. But she managed to do a decent job with the food before her, and by the time we sat nursing a hot cup of coffee each I began to think we were ready to move on.

'So...' Maya said.

Manohar exchanged a look with me, before speaking. 'I don't know how to say this, Maya, but your supervisor? Dr Sushant Kumar? He...'

'He's dead, isn't he?' she asked, matter-of-fact.

'Yes. A car accident, two days ago. Of course, it could be just that — an accident...'

She shook her head. 'It wasn't. Kind of figures, if you think about it. They follow us in Delhi but lose us. They probably went back to see what Sushant knew. They finished him off and got back on our trail to grab the pieces...'

'Piece,' I corrected. 'The Somnath fragment is with me.'

'But they've got the other one,' Maya protested.

'Which is useless unless they get the one we have and the one that's yet to be tracked down. That is, of course, assuming that we put all three together and...something happens.'

'So, it's a race to the third piece. I like that!' Manohar declared.

Maya drew in a deep breath and let it out, before saying, 'Let's do this, Professor. Tell us, where next?'

I put down my coffee cup. 'Kashi.'

'Varanasi?'

'Yup.'

Neither Maya nor Manohar showed further curiosity, so I elected to go ahead and explain, 'Maya had this insight last evening. She was suggesting that we follow the allegorical triad of ingredients to look for the third fragment in a place where not only is Shiva associated with fire, but which also has some connection to arsenic – in the form of life-breath or air. The place that came to mind was Kashi.'

Maya appeared embarrassed at being given any credit and tried to hide it behind confusion. 'I don't get it. What's at Kashi?'

Manohar knew what I meant. 'The temple of Vishwanath at Kashi houses one of the jyothirlingas – jyothi meaning fire as well as light. As for the life-breath: there's a well that was once part of the temple – now it's on the grounds of the mosque next door. Legend holds that the Shivalinga that used to be there was placed inside the well, the Gyanvapi it's called, and that the well is the *axis mundi* – the centre of the world, the point from where the world came into existence, which will remain when the world is destroyed.'

'Oh!' Maya's response, though not lacking in genuine enthusiasm, was subdued. Her scientific interest, however, wasn't as easily quelled. 'How do we know for sure this is the one? I mean, out of all the sacred places associated with Shiva, how do we know *this* is the one?'

It was, in effect, the same problem that I'd thrown back at her last evening. I didn't care to explain the whole chain of reasoning that had brought me to the particular conclusion but got straight to the point.

'Because,' I said, 'there's another part of the puzzle that points to Kashi. Triangulation, see. We use different bits of the metaphor to see if we can arrive at the same thing. I'm beginning to think that our dear friend Nagarjuna had a better sense of humour than I first gave him credit for. *My life is alchemy*: He wasn't being dramatic when he spoke his last words, he was telling his interlocutor where the three fragments were to be hidden – where he was born, where he died, and…?'

I stopped, in invitation to smart answers. Neither of my companions took me up on it. I continued, 'A scholar of old, one of the *dwija*, would think of few places as more important than where his true journey begins. Nagarjuna was educated at Kashi; that's where he'd have received his initiation and begun his life as an alchemist.'

'Fair enough,' Manohar said. He couldn't fathom my disappointment, for in this day and age, the concept of initiation was hardly of any importance. But to me, to those before me, it had meant more than could ever be explained, for it was the true beginning – the epiphany that the purpose of mortal life was to discover what lay beyond.

I could never forget that moment, nor could I remember it in totality, for it had held too many emotions. Fresh from a purifying bath, I'd been sprinkled with sacred water as though I were a seed to be nurtured and germinated, anointed with butter, and then sent into a small hut, dark like the womb I'd come from. Oblivious to day and night, to sunrise and sunset, I'd sat alone, contemplating with the full faculties of an adult the mysteries of life, of divinity and creation. When I was ready, and only I could say when that was, I was covered with a thin membrane-like substance over which the priests had draped a black antelope hide. From within this symbolic womb, I'd emerged into the bright daylight, a child taking birth all over again. And I wore a sacred thread as a reminder of what that rebirth had been like.

'How do we get there?' Practical, tactical Maya interrupted my reminiscing.

'We have a car. A comfortable one, I hope?'

Manohar replied, 'Comfortable enough. It's a spanking new Pajero. Even has a GPS system and a DVD player, though I must say the movies that come with it totally suck! But we can always pick up something for time-pass...'

Maya asked, incredulous, 'You want to drive all the way? We're on the western coast of India. Varanasi must be what... a good thousand kilometres off?'

'Sixteen hundred plus,' Manohar corrected. 'But the roads are good. We can get in a good seven hundred kilometres today, if we leave soon. That should bring us to Indore. Then, if we leave early tomorrow morning from Indore, we can reach Kashi some time tomorrow night... Late night, that is.'

'But why by road?'

'Guns,' I replied. 'We need guns. Can't fly any more.'

'I will be ready to leave in ten,' Maya declared, standing up.

'Me too,' Manohar said.

'I'll see you both shortly, then,' I said. Manohar left the room. Maya stayed.

'Err, Professor,' she began.

'Don't get all formal on me now, Maya,' I said. 'No thanks, no sorry, please... In fact, *I'm* sorry you had to go through such a horrible time; I can't see how those bastards picked up our trail without my knowing it. I've been lax, terribly lax, and I'm the one who owes you an apology for that.'

'I...It's...it's not about that. It's something else...'

I groaned silently. This was an emotional dump. Reluctant but empathetic, I said, 'Maya...'

'I'm sorry for what I said...yesterday evening.'

'Forget it. It's nothing.'

'No, Professor, please... It's not done by any standards to insult someone's birth. It's just that...I'm Brahmin too, on my mom's side. But except for my grandmom, my family was nothing but a bunch of orthodox idiots, who decided that because Mom had married a white guy...

'Anyway,' she continued, clearing her throat, 'I know it's wrong of me to think that all of you...them...*us* are narrow-minded idiots. I've met my fair share of decent, progressive thinkers. My stepfather, for one. The family forced Mom to marry him but it turned out that he was far more liberal, radically so, than they'd expected. That lot of jerks couldn't conceive of the possibility that not every man is a... Well, he'll be ashamed of me when he hears of what I said, yesterday. I'm sorry. I don't know what got into me...'

The intensity of her confession took me by surprise. In all sincerity, I told her, 'It's fine. Really...'

'Oh...'

The awkwardness continued. I searched for more to say, but I had no words to heal her past. Some things were just too private.

'Sorry again...' Maya finally said. 'I didn't mean to embarrass you either, you know.'

'It's okay. And for the record, you can call me a fucking idiot for all I care. I promise I won't go all parochial on you.'

Maya beamed, dispelling the last touches of tension between us. 'Why, Professor. I believe you do use the f-word after all.'

'Indeed.'

And I could say it in Sanskrit too.

19

The Pajero made good on our estimated schedule, and I silently thanked Kamal-bhai for one more favour done well. It had been quite a while since I'd met him, wanting to avoid suspicion at having hardly aged in the many years we'd known each other. Kamal-bhai and I went back a good three decades, for he was that archaic creature found these days only in Hindi movies – the ethical gangster, the don who had taken up arms, not out of greed but from a need to protect his people. Kamal-bhai didn't deal in girls or drugs, though it admittedly was duplicitous of me to impose moral limits on a man who didn't balk at extortion, murder and smuggling. Duplicitous, inconvenient and unneccesary.

Given that I was relegated to the invisible role of an ageing contractor of sorts, Manohar had become my main contact with Kamal-bhai and his network. I'd expected it to be more difficult, but he had built a bond with the gangster much faster than I had. Manohar's boyish good looks and his easy manner first inspired suspicion in many, but when that sentiment passed it always left in its wake a rock-solid trust, for he was the kind of man who considered personal honour a fair assurance and would move heaven and earth to keep his word. And when one had spent enough time with him to see the courage and humour that went with it, it was difficult not to like the young man. I was particularly glad of his cheerful company as we set out in the Pajero – he kept Maya engaged in conversation on music and movies, while I played the silent driver enjoying their companionship.

After an uneventful night at Indore, we were back on the road. At first the camaraderie of the previous day flowed over, as did chatter. By midday, Maya was curled up on the back seat in restful slumber. Clearly, she hadn't slept a wink the night before. She woke up after a couple of hours and offered to take the wheel, but I refused. She didn't insist, but shrugged and soon went back to sleep. Manohar and I exchanged sporadic monosyllables, but he mostly kept himself occupied reading and gazing out the window. I didn't mind. There was much to be said, but I didn't want to say any of it. Not yet.

At sunset we were still a good three hundred kilometres from Kashi. Darkness was beginning to settle over the rustic landscape. Occasionally, a light flickered in the distance, the solitary hut of some farmer watching over his lands, but for the most part, we were in the middle of serene nothingness. I made a quick calculation and then drove the car off the road and on to a rough clearing that abutted the tarmac. 'Bathroom break,' I declared. 'Five-star facilities to your left.' I jerked a thumb at the clump of trees nearby.

'Here...?' Maya sat up, groggy.

'We take the bypass road from here on. No more villages and hamlets. Just a long, lonely road with hardly any traffic, not even trucks. Given a choice, I don't want to stop anywhere. These aren't the safest parts of India...'

'Like what, robbers?'

'In one form or the other. So stretch your legs, whatever... You need the torch?' I called out after her, as she got out of the car and headed towards the thicket.

She held up her mobile phone in reply. I waved and walked away to do my own business. I could hear Manohar yawning loudly close by. No way was he driving, I ruled, splashing some water from a bottle on my face to freshen up. Back in the clearing, I lit up a cigarette and walked around our Pajero, checking the tyres and making sure all was fine. Manohar stood contemplating the evening sky. He always got very quiet when he was sleepy.

'I don't suppose you have a smoke to spare?' Maya's voice cut in.

I turned around, surprised, but held out the pack. She took a stick, and I helped her light up. 'I thought you don't approve?'

'It's not about approval. I don't want to die of bloody cancer, that's all.'

'And now...?'

'I guess the probability that I'll drown, fall, be beaten or shot to death is higher now...'

I laughed. Maya said, 'You look so different when you...'

'Yeah, I've heard that,' I cut in.

'I mean it. You look...nice. I mean, you look good even otherwise; I didn't mean... I mean, you're a handsome guy, but you look...nicer, know what I mean?' she babbled, flustered by her own candour.

Manohar, who found the episode amusing, called out, '*Arre*, mutual admiration society. *Chalein kya*? Shall we go?'

'Lighten up, Manohar. You have a laugh too,' Maya admonished.

'Hey, you want a laugh, I'll tell you my Donald Trump joke again.'

With a loud hoot of protest, I climbed in behind the wheel. Once Maya and Manohar had settled in, I pulled out from the clearing and got back on to the road.

We'd hardly driven for an hour when we ran into a roadblock – a makeshift one comprising a row of drums, the kind used to transport tar. A handmade sign in fluorescent paint proclaimed road-works ahead and pointed us to an off-road detour.

'What the...' Manohar swore as I screeched to a halt. There was no one in sight. We exchanged meaningful glances. He took a gun out of the glove compartment in front of him and slipped it into the waistband of his jeans. With a last look at the desolate road behind us, I turned off on to the dirt track.

The bumpy way made for keeping us all wide awake. Besides, we had to keep a lookout for any sign of the highway – light, traffic or anything other than the dull up-and-down of a dark ride into nothingness. Half an hour later, I came to a second stop.

'Shit!' Manohar cursed as the headlights shone on a

dilapidated brick structure. 'Dead end. This road was meant to lead to this brick kiln, that's all,' he stated. It was, I knew, the unstated that preyed on all our minds.

'There's no one behind us,' Maya said. 'I've been watching; no one's following us.'

'In that case, let's get out of here.' I swung into gear and turned the vehicle around with a squeal of tyres.

Before I could drive away, we heard another engine roar into action. A black Land Cruiser spun out from behind the brick kiln and right on to our path. Squinting against the glare of the headlight, I floored the accelerator. The driver of the Land Cruiser wasn't inclined to budge. Undeterred, I kept going. He still didn't move. He wasn't going to. I saw the gun just before a shot rang out.

'Down!' I shouted to Maya and Manohar as I jerked the steering wheel hard, trying to dodge. I needn't have bothered. He wasn't shooting at us, but at our tyres. And his aim was good. We lost pressure in one of our rear tyres just as he rammed the right front wheel, sending the car into a sharp spin. I knew better than to wrestle against it. I hung on tight, trying to keep the car on its self-propelled trajectory towards a pile of bricks.

The Pajero crashed into the bricks, punching through them with ease. For a moment, I thought we could keep going. But with a burst tyre, a chase could only end one way. The already-dented rim of the wheel caught in a pool of rubble and sand. It spun in place, while its partner at the other end of the axle thrust ahead. The Pajero flipped over, turning many times before it crashed to a stop, upside down. A window broke, spraying glass inwards, and the windshield cracked but remained intact. I coughed as sand and brick dust hit me in the face. By the time the dust cleared, our attackers had got out of their vehicle and surrounded us.

'Professor, you okay?' Manohar was undoing his seatbelt and trying to crawl out his window.

'Yeah. I'm all right. Maya?'

'I'm fine,' she said. She was already halfway out. I didn't bother with haste, suspended comfortably upside-down. The petrol tank was intact, which meant the car wasn't going to explode. Getting out was only going to be like jumping off a wild horse's back into a charging elephant's path. The ancient saying came true as I heard Maya shout.

Resigning myself to the situation, I tried to slide out the window but found myself wedged between the seat and the bent steering wheel. I felt someone grab at my legs through the passenger window and resisted, intending to wriggle out, but my dubious saviour was more interested in expediency than my comfort. He yanked hard at my legs. My neck jerked back and my jaw crashed against the steering wheel as I was bodily evicted from the car and thrown on to the ground.

'Don't move!' The man who'd dragged me out ordered. I'd not seen him before, but he was a huge man, larger than the gorilla from Maya's room. Said gorilla was also in attendance, holding Maya in a vice-like grasp, closer than he had to for the purpose of restraint. A third man stood less than an arm's length away, his gun trained at Maya's forehead.

'Get their phones. And his weapon,' a calm voice

commanded. I recognized the fellow from our two previous encounters – Maya's second attacker and my old friend from the beaches of Somnath.

One of the captors went around collecting our cell phones. Another frisked Manohar, appropriating his gun as a result. He then gave me a quizzical look, at which gorilla number two stamped down hard on my stomach. I doubled over as a stabbing sensation shot through me, but within seconds, trained instinct kicked in. I spurned the discomfort, pushing it out from mind and body till it ceased to exist.

The calm man – undoubtedly the leader of the lot – looked at me before drawing back the safety catch on the gun he held to Maya's head.

Though it wasn't worth much to me as a threat, I needed to know who the man was and what he wanted. I pulled my gun from where I'd tucked it into my pants, against the small of my back, and threw it aside. Gorilla number two picked it up. I tried to take advantage of my obvious disarmament to sit up, but was shoved again to the ground.

'I said, don't move!' gorilla number two growled, bringing the heel of his heavy boots down, first on my hipbone and then on the fingers of one hand. I didn't dodge, but it took all my preparedness to not wince. The man was a professional. He didn't bother with the wild and ineffective punching and kicking that most people mistook for fighting, but struck to hurt and could certainly strike to kill. As if to prove the point, he raised his knee up high and brought his heel down again with all his strength. I grit my teeth against the inevitable as his heel pounded down on my ribs. The crack sounded loud in my ears as one, maybe two, of my ribs broke. My breath caught in my chest, and my mouth filled up with blood. It spewed out in a thick blob as a cry escaped me. Something had punctured. Most likely my lung.

'Enough, Pratap!' the calm voice ordered again. He went on, 'I'm sorry, Professor. These brutes don't understand the meaning of redundant...'

'You mean,' I managed to wheeze, 'like your charming apology...'

The man said, 'I like your sense of humour, Professor. I also like that it's impervious to pain. Or is it? Perhaps Pratap's exertions aren't redundant after all...'

I lost the mood to banter. 'What do you want?'

'Stupid question, isn't it?'

'Not as stupid as thinking I'd carry the fragment on me...'

The man wasn't at all thrown by the mention of the Vajra. 'In that case, where is the fragment, Professor?'

I said nothing.

The man sighed. 'You know, I've heard about you. I believed you were a man of principle. And yet, if the money's good enough, you'd sell your principles too.'

'While you lease out yours by the hour?' As a retort, it was far too corny to be effective, but it was the best I could do. And it had the other, fairly important effect of eliciting the kind of response I'd wanted.

'I'm not in the buy-and-sell business, Professor. Some things are best left lost in history. Like these fragments... Either you're too sceptical to think that the Vajra is anything more than a bauble, or you just don't care. In any case, your lack of belief is dangerous. I'm sorry, but we can't let you go on. I hope that you'll change your mind about the situation, now that you know me and my motives. Nothing good can come of the Vajra, so please tell me where the fragment is.'

I remained silent.

The man addressed his companions. 'Bring him inside. These two as well.'

Pratap, or gorilla number two, directly followed the order by grabbing my arms and dragging me across the brick debris. I tried to stand up and walk, only to have him kick my legs out from under me. I suspected he found dragging me across the rubble more entertaining. *This asshole sure has issues*, I noted and gave up. For the time being.

20

'Inside' turned out to be a large chamber that adjoined the decrepit kiln. Our captors had already hung a single camping light from an old hook, and it spun around slowly, casting long, moving shadows across the floor and walls. The room looked as though it had once been a storage area or even a caretaker's residence, but all that was left of it were grimy walls and a roof that was crumbling in various places. The floor was covered with dead leaves, odd branches and dried mud. All we needed were a few dust eddies and the effect of whistling wind for this space to qualify as a movie set arranged for an action sequence. I sure as hell had no intentions of playing the hero.

In real life, men who took a beating from twenty other men didn't stand up, spew punchy dialogues and then pulverize their opponents. They simply rolled over and died. In my case, the latter wasn't an easy option. But then, I wasn't the kind to roll over either. The conviction shot through me as a thrill, the electric shiver of battle. It was a taste on my tongue, a delicious, juicy anticipation.

Before I could act on the impulse, the goon who had dragged me in forced me up on my knees. Whatever the intention for positioning me in an execution stance, it certainly gave me a better view of things than being down on my face had. I breathed in as deep as I could with a partly functioning lung and took better stock of the situation. Manohar lay on his side in the corner where his captor had thrown him, hands tied behind his back, his eyes never leaving me as he waited for some sign as to our next move. Maya had been similarly bound and tossed into another corner. 'Please!' she implored the young man in charge. 'Please don't hurt him…'

'I've no intentions of hurting anyone, madam. All I want is the other fragment; the one in the Professor's keeping. Get him to give me that and we'll leave you be. You'll have an uncomfortable night here, but in the morning you can walk down to the main road, hitch a ride, go home and forget any of this ever happened. Or…'

As if to emphasize his words, he kicked me in the stomach. A scream built up in my throat as my broken rib shifted, drilling through flesh and skin like some surreal internal dagger, but I willed myself to not give it voice. More blood flooded up into my mouth. I clamped my teeth down to keep from spewing it all out. This was not going well.

The gang-leader seemed to have reached the same conclusion. 'This isn't working,' he declared. 'Oh well…' Walking over to Maya, he placed his gun to her forehead, point blank. 'Tell me where it is, or I kill her.'

I swallowed blood and saliva and declared, 'I don't have it. And I'm not lying.'

'Bastard!' Pratap was vehement. 'Leave him to me, Moorthy. Give me ten minutes. He'll tell you all you want to know.'

Gorilla number one added, 'He must have it! Strip him!'

The man named Moorthy said, 'Shut up, you two. You need to know how to look into a man's eyes and tell if he's lying or not. The Professor here says he doesn't have it — it's the truth: he doesn't have it. The point is, who does?'

'These two?'

'No, I don't think so.'

'We can always check,' Pratap proposed, leering at Maya.

Moorthy addressed his other henchmen. 'What hotel were they at? At Indore?'

'Fortune Landmark,' gorilla number one replied.

'Number?'

The goon searched one pocket and then the other to retrieve a crumpled piece of paper.

'Er... 4347788. The code is 0731.'

Moorthy whipped out his phone and began to dial. I felt a grudging respect for the man. He was smart, I had to grant him that.

'Yes, Landmark Indore?' he spoke into the phone. 'Good evening. My name is Professor Bharadvaj, I was a guest at your hotel last night. I'd left a package to be sent by courier when I checked out this morning... It's been sent to Varanasi? Oh good! Actually, sir, can I trouble you for the tracking number? This is a very important sample that has to reach a client... Great! Okay...321119864. Thanks. Goodbye.'

He hung up and, regarding me with smug contentment, repeated the tracking number under his breath, committing it to memory. Then he turned to his cronies. 'Come,' he told them. 'The fragment should reach Kashi by tomorrow. We'll pick it up from the courier office in the morning.'

'What about them?' Pratap asked.

'Check their hands. Make sure they're tied tightly. Leave their legs loose. By the time they get anywhere, we'll have the fragments and be long gone.'

Maya let out an audible sob of relief. Manohar glared daggers at our captors, but said nothing. Moorthy was looking at me. 'Except him,' he suddenly announced. He assessed me for a few seconds more and then repeated. 'Yes, except him. Ayya was right. This guy is too dangerous.'

'Your Ayya's a good judge of men,' I said.

'As am I, Professor,' Moorthy replied, without missing a beat. 'Pity. I'd have liked to play our cat-and-mouse games for longer. But...' He called on his lackey, 'Pratap! You might want to...work a bit on the Professor here. I don't want him getting in our way again.'

Pratap welcomed the orders with an evil snigger and stepped forward to tie my hands behind my back.

'Making it an even fight?' I needled him, and was rewarded with another punch. He hit the bundle of nerves concentrated in the solar plexus area. Nothing could hold back my howl of agony as acute pain shot through my gut and into every part of me.

'Okay, that's enough then. Move out, the rest of you!' Moorthy ordered. He held his gun out to Pratap, close enough for me to see the filed-off serial number that made it untraceable. Pratap declined the weapon with a shake of his head. Reaching down the back of his shirt, the huge man drew out a crude, but no doubt effective, iron blade.

'Keep this anyway,' Moorthy ordered, thrusting the gun into Pratap's hand. 'We'll also leave the bike for you. Finish up and meet us at the camp. Kumar, Arul, come on. Pratap's going to take some time.' He turned to go.

'Wait,' I commanded. Moorthy turned around. 'Do I have your word that your orangutan here won't hurt my friends?'

Moorthy was taken aback. He walked back to where I knelt on the ground and, bending, grabbed hold of my collar to haul me up and prop me against a wall. 'You want my word? Kind of old-fashioned, aren't we, Professor?' he taunted.

'Only a man who tells the truth knows if another is lying. I'll accept your word for what it is,' I declared.

'How dramatic! But yes, you have my word. They won't be hurt. Is that clear, Pratap? Do you understand?' The tone left no doubt that Pratap would face the consequences of any disobedience.

Pratap signalled his acquiescence. I knew I'd pay the price for his embarrassment, but not before Moorthy and the rest of his men had left. True enough, he waited till his companions had got into the Land Cruiser and driven away before turning back to the three of us with an eager smirk.

'Orangutan?' he asked me, chagrined.

'You know what that is? I'm impressed.'

Pratap reacted by lashing out with the back of his hand, catching me on the side of my face. Manohar scrambled to his feet and tried to dash forward, only to find that his captor had also secured his hands to an old iron pipe that was fixed on to the wall. Laughing at the show of impotence, Pratap slapped me again. I felt my eyes blaze golden. He unwittingly took a step back, but then pulled himself together.

'You're all in big trouble, you assholes!' he taunted.

None of us cared to reply, but my mind filled with the choicest of Sanskrit phrases, mostly suggestions that involved stuffing various large implements that had no clear modern-day equivalents up certain orifices. Pratap appeared undaunted, even pleased at our hostile speechlessness. It soon became clear why.

His hand instinctively rubbed against his crotch. Like many scumbags I'd met before, the man was turned on by the mere prospect of violence. And his friends were no longer around to stop him from acting on that instinct.

Desperation filled the room at that sudden insight. Maya began shouting, her words an incoherent mix of rage and fear, as Pratap started towards her. 'What say we do it right here; let your boyfriends watch?' he taunted and began unbuckling his belt.

Manohar tugged at his bonds, his panic and frustration coming through as he kicked and wrenched at the rusted piping in a bid to get free.

Three blows to kill a man.

I thought of how easy it had been, not once, but again and again, through lifetimes of battle, and how I'd felt so agreeably ephemeral each time. Karma, it was said, was the pursuit of ultimate perfection; the pinnacle of what could be achieved through human action and choice. If so, then this was my karma, for there was nothing I did better, and no one could do this better than I. *We worship the sacred with our actions, for all actions are sacrifice.*

It took just a few seconds, yet time slowed down as strength crept up my legs, blazed as lightning along my back, and set my nerves deliciously afire. I was alive. I was boundless energy, the endless potential of existence.

Jumping up in the air, I drew my legs up to my chest to bring my tied hands from under me and in front. Then I charged at Pratap. As I'd expected, he reacted quickly and came at me with his long knife; I caught him at the wrist with both my hands and pivoted outwards, hoping to throw him off balance. Pratap responded with a grace that his size belied, spinning through the air and landing firmly on both feet. I didn't give him a chance to recover, butting my head into his.

Trained to endure pain as much as he was to inflict it, Pratap became further infuriated by the attack. With a roar, he used my grip on his wrist to yank me close and twisted his hand to stab at me. I felt the knife catch me on my left, close to where my broken rib had begun piercing through my skin. The serrated blade brought unexpected relief as it ripped a passage for the rib to emerge through. That gave me that extra burst of strength I needed, and I pulled down again on his wrist, harder this time, and felt his bones crack under my fingers. The knife clattered to the ground.

'You fucking...' Pratap swore and brought up his knee. I dodged him. He missed my groin but caught my hip. I stumbled, using the apparent handicap to move in closer to him. Unaware of my ploy, Pratap reached for his gun with his free hand. I grabbed his other arm. The gun went off, twice. Maya cried out, and I wondered if she'd been hit. This time, though, I let nothing distract me — not concern about Maya, not the molten sensation in my chest, the tremors that wracked my spine, the incessant pounding in my head.

Blow one. I let go of my hold on Pratap's arm and swung my right leg up and across, moving it across his body. He took my knee squarely in the chest and staggered back from the impact. I didn't stop.

Blow two. I continued with the same motion, but pushed off from the ground with my other leg, tilting my upper body in counterbalance as though intending a sideways kick. Pratap moved to avoid the feigned blow and into the exact position I wanted him in. Swinging my raised leg back, I brought my heel down on the nerves of his neck. Pratap cried out and his knees buckled under him, but he didn't fall. It didn't matter. I wasn't done yet.

Blow three. Curling my right leg as it swung through, I caught his neck in the crook of my knee. My shin was wedged tight under his jaw, so that he couldn't move his head. I squeezed, the simple move pressing down on his windpipe. Thinking that I meant to strangle him, he began to claw at my leg. But I had other plans. I jerked my right knee downwards. His cry of panic choked off mid-way as his neck snapped. I let his limp body fall to the ground before bending over to pick up his gun.

The silence that followed was sudden, but not unwelcome. I smiled, though it was more of a snarl – the grim taste of victory never lost its malty headiness, no matter how many times I sampled it. I recovered Pratap's knife and used it to cut the ropes around my hands before staggering over to where Manohar was. With one stroke, I had him free of the pipe. I then handed him the blade.

'Professor...' he began, his voice hoarse.

I smiled, reassuring, but even so he recoiled, his eyes showing a hollow dread that went deeper than the immediate gut-churning spike of mortal peril. I looked at Maya. She too was deathly pale, as though she had seen a metaphorical ghost. Perhaps not all that metaphorical, I realized.

I could feel the adrenaline of the fight ebbing. Unbearable heat radiated outwards from my chest like ripples of electricity. And then came awareness, followed by bemused comprehension. I'd been hit. Those two shots had gone right through me, hardly a few inches from my heart. Any man in my position should have been dead. No wonder then that Maya was staring at me with a mix of bafflement and fear. 'I'm okay...' I wheezed, '...flesh wounds, that's...' It was all I could manage before a fresh surge of blood filled my mouth.

Steady. Breathe. Breathe!

I turned away before Maya could say anything. 'We're... six kilometres or so...from the road,' I panted. 'The bags... we need to...'

Blackness and dizzying nausea hit hard. I couldn't see past the throbbing sparks that shot through the sockets where my eyes should have been. I felt my legs give out from under me and then dirt in my nostrils as I fell face down on the ground. Spasms racked my chest, and blood spewed out of my mouth.

'Professor! Oh my God, Professor...' Maya shouted.

Her voice tore through my ears and made me bring up some more blood. Needlessly I rasped out, 'Shut up!' My mouth kept filling up. I spat on the ground and wiped my lips with the back of my hand, before trying to push myself up. But my arms failed me, and I met the ground again.

Maya continued to stare at me, astonished that there was life left in me after all that had happened. Or was she? Her cries had seemed to hold the bitter sound of pretence, and I saw a glimmer in her eyes that ought not to have been there. Triumph? Fear? Panic that I was going to die before finishing the job for her? No, it was something else.

Slowly, I hauled myself up off the floor and stood facing her. Manohar moved to help, but knew better than to actually offer. I nevertheless waved him off.

Maya's expression went from confused to concerned and then to one of fear. I clucked my tongue, as if with false pity. She grimaced.

Her reaction spurred cold rage, the only kind of anger I have ever felt. I took an unsteady step forward and grabbed her hands. She resisted, but I didn't let go. I wanted her to see me, the *real* me, a man of rent flesh and bloody wounds and deathlessness.

'No, please...' she began, unsure of what it was she was protesting against. Laughing noiselessly, I pulled her closer. Wrapping my fingers around her small hands, I made her unbutton my blood-stained shirt. She struggled, tried to look away, called out in vain to Manohar for help before giving in with a sob and turning to face me.

A hush.

I let go of her hands. She staggered back, tripping over in her haste and falling flat on the ground. 'I'm sorry...' she gulped.

But my wrath hadn't had its fill. I peeled off what was left of the shirt, wincing as it stuck on where the blood and flesh had already begun to congeal on the fabric. It was all I could do to not scream as the cloth caught and tugged at my exposed broken rib. I pushed aside the flap of skin that hung from me like a tattered hide on a tanner's line and tried to force the bone back into place.

A mass of loose flesh, offal and blood spilled out.

Maya retched but continued to stare, as though unwilling to miss the macabre sight. Manohar, unable to contain himself any longer, ran outside to retrieve our bags from the overturned car. He was back at once, and set about rummaging in his backpack for a first-aid kit.

I sat down on some discarded cement blocks and shut my eyes, letting the promising rustle of miscellaneous items inside canvas calm my rage as Manohar cleaned out the wounds as best as he could and, leaving both bullets as they were, focused on stemming the flow of blood. He knew, as I did, that movie-style digging into the flesh with a knife was no use against modern, high-powered rounds. All he could do was keep infection at bay and try to stop the bleeding before I went into hypovolemic shock which, in my case, would result in eternal brain death. It was one messy scene. I knew that for many nights henceforth, Maya would wake up sweating, screaming, as she remembered what she'd seen.

After all this time, I remembered.

Burnt flesh and white bone. Limbs folded at impossible angles, faces contorted beyond recognition with fear, bodies mangled, pounded into pulp. But those remains had been lifeless and, thus, harmless. The dead did not see themselves, and if they did, they wouldn't care. We, the living, were left to try and find beauty in our violence, symmetry in atrocity.

Maybe I was blessed, or maybe I wasn't. I'd seen my own body lie as carrion for vultures and crows. I'd seen my guts spill out into my own hands, watched as I threw up pieces of bone. I'd done it enough number of times to diagnose my condition with antiseptic precision. I held no illusions as to how I'd look when, someday, I died. It would be ugly. It would be beautiful. My body would burn on a pyre. Agni, my ancestor, would rise to embrace me. His effulgence would become mine, and each cell, each pore of my manifested being would light up on the inside, peaking in a crescendo of flame and freedom. And then it would subside, burn into the grey dust of nothingness to be carried away by the wind into the vastness of eternity. In the red embers, my soul would simmer, ensconced in the golden womb of creation. No more being, no more living, just knowing. Just feeling oneness.

I gasped with delight and submitted completely to the illusion. Then it faded, and the pain seared through me again, though a bit duller than before. 'Hang in there, Professor,' Manohar urged as he rubbed a spot on my arm in the telltale after-manner of a needle-prick. I tried to get past the morphine-induced haze, searching for Agni, who had been there just moments ago. Like a lost child, I cried out to him, 'Father, where are you?'

The voice that replied was neither human, nor demon, nor divine. It said, 'Within.'

It could have been the morphine. It could have been something more. I fell back on to the bundle of bag and jacket that Manohar had hastily arranged as a cushion for my head.

Immortality is so much more bearable when death isn't your only hope.

21

I rose to fading sunlight and a familiar face, complete with white beard and intent eyes partly hidden by a thick cloud of smoke emerging from the snout of a burning chillum. 'Hari…' I croaked by way of greeting.

In a loud voice, Hari declared, 'You're an asshole, Asva. You had a gun and yet here you are, all beaten up like some drunk teenager who messed with a bunch of wrestlers. I thought you were a fearless warrior and all that. Turns out you're a complete idiot.'

'In more ways than you know,' I muttered.

Letting out a groan, I sat up and looked around me. This was a hotel room, and a known one from the smell of it. Clean sheets and cleaner bandages were an effective antidote to the excruciating rawness I felt all over, and the rumbling of hunger promised that I was quite on the path to recovery. 'Kashi?' I asked.

'But of course. As it happens, one of my…err, disciples happens to be an excellent surgeon. An attractive lady, discreet and cooperative too. Any other person might have wondered how you ended up with two bullets in your chest from a car accident…'

I pushed away the white sheet to look down at myself. The stick-on plasters implied a typical American first-aid kit, but the tight crepe bandage around my ribs was Indian. I could feel the ribs set into place, and I had the strange, possibly imagined, sense of the bones sealing back together. The bullets had been removed, and jagged, redundant stitches held the skin closed. I was healthy enough to heal faster than the average human, but not abnormally so. Thankfully, my body didn't associate a long life with indefinite healing time, my mythical curse of permanent disease and pus notwithstanding. That would have been…inconvenient, and for once, I was grateful to be as I was.

'When…?' I retained only a vague, drug-addled memory of how I'd got there, but from the way my wounds felt, I guessed it to be a couple of days ago.

'Two days ago,' Hari confirmed. 'Not including the night you were hit. We had you here by dawn, and today's the third day since.'

'How did you…?'

'Manohar called me.'

'They took our phones.'

'Your dead man had one on him.'

'Smart,' I said and settled back on to the pillows with a grin.

'You've taught him well,' Hari observed. 'You should've seen the way he's had control of the situation. He's learnt your calm, dispassionate manner of dealing with crises. Speaking of which…' He sat forward, concern writ clear all over his face. 'What happened, Asva? What sort of a stupid mess have you got yourself into?'

'You know what's stupid, Hari? The fact that I let myself listen to you the other day – your whole sermon on normal life and all that nonsense... No, I can't lay that at your doorstep. It's my mistake and I take responsibility for it. I should've let the Professor go that day.'

'You really want to take responsibility? Then take it for the right thing. Admit that every time you change personas, you're not dealing with reality but running from it. Admit that this job was a bad decision from the start. Admit that it's your ego driving you and nothing else. And then let it go. Tell Maya you're sorry, give her back her money and be done with it.'

Maya.

'What have you told her?'

Hari took a deep drag of his chillum and replied, 'If you're asking me whether she knows about you, the answer is she doesn't. Manohar handled that.'

'Good.'

The response amused him. He chuckled and said, 'You're attracted to her, aren't you?'

'Attracted? Me?'

'Why not? Are you beyond such virtues?'

'I've managed well for a long time...'

'That's neither here nor there, Asva. Just because you've managed to stay a complete and consummate idiot for so many years doesn't mean you're incapable of emotion.'

'I *am* incapable of emotion. I was brought up to be an instrument, a means of action. I've never dreamed of...'

'And here we go again,' Hari interrupted. 'Do I have to remind you of that time in Africa just a couple of years after we first met? When that guerilla group, the Oromo Liberation Front, wanted to take us hostage? Not that they'd have got much for us but...'

I could see where the conversation was going, and I wasn't sure I liked it. Hari used my discomfort to his advantage. 'They had a gun to my head, Asva. I was your friend. And yet you called their bluff. You didn't give a damn about me; you smooth-talked that bastard of a mercenary, bargained your way out of that situation as though Saraswati herself were on your tongue.'

'As I recall, I got us both out of there in one piece. Each.'

'Which is more than you can presently say for yourself. I could've been killed back in Africa, but you didn't let that affect your judgement or your commitment to the life you have chosen as Professor Bharadvaj. Those qualities made you a master strategist, and make you one still. But this last escapade of yours... The way I heard it, you were acting like some corny hero in there – beat me up but leave my girl be!'

'Hari...'

'Which isn't wrong. Maybe you want to be with her... Or maybe you *want* her. You're not a saint. But you're letting it affect your rationality.'

'So you agree, then, that I should remain a dispassionate instrument?' I retorted.

Hari wasn't impressed. 'Don't be stupid, Asva. It's not being *devoid* of passion that's affecting you, it's your denying it.'

'Dammit, Hari! For the last time, Maya means nothing to me. I wasn't playing a tragic hero; I was biding my time... bargaining, as you called it, till I got what information I could about them. It also didn't hurt that I had to deal with one man instead of ten. It doesn't get more dispassionate than that.'

'Then it's over. This project is done, and you and I are going to get high, talk pseudo-philosophy and forget everything that's happened this last week.'

'No,' I said, shaking my head. 'It's not that simple.'

Hari groaned. 'It's never going to be simple, Asva, not as long as you keep denying your identity to gratify your overinflated ego. So what if you...'

'And what identity have I denied? Professor Bharadvaj can no longer...'

'You're *not* Professor Bharadvaj!' Hari snapped.

'And I can't be Asvatthama.'

'Then you're the worst sort of man. You're a man without a self, without a soul. You're as good as cursed, the way the old stories go.'

The declaration stung, all the more so for knowing that Hari believed in what he had just said. I hadn't realized that he thought so poorly of me, or that what he thought mattered to me.

'Perhaps I am the worst sort of man, Hari,' I admitted, my voice unusually hoarse. 'But do you not see why I've made this choice? A man with a destination cannot wander.

I would have willingly carried endless life as a curse, if only to rail against the injustice of my punishment, of all that was stolen from me along with death – affection, belonging, even my history. I'd have stood tall under eternity's shadow, bearing the scars of betrayal with pride. But the price I truly pay…its unconscionable.'

'Loneliness? The heartbreak of loss, of outliving those you love? I'd expected this to be about redeeming yourself; proving to the whole world that you aren't the murderer you've been made out to be. But, clearly, it's a lot more self-indulgent. After all the shit I've heard from you, all your pontificating about rationality and philosophizing about the universe, it's going to come down to the same old cliché, isn't it?'

I had an incongrous desire to laugh, not in amusement but out of disgust, for Hari's words had painted an image of him watching vampire and werewolf serials on Netflix in a quest to empathize with me. Much as I disliked having to explain myself, this once I had to supply the paramount vice of needing to be understood. I chose my words carefully.

'If I walked out of this room, Hari, and said to the first person I met that I was Asvatthama of epic times, that I hadn't died, couldn't die…what do you suppose this person would do?'

At first, Hari did not see; he stared at me with puzzlement and a touch of irritation. A few moments later, it hit him. 'He'd laugh,' he admitted, looking at me with surprised horror. 'If that's what you said to him…or her…they would laugh.'

'Yes,' I said. 'Anyone would laugh. You see, myths aggrandize. In legend, even the worst of villains finds glory by dying at the hands of a hero. But to live on forever as the execrable symbol of defeat... It turns the larger-than-life villain into a simple, despicable monster; a laughable freak. The man called Asvatthama is an idea, a concept; nothing I say or do can absolve him, not without shattering the fantastical context he is embedded in and making him a pitiable laughing stock. It is why I've been so careful to conceal my identity, the fact of my immortality, all these years. People may *believe* that Asvatthama, son of Dronacharya, lives forever, but they will never *accept* that he does...'

Comprehension flashed in Hari's eyes. I'd expected he'd be able to see the difference, the fact that needing to believe in something didn't make it admissible as reality. If that were truly so then most of us would have been living life as shown on television, or not at all.

'I don't fear loss or the aftermath of attachment,' I continued. 'But I could never risk ridicule. Ego, you say? Perhaps it is, but I call it honour and there is none left to me but in legend. And that is why, Hari, I can never be Asvatthama. He is a ghost, and infallible only as long as he remains one. As for Professor Bharadvaj – his meaning came from his purpose, and now that he can no longer fulfil that purpose...but you've heard that story before, so I'll spare you the *pontification*.'

I smiled in an attempt to temper my melancholy. The occasion had far too many words and far too much emotion for my liking, and Hari was looking at me with the one look I despised most of all – sympathy. Thankfully, his rational side soon took over and, bringing his hands together to make a steeple of his fingers, he began to process what I'd just said.

At length he asked, in all sincerity, 'Then who are you? What are you, Asva?'

That question, I had the answer for. I'd had it for a long, long time. 'All forces in the universe occur in pairs – Newton's third law: equal and opposite action and reaction, the infallible symmetry of the universe. Life has its symmetry in death, whereas I...I am an aberration, an aberration for which I must take responsibility. And, like all aberrations, I must come to a natural, logical end.'

'What the fuck is that supposed to...?' Hari began, but then trailed off as wisdom prevailed over words. He made a few attempts to speak, resulting in a series of incoherent monosyllables, before pulling himself together. 'It never really was about finding out what made you this way, was it Asva? It was never about reclaiming what you lost. That is gone forever, for the legend of Asvatthama must stand untouched. But you, the living man...you are neither he, nor can you be anyone else... In fact, you think you ought not to exist because it disturbs the balance between reality and myth.'

'Yes.'

'An anomaly... What was it you said? An aberration. Something that should have been set right, that your family should have set right, but failed to. That is why you think they betrayed you. That instead of using their science to help...or destroy you...they claimed ignorance in order to save their own skins, given the political turbulence of the times.'

'Yes.'

'And so your karma, your purpose...this whole "taking responsibility". You believe you must do the job that they didn't have the balls for.'

'Yes. You're on a roll, Hari.'

He attempted to ignore the trite remark but the effort only made him look sadder as he said, 'You're looking for a way to die, Asva. All these thousands of years, you've just been looking for a way to die.'

To have heard it said so patently was liberating. With all the imperiousness that I had once legitimately possessed, I admitted, 'Yes. I am. It is the only thing left that gives meaning to my life.' Without waiting for a response, I closed my eyes, indicating that I was done with the conversation.

I could sense Hari study me for a while then heard him as he stood up to leave. In a soft tone, he said, 'Talk to Manohar. The boy is concerned and confused. He blames himself for this whole mess; says he was the one who pressed you into taking the case. Talk to him.'

I frowned, surprised at that, but dismissed it as something I didn't care about at the moment. 'Later. I want to see Maya. In exactly fifteen minutes.'

Shaking his head in disapproval, Hari made his way out.

22

Throwing aside the covers, I got out of bed. More spasms, not unbearable this time, shot through my side but ebbed to a dull burning that pushed all previous thoughts of food from my mind. Fortunately, the pain didn't grow worse as I unwound the crepe bandage and then pressed on the stick-on dressings to check if they were waterproof. I was desperate for a shower, and I needed some time to think before Maya got here.

Maya.

The need to see her, to make sure she was all right, was part of the throbbing discomfort that filled me, and I was far from ready to accept the explanations that Hari had given. I had no need to deny that I considered her – or anyone else for that matter – desirable, for I was sure that any actions that came thereof were the result of choice and not emotional compulsion. But there was something more at play, some niggling sense that I could not accurately place, which made me more keenly aware of and interested in her, beyond basal desire. Intrigue? Perhaps she was to me a symbol of the mysterious goings-on and needing to see her safe was a way of affirming my hold over the situation? Or was it just lust after all, heightened by the adrenaline-surge of danger and violence?

I settled on dominance as the explanation, the need to wrest back control over events that I'd lost when she had turned up with her silly theories, forcing Manohar to call me and... Letting out a hiss as the sharp, scalding spray from the shower finally turned into soothing pressure on tired muscles, I notched up one more complaint against Ms Jervois: she had made me examine my motives and logic far more than was required for the purpose of alert self-awareness.

I stayed in the shower for as long as it took to completely rein in my mind and then stepped out. Drawing on clean trousers and fastening my belt, I reached out for the brand new sacred thread that Hari had considerately procured for me. Putting it on with a habitual prayer, I set about changing the stick-on plasters for the spares that had been left on a table, when there was knock at the door.

'It's open!' I called out.

Maya made her way in. She looked overwrought, but beyond that bore no visible sign of our recent experiences. I tried to disregard the obvious streak of relief I felt at that and went back to replacing my dressing.

'Let me do that.' Maya stepped up. 'I...' she wavered and then went on, 'I heard Hari call you Asva, when he and Manohar were talking... Is...is that your name?'

'Yes,' I said, in a tone that brooked no further conversation on the topic.

She said nothing and avoided meeting my gaze, feigning preoccupation with the bandage in her hands as she peeled off its backing. Holding her breath, she stepped closer and pressed the self-adhering plaster over one of the sutured bullet wounds on my chest. I breathed in deep, taking in the smell of her hair, a new shampoo – perhaps the one from the hotel. It mingled well with the scent that was her own.

Maya finished dressing the second bullet wound, smoothing the bandage over with her hand for good measure. She ran her hand across my torso, feeling first the taut muscles of my abdomen and then the scars. Once, there had been many marks there, the relics of war, but they had faded over the centuries, leaving mostly the lesser signs of my current profession.

'How…?' she asked, fingers resting on a more recent memento – an eight-inch gash that ran from the side, under my left rib cage, down to the front.

'Knife wound,' I said. I didn't add that it had come from the katana samurai blade of Tomoyuki Yamashita, a general of the Imperial Japanese Army, whom I'd encountered during the Second World War. When the Japanese had attacked civilian settlements during the Battle of Singapore, I had been one of the many random non-combatants who had been thrown into the fray. I'd survived the short skirmish, wounded by none other than Yamashita himself and been thrown into prison – a fate far more fortunate than that of others. Eventually, I'd been recruited into the Indian National Army – though I had been part of its ranks briefly and well before Subhash Chandra Bose had taken command – and thus found my way into being part of India's independence movement.

That once, just that once, my actions had been motivated not by my god-forsaken purpose, my futile search. Loyalty? Patriotism? No, those notions were noble, while my motivations ranged only from partly selfish to fully so. But something had dragged me back to the land of my birth. Maybe it had been the prospect of having a purpose bigger than myself, something larger to fight for.

I let my mind wander further along those lines in a bid to overlook Maya's touch, but her hand remained on me, lingering needlessly on my scar.

'I'm sorry,' she whispered. 'I'm so, so sorry. I didn't think it would be like this. If anything had happened to you...'

I didn't care for her explanations, nor did she get to tender them in full as, at last, I tasted her lips. Again, I breathed in the smell of her hair, a mix of mint shampoo and just her. She was much shorter than I was and would fit snug against my chest. As though she perceived what ran through my mind, she pressed her body flush against mine. I pulled away, ending the kiss. She looked up at me, her desire laced with inquiry.

My next words were an exercise in self-restraint, part of a routine rehearsed over many years. 'Don't, Maya. You'll regret it.'

At once, the questions were gone, replaced with blazing defiance. She let go of me and took a step back. It made me want her all the more. 'I know I won't,' she declared. 'But if *you* will...'

'I wouldn't. I won't. But this isn't a good idea.'

'Why not?'

'I'd explain, but you wouldn't agree with me. We'll end up arguing over nothing...'

'I'm not going to argue with you.'

'Good.'

I expected some pithy repartee, but she said nothing. She trailed her fingers down the side of my face before bringing them to rest on my cheek. The tenderness in her touch made me want to throw up and slap her, both at once. Instead, I tugged at her light linen shirt, my lips back on hers, rough and demanding. She responded with eager ardour. Her skin was cool against my fingertips as I traced the outline of her form, pulling off her shirt, then her jeans, before finally tearing at her underclothing, pausing only to chuckle at the tattoo I'd seen earlier on her collarbone. It was an ouroboros – the Greek mystic symbol of a serpent eating its own tail in a sign of eternal renewal.

She gasped, startled, but didn't protest when I twined my fingers through her hair and yanked her head to the side, seeking access to the graceful lines of her neck and shoulders. Eyes closed, she yielded completely, stirring from her trance-like state only when I stopped and let go of her. Her gaze admonished and encouraged, and she playfully tapped a finger against the buckle of my belt. I gave her a cheeky smile and, sparing her the trouble, undressed myself before claiming her mouth again. I half-walked, half-carried her to the bed, laid her on it and stood drinking in the beauty of her naked body, slender but strong, like that of a Yogini of yore.

Reaching out, Maya made to pull me down to her but then paused, wary of my wounds. In response, I grit my teeth and closed the distance that remained between us. We both cried out softly — she at the rapture of contact, I at the exquisite flash of red-hot pain across my chest, but neither of us stopped. Neither of us could. Our bodies fell into an age-old, primal rhythm, and my death-deprived faculties surrendered to its pulse, seeking affirmation of life. She whispered in my ears, incoherent endearments I cared little for, and sank her fingernails into my shoulders as she arched up against me, taking pleasure even as she gave it.

I responded with a vengeance, with violent passion and an anger that was all too familiar and felt far worse than the searing ache that filled my every fibre. Then, and now, it was betrayal that hurt the most.

23

Sunlight streamed into the room through a narrow slit between the thick drapes on the windows. Next to me, the bed was empty. Maya had left soon after she thought I'd fallen asleep though, in fact, I had not. I hadn't stopped her.

I ran the night's events through my mind, savouring again the raw magnificence of her unclothed form. I was, in many ways, the worst kind of man, one who made no apologies for being that way and resisted all provocation to behave otherwise. It dawned on me as I lay there, aware of how the sheets held her smell, that I'd wanted her since she'd walked into the office at Paharganj. I brushed the admission aside, unwilling to admit that Hari had been right after all.

A knock sounded at the door. 'Yes, just a minute,' I said, glad of the interruption to my idle reverie. I got out of bed and, picking my pants up off the carpeted floor, put them on as I went to the door.

'Professor!' Manohar stood outside, showered and ready for the day, except in spirit. His eyes held hurt and confusion from my pointed refusal to see him the previous day, now compounded all the more by my gruff manner.

I held out my hand. 'Pratap's phone. Hari said you used it to call him.'

Manohar appeared further downcast. 'I don't have it. I broke the SIM card and the phone, just in case. I didn't want to risk those guys trailing us through it. For all you know, it might have got the police on our tail – God knows what else that bastard was involved in!'

'You junked it.' It was a statement and an admonition too. Manohar had destroyed what may have been our one chance to track down the fragments that had been taken from us. The reasons he gave were far from illogical, and in any other situation I would have approved of what he'd done. This time, though, the risks would have been well worth it.

'I'm sorry. I...'

'Anything else?'

He gave me a shocked look and then pulled himself together. 'We have a meeting with a historian who's associated with the Gyanvapi mosque – the one adjacent to the Kashi Vishwanath temple. I had Hari use his contacts and bring this man in, so we could find out about the Gyanvapi well. They are in the coffee shop downstairs. Hari had said you should be well enough to do stuff today, so I'd fixed it up. I'm sorry if...'

'Don't worry. I'm fine. Does this man know what we're interested in?'

'He doesn't know about the fragment but thinks we are interested in the original source of the Gyanvapi waters. I spoke to him on the phone, and he sounded like a rational, sensible chap; someone who isn't going to make a big deal of…sensitive enquiries if they're made in good faith.'

'Fine. I'll be downstairs in ten minutes.'

Before Manohar could say anything more, I shut the door in his face.

I arrived at the coffee shop to find the others already there. Maya flashed me a smile of welcome, a clear message that she had neither forgotten the events of the previous night nor regretted what had happened between us. She was in the midst of an animated conversation with Hari, Manohar and a man who was introduced to me as Dr Shahbuddin, a historian and one of the advisors to the trust that ran the Gyanvapi mosque. I took an instinctive liking to the tall, well-turned-out man and engaged in brief chit-chat before getting to the point.

'I believe Manohar has already told you what our interest here is. To confirm or refute my research premise, I need to get in under the mosque. By my calculations, there should be an entranceway in or around the original source of the Gyanvapi, the well of wisdom. Hari here can vouch for my intentions, and if anything goes wrong, I'll take complete responsibility for it.'

Dr Shahbuddin said, 'Hari has told me about you, Professor. I have no doubt that you mean no harm of any sort to either the temple or the mosque. But I must disappoint you. You see, there is nothing under the mosque.'

I glanced at Hari, trying to evaluate whether Dr Shahbuddin's response was a stock line or arose from genuine ignorance about the possibility. Hari's eyes held a third likelihood. They were full of disappointment, I supposed for more than one reason.

Dr Shahbuddin noted the overall air of discontent at his statement. He explained, 'The mosque has its own historical records right from the time of Aurangzeb. I can assure you, there is nothing under the mosque. No passageway, no chamber, no ruins. Nothing.'

'How can you be sure?' Maya challenged.

To his credit, Dr Shahbuddin took no offence and launched into an explanation. 'The mosque was built in 1669 – recent enough for us to have detailed construction records. I won't deny that the foundation level stands on the ruins of a previous structure, presumably the old Kashi Vishwanath temple. It is also common knowledge, as well as obvious to the eye, that the western wall of the mosque would originally have been part of the old temple. From what Hari tells me, this is a matter of history and not religion to you, so I assume you won't be upset by that admission?'

'No,' I shook my head. 'But do forgive me for asking this again: are you sure...?'

'I am,' Dr Shahbuddin insisted. 'Not only about the mosque, but also about the Gyanvapi well. Till some years ago, people used to jump into the well in a bid to commit suicide. I assume they believed that dying in the holy water would lead to salvation. But the point is this: The men who used to retrieve the bodies from the well came from a particular family, a family that did the task till just a generation ago. The last man to have held the job is long dead, but you can talk to his son if you like. The family still lives here. The fact is, it's nothing more than a ground-water well from a conventional precipitation aquifer – there are no mentionable inlets or outlets that lead anywhere.'

I stood up, ending the meeting. 'Thank you, Dr Shahbuddin. You've been immensely helpful, and I suspect you've also saved me much time and effort.' Despite my words, I felt an inexplicable tiredness and the prickling of my wounds overcame me anew. I steeled myself against both sensations and took Dr Shahbuddin's hand as he said his goodbyes.

'Well?' Manohar began, as soon as our visitor was gone.

Hari said, 'If you want my opinion, such as its worth, it's over. Those bastards have two of the three fragments, and the third is untraceable. You might as well give up and count yourself lucky to be in one piece!'

'Let me think...' I said.

Maya said, 'We can't give up! You know what these guys are capable of! God knows what they will do with the Vajra if they find the third fragment. They've already killed for it, and they won't hesitate to kill again. These men are animals, power-hungry animals. We can't let them get their hands on something...something that has the potential for unthinkable destruction.' She realized she was on a rant for she stopped and lowered her voice. 'Asva...' she used the name tentatively, even though she'd called it out more than once the previous night. Perhaps it was the lack of a positive reaction from me or the fact that Manohar was visibly taken aback, but she quickly corrected herself. 'Professor, I know you don't think the Vajra is anything much at all, but please remember that a few days ago you didn't believe it even existed. After all that we've seen and been through, can you honestly bring yourself to walk away from this mystery and leave things to fickle fate?'

Manohar said, 'Not all mysteries are meant to be solved.'

'What do you mean, Manohar?' She turned on him.

'I mean...' He drew his shoulders back, as though coming to a final decision on an issue he'd been struggling with for some time. 'I don't think those guys are...bad. Okay, that Pratap was a bastard, but he was only a hired gun. That man...Moorthy...I don't think he means harm. I...I don't know, I can't explain it.'

'Don't think he means harm? You're kidding, right? What do you suggest we do – we just leave their trail, let them take the Vajra, do what they want with it?'

Manohar sounded strangely tenacious. 'Maya, if this thing is truly that powerful, how can we trust ourselves with it? Even if we don't use it to ill ends, can we protect it from those who would? Moorthy and his lot seem to know what they are doing...' He placed a hand on my arm. 'Professor, you're the one who taught me that not all things can be made sense of in the present...that some secrets are best kept secrets till they can be explained. What I've just said comes not from analysis, but from instinct. As for what we ought to do now, I leave that decision to you and...'

Maya cut in. 'I don't think the Professor's in the mood to give up, Manohar. And you, Hari, I'm astonished that you agree!'

Hari shrugged, nonchalant, as though he didn't care either way.

'How do you know what the Professor wants?' Manohar snapped. He was, I knew, irked by Maya's sudden claim of familiarity.

Oblivious to his ire, Maya went on to address me. 'Well? How about it?'

I stood up. 'I said, let me think. And I think best on my feet. I'm heading to the temple.'

Manohar said, 'You should rest.'

'I don't want to rest, Manohar. I've rested enough. I need to do this.'

Manohar gave me a searching look and then appeared to understand. 'All right,' he said, also getting to his feet.

'Wait. I'll come with the two of you,' Maya said.

I shrugged. With a word of goodbye to Hari, we left.

The three of us made our way to the temple, past the crowd at the main arched entranceway of the temple complex and through narrow streets lined with shops selling devotional and secular items alike. Reaching the temple, I didn't bother heading to the sanctum, but walked instead towards the northern side of the precinct and the mosque that lay beyond. Between the two places of worship was a courtyard, with a raised dais that served as a small shrine and Nandi, the bull, next to it. Further ahead was a pillared hall, inside which a low, latticed wall in the shape of an octagon sealed off the Gyanvapi well.

A priest sat near the wall, attending to the devotees who stood in a haphazard line, waiting their turn to receive a handful of the sacred water. I fell in behind a wizened couple, feeling every care temporarily fade as I saw the warm contentment in their deep-set eyes, the wisdom on their crinkled-parchment faces. Age and, as far as I could tell, weather from their outdoor occupation – probably hard farming on a small, near-barren patch of land – had taken a toll on their appearance, but not their spirit. The two radiated serenity, the well-earned anticipation that comes at the end of a life lived to completion.

Content with the modest blessing that was a teaspoon of water from the Gyanvapi, the couple moved away, their steps sluggish but self-reliant. I reached the head of the line. The priest eyed me with mild curiosity as I placed a hundred-rupee note on the offering plate and held out my right hand, palm cupped. He doled out the ritual spoonful, and I moved away. With a silent prayer to Rudra, I sipped the water, draining my small quota.

Wordless, I began making my way out of the temple, Manohar alongside. Maya ran after us. 'Wait! What was that all about?'

I didn't break my stride as I answered, 'This isn't it, Maya. The third element – arsenic, life-breath, whatever you want to call it – isn't here.'

'You know that just by drinking that water? Come on, that's ridiculous!'

'Not by drinking it. I know, because it doesn't fit in. The clues, the connections, they don't make sense.'

She grabbed me by the wrist, bringing me to a stop in the middle of the crowded street. Manohar came to stand next to us, looking very much the uncomfortable spectator to a couple's tiff. 'What the fuck is going on here, Professor?' Maya hissed through clenched teeth. 'We decided that this was it. *You* decided…'

'This can't be it,' I explained, not without showing some of the frustration I felt. 'Look, I made a mistake. The legend goes that this was where Nagarjuna studied, where he was initiated into the order of alchemy, and that part fits. But…'

I trailed off and into silent inner argument. It hadn't been just Maya's premise or the fact that Nagarjuna had been initiated at Kashi that had led me here. There'd been more: Jabir's insistence that belief was the key to unlocking the secrets of alchemy. I'd dismissed the approach as irrational, but for many days after that particular conversation I'd wondered if he had perhaps been testing me, my mettle as an alchemist, and I'd failed for lack of faith – an error I'd tried to avoid ever since. But in spite of my best efforts, I'd failed again and more deplorably than I'd realized.

What if it wasn't the arcane principles of alchemy that Jabir was asking me to believe in? What if he'd been asking me to have faith in myself, in my fellow human beings?

I refused to affirm the premise but was wary of rejecting it completely and so left it for future consideration. Returning to the present, I noticed Maya staring at me.

She opened and shut her mouth a couple of times in an attempt at speech. Then she shook her head and declared, 'You know what, don't say another word! Stop with all this lecturing and theory, I'm sick and tired of your patronizing question-and-answer routine. In fact, I don't think you're really a professor anyway, so screw it. And screw you!'

She made to walk away, but I grabbed her arm. 'You're right,' I told her. 'I'm not a professor. I never was. But I am what I am, and you will speak to me with the respect that I deserve!'

It took me a moment to realize that I was shouting. I, Asvatthama, the man who hadn't raised his voice even in the most infuriating of situations or at the worst of men, was shouting at a girl – a veritable child as far as I was concerned – in the middle of a busy street. My words, however, were largely lost in the bustle around us and though a few passers-by gave us inquisitive stares, no one intervened.

'I'm sorry,' I continued, in a quieter tone. 'I am. From the day I agreed to this stupid search for the Vajra right up to this bloody second, I've been making one mistake after another. You want your Vajra; I'll find it for you, if it exists. Now leave me alone so I can figure out what to do next.'

Manohar shuffled where he stood. He obviously didn't like being privy to the conversation, but was placed in a delicate position where he couldn't walk away without appearing rude, or worse, derisive. His discomfort sobered me more than Maya's apparent hurt. I turned inwards, looking, searching, for the voice of reason. All I had was a feeling of someone watching me, amused. Hissing an indistinct expletive, I looked at Maya.

She burst into apology. 'Professor, I'm so sorry! I…'

'Please!' I let go of her arm and raised my hand in a sign for her to stop. 'Please, both of you... No offence, but I just need to get my wits together on this... I don't react too well to being wrong, do I? So...why don't you head back to the hotel and get comfortable. There's nothing more to be done here...'

'Fine,' Maya reached out to squeeze my hand.

Manohar didn't say anything, but frowned, betraying his reservation. On impulse, I patted him on the shoulder in a paternal gesture. The act left an unpleasant taste in my mouth, the cloying but compelling tug of affection, the promise of family and the allure of life lived to the full and left behind in vain. Only the sober friendship of the dead could take that heavy taste away.

I began walking towards my beloved ghats and their dispassionate funeral pyres.

24

It was past two in the morning when I made my way back from the burning ghats to the hotel room. I'd sat on the steps of the ghat for a long time, first praying to and then arguing with Agni. At some point, I'd descended into a tired inner quiet and then into wholesome sleep. The *dom*s who worked the pyres were no strangers to the many varieties of ascetics and mystics who meditated amongst the dead or spent their time lying in a spiritual or herb-induced daze between rows of bodies that awaited burning. But I neither looked nor felt the part, and one of the *dom*s had woken me up to ask if I were well. I'd spent a few hours in casual conversation with him and some of the other pyre-workers and less contemplative ascetics gathered there. A few *kullad*s of sweet tea and a great many cigarettes later, I'd wished them a good night, or what remained of it, and left.

I let myself into my hotel room and made straight for the shower, needing to wash off the strong smell of burning wood and flesh that clung to me. Behind me, the light came on, affirming what I'd guessed the moment I'd stepped through the door — that Maya was in my bed and she was now awake. When I emerged from the bathroom, she was sitting up, attentive and eager to talk. I switched off the light and slipped in under the sheets, keeping a casual distance between us. I felt her lie back down before reaching out in the darkness to place a hand on my bare chest. 'We screwed up, Professor,' she began.

'We?'

'I mean, Manohar and I. He'd said, and I'd agreed, that Moorthy and his men must have picked up the fragment from the courier office as they'd planned, and so we didn't even think to check. It was a mistake. If we'd gone there as soon as we'd arrived in Kashi, there might have been a chance… The package was delayed in transit because of some stupid roadblock. But…Manohar…he was sure that those thugs must've reached before us and, of course, you were in bad shape, so we weren't thinking too cogently. I certainly wasn't.' She added the last bit in an embarrassed hush.

'When did you find out?'

'Manohar and I passed the courier office when we walked back to the hotel, yesterday, after…after we'd all gone to the temple. I don't know why, but he suddenly decided to check on the package, after all. That's when we came to know that the place had been ransacked just the night before last. The manager reluctantly asked us if we wanted to file a police report and claim the basic compensation. I think it was a few hundred rupees. Manohar declined. I…I wasn't sure whether to insist. I have to say, his recent behaviour surprises me. It's as though he's just given up. But then, I don't know him that well.'

'Hmm. Yeah,' I managed to grunt, glad of the darkness, for it hid the anger I felt. How had I assumed, just as the others had, that Moorthy had already got hold of the fragment? And how had I not wondered how our pursuers were always one step ahead of us? Rather, I'd had been more interested in jumping Maya like a hormonal teenager.

I didn't dispute the inner injunction, but temporarily ignored it as my resentment turned outwards. My own faults inspired enduring guilt, but the faults of others were easily fixed with vengeance. Perfidy, in particular. Right then I felt as though I could never trust a living soul again. But time had taught me never to be hasty with judgements of treachery and deceit.

Around 480 BCE, I'd found myself a *satrap* – a vassal lord – under the Persian emperor, Xerxes the First. My position with him had not come by accident: The Persian magus Avastana, or Ostanes as the Greeks had called him, had been employed by Xerxes's father Darius to search for that which all conquerors sooner or later aspired to – eternal life. Ostanes had proved to be of more political than alchemical use, for Xerxes had, on ascending the throne, claimed to have been transformed into a god-like creature of incredible strength.

Of course, all that had come later, and at our first battle together at Marathon, Greece, he'd been a young prince and I a hired soldier. Beginning with that monumental loss, not long after which the prince rose to become king, my journey with him lasted over ten years, through his suppression of rebellion in Africa, right till his decisive defeat at the hands of the united Greek states in the Battle of Salamis. Much happened in that decade and was recorded in history, but not as I remembered it, for the story of those times was told by a Greek named Herodotus, who cast it as the heroic tale of freedom-loving peoples who defied Persian tyranny.

In truth, there had been heroes on both sides; men and women willing to fight to the last for what they believed in. I'd looked into the eyes of Leonidas, the Spartan king whose deeds are now the stuff of blockbuster films, and seen his true courage. I'd been a friend and counsellor to Xerxes – Kshayarsha in his own tongue – a man of tremendous political and technological foresight, who had believed that the divided Greek states had been far from prosperous or efficient. Above all, I'd stood shoulder to shoulder with Ephialtes, the so-called traitor of Thermopylae, whose betrayal had led to the fall of the three hundred Spartans who had stood between Greece and the hundred-thousand strong Persian army.

Far from the bitter, deformed cripple of digital posterity, Ephialtes had been a tall, fair-haired man, and his sparkling blue eyes had held wisdom. He'd seen what many had refused to see – that as long as Sparta continued to claim its superiority over and independence from the other Greek states, there was no hope for a united Greece. Sparta had to fall for Greece to rise. Yet history recorded Ephialtes's treachery, not his sacrifice.

And just as on that fateful day, when I'd led Xerxes's elite troops along the secret mountain path that Ephialtes had shown us to mount a surprise attack on Leonidas and his men, in this instance too, I didn't know whether the company I kept was a traitor or a true guide. And only one person could answer that question for me – my adversary.

My mind made up, I emptied it in preparation for a good night's rest. Maya waited for me to say more, to share my decision. I turned on to my side, my back to her, and was soon fast sleep.

I woke up before dawn, dressed and made my way out of the room without waking Maya. My steps quickened as I passed Manohar's door and I didn't let up till I reached my destination: Shankar Plaza, a modern office building with a small signal tower on its roof serving as evidence of the lopsided commodification that few places in India were free of. For once, I brooked no resentment against the monstrosity that sat on top of the building, for it made my task a lot easier than I'd expected.

A large hoarding proclaimed the existence of the courier office I sought on the second floor of the building. The board also served to affirm, in case one might be tempted by the early-rising habits of Kashi's residents to think otherwise, that the office was shut at that time and would remain so till a later, more respectable, hour. I, however, had need of neither the office nor its administrators. In fact, one more query in connection with the same package might serve to invite unwelcome attention and there was nothing to be gained in this instance by risking it. All I needed was to see the building, its surrounds, to be there in the same space as the man I was after. Building a temporal bond with the quarry was always the first step of the hunt.

The hunt. The words filled me with a familiar exhilaration. For the first time in days, I felt completely in my element. The feeling grew as I began surveying the area, my gaze finally settling on a large, misspelt signboard that pointed to a public telephone booth tucked into a small by-lane in the space between two rows of houses. The same signage proclaimed, without error, that the booth and the general provision store that it appeared to be an offshoot of, remained open twenty-four hours a day.

Moorthy, I was sure, would have scoped out the courier office before staging a theft, and a man of his intelligence would certainly have avoided using his cellphone within such proximate radius of a specific signal tower, in case the virtual location register logged the presence of the number. Of course, there was the possibility that he might have used his mobile phone but then thrown away the SIM card or done a hundred other things to hide his tracks, but I had a feeling that he was a man brought up to view thrift in all its forms as a virtue. And I knew by now that he was also a man who valued secrecy as much as I did. It had been his weakness thus far, for he'd been forced to rely on men like Pratap — my dead attacker — who were less suited to the delicacy of the task at hand, but needed to know nothing, registered little of what they saw or heard, and were entirely dispensable. And this flaw would now help me find Moorthy.

I made my way to the public telephone. A local stray eyed me warily from his place under a fruit hawker's cart, but didn't bother to vacate the space. I smiled at him as I walked on, wrinkling up my nose at the persistent stench from the garbage that waited to be cleared away.

The telephone booth was the standard, nondescript yellow tin box that allowed standing space for one. It was built right into the frontage of a small shop that sold sundry items, including an assortment of soft drinks and cigarettes, not to mention a bevy of two-inch sachets hanging from thin strings that ran from wall to wall, forming a persuasive method of display and storage. Shampoos, toothpaste, cooking oil, fairness creams and even condoms were available in single-serve packages, in evidence of the bottom-of-the-pyramid marketing trend and its success.

At that hour of the morning, the shop was manned by a young boy, hardly nine or ten years of age. He was already scrubbed and dressed in an inexpensive but clean school uniform. The sight made me smile wider still. Evidently, the boy helped out in the shop before heading later to school.

As I approached the counter, the dog emerged from under the cart and appeared at my side, striking a pose in a perfect 'sit' and looking intently up at me. The boy said, in English, 'Bun, sir? For doggie?'

I nodded and replied, '*Ek* pack Marlboro lights *bhi*, please.' On impulse, I dipped my hand into one of the many glass jars that stood on the counter and took out two bars of chocolate, which the boy added to my bill – a piece of white paper with some numbers printed on the reverse that I recognized at once. I watched as he took my money, counted it carefully and then tucked it into a drawer that he immediately locked. That done, he looked up, clearly pleased with himself at having concluded a big transaction this early in the day. I held out one of the two chocolate bars to him. He hesitated, but then took it with all the earnestness of his age.

The three of us – boy, man and dog – munched on our respective treats in companionable silence. Around us, the city stirred. Temple bells rang clear in the morning air, mingling well with the first *azaan* of the day. The gentle swish of a broom as someone swept the threshold of their house, the rhythm of human activity that had yet to give way to the harsher grunts of vehicular traffic and the lilting cries of vegetable peddlers as they went from door to door, selling their fresh wares – sounds of an Indian dawn that remained the same in spirit no matter which city one went to.

Finishing the bar of chocolate with relish, I lit up a cigarette. The boy licked his fingers clean and flashed me a wide grin. The dog too settled into a wholesome stupor, his back to one wall of the phone booth. Thus bonded, it was easy to strike up conversation. I began by asking the boy about himself, about the shop, the surroundings, what he wanted to be when he grew up, who manned the shop during the night and how many customers came in every day. The boy told me, continuing in English, 'for practice', that his name was Kishen and that he was the third of four children, that his brothers and his father took turns to run the shop through day and night, that this was a bustling neighbourhood during office hours though there was little activity after ten at night, but in all they had enough customers to make ends meet, and once he grew up he wanted to either be a doctor or have his own departmental store.

That conversation done, Kishen came around from behind the counter and sat next to me on the small wooden bench that a neighbour – a shack selling tea and bread-omelettes – set out as he opened up for the day. I ordered tea for the both of us and a bread-omelette for the dog and we began to play noughts and crosses on the small scraps of paper that Kishen had stapled together for use as a rough bill-book. We played many rounds over the next half-hour, tearing off the sheets one by one and throwing them into the nearby wicker basket that served as the tea-seller's garbage bin. Eventually, I threw my arms up and out in a lazy stretch before sitting up straight with the finality of one who has had much fun but needs to return to mundane existence.

'I have to make a call,' I told Kishen, 'and you better get back behind the counter before your father comes in and has words with both of us!'

Kishen giggled and stood up, holding his hand out for the homemade bill-book and the pencil we'd been using in our game. I tore off the last sheet that we had scrawled on and handed the two items back to him. As the boy went back in to tend to his tiny store, I glanced at the piece of paper in my hand. Kishen and his family used the reverse side of the billing paper spat out by the electronic meter in the telephone booth to scribble their own bills. It had just been a matter of going through the scraps long enough to find the receipts for the calls that had been placed the night of the burglary, after office hours. In fact, the slip I held attested to only one call having been placed that entire night, at just a few minutes short of midnight. I had no doubt that the police had, as part of the enquiry, checked with Kishen's father as to any unusual activity. But a calm, confident man making a phone call was hardly unusual in a tourist-filled city such as Kashi, even at that late hour. After all, thieves didn't hang around in the vicinity to chit-chat on phones after the crime had been committed. Moorthy, however, was much more than a common thief.

I memorized the phone number – a landline number along with its area code – and let the piece of paper join its fellow scraps in the rubbish bin before asking Kishen, 'Do you have a telephone directory?'

By way of reply, the boy handed me two thick volumes from behind the shop counter. I needed only the first. I flipped it open to the front pages where all the cities and towns of India were listed by their long-distance area codes and confirmed what I'd already suspected. Or had hoped for. Moorthy had made a call to someone in a place where Shiva was fire, but his spirit was life-breath.

I handed back the volumes and stepping into the semi-private phone booth punched the numbers with clear purpose.

The phone rang five times, before it was picked up at the other end. A man's voice said, 'Hello?'

I waited, not saying anything. 'Hello?' the voice repeated. I cut the line, lingered a couple of minutes and then dialled again. The same voice answered. 'Hello? Moorthy? Is that you? *Yenna pa?*' Continuing in Tamil, he asked, 'Is everything all right?'

The man's voice grew faint as he said, ostensibly to someone next to him, '...it's the same number he called me from the other day...' He spoke again into the receiver, 'Hello? Hello? Who's calling, please? *Yaar pesaradu?*'

I paused a few seconds more, letting my interlocutor feel the weight of the moment. My tone was neutral as I said, in the same language, 'We need to talk.'

Silence at the other end and then, 'Who's this?'

'You know who I am. I know why you're after me. I think there are some issues between us that we need to sort out before this gets out of hand. Neither of us wants to draw attention, nor do we want people to be unnecessarily hurt.'

'Fine.' Gone was the initial wonder and in its place was a cool composure that matched my own. 'I'm listening, Professor.'

'No,' I refused. 'We do this in person. Tell Moorthy and his friends to wait for my team and me in front of this phone booth at twelve noon, and we'll all head to the airport together. If your budget doesn't allow for air travel, I'll be happy to cover it.'

The man at the other end chuckled at that. 'You're a persuasive man, Professor. All right, I'll tell Moorthy.'

'You might want to add that if he gives me trouble... Well, best if he doesn't give me trouble.'

'He won't. Moorthy's a good chap, unlike…what was it you called that other fellow? Ah, yes, an orangutan. You might even enjoy Moorthy's company on the journey here. I'll see you tomorrow, then.'

'Hmm…' On impulse, I added, 'Thank you.'

The man laughed. It was a wholesome sound; one that made me like him, though grudgingly. 'You really are a gentleman,' he said. 'And you're welcome.'

I replaced the receiver and stepped out of the booth. By the time I'd paid for the calls, smoked a contented cigarette and walked back to the hotel, I was in positively good spirits. I made my way to Manohar's room and knocked on the door.

'Coming, coming!' I heard him shout from inside. The sound of much bustling and hurrying followed. He then opened the door, his hair wet and a towel around his waist. 'Oh, Professor! Is everything okay?'

'Everything's fine, Manohar. Get dressed and then get packed.'

He gave me a quizzical look, but it lacked the confusion and uncertainty I'd seen so often in these past few days. This was an expression that bespoke excitement, curiosity and, above all, complete trust. The hunt, he too had sensed, was about to begin.

I smiled and said, 'We've got work to do.'

25

Sharp at noon, Moorthy climbed out of a minivan that had rolled to a stop at the head of the lane where the phone booth stood. Maya began to fiddle with the red string that Hari had tied around her right wrist as a protective charm, after first asking her whether she believed in God, prayer and talismans, in that order. I hadn't seen the connection between the three, nor did I think the string was anything more than the meaningless standard-issue placebo that Hari offered as Baba Shivdas to visitors. But his mild manner and kind words had calmed Maya, and when he'd placed his hand on her head in blessing, it had come with genuine wishes. Maya had taken some strength from that, for she stopped fingering the string and drew her shoulders back in a resolute stance.

For his part, Moorthy was very much aware of her discomfort and he addressed her first. 'I'm sorry. It was a grave error in judgement. If I'd had the least inkling that Pratap would try to hurt you...'

Maya appeared mollified by the apology, but Manohar snapped. 'How did you...?'

Moorthy cleared his throat, embarrassed. 'I saw the body.'

'You saw the body? But...?'

'Yes, I know. You left him hidden under a pile of rubble. We went back to cremate him because even scumbags deserve to rest after death. Also, we didn't want him being traced to us. That's when I saw that Pratap was...well, his belt was undone and his pants unzipped. I see no reason why any of you would have bothered to do that... Be that as it may, Pratap was a hired hand, as were the others. But that isn't a mistake I will make again. The men you see with me today are as brothers to me. I've known them for years, and we are all sworn to the same cause.'

I said, 'And what cause is that?'

Moorthy exchanged glances with his colleagues. 'Don't you know, Professor? From the expression on your assistant's face, I dare say he's deduced it.'

I was about to make the instinctive correction that Manohar was a colleague and not an assistant when he said, 'You are protectors of the Vajra, aren't you?'

'Yes,' Moorthy said. '"Custodians" is the word we use for ourselves. I know you have many questions on who we are and what we do, but I'm not the right man to answer them.' With that, he stepped aside, indicating for us to get into the minivan.

I got in without protest. Maya and Manohar had no choice but to follow.

'I hope you know what you're doing,' Maya whispered. She was sitting between Manohar and me, and I wrapped a protective arm around her shoulder. As though he neither noticed nor cared, Manohar turned to look out the window on his left. None of the others witnessed our brief scene. Moorthy was busy giving instructions to the driver of our vehicle, while his colleagues chatted amongst themselves. Despite the casual air of the situation, as well as Moorthy's undoubtedly genuine apology, I didn't think him any less dangerous. But our interests were temporarily aligned, and our destination was the same. It didn't make sense to rethink this plan on account of residual unpleasantness.

We found tickets waiting, along with pre-assigned seats that suggested Moorthy had put some thought into the arrangements — his men were consigned to the rear of the small plane, enough rows behind us to be temporarily forgotten. He, however, sat with Manohar, and the two of them were soon deep in conversation. At first, the exchange was antagonistic, even mutually inquisitorial. But after some time, an odd understanding grew between the two of them. I wasn't surprised.

Maya tried to behave as she always had with Manohar, but he remained intent on snubbing her. If Moorthy caught on to the underlying tension, he said nothing, other than when he asked us, on arrival at a four-star hotel in Chennai, how many rooms the three of us wanted. Maya shrunk to my side. I replied, 'Two.'

That night we made love again, and I performed without protest. Maya was eager for tenderness and warmth and I obliged, and the bonding was a lot more pleasurable than I'd expected. The sound of my name on her lips as she cried out in ecstasy, the most intimate taste of her, her fiery willingness to please and be pleased: I was acutely aware that I enjoyed these things.

As I fell asleep, my last thought was of the only woman whom, many millennia ago, I'd admired beyond limits of propriety, for she hadn't been mine to so regard. When at last I'd made love to her, hardly hours before my fateful self-sacrifice, it had been an act of worship, not lust. I'd never seen her again after that day, nor did I know what had become of her. There was no place, even in folklore, for a defeated king's widow. Her memory haunted me through the night and into the next morning till, five hours, three filter-coffee breaks and two-hundred-odd kilometres later, we reached our destination.

Mount Arunachalam rose majestic and imposing in the distance as we drove up to the small town of Thiruvannamalai. Believed to be a naturally formed gigantic Shivalinga – an earthly manifestation of Shiva himself – it was deemed one of the holiest sites in the world. Thiruvannamalai's claim to fame had grown with the many parables and stories that were associated with the place.

The most oft-told of these was the tale of how Brahma and Vishnu had tried, without success, to measure the physical being of the third member of their Divine Trinity: Shiva. Many of the scriptures described Shiva as a column of universal breath or *prana* – what the Greeks called *pneuma*, the active force of life. But Shiva wasn't just some intangible concept on a formless plane; he was rooted in earth, the embodiment of Shakti or the manifested world, but he also extended beyond her bounds, infinitely into space. This description, in fact, was what gave Shivalingas their form. Phallic or otherwise, Shiva was a symbol of the infinite, and also a reminder that infinity was real, and primordial energy immeasurable.

And so, when it came to the Divine Trinity's measuring competition, Shiva had taken his form as an endless column. While Brahma, the creator, set out skyward as a swan to measure the upper half of Shiva, Vishnu, the protector, had assumed the form of Varaha the boar to plunge into the core of the earth. Vishnu returned to confess his inability to measure the lower half of Shiva's being, affirming that it went on well past the physical limits of the earth, but Bramha claimed that he had reached the upper extent of the column when, in fact, he had not. That lie, it is said, is why there are so few temples to Bramha in a land that is filled with shrines to every one of the three hundred and thirty million gods in Hindu religious lore. The particular contest having been settled — successfully or unsuccessfully, as it were — Shiva was then said to have assumed the form of Arunachalam, the mountain of fire. *The place where life-breath turned to fire.* It was also the place where Shiva and Shakti — or meaning and form, to use Jabir's terms — had merged, the tale setting up a strong connection to the alchemical *siddha*s and, as I'd realized lying next to a burning pyre at Kashi, where the third fragment of the Vajra was undoubtedly hidden. As for dear old Nagarjuna, this was where he had seen the true state of all living creatures and come to terms with his own meaning – not as an alchemist but as alchemy itself.

Perhaps that was the divinity at work in this place, for many had discovered the meaning of meaning here, none more famous than Ramana, known as the Maharishi. I'd known him for a very short while – hardly months – before he had passed on, but had come away humbled by his approach to spirituality. Maharishi Ramana had believed that self-inquiry was the best means to enlightenment and that all answers lay within. Despite his guidance, I had failed to find the answers I sought – within or elsewhere. But then, he had been a kind and noble soul and I…I was who I was. The days I'd spent with him had been full of peace.

Even today, Thiruvannamalai radiated serenity, though it had long since turned into a bustling temple town complete with ashrams and yoga centres, as well as hotels that catered to tourists of all budgets. It was to one of the smaller ashrams that dotted the circumference of Mount Arunachalam that Moorthy led us.

We were each given a room to ourselves – a clear sign that Maya and I were expected to maintain the sanctity of the hermitage. Other than that minor inconvenience, if I cared to call it that, the surroundings were pleasant and our rooms comfortable. I gladly accepted the hot filter coffee that was brought to us, its aroma blending with the natural smells of camphor and medicinal herbs that filled the entire ashram.

Moorthy said, 'I'll leave you guys to relax. If you'd like to go out, please do so.'

'Not keeping a tab on us, any more?' I asked.

'There isn't much you can do here that I won't know about, Professor.'

'And your leader? When do we meet him?'

'You make him sound like an underworld don. He's just an ascetic. As for when you will meet our Ayya, as we call him, that's up to you. He's brought you this far for a reason, but he sees no need to meet you unless it's necessary.'

'What do you mean?' Manohar asked.

I said, 'He means we need to find the third fragment on our own. And once we find it...'

Moorthy corrected, '*If* you find it...'

I didn't accept the correction. 'Once we find it, we will find your Ayya too, I expect?'

Moorthy neither confirmed nor denied the premise. All he said was, 'I'll be around the ashram if you need me.'

'Thank you,' I said.

Maya waited till the three of us – she, Manohar and I – were alone. 'He's toying with us!'

'Not toying. Testing,' Manohar said. 'In any case, the third fragment is what we want, along with getting back the other two. We just need to figure out how to get it.'

'If we go by the same pattern as before, we should look in or around, even under, the temple...'

Manohar shook his head. 'The temple isn't such an old structure, though we could always argue that it's built on an older, existing foundational structure. But there's no evidence to suggest that.'

'How about the Adi Annamalai temple on the other side of the mountain? The idol in there, the story goes, was installed and worshipped by Brahma himself, in order to atone for his lies... I assume you know the story?'

'Who doesn't? But...there has to be more to it than that. The problem is, this whole place is full of hidden caves and mystical sites. Apparently, there's a secret passageway that Maharishi Ramana saw in a dream or trance, leading out from the Adi Annamalai temple to a cavern within the mountain filled with waterfalls and fountains, where Shiva himself sits in perpetual meditation, as a *siddha*. There are also some other caves up on the mountainside, each with intriguing folktales of their own. In a place like this, we could keep searching for days. I doubt this Ayya has that kind of patience with us.'

'What do you think, Professor?' Maya said.

'I agree with Manohar. We need to find a pattern that tells us where and what, like at Somnath.'

Maya grinned. 'Come on, then. Walk around, do whatever it is you do. You'll work it out like that, I know!' She snapped her fingers.

'Don't, Maya!'

The admonition came not from me, but from Manohar. He had a look on his face I'd rarely seen, an irritation that was unusual by its occurrence and justification, both. Reluctant to get involved, I said, 'Take a nap, both of you. We may have a long night before us.'

26

Leaving Manohar and Maya to their own devices, or an argument if they were so inclined, I set out for the sprawling Arunachaleshwara temple and arrived just as it opened for the evening. I took my own time to wander around the five *prakara* or circumferences that made up the twenty-five-acre complex, taking in the majesty of each of the nine gateway towers. Of these, the famous eastern *gopuram* stood at a massive sixty-plus metres. As far as historical architecture went, the temple was eclectic – having been built over the reigns of many royal dynasties, from the Pallavas in the ninth century CE to the Vijayanagara kings of the fourteenth. But the core of its presence was far older than even I could imagine, and far more elemental.

I made my way to the massive temple tank. Wrapping my shirt around my waist as a sash – the act of removing the upper garment a symbol of surrender to a higher power – I joined the many devotees there in a sacred bath, all the while looking up at the peak of Mount Arunachalam. I then sat on the steps, thinking, mentally sifting through every combination of scripture and fact that I could think of, but it led me nowhere.

As the skies darkened at dusk, I sensed desperation creep into my mind and take firm root as futility. I tried to focus, to regain my slipping purchase on the present, but in vain. Mount Arunachalam stood firm before me, taunting me with His existence, reminding me of the many things that I'd seen and could never forget; death and again, death, and one death above all that I had not caused but had done nothing to prevent.

I'd met him in Jerusalem, where, during the times of Tiberius Caesar, I'd eased my way into the service of the Praetor of Judea, as a soldier. The man had been young – hardly thirty or so – and handsome in a gentle way. I was told that they had arrested him sometime during the night, but I'd only seen him around dawn, in the garrison courtyard, surrounded by soldiers. They had beaten him, kicked him, and turned his back into a bloody mess with the 'scorpion' – a barbed whip. Against it all, his brown eyes had held fearlessness and a conviction that had shaken me – a man who'd seen more savagery than could be imagined by the most depraved of minds – to the core.

The soldiers had been laughing; they'd invited me to join them, handing me the scorpion so I could take a turn. Before I could react, someone had called out orders, others had dragged the man out of the garrison, tied him to a heavy wooden transom, paraded him to Golgotha on the outskirts of Jerusalem, and there, driven nails through his wrists and feet and raised him up on a cross. Three torturous hours later, as the agony of torn spinal nerves and collapsed lungs had become unbearable, the young man had looked to the skies and asked his maker why he'd been forsaken. Then, he had died.

At that moment, I'd realized that the question he'd asked of his god was the one I'd refused to ask mine, and with good reason. He had been sure of his ultimate vindication. I had never held such a hope. My world was nothing but shrivelled darkness, a black desolation that I'd first known the night of the massacre at the end of the Great War. It was the same darkness that surrounded me now.

Heaviness settled on me, a nauseating despair, and guilt rose bile-like in my throat. I ran, frantic, towards the inner sanctum of the temple. It was a mistake. The cacophony of mantra-chanting priests, fervent devotees and excitable tourists filled my head till I felt it would explode. I longed for silence, to shut them up even if it meant killing them all.

Yes. Kill. It was what I did best. It was pleasure, it was prayer, it was meditation. It gave me a reason to exist. It didn't matter that I had no weapon; I could slay with my bare hands, reassembling the horrible assault of smell and sound around me into a symphony, a smorgasbord of snapping necks and rent intestines, flailing limbs and heads torn apart, not by the force of a blade but by sheer brute force. What a fool I had been to think my life could ever be free of violence. Was there ever – would there ever be – such a luxury?

Never had I regretted my actions during the Great War, for I had been bound by duty and loyalty. But the choices I had made then condemned me to kill, again and again, for the rest of forever. Such was my true punishment, though I had no knowledge of my original crime. So it would go on, till it no longer mattered whether I had deserved this endlessness, this life in the shadows. All that would remain was a pain without penitence, the hellish state of not knowing why I suffered but wanting to believe it wasn't without cause.

I screamed, or did I? I imagined I was covered in blood, but it may have been the water of the temple tank. I was in a shrine. I was on a battlefield. I could smell the *vibuthi* and the fragrance of burning camphor. I could taste the charred flesh and smoking wood of a funeral pyre. But it was I who burnt.

Immortality is so much more bearable when death isn't your only hope.

The recollection…or was it a voice…was as a light. I held on to it. Not just to the words but also to the soft tone in which it had taken form till, slowly, shadows and darkness faded. I opened my eyes. A child, a dark-skinned girl, maybe nine or ten years old, stood before me, concern in her eyes. I placed the voice I'd heard moments ago as she asked me, in Tamil, 'Anna, are you all right?' I didn't respond, though I became aware that I was lying sprawled against a large pillar, drenched in sweat, my chest heaving. No wonder I had drawn the girl's attention. She put down the basket of jasmine strands that I gathered she was selling and pulled out a dented plastic bottle that had once held a soft drink but was now filled with foggy-looking water. She passed me the bottle. I took it and, dismissing all thought as to the water's dubious source, emptied it in a few gulps.

'It's the heat,' the flower-girl knowingly declared as she reclaimed the empty bottle. Seeming satisfied with my recovery she smiled, loaded her basket of wares back on to her head and walked away. For all the fragrant blooms in her basket, her thick, long plait of blue-black hair was unadorned.

I turned my attention to the world around me, to the bustle of worshippers who walked on by, heeding neither my presence nor my former state of distress.

My heart was racing, as though I'd run a great distance. But my mind was at rest now, and before me was an idol, a mountain, both of one form, one meaning. I'd once heard Ramana say that Arunachalam was the Self, and the Self lay within. And that was the key to where the third fragment of Nagarjuna's Vajra was hidden.

I took a few minutes to pray, as always giving thanks for the strength to go on and asking for nothing, not even that which I wanted the most. Then I made my way back to the ashram.

'What the...?' Despite my words, I was far less angry than I ought to have been. I attributed it to the satisfaction of having been right – Moorthy's behaviour, the whereabouts of the third fragment, my abrupt despondence at the temple...all of it fell into place the moment I re-entered the ashram. But I tucked the reactions away and directed myself to the scene in front of me: Maya pointing a gun at an enraged Manohar, who hankered to launch himself bodily at her but for the fact that three of the Custodians were holding him back. Moorthy, it appeared, had tried to intercede and had received a cut lip and a blood-stained white shirt for his efforts. He sat to one side, nursing the lip and a quickly-swelling jaw, but not without amusement.

'Stay where you are!' Maya barked at me, as I approached her.

I slowed down, but didn't stop. 'You know,' I said, 'this is the second time you've pointed a gun at me. I might get the impression that you don't like me.' The gun wavered; her confusion became obvious.

Manohar cried out, 'Don't go near her, Professor. She's just using you, the bloody bitch.'

'What did you call me? I'll show you exactly what a bitch I am.' Maya trained the gun back on Manohar and I had to shift to stay between them. Moorthy let out a loud guffaw. It got on my nerves. I strode over to Maya and grabbed her hand, bending her wrist inward. She let go of the gun at once. She'd had no intention of firing – I knew that from the complete lack of pressure on the trigger as she'd held the gun, but having lost the weapon she lunged at me like a tigress. I dodged and grabbed her by the back of her neck. Tempted as I was to slap her, I realized it wouldn't be enough. I dragged her over to an old-fashioned stone water-trough and dunked her head into it. She didn't struggle, thinking I meant only to shock her. But when I continued to hold her down even as she ran out of breath, she began to panic.

Manohar let out a yell and a slew of abuses that made it clear his fury had now turned against me. I addressed the men who were holding him back. 'What the hell are you waiting for? Bring him over here and dip him in, will you? Moorthy…'

Moorthy gestured to the men, and they complied.

'How long?' he asked me, watching the bubbles rise.

'You know how long. Till they start to panic. Till the body starts releasing adrenaline – enough to counter the effects of whatever it was you put in our coffee.'

'Smart! But how did you...?'

I glared at him till he shut up, hardly in the mood to explain how my body was trained to fight these very toxins, and many others like them that his great-great ancestors had not even dreamed of. 'I don't get it,' I said. 'Why try to intercede but then give her a gun?'

'Our intent wasn't to let either of them hurt or be hurt. It got out of hand when Manohar said she was sleeping with you just to...well, she lost it then and slapped him and said he was a jealous...you know, and then he smacked her back and... Anyway, I tried to separate them. Unfortunately, not only did Manohar land a good right hook, but also, Maya took my gun. You saw most of what happened after that.'

Feeling Maya's resistance let up, I pulled her head out of the water before she took water into her lungs. She fell to the ground, gasping for air. I was ready, in case she was still under the effects of the herb-hallucinogen or whatever it was, but she'd had enough. She quietly curled up on the ground. Manohar, on the other hand, took one more round in the water before he went into a daze, leaning back against the water-trough where the men had lowered him.

'In Rudra's name, Moorthy, give them the antidote or whatever it is they need.'

'In Rudra's name, Professor? You sound like a man who believes...'

'...in the goodness of human beings. When Nagarjuna left the fragment here, in the keeping of fire and life-breath, he trusted in the goodness of men; the goodness of you lot who call yourself "Custodians".'

'No, Professor. He trusted its safety to the evil inside men...and women. He made it such that anyone who comes near the Custodians must pass through a grove of trees – the grove doesn't exist in that form any more but the trees do, and their crushed leaves were added to your coffee. All one had to do was set the inner animal inside humans free and then, driven by their own fears and ambitions, they would squabble and fight and kill each other long before they reached the Vajra fragment. But you...your mind is strong and your heart is pure.'

I chose my next words with great care.

'Fuck you, Moorthy. We could have done this the easy way a long time ago. We could have avoided a lot of trouble.'

'There never was any trouble that wasn't worth it. No ancillary casualties or damages. Yes, we could have done this the easy way, but unlike you I'm not so free with my trust.' Moorthy gave instructions in a low voice to one of the other men. The man passed over a small bottle filled with a viscous liquid. Moorthy tipped some of the liquid first into Manohar's mouth and then Maya's. Immediately, a touch of colour returned to their skin.

'They'll be fine in a few minutes. A bit tired, but no worse for the experience as a whole.'

'Then there should be no problem setting out in an hour or so.' Before Moorthy could protest, I added, 'You're taking us to see your Ayya, Moorthy. I think you'll find he is ready to see us. And now, if you don't mind, I'd like some *real* coffee.'

27

It took us about four hours to climb Mount Arunachalam. By the time we set out along a less-frequented, difficult route on the westward face of the mountain, daylight had faded. Still, the sky was clear, and there was enough of a moon to help us climb without needing flashlights. I was relieved that we were many days off from a full moon, when the circumference of the mountain and the main route to its peak would be packed with pilgrims – an estimated five hundred thousand of them making the trek every month, in hopes of a vision of Shiva or at least of karmic merit and expiation of sin.

Maya and Manohar walked side-by-side, exchanging occasional words but not saying a thing to anyone else, including me. It was difficult to tell whether their grimness was a result of ire or embarrassment over the things they'd said under the influence of the herbal concoction. At any rate, they clearly felt the need to show solidarity in their opposition to the general way things were going.

I fell into conversation with Moorthy and his fellow Custodians on topics related to our surrounding: The loss of the once-diverse wildlife in the area due to deforestation and the recent attempts at reforestation; the caves, the meditation sites – some of them occupied by mendicants, others by foreigners seated in perfect lotus postures. I observed that Moorthy and the others had taken off their shoes and stuffed them inside their backpacks, as had Manohar. Maya kept her shoes on, as did I.

We reached the highest of the mountain's three peaks, a narrow, tabletop feature that rose sharply at one end to form a crag. The area was black and slippery with oil and ghee from the enormous, man-high brazier that was lit atop the mountain once a year, when the full moon lay in conjunction with the Pleiades constellation, to commemorate Shiva's appearance at the very spot.

Below us, to the east, the city lay in a pattern of soft light – the temple the brightest cluster by far. The four main *gopuram*s as well as the outer walls of the complex were connected by what appeared at this distance to be an unbroken chain of bright dots. Within this perimeter, more plays of shadow and light. The thousand-pillared hall was lit from within, its glow fading into the solemn but rippling darkness of the temple tank. And yet, against this mind-blowing panorama, the eye fell on the pinpoint of light that was the flickering lamp outside the main sanctum, a sign of the inextinguishable fire that burnt within.

'It's an ideal place to sit and meditate, especially at sunrise,' Moorthy said. 'I'd be happy to stay back with you till morning, if you like. The others can stay or go, as they wish.'

'That's a lot of goodwill from a man who just tried to poison me and my friends.'

'It wasn't poison, Professor, and you know it. You didn't complain about what you had to go through to get your hands on the other fragments, so why begin now?'

A new voice, kind and warm in tone, added, 'We trusted in the different powers of creation to keep them safe, my son.'

I turned around to see an old man, his hair and beard as pristine white as the short *veshti* he wore, emerge from the shadows at the base of the crag. Around his neck was a string of *rudraksha* beads, and *vibhuthi* ash was smeared across his forehead and arms in the typical fashion of Shiva-worshippers. But it was the light in his eyes, the spark that showed contentment, clarity and complete surrender to a superior power that told me who he was – a *siddha* – not in the sense of a magical shaman, as some believed them to be, but a man of enlightenment. 'Ayya!' Moorthy bent down to touch the old man's feet, as did the other Custodians. The old man placed a benevolent hand on each of their heads and exchanged a few hushed words with Moorthy, who then stepped away.

The *siddha* beckoned me closer. I complied without hesitation, driven more by instinctive trust than the absence of danger. The man said, 'The Srisailam fragment was left in the keeping of wild creatures – cobras and vipers, to be precise. At Somnath, we trusted in nature, a force that you tamed in the only way possible – by surrendering to its might. And here…well, you've already figured that out, haven't you?'

'Yes, but whether I'm right or not remains to be seen.'

The *siddha* raised a closed fist to his chest and whispered a few words I didn't catch. Then he held out his gnarled hand. The third and final piece of the Vajra shone dully on his rough palm. Against my eagerness, I waited. The *siddha* laughed noiselessly and then dipped his other hand into the waistband of his white dhoti and took out two familiar-looking canisters. Palms open, he offered all three items to me. 'Put them together,' he urged.

I took the two canisters, unstoppered them one by one and slid the fragments out on to my left palm, slipping the empty cases into my pockets. Then, with my right hand, I picked up the final fragment and arranged the three pieces on my plam. With an enquiring look at the old man, I snapped them together like bits of a jigsaw puzzle.

A smooth, seamless disc lay in my hand, as though it had always been whole. I couldn't find the edges where the pieces had joined, so precise was the technology behind this centuries-old Rubik's-Cube like device. The dots and lines on each of the pieces had now fused together to form a symmetrical-looking pattern, like a design blown inside the best Murano glass. It resembled the more commonly known Vajra – the diamond sceptre that in Buddhist traditions signified spiritual power, but it was also more.

I held out the Vajra for the *siddha* to see, my expression an unspoken query.

He said, 'Yes, you're right. What we protect isn't just these fragments, but also what they lead us to.'

'A symbol within a symbol. A myth that obscures another,' I said, understandingly. 'Over time, people begin to focus on the Vajra and not what it leads to. Nagarjuna sure had foresight. But what did he create that he wanted so much to protect?'

'Not create. Find. Nagarjuna wasn't very different from you, Professor. He wasn't attempting to make something; he was trying to find what had already been created.'

'And that was...?'

'Why, what he said he was looking for. Again, not unlike you, Nagarjuna was a man of veracity.'

'A substance that transmutes elements? That gives eternal life?'

'Do you think it impossible?'

'And this is it?' I weighed the Vajra in my hand, contemplative.

'This is what it is,' the *siddha* replied. 'A pointer...sign... guiding mark...what would you like to call it?'

'A pointer to what?'

'To a destination, naturally. Think about it. What are destinations, my son?'

'It depends.'

'On what?'

'On whether one is a traveller or a wanderer. Destinations can be the end. They are also the beginning.'

'I was right about you.'

'Ayya?'

'I am a healer of old. A healer of body and spirit, both. And that is why I can tell that you aren't what you seem. Your eyes have seen much and your heart is uncorrupted. There's a smell about you that says you were conceived on a bed of kusha grass – *darbhai*, we call it in Tamil. Your parents must have been of a holy order. What lineage do you come from?'

I hesitated, then said, 'Angiras. Bharadvaja *gothram*.'

'Hmm. Did you know that once the ancient Angirasas were men and women of science, wise seers and scholars. They would've seen through this puzzle at once, as would you. But look at you. Caught in the identity this world has given you, you've lost your sight. You've lost your curiosity, your oneness with things around you. You hold on to this transient personality, like a soul that clings on to the manifested world, wanting back its mortal shell. But the soul is eternal. One glance inwards, and this whole mystery is solved. But you won't believe, will you? You search for rational explanations, pretending that you, the anomaly to all limits of science, don't exist. Is it so bad to accept that your existence is as rational as everything else?'

I frowned at his words, unsure whether he was merely being mystical or if his words did indeed hold a deeper meaning. Perhaps the old ascetic knew...

Unlikely. A touch of condescension entered my voice as I recalled the expressions of disgust and fear, the abhorrence with which those lauded Angirasas had declared me a forsaken soul and doomed me to wander, homeless and nameless.

'Acceptance implies faith,' I said. 'Rationality implies inference. The two don't go together. My ancestors, whom you regard with such fondness, would have been the first to refute the eternal nature of any form of existence, on the grounds that it is irrational. I don't doubt their interest in science or in spirituality. But that doesn't make the two concepts identical.'

The *siddha* laughed. 'You can weave together many things and make a story, a story that may even hold up to all scrutiny by reason. But sometimes, to find a missing piece, you must take a leap of faith. One day, you will find the faith that completes you. Till then, I shall leave you to your rational scepticism.'

His words held acceptance, a repletion that came only from knowing more than could ever be put into speech. I suddenly felt embarrassed by my own self-assured words and arrogant behaviour.

Slowly, I knelt down before the *siddha* and prostrated myself at his feet, wordlessly asking him to show me the way. I stayed there for a while, aware of the way the rough skin of his feet felt against my forehead, under the skin of my palms; the cold rock under my nose. Thought ebbed.

And then, a gnarled, wiry hand was on my head, its warmth filled with blessing. 'Be at peace. Be at peace with who you are.'

Blinking away the tears that I hadn't noticed so far, I sat up on my knees, my palms together in salutation. Looking up at the *siddha*, I said, 'Then you will forgive my disbelief. You will forgive me for thinking that wherever the Vajra leads, it isn't to what I seek.'

'You deny the possibility of transformation.'

'Never the possibility. Just the probability.'

'Do you still intend to find this place?'

'Yes.'

'Why?'

I answered, 'Because untested disbelief is nothing but dogma.'

He nodded, satisfied. 'And faith is meant to be tested. You know where you must go next?' His hands pressed over mine, pushing my fingers down against the disc, against the pattern within, as though I could reach inside it to pull out the Vajra within the Vajra.

'Yes, Ayya. I do.'

'Then go in safety. Bless you, my son.'

'Thank…'

But I didn't finish the sentence, acting the split second I heard the muffled thud of the gunshot. The bullet whizzed by my cheek as I sprang up, but I was too slow.

I caught the old man as he fell; blood spurting out of his emaciated chest and flowing down to soak his *veshti*. Behind me, I was vaguely aware of people moving, Maya yelling at someone, the sound of more gunfire. Moorthy's voice rang off the stones, frantic and angry.

An unwelcome chill ran through me as I realized that I'd made a mistake after all. It was the worst time to engage in idle analysis but, in a vague attempt at escapism, I began contemplating the varying species of fault, in particular the proposition that an error of action was far less heinous than one of inaction. I'd been part of the audience when the definitive lecture on this topic in the history of humankind had been delivered, on a battlefield no less. I should have paid more heed to it then but, in my defence, there had been a war to see to.

Around us, more dull thuds, the typical sounds of silencer-fitted guns. More shouting and screaming. It felt suddenly like a dream that continued to play out even as the mind, recognizing it was asleep, struggled to wake. Someone said they were hit. I didn't know who it was. I didn't care. I was back on my knees, cradling the *siddha* in my arms.

'Arunachaleshwara!' He called out to the god he had served with every last scrap of his soul, uttering the sacred name as he would that of a loved one. Then he regarded me with triumph and whispered, 'This...is illusion.'

I smiled at him. 'I know.'

The man crumpled in my arms, like a child going to sleep. Gradually, his breathing came to a stop. I laid him gently on the ground and stood up. Orders to cease fire cut through the mayhem. The gunmen complied, and a tentative hush fell over the night.

My eyes still on the dead *siddha*, I said, 'You didn't have to kill the old man, you know. He didn't have to die.'

In a breezy, lilting voice, as though he were commenting on the weather, my friend of many years, Hariprasad Namdeo of Kashi, replied, 'But of course I did, Asva. This man murdered my wife.'

28

We were surrounded by silence and a small army of about twenty people, a few of whom held Moorthy and his remaining associates at gunpoint. A rather impressive show of sub-machine guns, I noted. To his credit, Moorthy was as calm as he could be under the circumstances, though I could tell that he wanted nothing more than to rush to embrace his Ayya. Manohar was crouched on the ground next to Maya, who had pushed herself up into a sitting position and was staring, unblinking, at the new arrivals. I turned to face my nemesis.

Hariprasad Namdeo, the man whose life I'd once saved, the man who'd become my closest and sole friend. The man who'd accepted who I was with neither doubt nor greed… Or so I'd believed. I had questions, many questions, but they were so obvious that to voice them out loud felt downright stupid. He knew what I was thinking; he knew me well. He knew I wanted explanations: For his treachery, for his actions and, most importantly, for his motivations. I didn't budge as Hari walked up to me. He cast a look at the fallen *siddha*, and lay a hand over his heart in silent prayer. Then he held out the same hand. I dropped the Vajra on to his palm.

'Where next?' he asked.

I didn't reply. Hari gestured to the man nearest to us, whom I placed as one of the hired thugs who'd been with Moorthy the day he and Pratap had attacked us. Moorthy obviously recognized him too, but remained expressionless. His mistake had cost his Ayya's life. I wanted to say words of comfort, but it was a yell of protest that escaped me as Hari's man strode over to where Manohar and Maya were on the ground and summarily disposed of Manohar by clipping him across the face with the butt of his weapon. Then the thug bent down to grab Maya.

Maya started in alarm as the goon tied her arms behind her back and stuffed a rag into her mouth before leading her away down the hill and out of sight. My stomach cramped at that, but I said nothing.

'I'll keep her safe as long as you cooperate,' Hari assured me. 'And once we're done I'll let her go. If not…'

'You'll kill her? You think that scares me?'

'Killing is easy. There are worse things in life than death.'

'Like watching your sappy soap operas?'

Hari said, 'Drop the action-hero act, my friend. We both know that you don't get forced into doing things you don't want to. But the point is precisely that. You want to find whatever it is that this Vajra leads to. You made that absolutely clear the other day. If you're resisting now, it's only because I'm forcing you to do it. Left to your own devices, you'd have run off to search for it anyway.'

'In that case, why not continue your charade for a little longer? Why not wait for me to do whatever it was that you expected me to?'

Pointing to the dead *siddha*, Hari said, 'It was because of him. I couldn't let the opportunity to finish him off pass me by. There's nothing quite so stressful as a useful enemy, you know. I needed him, I needed him in order to find the third fragment, and I also needed him to tell us what the next step was. But he has served his ultimate purpose, and I'd be a scum of the worst order if I left him alive. He was a treacherous adversary to have and, worse, a man without conscience. After all that I'd done for him, the moment he decided I was more of a liability than an asset, he didn't think twice about coming after my family. His battle was with me, but he took it out on my wife, *maaderchod*!'

I snorted at the allegation that the frail recluse could have been a threat to anyone in any form, but didn't doubt the possibility. The *siddha* had, after all, been the force behind Moorthy and his actions. He could well have been the mastermind of other schemes too. Right then, however, I placed a lot more trust in his integrity than in Hari's.

'Besides,' Hari continued, 'his days were over. The world is about to change in ways he would seek to defy, time and again. I'd have to keep looking over my shoulder if he were left alive. Believe me, Asva, I had no choice. So, shall we get a move on?'

'Move on where? You have Nagarjuna's Vajra.'

'Oh please! Do you think I'm an idiot, or hard of hearing? Either way, you do me injustice. What was it you said…? Ah yes: *A myth that obscures another.* We both know this trinket isn't the ultimate prize.'

I responded with a question that I should have asked a long time ago: 'Who are you, Hari?'

'Don't you know, Asva? I think you do, and that the question is purely rhetorical.'

'You were a Custodian, weren't you? One of those charged to protect the secret of Nagarjuna's Vajra, like Moorthy here. Except, you grew…I don't know…you grew tired of it? Or did greed get the better of you, and you reckoned you could profit by selling out? No, wait: You needed me to find the other fragment for you… So that means you weren't a Custodian after all; at least not one of any consequence. Was that why you did it? Spite? And so you built your private mercenary army to get even? Or are some rich investors funding your operations? God, that makes you sound more important and powerful than you deserve! You're just a thief and liar, aren't you? A man who had to run and hide under the guise of a hippie-guru to save your skin. What happened then, Hari? Between the wannabe Custodian and the fake Baba? What happened?'

'You happened, Asva,' Hari said. 'Didn't you ever wonder how it was so easy for me to accept the truth of who…of what you were? Or were you grateful that I did? I believed you were the solution to it all – the number of tests I've run on your blood, the cultures of your tissue that I've had examined, the discreet and indiscreet ways in which I have studied you…but I found nothing! *Nothing.* And yet, here you are. So many times, I toyed with asking, even begging, you to help me. But your cynicism was overwhelming. You were the reason why I began to keep an eye on the Custodians and their activities once again, more than a decade after they'd destroyed my life. And that's how I came to know that the NDRO had the Srisailam fragment.

'I thought it might be time to tell you the truth, to offer you hope, the chance to finally be at peace... I used Dr Sushant Kumar to manoeuvre Maya – she acted just as I had predicted she would, and contacted Manohar. I expected you to jump at the chance; but before things could fall into place, you turned up at Kashi. I couldn't risk telling you the truth after that, Asva, nor could I let you be. I had to keep you on a tight leash, force things along. Unfortunately, my activities drew the Custodians' scrutiny. Oh well, I suppose they would have got on to you sooner or later – they aren't all that incompetent. The rest is self-explanatory and, if it's all right with you, I'd rather move on to the future than dwell on the past. The Vajra isn't the end in itself, but a means to an end. And I insist on reaching that end. Tell me, where next?'

I maintained a stubborn reserve.

Hari sighed. Turning, he shouted so that his voice would carry, 'Rohit, the Professor here needs a small demonstration, please.'

An ominous quiet ensued, but it didn't last long. A scream rent the air, then another and another. I didn't want to speculate as to what the brute was doing to make Maya cry out that way.

'Stop!'

'Then tell me, Asva. Where next? We don't have to hurt her any more than you want her to be hurt.'

Maya screamed again.

'Please!' My voice cracked, astonishing Hari as much as it did me.

'That's enough, Rohit,' he called out.

The screaming stopped. I thought I could hear Maya sobbing, but wasn't sure. I didn't want to test her resilience. 'It's not going to be easy, Hari. What you seek…it's not an easy place to get to, let alone find.'

'What the…' Hari began, upset at what he determined was my lack of cooperation.

'Pakistan,' I said. 'Pakistan. That's where we need to go.'

'Where in Pakistan?'

'The Makran desert.'

'Why?'

'That's where the ancient scholar Dadhichi had his ashram – around Gwadar in the Balochistan province.'

'Dadhichi? The mystic scholar who sacrificed his life so that the gods could make a weapon from his bones? The weapon that Indra used to destroy the dragon-demon Vritra?'

'Yes, that's the story in the Vedas. You know Indra as the god of rain and Vritra as a demon who steals cows. But Indra's weapon, many scholars hold, isn't quite a lightning bolt. Rather, it is a symbol of ploughing the land with implements, and the whole thing is a metaphor for the transition from a nomadic society to a settled, agricultural one.'

Hari frowned. 'But now the literal meaning fits too, doesn't it? If we consider alchemy as the transformation of the human body, then one of the oldest instances of such alchemy is that of Dadhichi. His spine was made hard, hard as diamonds, and the adamantine metal was then forged into Indra's thunderbolt. And when Dadhichi was thus transformed, he was given a new name: Asvasirisha, because he was revived with the head of a horse. But weren't you the one who once explained to me that Asva – your name – is *A-sva*: Not temporal, neither of today nor tomorrow. Eternal...'

'That appears to be a logical link...of sorts. Personally, I think he was nothing more than a metallurgist who transformed agriculture. This X-Men-meets-Vedas kind of bones morphed into thunderbolt story sounds way out.'

'And the place of this transformation...be it of his person or of society... It's in Pakistan?'

'Yes. There is historical evidence that a battle – most likely the battle that was the seed of the Indra-Vritra legend – took place in what is today northern Pakistan, alongside a river that historians have identified as the Indus. But the legend is quite unequivocal in stating that the river along which the battle was fought flowed north. The Indus, however, flows mostly from north to south, except for a very short tract near...'

Hari interrupted, 'So the Indra-Vritra battle was fought in northern Pakistan? Then why are we going to Gwadar?'

'Stop making me repeat myself! The arms for that battle – the ultimate weapon Indra used to defeat Vritra – came from Dadhichi's hermitage, which is in the south-west of the country.'

'Thank you for the geography lesson. What does all this have to do with Nagarjuna?'

'Are you really asking me this, Hari? Don't you know what Indra's weapon, the weapon made from Dadhichi's bones, was called?'

'It was called the Vajra. Is that all you have, Asva? The fact that these things share a name? One was a weapon and the other…'

'I'm not responsible for your scepticism. You've forced these answers out of me. Whether you believe what I say is up to you. I won't shirk from saying that I think Balochistan may hold historical relevance, but that doesn't make transmutation or the Vajra real.'

'Such callousness won't suffice, Asva. Not for Maya. I want to know you're not taking me on some wild goose chase – or wild horse chase, as it may be. Tell me what the connection is between Nagarjuna's Vajra and Indra's thunderbolt.'

I resented being quizzed, especially in a situation where I had no choice but to answer; all the more so when the truth was something I had no desire to share. The *siddha* had spoken of my ancestors. Dadhichi had been amongst them.

I settled for disclosing a different factoid instead, though it didn't fully answer Hari's question. 'When Nagarjuna went through his process of alchemical discovery, he faced certain trials. Each of the elements: Earth, water, wind, fire and space tested him. In the end, the combined energies of the elements rained down on him as thunderbolts – Vajra thunderbolts. Of course, the whole thing could be an allegorical reference to how he conquered the elements within to achieve human transformation, or enlightenment, if you will. Or, it could be less metaphorical and more of a factual link... Look, do you want a PhD thesis on this? Or do you want the bloody conclusion?'

Hari appeared less distrustful, but far from committed. He said, 'And how is it that no one made these connections before? Jabir had once said...'

Because I cut in, 'I know what he said. And that's precisely why: Because no one takes these incredulous stories of horse-headed men and alchemy seriously enough to act on it. *I* didn't take them seriously.'

'And now? Do *you* believe?' The question came abruptly from Manohar.

I said, cautious, 'The *siddha* did. All I'm doing is walking the trail of his belief. The mark of the Vajra – Indra's thunderbolt – that is what the old man wanted me to follow. He was the one who pointed me to Dadhichi's ashram. I wouldn't have made the connection myself, not in a million years.'

Hari weighed my words. 'I suppose it adds up,' he declared. 'But...'

'I have nothing more to offer, Hari. We can go or not, the choice is yours.'

'You're an obstinate bastard, Asva, and I know better than to argue with you. Fine. The Makran it is.'

Moorthy finally reacted, 'Wait! This is ridiculous. There's no way we're getting to Pakistan while you're pointing that gun at us. Never mind the gun, we're not getting to Pakistan any way – it's near impossible to get a visa.'

'Visa?' Hari snorted. 'Moorthy, are you seriously this naïve? Don't worry; Professor Bharadvaj has his ways of getting us in, with whatever…erm, papers may be necessary. Don't you, Asva? I presume a certain friend of yours maintains contacts at the border outpost at Samba?'

He didn't wait for a response but began making his way down the mountainside. One of his goons fell in next to him with a flashlight. I was about to follow but stopped as I felt a light prick on the back of my neck. I had just enough time to let out a resentful expletive at what would come next. Then everything went dark.

29

I was dreaming again, suspended somewhere between reality and a greater reality. Maya. She was asking me why I was so obsessed with showers. I replied that it was because there were no rivers in which to wash off the blood. She rebuffed me, eyed Manohar and said, 'That's it?'

'That's it,' he replied, winked at me and then was gone.

I was walking along a wire fence, which disappeared without warning. I stumbled through the darkness and someone caught my arm. There was light, a campfire and a group of shepherds sitting around it. One of them stood up. He threw off his frayed shawl to reveal a blue pin-striped shirt and cream trousers. With a witless cackle, he picked up a brown goat and ripped it apart, limb by limb. I wanted to tell him to stop, but I was speechless, powerless. The goat bleated its agony, and I writhed. An amorphous voice boomed: *Leave him be.* There was silence.

'This way, Professor,' a man said, appearing out of nowhere. His accent was crisp and had a touch of Britain about it. There was a trapdoor in the ground. 'Is there a shower in there?' I asked. He said yes, but he was lying. There was no shower, only a narrow, man-high passage.

Maya had returned on the scene and was claiming she couldn't breathe. Pinstripes pointed out the system of ventilation through a series of pipes, battery-operated lights and the occasional wooden beam that served to reinforce the roof of the tunnel. She pouted and said, 'You'll have to carry me.'

I lifted her in my arms and carried her to a bed that appeared out of the floor, a bed made of blue plastic cans. Manohar materialized too and pointed to the cans. 'Acetic anhydride,' he said. 'It's a precursor chemical used to extract heroin. They take it from India all the way through to Afghanistan – the world's largest producer of illicit opium. And they bring the heroin back the same way – across the northwest frontier of Pakistan, into India. From there, Kenyan and Nigerian cartels route it to Europe and other parts of the world.' Again, he was gone.

'That's flammable stuff,' Maya said, seductive, as she took her clothes off. 'You shouldn't smoke in here, Professor.'

'It's safe as long as it's on a blue truck. It's the green trucks that are risky.'

'I liked the pink one. I wish we could have ridden on that.'

Moorthy appeared. 'No pink trucks for you,' he shouted at Maya, then pointed at me. 'No showers either. You killed Ayya.'

The dead *siddha* joined in, blood-stained *veshti* and all, waving to me. 'Vipers and cobras,' he said, 'all-powerful Sesha himself protects me. But who protects you?' With that, he turned into a giant snake and lunged at me.

His venom felt cool and heavy, as though I lay at the bottom of the ocean. I wanted to remain there, away from the voices, away from cognition. But I couldn't. I had to swim and I did, moving sluggishly through the dark void till, in the distance, it turned reddish-brown with the promise of the sun. I kicked my legs hard, the weightlessness of anticipation floating me upwards, through redness, now golden, now white, a brilliant white.

My eyes opened slowly, resisting light. I was in a small, mud-walled room with a single door and an oval window. My back felt stiff: I lay on a hard mattress that smelled as though it had known many fluids other than water. Turning, I realized my bed was little more than a narrow bench.

'Bloody horse tranquillizer!' I grumbled, trying to sit up. The effort sent me spiralling back into the rust-hued eddies of my mind. Manohar was immediately at my side. Moorthy, I saw, was also nearby, sitting on one of the two mattresses that were laid out on the floor, occupying the rest of the space in the tiny room. The door, rudimentary as it was, had been latched from the outside. Hari still had us on a leash.

'How long?' I asked Manohar.

'Just short of thirty-six hours. All I can say is that, for a phony baba, Hari sure has money.'

'We're in?'

'Yes. He called on your contact immediately.'

'How?'

'Tunnel. Right under the Indo-Pak border.'

That explained the dreams...the colourful trucks, the talk about chemicals and drugs. We'd been smuggled in with the barrels of precursors that had been taken across the border through underground tunnels and then moved across Pakistan by road. As for the showers — that was subliminal guilt. Right after the Great War, I'd spent days in a river, risking hypothermia, trying, in a pathetic, Lady Macbeth kind of way, to wash the blood of hundreds off my body.

Manohar went on. 'We took a private charter plane from Islamabad to Karachi. Left Karachi before dawn and drove here. We've been here for a couple of hours. Hari locked us in, and a couple of goons are standing guard outside.'

'He didn't have to knock me out. I'd have come along without trouble. This is what I call overkill.' Neither man responded to the comment. I couldn't help but note how steadfast they both were. It was a characteristic that I associated at once with Manohar, but to find Moorthy so stoic was heartening.

I set about saying what had to be said. 'I'm sorry, Manohar. I should have seen this coming.'

He responded with familiar grace. 'It's all right, Professor. Quite a feat really, keeping you in the dark for so long.'

'Well, I certainly didn't think Hari capable of such fine stratagem…' I didn't elaborate on the further implications of Hari's duplicity, turning the chain of thought that followed into a question instead.

'Maya?'

Manohar stiffened but said, 'She's here. At least, she was. Haven't seen her since we arrived.'

'Where are we?'

'Hingol National Park. I believe this is "headquarters", though you wouldn't know it. There are two more huts like this for transients and campers like us, and an air-conditioned office room with barracks for the park ranger and his two men. That's all there is out here.'

I stumbled off the bench and made my way to the nearby window. It wasn't barred, but hardly presented an option for escape given the landscape it opened out on to – a terrain that had even defeated Alexander the Great. But failure was something I understood only too well, and the tired, delirious man I'd met at Babylon some days before his death hadn't diminished him in my estimate, though his condition had raised my respect for the mighty Makran.

In modern terms, these remote lands would be described as lunar – a stark, harsh desert pitted with craters, quicksand pits and gnarled prehistoric rock formations. The sun shone down, relentless and resplendent, on a never-ending array of peaks and valleys that ran jagged and lightning-bolt-like over the entire landscape, right up to the horizon. I felt a lump in my throat as I surveyed each crag and crest. These mountains were strangers to me; nevertheless, the immutability of their existence made me feel gratefully mortal. They also reminded me of the mountains I had once called home, my long-lost brothers and sisters.

Images came floating to me, fuelled by the after-effects of the tranquillizer. My glorious palace, lit by bold braziers and protected by a moat filled with mighty-jawed crocodiles. Few had dared attack Ahichhattra in its history, and none at all during my time. *My time.* Even in memory, it was rather excessive hubris for a man who had so miserably failed to see through his enemies and succeed in his plans, as I had these past few days. Thus self-chastised, I turned back to my companions, only to meet Moorthy's hateful stare.

'You don't like me, do you?' I asked.

'No, I don't.' Moorthy was candid.

'Because of what happened to Ayya?'

'Because you're the kind of man who makes a fuss about segregating waste and boycotting brands for using child labour, but you won't think twice about paying a bunch of terrorists – that's what they are, no matter what else you call them – to help you get to where you want.'

'I think you have me confused with Hari.'

'You're not very different from him.'

'None of us is different from the other, Moorthy. We are all failed, flawed men. We can either accept our limitations and work with them, or give up. What's your choice?'

'It's certainly not the same as yours.'

'I'm not surprised. It takes balls not to impose self-righteous judgement of good and bad on people and contexts you've no clue about.'

'Self-righteous? I think there's nothing self-righteous or ambiguous about terrorism and treachery. You do know where we are? And the fact that we are here illegally? Not that being here with a passport and visa might make me feel any safer!'

'Safer? You're worried about being safe? You mean, because...'

'Yes.' The pre-emptive answer showed his instinctive need for political correctness, woefully out of place in these surrounds.

'One should fear good men the most, Moorthy. They do things on principle, and that is the most powerful motivator of them all. Evil men are a scary proposition, but less so than good men, for they are motivated by anger. I'm willing to bet whatever thugs Hari has outside are driven by nothing but greed. They're not worth fearing.'

Moorthy mumbled something about giving a million dollars to see my bravado when those thugs took off my pants. I disregarded the statement and its multiple meanings. He had, I expected, gone from blaming himself to blaming me for his mentor's death, but what held him back from showing it was guilt at having come with me and, worse, at having done so in a way that tore at his conscience. The temptation to put him in his place, to shatter his naïve notions of piety and goodness fell away as I admitted my own complicity and, thus, helplessness. Needing to do something in order to regain a sense of control over the situation, I strode up to the door and knocked, then banged on it.

A series of shouts and a prolonged discussion later, the door was opened. The sight of Hari and his henchmen did nothing to ease my building irritation; nor did it help to see a piece of linen tied around Rohit's wrist like a bandana, the cloth remarkably similar to that of the top Maya had last been wearing. The goon slid a serrated knife out of his shirtsleeve and held it in view. I ignored him and favoured Hari with a disdainful scowl.

Hari made light of my reaction. 'I'd have expected Mount Kailash, Manasarovar, that sort of thing. Why here, Asva?'

'I'm sorry to disappoint you, Hari. But I'm not writing a thriller. I can't shift history and fact around to suit your sense of the dramatic.'

'Well, at least tell me why.'

'Just the why? Aren't you interested in the what?'

'Stop playing games, Asva. It didn't take much to find out what the various places of interest here are. Your particular concern is the Hingol or Hingula Devi cave temple that's in these parts.'

'That is smart of you!'

'Don't be ridiculous! You'd already mentioned Dadhichi and his hermitage. I happened to learn that he is credited with having composed the mantra in praise of this particular goddess. And that *hingulam* is the Sanskrit word for cinnabar, a primary ore of mercury. It doesn't take a historian like you to work out where in the Makran desert we need to go next. But what after that?'

'I don't know.'

Hari signalled to Rohit. I didn't need to be told what the implicit threat was. Before Rohit could move, I said, 'I don't *know*, Hari. I've already told you that it was the *siddha* who pointed me here, to Dadhichi's ashram. Beyond that, I don't know.'

'But you can find out?'

'Unless you think it doesn't take a historian like me to work out these things.'

Hari said nothing, but took out a thickly folded sheet of paper from the pocket of his kurta and unfolded it. He smoothed it out against his thigh and then held it up, studying it keenly. A satellite map – I might have guessed. At length, he folded it back up and handed it to me. 'There are some men outside – a local guide as well as some guys who can get us equipment, so you may want to talk to them about how long this will take and what we will need. Of course, these are decent people who think we are yet another bunch of crazy adventurers and good-for-nothing archaeologists. I'm sure you'll help keep that image intact. Otherwise…'

I waved off the reminder. 'There is one more thing,' I said, as he headed for the door. 'You know what it is.'

'Right. But of course. Once this is done, the four of you are free to leave, *if you wish*. You have my word. But if you try anything smart before that… If you think you're going to pull some silly trick to escape… Well…' He patted his abdomen, above his belt. The metallic clunk that resulted made it clear that his threat had no gastronomic associations. 'My men are armed too. They won't be as reluctant to kill anyone as I am. So I can't emphasize enough the importance of your cooperation.'

'We get the point, Hari. And tell these idiots to not lock us back in here. I want some fresh air.'

He motioned to Rohit to leave the door open.

I waited till Hari and Rohit were gone and then stepped out of the room. Three men lounged outside our door, indolent in the partial shade of the hut. One was dressed in the traditional whites of a Baloch man while the other two were in trekking khakis. At the sight of me, the guides, such as they presumably were, exchanged grins and quips before breaking out in guffaws.

I ignored them and walked a few steps ahead, looking around. The surroundings were exactly as Manohar had described them – two more small cement huts with rough but sufficient wooden doors. Only one of the two was padlocked, and I suspected that Maya was inside. About ten metres away was a rudimentary fence, with a gate that had been left wide open. A rectangular building with a corroded air conditioner affixed to the only visible window announced itself as the office Manohar had mentioned. Beyond that was a de facto parking area, with two old jeeps that bore the fading insignia of the national park.

I turned to the guides, only to have them break into laughter again.

Manohar came to stand next to me. 'They've been doing that since morning, every time the door opened,' he grumbled. 'Peering in at us and sniggering. Can't make out a word but it sure doesn't sound complimentary.'

'It's for the best,' I assured him. 'What they said just now wasn't in any sense a compliment, though I think they meant it in jest.'

I approached the three men, offered them a cigarette each and then proceeded to dress them down with some choice words in the same tongue they had just used. By the time I finished, we'd progressed from sharing cigarettes to rounds of the hot tea that was being made over a small campfire, and I could feel an appetite for lunch building up. I directed the men to business, making further enquiries as to the lay of the land and giving them clear instructions on the equipment we would need. Manohar and Moorthy observed, but said nothing to interrupt. Only when we were back inside the relative privacy of our hut did Moorthy ask, 'Are you even Indian?'

India was a recent concept, a relative concept. My natural allegiance was to a kingdom that in present times was just half a state and to an empire that extended much beyond what today's international borders marked as mine and not mine. 'Yes,' I replied.

'But you speak...?'

'Pashto. That was Pashto. But my accent is terrible.'

'Isn't that what they speak in Afghanistan?'

'Some parts, yes. Along the border with the North-West Frontier Province mostly.'

'You speak Pashto. And you wear a sacred thread. Exactly who... I mean, how can I trust you?'

I had patience for his genuine complaint against me, but not for his misguided anger. 'It disappoints me that you come back to this again and again, Moorthy. I have no problems with men of faith, no matter what faith they are of. But I do have a problem with fanatics, no matter what their nationality. So choose your next words very carefully.'

He did. He said, 'I'm sorry. Ayya wouldn't be proud of me for behaving this way. It's just that I...'

'You're scared,' Manohar offered. I noticed, for the first time, the dark circles under his eyes. I doubted he'd slept at all since we left Thiruvannamalai.

Moorthy went on, 'I am. But I'm also... I mean, do you think it's possible? Alchemy?'

Manohar said, 'I don't. But I'm amazed that you don't either. Or have you spent your adult life, and perhaps a fair part of your childhood, protecting what you don't believe in?'

Moorthy frowned. 'Sometimes,' he said, 'it's easier to stand by a formless principle than to have it examined under the harsh daylight of experience. Yes, I did believe in the notion of transmutation and endless life, but to believe that those three fragments are tantamount to something real... is difficult.'

I understood only too well how he felt.

As the day faded into night, we closed our door from the inside to protect ourselves as best we could from the strong gusts of wind and sandstorms common to these parts. Moorthy and Manohar left the bench to me, for no ostensible reason other than that I'd already spent a few hours on it. I slept, partly out of discipline but also from the residual effects of the tranquillizer. This time, there were no dreams.

The shadowy figure standing over me was familiar, though his stance wasn't. I didn't wait for explanation or enquiry but dodged as he let fly his leather belt as a whip. The heavy buckle caught the side of my face – not hard enough to draw blood, but enough to sting. The assailant made good on the advantage and moved in. But before he could finish looping the belt around my neck, a strong hand towed him back. The scuffle lasted just a few seconds.

Moorthy cried out as he was smacked into the wall behind him. A seething Manohar stood between us, ready to take him on if he tried to come at me again. But Moorthy's mustered courage had already failed him. The man had never been a cold-blooded murderer.

Manohar flicked a cigarette lighter, used it to light the hurricane lamp in the room and came back to face Moorthy again. 'What in the...' he began.

Moorthy cut him short. 'It's the best way. He dies, it's all over.'

'He? You mean the Professor?'

'I should have killed him right then, at Thiruvannamalai. We can't let a scum like Hari get his hands on...'

'On what?' Manohar growled.

Moorthy was breathing hard. 'We know what it is that we – the Custodians – protect. And it's not too difficult to deduce why. Whatever the source or cause of transmutation may be, the actual process of changing an element into another would involve changing the atomic structure of the element by means of...'

'Fission or fusion,' Manohar completed. 'You're afraid this thing has nuclear potential.'

Moorthy nodded. 'In recent times, some of us have tried to come up with more coherent theories, to operate on the basis of scientific facts instead of blind tradition. We have our records, old records, and many of them support this conclusion. In fact, they suggest *this* is why we were created – to prevent nuclear catastrophe by guarding this secret.' He turned, eyes entreating, to Manohar. 'Now do you see what I mean? Don't you think the lives of millions are worth a single man's death? It's a sacrifice, a worthy sacrifice, for the sake of...'

I didn't wait for him to finish. 'Go back to bed, Moorthy,' I said. 'We'll talk about this in the morning.'

'But...'

'Didn't you hear the Professor?' Manohar cut in. He added, more gentle, 'Besides, what you're saying... It can't happen. In scientific terms, both fission and fusion are transmutation, yes, but no living being would survive the process; the energy that is released would pretty much destroy the participant. I know that sounds like a casual dismissal of ideas you've worked hard on, but please trust me when I say we...the Professor and I...have considered this and ruled it out. Even if your secret thing exists, I doubt it can be weaponized. Now, go back to bed.'

Moorthy was bewildered. 'Do you want me to leave?'

I answered, 'It's fine. Go to sleep, both of you.'

Manohar waited till Moorthy had got back into his makeshift bed. He then came up to me and paused, studying me in the semi-darkness. 'We can't let him have it, Professor,' he eventually stated. 'We can't let a man like Hari have it.' The imperative in his tone was new, but I didn't find it offensive. On the contrary, it spurred a sense of pride.

'There is nothing to be had, Manohar. The reason we are here is because we have been forced to come here. And yes, I'll admit I have far too much hubris and want to solve the puzzle, to find my way to the end of this maze just because it is there. But it's only a puzzle, nothing more. Trust me, Hari will find nothing.'

'How can you be sure? Why would anyone go to such trouble to hide something of no value?'

His insubordination too was new and not as inoffensive. But his question compelled an answer since it came on the trail of much-worn patience. I, however, had no answer to give. 'What do you want me to do?' I barked.

Manohar did not back down. He said, 'Moorthy is right, Professor. We need to walk away from this, no matter what the consequences.'

'You're making us sound braver than we are.'

'We've always been brave, in a way. We've done many risky things in life, but not necessarily for noble reasons.'

'Nobility is overrated and, in this case, irrelevant. There is nothing there. Hari is on a meaningless hunt, and I want to be there to spit in his face when he admits defeat and hopefully kills himself.'

'Hari knows you well, doesn't he?' Manohar said. 'Which is more than I can say for myself. He knows your motivations. That is why he can leave this door right open, yet be sure that you won't do a thing he doesn't want you to.'

'What Hari wants doesn't exist,' I repeated, stubborn.

'Perhaps it's best that it stays so in the eyes of the world.'

I glared at Manohar. He regarded me with certitude. Only then did I realize that I was angry, that I stood with clenched teeth, heaving chest and a frown that made Moorthy, who was now sitting up in his bed, visibly nervous. Manohar merely waited, well aware that my rage could never outlast reason.

Not wanting to give him the satisfaction of being right, I left without another word, making my way out into the moonlit desert night.

It didn't take much to see which of the other two huts Hari occupied. The door was closed from the inside, and it lacked the messy confusion of bags and garbage that characterized the threshold of the third. I strode over and knocked. I didn't have to wait long before Hari opened the door. The subtle but familiar smell enveloped me at once, and it was all I could do to not react.

'Asva...?' Hari began.

'I want to see Maya. I need to know she's all right.'

Hari placed a hand on my shoulder. I didn't baulk. He said, 'You can always tell when a man is lying, can't you? Then look at me as I say this: Maya is fine. You'll see her in the morning.'

I walked away without argument. The smell, the sweet smell of Maya, followed me all the way back to our hut and haunted me for the rest of the night.

30

It was still dark when one of Hari's hired hands entered our hut. I'd been awake from the moment he'd stepped on the threshold, but lay motionless till he gave me a rough shake and told me to get ready to leave in a short while. I sat up, tempted by his behaviour and the residual ill humour of the previous evening to begin my day with the choicest of expletives, but was mollified as one of the guides came in bearing cups of steaming tea. Sipping on the strong, overbrewed tea, I made my way outside to find the equipment I'd requested laid out by the smouldering campfire. Calling out to Manohar and Moorthy to pitch in, I began to take stock of the materials and check their condition.

It was Manohar who noticed her first.

'Maya!' He sprang to his feet and, contrary to the strained tones he'd used to speak of her but a day ago, ran forward to meet her with a friendly, protective hug. For her part, she took comfort from the embrace and returned it with sincerity. Drawing back, she greeted Moorthy with a nod and then moved to hug me as she had Manohar. I mirrored her gesture but without warmth, focusing instead on the fact that she'd changed out of her kurta into an oversized cricket T-shirt such as might be bought in any street bazaar in Pakistan.

'It's good to see you, Manohar,' she declared. 'And you, Professor. Are you all right?'

In another place, another time, her concern would have pleased me. As it was, I felt unaccountably satisfied that the sight and sound of her – unhurt – brought nothing more than mild satisfaction. 'I'm fine,' I said. 'You're all right, I hope?'

'Yes.'

I nodded and continued checking the climbing equipment the guides had managed to get for us. Maya turned away, looking pensive. I suspected she was trying to reason through my behaviour, to justify my recalcitrance by arguing that I was feigning lack of interest to reduce her utility as a hostage. Or perhaps she didn't care why I did what I did. Perhaps she faked that too. *Asva, you complicated bastard,* I chided myself, though amused by my own over-analysis.

Hari noticed the interaction, or relative lack thereof, and shrugged as though he were nothing more than a wise old man who knew best to leave lovers to their spats. Rohit, who was close to winning my unqualified endorsement for being the most despicable thug ever, passed a vulgar comment, which made Maya spit on the ground in front of him. I tensed, in case he went at her, but he laughed and set about riling me instead. I imagined him lying half-dead on a battlefield, vultures picking at his face bit by bit, and allowed the scene to quiten my mind. It set me in the right mood for adventure, the strained circumstances in which it had presented itself notwithstanding.

Dawn glimmered in the east as we set out from camp. Our motley group consisted of the four of us, Hari and a division of ten mercenaries. In addition to Rohit, the undeclared leader of the hired muscle, and the four men we'd already had the pleasure of meeting at Thiruvannamalai, we were joined by three others, whom Manohar referred to as 'imported thugs': A lanky Slovakian soldier of self-professed Brazilian jiu-jitsu fame and two Polish brothers, both snipers and fresh from the Ukraine conflict. A bearded subcontinental of indeterminate nationality and a distinct British accent, who went by the name Piggy, and Rohit's younger brother Rahul made up the rest of the numbers. Mercernarism, it seemed, was often run as a family business.

After confirming our course one last time with the park guides who, upon my insistence, stayed behind at the camp, we began trekking towards the first of the many mountain ridges that formed the Central Makran Range. The dried-up bed of the Hingol river served somewhat as our guide, but it was difficult to tell the splintered earth of the bed from the desert plains it ran through. Red flags dotted the landscape, unambiguous warnings of quicksand that we did not ignore.

While a monsoon month might have made for better climate, it would also have left the track impassable – the Hingol, often in spate after the rains, was known to rise a good twenty metres or so and would have submerged much of what we saw around us. I picked up a pebble from the dried path and rolled the smooth, rounded stone over and over between my fingers. It felt good to touch this earth, old earth.

From a distance, the Makran range looked like a multi-level city of rock and mud, similar to some of the more densely clustered, near-inaccessible ridges of the Grand Canyon area. It progressed from a narrow eight-hundred-kilometre-long expanse of mountain that stood parallel to the coast of Pakistan, over the desert plains we were walking on to rocky terrain that then flattened out into the plateau of Balochistan. From there, the range blended into the vast north-south elevation that ran all the way up to the Bolan Pass and further north to the Khyber Pass and the Hindu Kush mountains.

True to its dreaded reputation, the Central Makran Range lacked wide, verdant valleys and undulating rivers, serving rather as a harsh home to many small streams that flowed in and out of each other after the rains to form a haphazard spider's web of trails that led into the unexplored heart of the mountains. The contrast of barren terrain with intermittent verdure made for an interesting mix of wildlife, and I'd heard from the ranger guides that though leopards and foxes were listed as rare, jackals were common enough in these parts, along with smaller animals such as wild goats, mongoose, lizards and the like. The fringes of the Makran range were less unsafe and they remained within reach of the determined traveller – which was why our declared intent to trek to the cave temple of Hingol had caused no stir. We, however, were probably bound for areas beyond that.

The riverbed became narrower and clearer as we neared the foothills of the range, and by the time we made our way into the first of many ravines to come the trail had taken on a consistent form. It also began to climb steeply as it wound its way through the mountains, the ascent easy at first, but far more than a casual trek in many parts. Our journey was as pleasant as could be under the blazing sun, though there were no complaints when Hari suggested we stop in the shade of an overhang to let the noon hours pass. None of us had the energy to propose lunch, but we fell hungrily upon the chocolates that were our ready food supply. We had enough to last us long, but water would soon become a concern – there was only so much we could carry and, already, we'd each consumed more or less two-thirds of our personal ration.

'Do you think we need to...?' Manohar held up his near-empty bottle.

'No. Based on what the guides told me, we should hit the river in a couple of hours.'

'You haven't been here before?' Hari asked.

'No, not these parts exactly.'

Hari frowned but didn't comment further. One of his henchmen let out a cry as a gust of wind snatched the bottle of water from his hand and shrieked away with it before any of us could react. His companions jeered. I said, 'Be glad we're not on the plains we left behind.'

'Why?' Rohit asked.

'Sandstorm. It comes and goes in minutes, but…' I shrugged and waved my hand in the path of the vanished bottle. He got the point.

'We should have brought the guides,' he complained to Hari.

'We don't need them,' Hari said. 'We have the Professor.' I would have appreciated the endorsement a lot more if it hadn't been accompanied by a malicious smile.

We resumed our trek a couple of hours after noon. Again, Maya walked ahead of me, having given up all effort at conversation. She'd accepted my reticence for what it was, though she appeared distinctly unhappy. I couldn't blame her, given the broader situation we were in: Four captives under the control of their former friend being led into the dry wilderness of Balochistan by armed escorts bearing brand new prototype-only Kalashnikov AK12 guns, which they now held in open view. But for that and the general air of disreputability that hung over these gentlemen, we might have passed for any one of the few but fervent groups of trekkers who chose to adventure in these remote parts.

For his part, Hari held my point from the previous evening as valid. Consequently, he made no effort to keep the four of us restrained or under too careful a watch. I, however, made up for the slack by keeping an eye on Moorthy, whether Hari and his men did or not. Moorthy had no faith in Hari's assurance that we were merely temporary hostages and not permanent inconveniences. Nor did he trust in my motivations or my ability to ensure that Hari would deliver on his end of our dubious deal. He had cause to be angry and little reason to be patient – a combination that made him prone to errors of judgement, including an attempt at escape. Not only did I want to keep him out of trouble for his own sake, but I also didn't want anyone else at risk. There was nowhere to go; if we did think to run, we wouldn't get very far.

A shout from Hari. Maya, I saw, had veered away from the trail and was pointing at a cluster of rocks up ahead as she strode towards them. Hari understood. 'Don't bother!' he waved back the goon who made to follow her.

'Women, eh?' he remarked in a between-us-boys way, as he came to stand next to me. 'Don't know why they have to make such a fuss about taking a tinkle. Considering it's the one thing standing between them and gender equality.'

I pointedly ignored him and stepped away as Maya jogged back across the rubble to join us.

We walked for an hour or so more, further into the valley till it narrowed into a ravine that was less than twenty metres wide. We also encountered, nestled in a bend in the riverbed, the first pools of water – its aquamarine tinge more fitting of the sea than a desert. From the bend, we could also make out the dark outline of the cave temple hidden at the base of the mountain. Clusters of saffron flags dotted the hillside, hoisted on sticks forced into the cracked clay-sand desert surface. The entire company came to a stop as one.

'Hingula Devi,' I declared. 'The locals call her Nani Bibi – named, as one story would have it, after the old Iranian goddess Nania.' I didn't add that Nania was a derivative of Inanna, an older Sumerian goddess who'd had her temple at Uruk and was said to have been brought back from the underworld by none other than Enki, from the immortality epic of Gilgamesh.

'A Hindu temple in the deserts of Pakistan. I don't believe it!' Rohit exclaimed.

Manohar was back in form, galvanized by the sheer adrenaline of doing what he loved to do. He said, 'For the record, there are about four hundred temples in Pakistan. Some of them are maintained by the state as historical monuments or sites of pilgrimage.'

'This one looks pretty deserted.'

'March and April are busy months. There's a festival then, which draws up to a thousand visitors, Hindu and Muslim both. But through the rest of the year, no one comes here except for nomads from Pakhtun. Speaking of which,' he added, the words obviously ringing a bell in his mind, 'there was a monastery of Tantric Buddhists in the Pakhtun area some time around the first or second century.'

'What does that have to do with this place?' Moorthy snapped.

'Patience, Moorthy,' Hari said. 'Let the Professor and his precious lackey do their job. Let him scramble for clues, find the ancient path or do whatever it is that he has to do. Surely you didn't think it was going to be as easy as walking into some buried crypt and picking up hidden treasure?'

I clucked my tongue. 'The problem isn't finding clues. Like Thiruvannamalai, or any historical site, really, this place too is full of clues, of traces of the past. There's an underground tunnel that leads to a hidden rock cave, there's a carved sign of the sun and the moon said to have been made by the avatar Ram. There are pools filled with sweet and salt water, and a bottomless well that is said to contain water from the primeval flood. Centuries of people have left their mark on this place. The problem is finding what is relevant to us.'

'We need to sift through the surfeit of symbolism,' Maya added.

'How poetic!' Hari barked.

Maya shrugged.

I said, 'She's right. But there's a simpler option too. We could just follow instructions.'

'Whose?'

'Dadhichi's. In the mantra he composed in praise of Hingula Devi, he describes her as nectar incarnate.'

'And?'

'Hingula Devi isn't a Shakti figure exclusive to this temple. In all other scriptures she is embodied as fire, not nectar.'

Hari waved his hands in a grandiose gesture. 'And our cryptic, everybody-else-is-a-jackass Professor is back. What the hell do you mean, Asva?'

'The river, Hari. The river is the goddess. The Hingula Devi temple is of no interest to us. The river is what we follow till she is, if I can borrow Dadhichi's words, "one with Shiva".'

'Rock. The mountains,' Manohar said, viewing the weathered and eroded cliff-faces on either side of us with new respect.

Hari interjected, 'The Hingol runs for five hundred

kilometres from source to sea. How do you expect us to get to wherever we're supposed to go?'

I said, 'We walk.'

For the next four hours there was nothing but the sound of our steps. We reached a section where the gorge we were in took a sharp turn to the west, the stream turning with it. Before us, the canyon wall rose in a sheer cliff for about two hundred metres. Even our dubious escorts were captivated. 'Bloody hell!' Rohit exclaimed.

'How...how old this place must be,' Manohar said, in a stunned whisper. 'Imagine how many million years it has taken the earth to sculpt these rocks into such shapes.'

It was Hari, unimpressed and undistracted by our surroundings, who noticed. 'Where's Maya?'

'Maybe she went to pee,' Rahul – our old friend Rohit's brother – scoffed. 'The lady has no place to pee here.'

'Let's wait then,' Rohit said. His tone implied that he wasn't making the offer out of courtesy and his next words removed all ambiguity: 'I had a feeling that bitch was setting us up. She kept going off to make sure we didn't get suspicious. She's been planning to escape the whole time!'

'Now, Rohit, relax,' Hari said. 'She's not that stupid.' As though on cue, Maya appeared from behind a cluster of rocks. 'There you go,' Hari said, flashing a benevolent smile.

The grin however faded when a disappointed Rohit took stock of the group again and growled, 'Where's that dickhead Moorthy?'

My stomach sank as I realized that Maya's disappearance had distracted me enough to briefly forget Moorthy. No doubt he had made good on my preoccupation, as well as everyone else's, to stage his escape. An escape that wouldn't last long. Not only would our escorts easily find him, but they would also make brutally sure that he dared not cross them again. 'You know,' I began, nonchalant, 'maybe he went off to take a leak too…'

But Rohit was not to be deterred. He and his goons were excited to have more than guard-work to do. A chase was as thrilling as it could get, even if their quarry was harmless. 'That's it,' he declared, swinging his gun off his shoulder and into readiness. 'Spread out. Find the bastard. Rahul, you stay here with these guys.'

'Hang on,' I protested. 'He's probably gone a bit ahead and is waiting for us to catch up. Like Hari said, there's nowhere else he can go.'

Rohit looked to Hari, as though awaiting instructions. Hari shrugged; he was irritated but not overly concerned. 'It's possible,' he said, as he prepared to walk on. 'He knows we were heading that way…'

His words pulled an innominate lever in my mind, and something that had been lingering at the periphery of observation fell into place.

'Wait!' I commanded, lifting a palm for emphasis.

'What…?'

'Shh!'

There was no doubt. Few creatures in the wild could stink that way, and the odour hung, faint but indisputable, in the hot, shimmering air. The lack of a breeze meant it moved slow, but that was no matter to these animals, who'd scented us from a distance even though we – no, *I* – had failed to anticipate their presence.

It's too late!

I discounted the fear at once. I smelled only mangy animal, not torn flesh and fresh blood. Still, it didn't leave me much time. Flouting Rohit's warning to stop or else he'd shoot, I began running ahead into the dry gully, sprinting as fast as I could over the rocks and stones that lay in my way. Without breaking my stride, I bounded up a pile of boulders, trying to use the elevation to find Moorthy amidst the many outcroppings that extended out from the cliff walls and into the narrow valley. I let out a sigh of relief at the scene that greeted me.

Moorthy was about a kilometre-and-a-half away, standing on a rock, backed up against the cliff wall. I chuckled to myself when I saw the small, tawny creature that had our would-be escape artist in such a position – a common wild jackal. The animal appeared to have interrupted his flight.

Behind me, Rohit and his look-alike, Rahul, were yelling and waving from a distance. I was beyond the range of their rifles – the gap between us a clear sign of how fast I had run. I waved to let them know all was well before setting out towards Moorthy at a jog.

The jackal slowly retreated a few metres at my approach before turning and trotting away down the valley, out of sight. Moorthy watched the animal go, showing way less trepidation than I had initially attributed to him. Then he hopped off the rock he had been on and faced me.

'I don't want to argue, Professor,' he began, categorical. 'But I did this to get you away from the rest of them. It is not I who must escape, but you. Without you, Hari can't…'

'Not this again!' I groaned. I was tempted to walk away and leave him to do as he wished, but then reconsidered. In his position, my actions might not have been any different.

'Come on,' I grabbed his arm, pulling him along as I began walking back. 'I've told them you were probably off taking a piss. Keep to that story. Tell them the jackal made you run. You won't hear the last of it, I know, but it's the safest thing to say. And for heaven's sake, don't you dare try to pull such a stunt again!'

'Professor…' He began to argue and struggle, but uncharacteristically cut short his protests. I stopped and followed his gaze to find that our animal acquaintance had returned and now stood a short distance away, observing us with renewed interest.

I silently cursed the last twenty generations of humanity and their ridiculous ignorance of nature before saying out loud, 'Relax, Moorthy! A lone jackal is hardly a threat, and certainly not this guy…he's just a harmless, mangy creature. Let's go.'

Moorthy did not move, but stared at me as though I'd turned into a mangy creature myself. That was when I saw them. The group emerged from behind an outcropping with all the drama that had thus far been lacking in the situation. I counted twenty-six, but more were now trotting down the cliffs on either side. It was a hunting pack, no doubt, for there were no pups or nursing mothers in the snarling lot.

'Harmless, did you say?' Moorthy hissed.

I shrugged. The canines, however, did not agree with my assessment of their kind.

Their cries grew into hacking, guttural growls as Moorthy and I took one measured step back and then another. Maws dripping, the jackals advanced upon us.

31

I once knew a man, a man I'd very much liked to have counted as a friend for the undeniably decent person he'd been, except that we'd ended up fighting on opposite sides in the Great War. That and the fact that I'd killed him in cold blood. He'd also been one of the best hunters and trackers of the time and had known things about the natural world that even my father had not.

'Animals,' he'd once said, 'are more complex creatures than we make them out to be. They're far from stupid and have as much system and structure in their lives as we do. A true hunter must recognize these creatures as a society in their own right.' Now more than ever, I relied on my old friend's advice.

'Listen up, Moorthy,' I said. 'Jackals work as a pack. When they hunt, they fall into a formation and they won't break it till they catch their prey, or the leader of the pack – that big, ugly fellow over there – dies. Once he's dead, they'll fall out of the hunt. To them, succession is far more immediate than the prey at hand.'

Moorthy gave me a scornful look. He said, 'And this animal psychology works how? We've got nothing to kill the leader with.'

'Rohit and the other guy...Rahul...are not too far away. We need to get the jackals running towards them. Once the pack is close enough, those guys will shoot them down.'

'But how do we send the jackals towards them?'

I felt a shiver run through me. The jackals had stopped moving, but it wasn't good news. There was that characteristic stiffening, the tensing up of haunches that meant they were getting ready to pounce.

'We use live bait. Ourselves.'

'What? You're out of your mind! They'll catch us and maul us to bits before we are even halfway there. It doesn't matter how fast we run!'

His fear made me falter. I snubbed the voice of doubt and told Moorthy, 'Jackals don't run fast, they just run hard till their prey tires. We don't have to last that long. Come on. Sprint. As fast as you can. Now!'

Moorthy set off, pumping his arms to run as fast as he could. I was right behind him. It took the pack only a few seconds to react. The leader let out a gruff cry that was part howl and part hacking bark. As one, the pack ran down into the hard, sandy bed of the valley and fell into their typical arrowhead hunting formation.

Less than a minute later – though it felt like a very long time, even to someone with my conception of it – our canine hunters were about a hundred metres behind us and holding that distance. Next to me, Moorthy glanced over his shoulder, cursed with what breath he could spare, tucked his chin in and picked up speed. I kept pace.

As we negotiated a gentle meander in the gully, I sent

up a silent prayer that we would find Rohit where I'd left him. If he'd turned back to join the others… I dismissed the apprehension as I spotted Rohit and Rahul, their heads together in discussion. I began shouting, trying to attract their attention. It worked and, after an astonished pause, the two men began running towards us, guns at the ready.

And with that the probabilities caught up with us.

I tripped on a vein of rock and flew through the air to land hard, a couple of metres away. I got to my feet at once, but the damage was done. As the smell of blood rose from my grazed knee, the leader of the jackals let out a spine-chilling howl and the pack picked up speed. They were ready for the kill.

'Run,' I told Moorthy as he stopped.

'But, Professor…'

'Go, get help,' I commanded. 'Go! It's our only chance!' I hoped that he would take the assertion at face value and keep moving. He hesitated a few moments more, but then took off again, a new vigour in his spirit. Perhaps, I mused, it was guilt that now spurred him. I would know – it was, after all, a familiar sentiment.

I turned to face the advancing pack.

Nothing reminded me more of the anachronism I was than the fact that what passed in current times for a heroic deed had once been just a job. Many a mercenary had, as recently as the past century, complained to me how people couldn't comprehend that fighting could be as normal a way of life as any other. I was one of those who did understand.

The jackals neared. They were larger than their cousins from the Deccan plateau and the Serengeti, both of whom could bring down a deer kid, but nothing bigger. Having said that, packs of this size were a rarity in any jungle and were best not taken lightly once they had scented blood. As the metallic tang filled my nostrils, I saw on the ground in front of me, a splatter of red where I'd fallen.

You never have to outrun your hunter, if you can outrun your friend. In this case, Moorthy needed to do neither. I was grateful when the jackal leader pounced, for it spared me from having to think about why I'd just done what I had.

The leader went straight for my throat, the typical hunting style of these animals being to knock down their quarry and then rip open the stomach and chest cavity to begin gorging on the flesh while the prey was still alive. A jackal his size could take on over three times his weight, and I only had split seconds till the others of the pack went for my legs.

I threw an arm up in front of my face and throat, letting the jackal leader sink his teeth into it, and with the other arm tried to grab him by the scruff of his neck. I tried to force the beast's head back with my forearm as I pushed down on his neck from behind, trying to snap it. It didn't work. He let go of my forearm, turning in the air to bite my other hand even as he dug into my chest with his claws. My right leg buckled as two more jackals slammed into it with all their weight. I felt myself toppling, taking the leader down with me. Age-old training countered the intuitive urge to struggle for balance; I let my other leg bend and swung my whole body around in an attempt to dash my first nemesis against the ground with the force of our combined fall.

The jackal crashed to the ground with a yelp, taking the brunt of it on his rump and hip, but then lunged again with all the fury brought on by his pain. I tried to bring a leg up to kick him away, but another beast came at my thigh. I rolled over, trying to throw them off and, at the same time, protect my throat and stomach, when the most welcome words I'd heard in a while rang through the air: '*Get down! Down!*'

Trusting a man who was as sworn an enemy as any, I spread myself flat on the ground, face down. Gunfire sprayed around me, bullets hitting animal and ground alike. Shrieks and howls filled the air. I felt the weight of a carcass on my back and one more on my leg, their blood soaking through my clothes.

'Stay down, Professor!' Rahul again called out. I didn't move till the gunfire ceased and, presumably, the jackals that weren't dead had dispersed.

'Professor!'

Both Maya and Manohar ran towards me, reaching me at the same time. Moorthy was right behind them. He opened his mouth to speak, but Manohar snapped at him: 'What? Are you scared of the dead ones too? Stop standing around and give me a hand!'

Moorthy didn't retort and came up to help as instructed. Together, the three of them pulled off the jackals from on top of me, one by one, and threw them aside.

'First-aid kit!' Maya shouted, to no one in particular. One of the hired men brought it to her. The others went forward at Rohit's instructions, following the blood trails left by the few jackals that had escaped. Around us, I counted, were twenty-odd corpses. Maybe it was the effect of Manohar's vehemence, or perhaps Rohit and his fellow henchmen were naturally lacking in officiousness, but neither commented nor showed undue concern at what had happened. Perhaps, as men of action themselves, they were aware that jackals, scary as they sounded, weren't in the same league as wild boars or bull elephants. I had no complaints. Whatever it was, the situation had deflected some of the attention from Moorthy's ill-advised escape attempt.

Hari walked up to join us; he seemed more amused than upset. 'You look like shit, Asva. And you, Moorthy. What the fuck were you trying to do? It's your fault this happened to him!'

Moorthy wisely held his tongue, while I considered some scathing Sanskrit repartees, wondering which one was best rendered in translation without any loss of derision. Before I could choose, though, Maya jumped in. 'We have to get him to a hospital. He needs rabies and tetanus shots. Not to mention stitches and...' Hari held a palm up, indicating for her to stop, but she went on, 'Please...we can't...'

'Shut up!' Hari barked. He turned to me, solicitous. 'You're all right, aren't you, Asva? Tell her. The poor thing is worried out of her wits!'

His false sympathy made me feel disgusted and dirty, far more so than did all the vermin blood that coated me from head to toe. I didn't bother to answer him and turned instead to Manohar. 'Water,' I said, needing to get the sand, grime and creature-stink out of my mouth and then off my whole body.

That was when Manohar asked, matter-of-fact, 'Where's the river gone?'

32

It took us a couple of hours to gather ourselves and our wits together and make our way back along the few kilometres to where the valley had taken a sharp turn to form the gulley. I was a little stiff, and the cuts and scratches on me burned as I sweated through every pore under the desert sun. I had a limp, which wouldn't take too long to heal but, without stitches, the wound on my forearm would need a day or two. The serrated marks of the jackal's teeth had left a jagged cut, and though Manohar had bandaged it up well, the skin threatened to split at the least attempt to move my arm.

All this became inconsequential against the more immediate problem: Not a drop of water, not even the smallest pond or stream was anywhere in sight.

'This is the riverbed, no doubt,' Manohar remarked, examining the rounded stones that marked the river's dried-up trail. 'Maybe a stream forms after the rains?'

Hari said, 'In that case, we should keep moving. We'll find the river again further upstream.'

'No,' I disagreed. 'We need to head back. I want to be absolutely sure about our trail.'

Hari began to protest, but I dismissed him and began trying to trace our route in reverse, hobbling along till I felt my balance return. Manohar and Moorthy followed, as did Maya. Hari and his lot had no choice but to fall in behind them.

We ended up at a point a good distance back on the route we'd taken. It was where we'd had the last clear indication of the river – a large rock pond formed by a natural indentation in the riverbed, which then narrowed into a rivulet hardly a metre wide. I took the chance to strip down and wash every bit of blood and dirt off me. Manohar helped replace my wet bandages with dry ones. I noticed then that Rohit too had a large bandage around his lower leg.

'What happened?' I asked, pointing at the thug's blood-soaked dressing.

'One of those fuckers wasn't dead enough. Bit me as I was walking by,' he explained, ungrudging.

I realized I hadn't as yet said what I ought to have, some hours ago. 'Back there...you and Rahul...and the others. Moorthy and I would have been jackal lunch if you hadn't...'

He looked amazed and uncomfortable at my gratitude. I wondered if I had as weird a look on my face – these were awkward words for men who wouldn't think twice about killing each other if they had to.

'God, I'm stuck in a B-grade Western,' I muttered. Manohar chuckled to himself and said what sounded very much like *'angrez-ki-aulad'*. I didn't mind: Calling me an Anglophile was as much politeness and honesty as I deserved at that point, but the dash of humour did nothing to ease the disquiet I felt.

'Are you thinking what I'm thinking, Professor?' Manohar came to sit next to me.

'And what are you thinking?'

'Sandstorms, attacks by vicious animals and a river that goes missing... Maybe it's because we survived the sandstorm without trouble that we fail to see these for what they are.'

'Traps?'

'Elemental traps. Not unlike the elemental challenges Nagarjuna faced in order to get to his hallowed secret, whatever it is. He could have used the same principles to set up snares for those who followed him, or else these natural hazards are what made this place so hard to find in the first place. I don't know. But see... Wind. Creatures of the earth. A water course that leads us astray. If you hadn't been you... I mean, if it had been left to us, we'd have followed Hari upstream, not come back here.'

I thought about it and said, 'You know what makes us totally crazy, Manohar? You and I?'

'Hmm?'

'We think the proposition that a bunch of dead scholars set up traps using natural elements to make sure that no one unearths a secret that doesn't even hold scientific credence is more tenable than the idea that we might have had a bunch of freak accidents out here in the wild.'

He grinned, gratified by my assessment of our sanity.

Smiling back, I said, 'So what shall we do?'

'Let's head to the cliff – the one before the valley turns and narrows into the jackal-wala gully. I have a feeling the river goes underground.'

'Oh?'

Manohar appeared like an overjoyed child showing off his newfound ability to a doting parent. 'You remember what you said about the river being the goddess herself, and following it till Shakti becomes one with Shiva? It may have meant the point where the river splits into two – a seasonal above-ground stream and a perennial underground tributary. The obvious course is the wrong one, and will lead us further into trouble… Whereas…' He stopped, abashed at his own zeal. I squeezed his shoulder in reassurance and stood up.

It took but a few minutes to explain things to the others. Maya and Hari received this news with varied endorsement; Moorthy took it with a scepticism that suggested a desperate attempt at denial. The others listened, sans opinion, in the typical manner of hired hands.

Rahul asked, 'Can it happen? Do rivers just go underground like that?' He was back to being his obtuse, nauseating self, which rid me of all residual gratitude. It was always less stressful to dislike someone who deserved it.

Manohar clearly felt the same way. 'It speaks!' he quipped under his breath. I chuckled, but was glad when he didn't repeat it. The last thing I wanted was a testosterone-driven punch-up.

We made our way forward, for the second time, to reach the cliff Manohar had spoken of. It appeared as uninspiring and innocuous as it had before. Hari was looking around at the valley, thrown into shadow here and there in the dimming light. 'Which way?' he asked.

'Up. On the cliffside. The next element stands in our way – sky, space, ether…whatever you'd like to call it.'

'Sky? Bit of a stretch, isn't it?'

Before Hari could go on, I said, 'We ought to wait till morning to be sure. There's a good chance we might miss things in the dark, not to mention it's been a very long day. Let's camp here and continue tomorrow.'

Rohit grunted his assent and then, a smirk on his lips, leaned in to whisper something to Maya. Evidently it was a lewd remark for she turned on him, eyes blazing. I expected her to slap him, but she seemed to decide against it. Throwing her backpack down right where she stood, she curled up with her head on it and closed her eyes, as though daring him to do what he would.

The rest of us set about the more mundane but essential task of setting up a small campfire with the few twigs we'd carried for the purpose. I placed my sleeping bag next to where Maya lay and settled down on it. The others laid claim to their own spots around the fire, till our company had settled into a loose circle with the reassuring blaze at the centre. Moorthy no longer needed watching. He would feel too obligated to me to attempt another getaway. For the moment, staying was the safer option for him, though I suspected dangers far worse than hired thugs awaited him in my company. But those were concerns for the morning.

Under the night sky, after such a long day, it was tough to feel anything but replete.

Leaving our captors to see to the perimeter guard and keeping watch, I gazed up at the thick blanket of stars till, eventually, I fell asleep.

It was dark, but the smell of morning was in the air by the time we were all awake and as well-breakfasted as we could be. The fire put out, we all rolled up our sleeping bags, Maya mouthing a word of thanks as she stuffed hers back into her rucksack – I'd woken her up during the night and told her to get into her bag before she developed cramps from the ambient cold of the desert.

I finished packing away my gear and then set a swift pace towards the cliff.

'Let me guess – you're going to use the rays to find a secret passage? Or some shadows or markings silhouetted against the sun?' Maya teased, in a whisper that I alone could hear.

'I've told you before,' I said, smiling despite myself, 'I'm not your whip-snapping, tomb-raiding type.'

'You *are* my type.' She reached out to give my hand a light squeeze before turning away. I heard her exclaim as the sun cleared the horizon to the east, its rays skimming the upper reaches of the mountain wall that lay before us.

'Unbelievable!' Moorthy whispered. He tapped me on the shoulder, inviting me to take in the spectacle that unfolded before us, but I kept my eyes on the cliff-face as the rising sun dyed the grey rock in shades of burnished orange and sanguine red.

I'd been a very young boy when my uncle – my mother's brother – had brought me to the temple of my forefathers at sunrise. I'd clapped and rejoiced at the startling burst of gold, the mythical chariot of the sun as it flashed across the eastern skies; his wife, the dawn, laying a blazing carpet to welcome his arrival. My uncle had placed his hands on my shoulders and turned me around to face the idol-less altar. It had filled with flaming radiance as the first ray breached the horizon to shine into that sacred space. 'And that is how the divine fire burns within you when enlightenment dawns,' my uncle had said.

I'd not understood then, but had nevertheless added my voice to his as we chanted the Gayatri mantra – the morning obeisance to the sun. By the time I was a man, I no longer gazed at the dawn. I'd stopped looking westward to the altar too. Light was everything and all light, I'd realized by then, lay within.

'There!' It was a soft, satisfied exclamation, but Hari heard me.

'What is it?'

'See, the rays bend...or appear to. There's an opening of some sort there. And there, more handholds. That ledge... I expect there's some sort of an opening that we can't see from here.'

'I don't see anything,' he protested.

'That's because you don't know where to look. Fifth-grade geography, Hari: Hanging valleys. In this case, a series of hanging valleys with a river that goes subterranean, if you even know what that means. Now, you must excuse me. I need to climb up.'

Hari eyed me with camaraderie and then, as an afterthought, clapped me on the back. I shrugged off his hand and went to set up my climbing gear.

33

Life, scientists said, wasn't a continuum. Rather, it was discrete, distinct parcels of time and experience crunched together. Human beings, however, perceived it as continuous and thus constructed from it meanings that didn't really exist – all because at five hundred milliseconds between stimulus and response, thought travelled slower than sound. Less politely put, our brains were too sluggish to see reality as it truly was. I supposed that was also why patience was such a lauded virtue – it took wisdom of a particular sort to see that the solution to this human limitation lay not in speeding forward but in slowing down. Manohar, I'd always found, was a remarkably patient man, which made him an excellent colleague in times such as these.

Our initial excitement at the breakthrough had been dampened by functional imperatives: Erosion had left the cliff-face sheer and smooth, and climbing it would take considerable skill. But Manohar hadn't been fazed. Acting with professional ease, he set up all that we would need to make the ascent up the bluff in pitches, or section by section. Once we were at the ledge, the plan was to let down a top rope, or even a double pulley, for the others.

I went first and had been climbing for about fifteen minutes when I started finding well-placed crevices in the wall whenever I reached out for a handhold. It didn't take long to fathom that the grooves were indeed worn remnants of grips that had once been set into the rock. People had been meant to get up here.

Once I'd set up a safety rope, Manohar quickly climbed up to join me on the cliffside. He need not have hurried, though – after that pitch, the climbing slackened. The handholds we had come across were eroded in far too many places to serve as a means of ascent. It served to affirm my premise that at one time, centuries ago, this had been the course of the river, but as it stood now it also made for some rather technical climbing.

'What are we going to do after this, boss? After this business is over, I mean...' Manohar asked. He was hanging in mid-air, suspended by ropes, a toe against the rock surface to keep him from swinging. I was similarly suspended a few metres above him, to his right. It had already taken us an hour to drive a single bolt into a cleft about ninety metres off the ground, halfway to our destination up the cliff – a step we might have skipped if we didn't have to think of setting up a ropeway for the others behind us.

I stopped hammering. Letting my arms fall to my side, I twisted away from the rock-face. Mountains ran, endless, along the horizon and seemed to flow upward into the sky. The earth bled silver-grey ichor, the living mineral forming a complex, unpredictable pattern on the surface of the mountains. From where I was, the jagged peaks appeared close, close enough to reach out and touch, for their sheer size made the distance insignificant. To my right, the sun was inching up the horizon, its warm redness turning into a fiery effulgence, recolouring the entire landscape around us. A glint here and there, like a diamond, as its rays hit the downstream course of the river. True to what Manohar had said, there was no water in the upstream valley for as far as the eye could see. What had appeared to be rock indentations and crevices from back in the gully were obvious foxholes and tiny caves from up here.

Fire, earth, water, sky, wind. Every element – malevolent or not – was present in the moment, and I felt content to hang there, suspended in nothingness, feeling the golden rays on my bare back and shoulders. Fortunately, everyone had been too preoccupied with the situation as a whole to comment on the fact that the jackal-wounds on my chest were already healing, my self-rejuvenating body fighting the otherwise-inevitable infection.

It occurred to me that if I let my hammer drop, well-aimed and unannounced, on Hari's head, it would be the end of all our troubles. *Or would it?*

'I don't know, Manohar,' I said. 'I wouldn't mind a holiday. Preferably in a cooler climate.'

'Hmm.'

'How about you? You're game for more work? Or think it's time to settle down in a decent job, have a steady relationship...?' This wasn't unlike the conversation that Hari and I had had barely days ago. Now, in the middle of the desert and with all that had come to pass, it felt as though that had been long ago and far away.

Manohar said, 'I... I don't know, Professor. Haven't decided. This trip... Well, it's been a bit of a bummer in some ways. Made me wonder what it is I really want to do with my life. I don't know; it's kind of tough to think straight right now. I'm sorry...'

'That's okay,' I replied. I suspected it was more than this particular assignment that weighed on his mind. It would only be a matter of time before he chose to quit this line of work. Which was just as well – he had a life to get on with.

It took us a further hour to reach the ledge, if it could be called that. It was more of an overhang, with a narrow doorway-like opening and a small pool of clear, clean-looking water in front of it. Both opening and pool were of human make – the former a precise rectangle, the latter a perfect square, similar to the pool at Somnath. The sudden appearance of water from under the earth's surface made it seem as though the mountains had squeezed forth the nectar of the earth.

'Whoa!' Manohar exclaimed.

'Yeah. Let's get the others up.'

With a top rope in place, it didn't take too long for the others to climb their way on to the ledge. Hari surprised me by making his ascent with a stamina and agility I'd never associated with him.

'What sort of a place is this?' Moorthy marvelled. 'I'd never have believed such places existed.'

'When was the last time you saw a mountain?' I asked him.

'I live in Thiruvannamalai!'

'Yes, but when was the last time you looked at it as anything but a mountain, a cohesive whole. These sort of features – hanging valleys, underground springs – they're all common stuff. We don't pay any attention to them because nature has become an indistinct blur to us. We think of all that's out there as "nature". But, as the saying goes, God lies in the details.'

'I think you mean "the devil".'

'Same thing.'

Hari turned to the Polish brothers, who had done nothing on this trip so far other than add to the multi-culturality of our posse. 'Stay here. Make sure this area remains clear and the ropes are secure.'

I was tempted to make a smart-ass comment about rope thieves being common in these parts, but let it go. In Hari's position, I too would prepare for the possibility of gate-crashers – law enforcement, private collectors and a whole spectrum of unscrupulous characters, depending on how much they already knew. That being the case, I had little doubt that between the brothers Wachowski, or whatever their name was, it would take a small army to get in behind us. Thus assured, I focused on making sure that the twisted knot holding the carabiner to rope was secure and then hooked the carabiner into a cam that I had set up in the rock. I tested the rope with my weight before winding it into a neat coil.

It was in good form to set the return route in advance, I reminded myself. *Whether we would need it or not.*

'You'd better be right about this, Asva,' Hari said, under his breath.

'Or else...?'

'Do you honestly want me to answer that?'

I didn't. Instead, I replied, 'I have faith.'

Hari was derisive. 'In God?'

'In Nagarjuna. The guy was no idiot. And unlike present company, he had a healthy respect for others. If he created a puzzle, he also left a solution.'

I made my way through the rectangular opening, with Manohar right behind me. Together, we flashed our torches around, taking in the smooth rock. It was dark — black, in fact — a remarkable occurrence given the sandy brown terrain outside. The tunnel had space inside for me to stand up tall, though it only allowed us to walk two abreast. 'A maze?' Manohar asked.

'Looks like it.' I turned back towards Hari. 'We should start heading in. I'll lead.'

'No!' Hari was emphatic. He gestured to Rohit, who picked out two of his men. They switched on the strong flashlights strapped to their belts, and a powerful beam cut through the darkness. One of them held his AK-12 in alert readiness.

Moorthy asked, 'What about air? We have only three emergency oxygen canisters between all of us. They won't last long and we have no idea how long we're going to be inside.'

'We won't need them.' I flashed the beam on to the ceiling. Five small round holes were set into the rock in the precise pattern of a plus sign. 'Ventilation channels.'

'No more excuses, then,' he muttered under his breath.

The men in the lead began making their way through the tunnel. We followed in twos, slow and silent at first. But soon, not knowing what to expect became too much to take and the sounds of fidgeting and muffled sighs interrupted the silence. We had gone about half-a-kilometre down the tunnel when Manohar leaned in close and whispered, 'We're missing a step.'

'The final element,' I said. 'Fire.'

'But…how?'

'I don't know. I also find these ventilation channels a bit funny – Somnath didn't have them.'

'Well, I'm not complaining about the fresh air. At least it doesn't smell…well…smell like anything in here.'

That's when it struck me. 'Switch off your torches!' I shouted. 'Off!' It took a few moments and some loud curses but everyone complied. One of the hired guns offered loud suggestions about a lighter.

'*Abey, saale*! Do you have cow dung in your brain? A *lighter*?' Manohar hissed through the darkness.

'What is it, Asva?' Hari asked.

'There's a reason why the ventilation holes start right from the entranceway. We aren't supposed to smell anything.'

'And what do you think it is we are not supposed to smell?'

'Gas. I'd say some form of methane from the mud volcanoes in the area, except…'

'Except?'

It was Manohar who replied, 'Methane doesn't have an odour of its own. There must be some other hydrocarbon, which gives it odour and increases its flammability. In the olden days, trespassers would walk through these tunnels holding flame torches or braziers and then... Boom! Our torches are powerful, and who knows what the heat of the beam can trigger off. Or does someone want to find out?'

'Fine. But how do we move forward? We can't just stand here in the dark...'

I said, 'This passageway was kept narrow for a reason. We'll need to feel our way through. I'll go first. I want everyone in a single line...' After some muttered discontent about school kids in a playground line-up, we set off again in single-file, Manohar right behind me.

We had barely covered two hundred metres or so when I had the peculiar feeling that the outline of the tunnel appeared sharper than normal night vision ought to allow for. I wondered if I was imagining it, when Manohar mentioned the same thing. 'It looks like there's a dim light up ahead, but it's...diffused.'

He was right. A few minutes later, we emerged from the tunnel into an underground crypt, not very different from the one at Somnath. Except, this near-square room had four passageways leading out from it, one set into each wall, including the one we had entered through. The other astounding thing was the wall of the nook – it emitted a dull green luminescence, dot-splatters that glowed in the dark.

'Some chemical in the rock, do you think?' I asked Manohar, as he studied the walls.

Maya reached out to touch the stone. I followed suit. A crumbly substance, not unlike moss of some sort, came away on my hands.

'A bioluminescent fungus, is my guess,' Manohar said, examining the residue. 'Symbiotic with some bacteria in the rock.'

I wiped my hands against the leg of my pants, glad that it didn't take up the shine. 'A bioluminescent whatever, all right. Point is, it puts us back in the safe zone.'

My reassurance apart, no one wanted to be the first to switch on their lights. Not that it mattered – if I were wrong, we would all go up in flames anyway. With a cluck of my tongue, I slid the tab on my small torch. I heard an inadvertent sigh of relief from one of the hired hulks, after which the more powerful beams of the bigger flashlights came on, one by one. Rohit and Rahul moved around, examining the three other exits from the room. 'There are stairs here. They go up,' Rahul called from our right.

'This way is down. But no stairs. More like a slope... gets steep.'

Rohit flashed his beam through the third exit. 'Stairs here too, about seven or eight of them. Turns into a passageway.'

I said to Hari. 'I need the Vajra.'

'Why?'

'Because it's a map that tells us where to go next.'

Hari grunted. 'Seriously, Asva? Do you have to press toggle-X on your controller to use it, or do you just pull it out of your virtual fanny pack?'

I didn't react to his silly joke; I simply held out my hand. He clucked his tongue and, digging the Vajra out of his pocket, gave it to me. Pleased at having got my way, I explained, 'The Vajra pointed us here, to this location, but that piece of information could have been held or passed on with or without this thing. If someone went to the trouble of breaking up the Vajra and hiding it in three different places, it implies that it has to be of more use than as a symbolic trinket. We need it to get inside.'

'Like a key?' Maya asked. 'Except it doesn't literally open doors, but shows the way, like the key on a map...'

'I guess that comparison works.'

I laid the Vajra out flat on my palm, and it slowly began to give out a faint glow, reacting, I suspected, to either the atmosphere within the tunnel, or possibly the magnetic field of the mountain as a whole. It took a while to see beyond the tessellated pattern of overlapping hexagons and circles to make out the hidden but irrefutable course pointers, like a path etched into the substance of the disc itself.

Moorthy was dumbstruck. 'We're going to follow *that*? It's going to take one hell of an eye to keep track of where we are on that thing!'

Hari grinned and looked all the less friendly for it. 'You lead, Professor.'

'My thoughts exactly,' I said. 'We go left. Through that exit and down the slope.'

The route we encountered wasn't a very difficult one to traverse, but was designed across three dimensions and multiple layers, making it impossible to memorize the way. Pathways opened up to our left and right, some of them stairs that led upwards and others, down. We followed the Vajra-map, its silver markings glowing clear in the dimness.

Initially, there was some curiosity as to where the other paths might lead. I cautioned against exploring them, the advice taken lightly till Rahul nearly fell off a flight of stairs that ended in mid-air. We risked flashing one of the smaller torchlights into the darkness below, but couldn't tell if the fall would have been a mere few metres, or a few hundred.

'How long do you think...' Moorthy asked me.

'Another hour, hour-and-a-half? We're about halfway to the centre...assuming the centre is where we need to go.'

'And if it isn't?'

'Then I'd have been right all along, wouldn't I? There's nothing in here worth finding, after all.'

Moorthy fell into a sulk after that. It extended over the group as a whole, coming to a head when we reached what appeared to be a wrong turn.

'We're screwed!' Rohit shouted and came charging towards me. 'You screwed up, Professor! You made a mistake. Or else, you did this on purpose. Either way, I swear I'll break...'

'Shut it, Rohit.' I advanced to examine the results of my alleged error. We were standing at the base of one more seemingly interminable flight of stairs that would have been apt in an Escher sketch, except we couldn't see the whole picture or even part of it. The landing at the bottom of the stairs was unlike the ones we'd encountered earlier. The dead end ahead, as well as the opening to our left, were of familiar design, but to our right was impenetrable darkness.

I tentatively reached out with my foot and then, kneeling, felt around with my fingers. But there was nothing there. Again, we risked a single, weak torchbeam. It faded into infinity, but not before showing us emptiness – like a shaft, except much larger. Nevertheless, the Vajra said right was the way to go, a very short right and then right again, forming an angular U-turn, like one of the funny false turns that one expected to find in a maze. If I had not been certain of my own diligence, I'd have been tempted to think it was the wrong way. As it stood, I wasn't sure how to proceed.

Hari regarded me with indifference. 'You find a way. We'll go that way,' he declared.

I sat down on one of the steps, waving to the others to get comfortable while I figured things out.

Some disgruntled murmuring and shuffling later, two of the goons declared, 'We're going to check out this passage,' they motioned to the path on our left.

'It's the wrong way,' I said.

'Is it? What if the map is wrong? What if *you* are wrong?'

I shrugged. 'Maybe I am. Maybe I'm not. But I don't like the air down that way.'

I heard Manohar mutter, 'Okay, Gandalf.'

The private joke brought a smile to my lips, which the goons took as reason enough to rub my face in it again. 'You guys rest here. We'll come back soon.' With that, the two men turned into the passageway. Their conversation echoed back through the tunnel as the two proceeded, unaware that they were favouring the rest of us with way too much information.

'Damn, is that stink you? Assumed it was bats...'

'And you? You smell like a garbage heap. Not that you care, but we have a hot chick with us, so...'

'Yeah... She smells nice. Couldn't tell back in there, right? I mean, our stench? But here... Hey, this funny fungus thing again. What do you suppose that smells like?'

'It's weird! Come on, I'm not going near that thing...'

'Get back!' I said, my tone brooking no dissent. Hari reacted swiftly. He ran, pulling Maya up from where she was sitting as he took the stairs up, two at a time. Manohar and Moorthy were right behind him, while Rohit and Rahul led the others, their faces set in disbelief. I took a step towards the tunnel, intending to call the two men inside to safety. But it was too late.

We felt the searing heat, and the blast, mild as it was, knocked us off balance. Moorthy hit his head against the wall and Rohit banged his knee, going down hard on the ground. The rest of us managed to steady ourselves and sank to the floor where we were. It was over before we could even look back to the base of the stairs. The perpendicular angle of the passageway, as well as the opening to the right, had saved us from the brunt of the blast, and barely a flame of tongue had flickered out of the opening towards us. Other than the trail of smoke and the distinct acrid smell of burning flesh, no clue remained of what had just happened.

34

'The luminescence is a false marker, isn't it? Only the Vajra shows the way?' Maya's voice sounded small in the dark stairwell.

We, all of us, had been sitting motionless for over twenty minutes. It was a reaction I'd seen before, particularly when armies were on the march. Just as it seemed that all was well, that the adventure was merely a riskier variation of a walk in the park, one was reminded of the real stakes, the looming dangers. That was why people enjoyed movies, the promise of adrenaline kicks at twenty-four frames per second, with the reassurance that peril and excitement lay waiting at the beginning of the next reel. Real life was less predictable and a whole lot more surreal. There would be anticlimactic dialogue when action was expected, and the action would come when you least expected it. And romance? It was never there, unlike dark comedy, which always, always, lurked in the background of every scene.

'Yes,' I said, in reply to Maya's query. 'Fluorescent fungus or not, they shouldn't have gone off the grid. I shouldn't have let them go.'

Moorthy glanced up. 'Hey, you're feeling sorry for the wrong guys here, Professor.'

'They were men under my lead, Moorthy. It doesn't matter what scum of the earth they were; I was responsible for them.'

'You told them not to go,' he argued.

'I didn't insist enough.'

'It's not your fault...'

'Drop it!' Manohar interrupted. He turned to me and said, in a gentler tone, 'Should we...?'

'Don't bother,' I said.

'But...' Rahul began, but I cut him off with a glare. He deserved credit for persisting. 'If they're alive... If they're alive, it's worse.'

'They're dead. Besides, what can any of us do?'

Rohit sighed; he wasn't done reflecting over the situation. 'How come we didn't get...you know...' he asked.

'Fried?'

'Killed.'

I stood up, as did the others, and we made our way back down the stairs, to the landing. Holding up the Vajra as a source of light, I pointed to the many rounded holes above the passage to the left. 'The ventilation system we saw earlier probably sucks the gas back in.'

Maya was visibly excited. 'I could spend a lifetime here...' she began.

Hari clucked his tongue in false sympathy. 'Pity, no one will ever come to even hear of this place. No one other than a few select individuals, who will know its true purpose...'

Maya opened her mouth to argue and then settled against it. With a last dash of defiance, she muttered, 'I'd love to get a look at the ventilation system. The bacteria management too... It could...'

I said, 'And if you don't mind, I'd prefer to leave it all to speculation. I don't plan to cross an inch over that threshold and off the path the Vajra says we should take.'

'The path we *should* take, you say. But *what* path will we take?' Hari pointedly asked.

Manohar and I surveyed the apparent nothingness to our right and then exchanged silent looks, after which he ran some calculations in his head before asking, 'Fifteen metres?'

I said, 'Make it twenty. Just in case.'

'If you crash...'

I knew what he meant. Falling just five metres would simulate the impact of hitting the ground with a parachute, assuming that one had been trained to land right. Near twenty metres was asking for big trouble – in my case, at the very least, a lot of pain. On the other hand, if the fall were shorter, that would be just as bad as jumping without a rope. 'Twenty,' I declared, with finality.

Reaching into his bag, Manohar took out a length of climbing rope as well as a harness. Buckling the harness around his waist, he passed the rope through it and knotted it tight. He ran the rest of the rope behind him, fashioning it into an easy-to-hold coil. 'Here, grab this,' he instructed Rahul, the biggest man of the lot of us. I picked up the other end of the rope and wrapped it around my waist in a sling.

As Manohar and Rahul stood braced, I sat on the edge of the landing, legs swinging in nothingness. Then I used my arms, fingers gripping the edge of the rock, to turn and lower myself down.

'Can you see anything?' Manohar asked.

'No,' I grunted. Holding on to the edge in a pull-up posture, I reached out with my legs till I was almost parallel to the landing – or ledge, as I now realized it was. I then swung my legs back and up, reaching as far behind me as possible with my heels. Nothing.

'Ready?' I called out and then let go of my hold on the edge, allowing myself to fall through the air. I braced myself for impact, but all I felt after a few seconds of falling in the dark was the hard jerk of the rope against my waist and thighs. With a groan of disappointment, I threw my head back and hung there in the dark, letting Manohar and Rohit take my weight.

'Hah!' I exclaimed as realization dawned. *Up! Not down, up!*

'Bring me up,' I shouted and could hardly wait as the two men took in the rope, hauling me back the seven storeys or so that I had fallen. 'Wrong direction!' I declared, as soon as I was back on the landing. 'Give me a boost, Manohar.'

He hoisted me on his shoulders, so that I could run the beam of the torch and then my hand over the edge of the ceiling. My fingers felt what could barely be seen – ladder-like indentations in the rock, similar to the ones Maya and I had encountered at Somnath. The way onward required climbing up the shaft to reach what I suspected would be another landing directly above the one we stood in, the former set so as to be invisible from below.

Easing myself off Manohar's shoulders, I swung myself on to the rock face and, feeling my way in the darkness, used the grooves to climb to an even-floored space about three metres overhead. It lay at the bottom of another stairway that I was sure would take us back into the maze-structure we had been navigating so far, but at another level. Undoing the rope sling from around my waist, I set it up for Manohar and Rahul to use. Once they had made the ascent, the three of us helped the others up. The whole process took about three-quarters of an hour and some significant use of arm and back strength, but we were all hardly the worse for wear at the end of it. Marvelling at the engineering ingenuity of Nagarjuna and his lot, we made our way up the steps with renewed energy.

And then, before we knew it, we were there.

The hall was massive. Not Renaissance cathedral-massive but nevertheless impressive for a hidden cavern in the heart of a mountain. It spanned nearly a quarter of a kilometre in each direction, and the ceiling transitioned seamlessly from the walls to curve and peak about a hundred metres over our heads. A cluster of green luminescence, set in a perfect circle right at the apex, bathed the whole chamber in a soothing light. The starkness of the chamber, its complete lack of embellishment, suggested a functional purpose.

From where I stood, at the threshold, I could see an opening set diametrically opposite, and a third exit was to our right. Also to the right was a row of stone slabs along the periphery of the chamber. These had likely been seats from which one could observe the proceedings the hall had been intended for.

I turned to my left, expecting similar, symmetrical arrangements but there was no corresponding passageway, no seating slab, only a wall. And in front of it, a smooth square block of familiar black stone, its presence that of an intimate friend.

'We did it, Asva! You did it!' Hari clapped me on the back. His eyes held an unearthly glow. 'This place? This place is it! It's what I've dreamed of finding my entire life. This is where the oldest of alchemists worked and worshipped. That is what Nagarjuna found and locked with the Vajra. He discovered the seat of alchemy, where magic might just be revealed as science. This is it, Maya. This is it!'

'Arunachaleshwara!' Moorthy couldn't help but be thrilled, despite the circumstances that had brought us here. Even the uninformed Rahul and Rohit appeared astounded and excited.

I was vaguely aware of their energy, their exclamations, their compliments – the low hum of conversation around me as, for a few moments, mortal enemies became friends, united by the primal ties of survival and success. But their elation paled against mine; against the cool bubbling sensation in the pit of my stomach as though a memory had come alive to give succour, for it was at an altar like this one, identical in its unadorned blankness and unshakeable presence, that I'd laid down my life in sacrifice to Rudra. It was at an altar like this one that I had been made immortal.

I'd come fresh from the last massacre of the Great War, covered in blood, and thrown myself into its stony embrace. I'd held it tight and wept; as though it were the only mother I'd ever known. A cry had spilled from my throat, a guttural call that was part prayer, part accusation. Invoking Rudra as both receiver of and witness to my sacrifice, I had pulled out my sword and raked it against every part of me, gasping with insane pleasure as life had spurted out to clean away the stains of blood-debt from my being. Like beams of sunlight bursting through clouds, I'd been a creature of fire and light and pure thought. Finally, I had drawn the blade across my throat.

The stroke was meant to behead me, but my tired arms had failed and a small flap of skin remained, keeping me conscious long enough to see my flesh splatter on to the altar, sticking to the surface in clumps. My last thought as I'd fallen forward on to the sacrificial stone had been that death was not an end, it was a threshold, the ultimate process of natural evolution that takes that portion of the constant universal energy known as life and changes its form.

And then something had happened to me.

I'd woken, alive. Forever alive.

I reached out for Manohar; like an old man I placed a hand on his shoulder and let him take my weight as the sudden sense of relief that coursed through me left me feeling strangely weak. He faced me. I smiled and whispered, so that he alone could hear, 'At last, Manohar. At long last...'

The concern in his eyes turned to pure dread.

35

For once, I couldn't be sure of what Manohar was thinking or feeling. He had that look of inscrutable anger that came so swiftly in youth, and I had long since forgotten what else went with it. For the first time, though, I wondered what my father had felt when I'd got the same look on my face. I suspected it hadn't been pride.

Before I could say or do anything, Manohar stepped forward, and his voice took on a convincing, commanding tone. 'We had a deal, Hari. Let us go. You don't need us any more.'

'Oh please, Manohar! Nagarjuna's secret isn't some weapon of mass destruction, and I'm not some celluloid Dr Doom standing at the helm of a missile, waiting for you lot to play James Bond. This isn't about world domination or such villainous things. I was once a doctor, a man who saved lives. I approached the Custodians in the hope that they could help me, that transmutation could be used to prevent cancer and AIDS and…and delay cell degeneration to save people from starvation, even natural disasters. But did they help? No! What do a few hundred thousand lives matter when there is a secret to be kept… Hah! And once I left them, they hunted me down with a vengeance. My wife paid the price for their zeal.'

'Spare us the explanations. You brought us here under duress. We have no reason to care about any of this,' Manohar retorted. He was brimming with contempt, part of it, I suspected, directed at me.

Moorthy opened his mouth but appeared to have nothing to add. I couldn't see Maya. Despite the persistent sense of euphoria, a stabbing sensation that I didn't want to name shot through my gut.

Hari turned his attention to me. 'You're exceptionally quiet there, Asva.'

Manohar took a couple of steps forward, as though to pre-empt my speaking, but Hari responded by drawing his gun and holding it up in obvious view. He continued to address me, 'Here we are, standing before the one thing that can set you free... But you have nothing to say. How is that possible? Could it be, that for all your philosophizing, your anger and resentment, you actually think you *deserve* this long, endless life?'

For once, I had no pithy retort. It wasn't a state I found comfortable.

Amused by my obvious paralysis, Hari gloated, 'Come on, Asva! Isn't this the purpose for which you were put on this earth? Isn't this your karma? You are at the end of a long and difficult journey, my friend. It is time.'

I tried to find the right words to counter Hari's premise, to show him how unscientific his conclusions were. But I couldn't, for the agony of being the conundrum that I was:

To end this deathless existence, to destroy the aberration, I needed the science of its opposite, its counter-force. But the very nature of my aberration was that it was a hideous distortion of universal balance; it had no counter-force.

Energy is neither created nor destroyed; it merely changes form.

Einstein's theory of mass-energy equivalence not only reaffirmed the theories of conservation of energy that earlier scientists had put forth, but it also established what philosophers had been saying for aeons, that creation was made of energy and matter in interactive equilibrium with each other. The thing about matter was that, sooner or later, it decayed, broke down into smaller and smaller pieces of matter and energy. Even the super-stable proton, which would outlive the rest of the universe twenty times over, could split into positrons and pions. One could manipulate matter to harness its latent energy by breaking the bonds between atoms – the everyday processes of organic and chemical change, or by breaking within-atom bonds – to release nuclear energy.

Yet I endured, ostensibly without decay. It simply didn't make sense. Or did it?

No wonder then that Isaac Newton, the father of modern alchemy, had so desperately insisted that even light was corpuscular – made up of particles. His hypothesis had mired him in a lifetime of controversy and dispute with another scientist – Robert Hooke, a genial hunchback with a kind voice who'd also been the pioneer of...

'Cell theory,' I said out loud.

As one, friend and adversary alike looked at me. 'Cell theory,' I repeated. 'Cell theory holds that life... New cells can be created only by pre-existent cells. When cells replicate, the telomeres – or "end parts" – of their chromosomes protect the integrity of the genetic code that is transmitted. But over multiple replications, the telomere string shortens till the cell goes through programmed cell death, or apopstosis. Stem cells are the exception. They can synthesize telomerase, the enzyme that replenishes telomeres, making them – and I use the word in the biological sense – immortal. But here's where nature's safety fuse kicks in – when stem cells transform into organ-specific, differentiated cells, they lose the ability to make telomerase and so must, one day, die. Conversely, if normal cells mutate to develop the ability to replicate without limit, they lose some of their intended functionality. These are what we call cancers. And so you see the paradox – the greater the self-replication potential of the cell, the less its functionality. The few immortal creatures that occur in nature tend to be primitive, mostly unicellular organisms that do nothing other than renew or propagate themselves so that the species survives. In complex creatures, such as human beings, uncontrolled cell replication is a disease. Unless human DNA evolves such that each cell in the body could produce its own telomerase without losing its basic genetic structure and function...'

No sooner had I said the words than I realized that I was telling Hari exactly what he wanted to know.

It makes no difference. These arguments are specious. Or are they?

For his part, Hari was not convinced. He frowned and said, 'We've had this discussion before, Asva. You've pointed out, and I've agreed, that evolution takes centuries, even millennia. Mutagenesis is a slow, iterative process. The faster the mutation, the less chance of the organism's cells adapting to retain their original genetic functionality. Of course, radioactivity from substances like cesium or polonium, or a nuclear explosion, might be powerful enough to cause alteration, but then the organism's cells die rather quickly as a result, as does the being. So how...'

I tried to salvage what I could of the situation. 'Like I said from the very beginning, Hari. The idea that one can live forever or gain spider powers or x-ray vision through transmutation is simply bogus. Genetically speaking, your options are to either die or turn into an amoeba for the rest of forever.'

Hari said, 'And yet, you, my friend, did neither.'

Moorthy spared me the trouble of finding a response I did not have.

'What on earth are you two talking about?' he burst out. I could see from his face that his imagination had already made him suspect the worst, whatever he may have thought that was.

Hari didn't care to console him. 'Shut up, Moorthy!' he snapped. 'I've had enough of you and your lot. One more word, and I'll... Piggy! If Mr Moorthy speaks again, please shoot him, will you? As for Professor Bharadvaj here...'

Hari turned to me again. His voice was suddenly the calm, precise tenor that he used with throngs of ardent devotees

– the benevolent voice of a mighty but loving God. 'Are you going to hide again behind science and probabilities, Asva? Mutagenesis, myth, magic...what difference does it make? To what end is this argument? Tell me, upon your honour, do you not see that which you've been searching for all your life?' He smiled, satisfied at the thought that he had me trapped, for he knew I would not lie.

I dared not reply. I was aware of Manohar's eyes on me, boring into me as though he could not believe what I was about to do. I told myself I didn't care. Hari was right. My long search was at its end. I had earned this reprieve, endured every suffering to find this one chance. Nothing else mattered. Everyone and everything faded out of existence.

My gaze moved to the black altar.

A forgotten grace fluttered in my heart, a sensation I'd not known in a long, long time. Hope. The feeling was so alien that it left me breathless, delirious with anticipation – the way I'd felt when, as the man I no longer was, I'd worshipped knowledge. I'd wanted nothing more than to revel in learning, to follow in my father's footsteps to teach and share without reserve for I'd believed the essence of humanity was to strive towards something greater, something good.

And I'd killed to preserve that noble way of life.

Like a man who wakes within a nightmare to the cold reality of being asleep still, I lived again through the slaughter and, in its savage wake, I saw the truth: I saw greed rule the world, disguised in the extreme as righteousness, but most often tolerated as politics and her constant companion: Trade. The world that would now follow would be no different.

I saw Hari, many Haris, lording over a new global empire in which, life had a market value and, in inevitable response, death created demand. Bio-terrorism, environmental anarchy – fears of low probability and far-away futures were suddenly immediate, and drugs for arms took on a new meaning. A more horrifying meaning, that would lead us to another Great War, one that would make the last look like a silly playground skirmish. I'd once killed to protect the knowledge that I had held sacred. This time, I'd do whatever it took... Just as my kin had done.

And we worship the sacred with our actions, for all actions are sacrifice.

It didn't matter how I'd been made immortal. It only mattered why. I was the product of science, of knowledge so powerful and terrible, precious and precarious, that my family had protected it by hiding it in the best place possible, where it would neither be destroyed nor discovered: In plain sight.

The world would never forget Asvatthama, the warrior of myth, or the tale of his curse. They'd believe that he existed, but would never accept that he did – just as they'd believe in immortality, but would never accept it as reality. I hadn't been an accident or an act of magic, nor had I been forsaken. I had been the last and most powerful weapon of a terrible destruction that had heralded rebirth and revolution.

I had been sacrifice.

If I walked out of here and said to the first person I met that I was immortal, they'd laugh.

At that thought, so did I.

Warmth spread slowly through me, not quite as a sensation but more like settling into a state, like rippling water becoming still, as purpose and potential, intention and action all came together. At last, I returned to the moment. I found Hari studying me with eager curiosity, as though I were a lab animal, the outcome of an experiment. His question still stood between us.

I answered, 'Fuck you, Hari.'

Hari sighed and used the sight of his pistol to scratch resignedly at his forehead, as though he'd known it was all too good to be true. In any case, he was ready. He said to one of his henchmen, 'Bring her here.'

A gun-for-hire grabbed Maya by her arm and dragged her forward from the corner she had been in. She made not a sound, but her eyes remained on me and they revealed much. Relief. Fear. Despair. Apology. But, above all, they held calm acceptance, the same look I had seen when we had been trapped in the undersea cave at Somnath. A look that said she had known all along what would happen and accepted it without demur.

What happened next, though I'd expected it, had even prepared for it, was a silent kick in the gut. Hari handed his gun to Maya and said, 'Shoot that son of a bitch.'

36

If I wasn't shocked to see the gun in Maya's hands, her fingers wrapped around it with expert self-assurance, I was the only one. Save Hari, that was.

'Don't tell me...' Moorthy began, bristling at the sight of Maya and Hari next to each other, a strange familiarity between them.

Manohar was the first to reconcile to the new situation. He came to stand next to me, as though wanting to show our adversaries that I wasn't alone, and said, 'So you've been this bastard's whore all along, haven't you?'

'Watch it, Manohar. That's my father you're talking about.'

'*What?*' Moorthy and Manohar exclaimed as one.

'She means stepfather,' I explained. The turn of events was unforseen but not inexplicable. *He'll be ashamed of me when he hears of what I said...* She'd used those exact words, not long ago, at Diu. The only words she'd spoken in the present, because her stepfather was alive and well, and screwing me over in every way he could.

'You *knew?*' she asked me, eyes narrowed with suspicion. I shrugged by way of response. Her disbelief was evident, as was Manohar's. After all, she'd gone to extreme lengths to keep her cover – including getting beaten up by Moorthy and his goons and losing her piece of the Vajra. But I had no doubt that the courage she'd shown at Somnath and on other occasions had been real. And she had kept her anger in check even when she'd come face to face with the man she recognized as her mother's murderer. That sort of fortitude had to count for something.

'Of course he knew,' Hari replied in my stead. 'But denial is a powerful force. Don't look so shaken, Manohar. You really think my daughter couldn't hold her own against the likes of Moorthy and Rohit? No offence...' he added, directing the last remark at the latter. Before the goon could react, Hari continued, 'You can call it miscommunication or a mistake, but she assumed they were acting on my orders and let them slap her around so that you two wouldn't suspect that she meant for them to take the Vajra fragment. Of course, she wasn't completely wrong – Rohit was and is my man, and I did get my fragment, so... As for the Professor, he saw what he wanted to see: A woman tough enough to turn him on, but not so tough that she didn't need rescuing and not so smart that he couldn't mansplain away to glory. Arrogance and denial. So predictably you, Asva.'

Maya appeared reluctant to accept Hari's explanation. She said, mostly mocking but not without a touch of wistfulness, 'Oh, I think the Professor here was a little more...involved than that. Weren't you?'

As always, I used innuendo to keep from having to lie, though I did want to believe that I had felt nothing for her and never would. 'Did you really think I was?'

Her knuckles whitened as she clutched the gun tighter in a bid to cover her uncertainty. She argued, 'And you saved my life? Why did you do that?'

'What the fuck was I supposed to do? Watch as you were raped and killed? Just because you're a bitch and your father's an asshole?'

Hari said, 'Ah, Asva. Chivalry? Or affection? Pity we won't find out! Shoot, Maya.'

'That threat is redundant, and you know it, Hari.'

'You've no idea what threats I'm capable of, Asva. Come on, Maya.'

I ignored him and addressed Maya instead, 'It was your father who told you how to get past the snakes at Srisailam, right?'

Pride shone strong through the many emotions Maya appeared to be struggling with. 'Yes. It was quite easy, you know. All I had to do was take the herbal antidote, and then stay calm and let the snakes bite as I moved through the tunnel.'

Hari added, 'Of course, in the olden days, even the antidote was unnecessary. *Siddha*s could use the power of meditation to bring down their heart rate enough to stay alive and let the venom pass out of their system. I expected my passionate, excitable daughter might have trouble with that, so I gave her the antidote. But she did me proud, Asva. Didn't panic in the least. A woman like her could do magnificent things with the Vajra and its power.'

'Honestly, Maya,' I interrupted, 'doesn't it make you sick when he talks that way? I've no idea what goes on in this creep's mind, but it doesn't sound pretty… And you, Hari, when did you go from using your daughter to do your dirty work to pimping her out? Was getting her to fuck me always part of your plan?'

Hari retorted, 'I don't know when you lost faith in yourself, Asva, but I didn't think you were susceptible to seduction. Nor could I have forced this girl to do anything she didn't want to. She acted of her own free will. As for my "plan", as you call it, as I said before, I'd have told you the truth, I'd have asked for your help rather than play you, if only your oversized ego hadn't got in the way.'

'Say what you like, Hari. It doesn't make you any less of an asshole.'

'Shut up!' Hari snapped, his impatience finally revealed. Turning to Maya, he again ordered, 'Shoot.'

Once more, Maya looked at me. My silence told her what she wanted to know. She dropped her arm, letting the gun point to the ground. Moorthy let out a gasp of relief. Manohar stood, unmoving.

I had hardly taken a step forward, when Hari grabbed Maya's hand, wrapped his fingers over hers, raised the weapon and pressed down on the trigger. The gun went off, twice in quick succession. The shrill after-shriek of speeding bullets rang around the cavern, ascending to a roll of echoes that drowned out Maya's shout of protest. I acted out of instinct, throwing myself at Manohar, taking him down with me behind the sacrificial altar. More shots resounded through the cavern; I fell to the floor. Moorthy was shouting over the din as he crawled towards me.

'Arunachaleshwara!' he exclaimed. 'Are you...?'

'I'm fine. It's Manohar. He's hurt.'

I didn't add 'badly' for that much was obvious. The bullet had hit Manohar in the chest, and only the fact that he was alive and conscious, though barely so, suggested that it had not gone point blank through his heart.

Moorthy ripped open Manohar's t-shirt. He retched at the sight left by the mushrooming bullet but then pulled himself together and set about fashioning a compress with his belt. As he pressed down, blood sprayed from the wound in an obscene fountain, splattering on to our faces. Moorthy cursed and wiped his face with his shirtsleeve. I didn't care. I murmured incoherent words of encouragement to Manohar and tried to lift his head. He let out a feeble moan; the sound was drowned out by a fresh burst of gunfire. Hari's voice followed, loud and mocking. 'It's your fault, Asva. I didn't want to do this, but you forced my hand. He's going to die unless you help him, unless you do what needs to be done.'

Moorthy scowled. 'What the hell is he talking about, Professor? He goes on and on about you...'

'Shut up, Moorthy,' I said.

He gnashed his teeth in response.

Around us, I could hear Rohit issue orders to his men. Just to make sure we knew where we stood, he let loose another round of gunfire. The bullets grazed the upper surface of the sacrificial altar, sending up small sparks.

'Stop!' Hari's command sounded over the shots. 'He's dying, Asva. You know it. You can save him.'

I tried to not listen to that wise voice, to ignore the conviction it held. A smell rose in the air, the smell of fresh blood and more.

'Does it ever get familiar?' Hari persisted. 'How many deaths lie on your head, Asva? Does the blood ever wash off? This is your chance. Give the human race the gift of eternal life and then we can tell the whole world who you really are. You needn't fear ridicule, because you would be their saviour; you'd be a god! Imagine that, Asva; just imagine that. Remember what it was like, to have a name, an identity, honour? And once there are more like you, you'd no longer be an aberration or an outcast; you'd be the first of a new breed of strong, noble humans, the kind the planet now needs. You can even have a family, your own family of immortals. Yes! You'd never be alone again. Come on out and help me save Manohar. Make him like you.'

The words painted a picture of the life that had never been mine, of the world that had been taken away from me once, and then time and again. I saw myself as a man, merely a man, spending days of quiet contentment. I felt happiness, the kind that needed no reason but that of being human. I knew love, and I swore to protect those whom I loved with all I had, and it shone within me as a blazing, blinding light. I watched as that dazzling amorphous affection moulded itself into the form of a brave, strong man, a man who as was proud of me as I was of him, for in his eyes, I was a hero of legend and not some murdering monster; I was a good man, as I could have once been.

Manohar.

'Professor, no....' Moorthy grabbed desperately at my arm. 'For God's sake, please don't...you can't tell him...'

He caught my gaze and stopped short. I knew what it was that he saw, what it was that seeped out through my every pore, threatening to burn everything in existence. Rage. Not the red-hot mindlessness of great anger but white heat and ice, the cold precision of a predator in the precise moment when teeth sunk through flesh to meet warm, sweet, *living* blood, and fury slaked its thirst on life. I felt my eyes blaze.

Shaking off Moorthy's ineffective grip, I stepped out from behind the altar stone.

37

Rohit was immediately on me. He swung the butt of his rifle into my face. I went down sideways from the impact. He took the opportunity to wring my right arm behind my back and used it to maintain a hold on me as he dragged me towards Hari.

'Let's be direct about all of this, Asva,' Hari said. 'We both know what this place does, the question is: How is it set into motion? The truth, please!'

'Can I ever speak anything but?' I snapped, biding my time. I was rewarded with an impenitent kick to my groin from Rohit.

As I doubled over in agony, held up only by the hired muscle's grip on my arm, Hari said, 'So, when it comes down to balls and brass tacks, you're just a man after all, aren't you, Asva? How pathetic!' He stepped up to lay a sharp slap, more humiliating than hurtful, on my face. It made me wonder how much he hated me.

A gleeful Rohit took the act as a sign to shove me to my knees. Then he pressed the tip of his gun into the back of my head and gestured to Rahul and the others.

Stealthy but steadfast, the men advanced upon the sacrificial altar. I heard the telltale click of the safety catch on their guns and then a snide whisper about wasting bullets on a dying man.

I moved.

My right leg shot back, muscle and bone acting as one to drive my heel into Rohit's kneecap. He screamed. I spun around, grabbing the barrel of the gun he had to my head, wedging my finger behind the trigger so that he couldn't shoot. In the same instant I drove the tip of my shoe into his pelvic joint and pulled him down by his hold on the gun, using the counter-force to lift and throw him. He took to the air with a diver's grace, cutting an arc to land head first behind me.

I wrested the gun from his grasp and was up on my feet at once, firing at Piggy, who was almost upon Manohar. A third man raised his gun to shoot at me, but Moorthy lost no time in tackling him to the ground. The Custodian's eyes held the courage of a man ultimately vindicated. I didn't complain, but turned to face the remaining three mercenaries.

Rahul was, in the emotionally inexplicable way of kin, shaking Rohit hard, hoping to bring him back to life. It gave me an edge that the de facto leader of the gang had been the first to fall, but now I had his infuriated brother to deal with. Rahul let out a blood-curdling yell and stormed at me, his clenched fists opening into talons. In his mind, he'd already sunk his nails into me, ripped my skin off my flesh with his bare hands. I didn't doubt that he could make good on his intent. I tried to shoot, found the clip empty, and had to settle for swinging my gun at him. The blow knocked his rifle out of his hands, leaving us even.

The new odds dawned on Hari. Snarling, he raised his pistol, but out of the corner of my eye I saw Maya grab his hand. Shots rang in the air – two, and then two more – but nothing caught me. Hari pistol-whipped Maya across the face and then ordered one of the mercenaries to subdue her. I saw the man, a big guy with a wannabe seaman tattoo on his arm, seize Maya from behind and push her down. She resisted, but her resolve was gone; her world as she'd believed it to be had been destroyed in an instant by Hari's actions. With quiet satisfaction, I turned my back to the scene. I was just in time: Rahul and the Slovak stormed at me.

I launched myself at Rahul, butting him head-on, wrapping my arms around his waist and running my shoulder into him again. He was a big man, and though he doubled over, he didn't fall. He grappled back, while his imported counterpart drove his elbow down again and again on my spine.

The Slovak had not bothered to carry a gun, and with good reason. He drew a long, serrated hunting knife from his leg-strap. At the same time, he used his other hand to pull out a small dagger hidden up his sleeve and flick it at my eye. I barely ducked in time.

Rahul used my momentary distraction to come out the better from our tussle. He drove his knee into my stomach and switched his grip into a chokehold on my neck. Using brute strength against me, he twisted upwards till he was standing right behind me, my head caught in the crook of his left arm, his right arm wrapped across in an arm-bar. I drove my elbow into his ribs, tried to crunch my heel down on his toe, but he was an experienced fighter and merely sneered at these elementary defences.

The Slovak twirled his knife in a fancy display that he probably thought intimidating. I felt sorry for him; he didn't know better than to face Asvatthama, son of Dronacharya, with a blade. I gave up trying to get out of the chokehold and used both my hands to grab my new assailant's wrist. Rahul continued to throttle my neck, while the Slovak slashed me once, then again, drawing blood. Then, despite my resistance, he thrust the knife more determinedly into my flesh. I saw Moorthy begin to run towards us, having disposed of Piggy, but he would be too late to help – between a broken neck and disembowelment, or both, I had about three seconds to avoid an excruciating experiment with eternity.

I yanked the Slovak forward. He yielded with a startled look, his immense weight driving the blade towards me. Adding my own strength to the thrust, I shifted. A hoarse shout escaped me as the knife's jagged edge caught me on the right, tearing through skin and onwards to its intended destination behind me – Rahul's liver. I added what force I could to the thrust. The blade plunged into Rahul's torso.

I returned my attention to the Slovak, pressing down on his wrist with my thumb, compressing the pressure point between his two tendons. It wasn't enough to make him fall down in a faint or even let go of the knife, but it gave me the traction I needed to wring his hand, and the blade with it. The knife drilled deeper into Rahul's flesh, cutting open a wedge-shaped wound. But I wasn't done.

Using the weight of my entire body, I pressed the hilt outwards and up, changing the angle of the blade within Rahul's body. It ripped through his stomach to strike his kidneys and sever the muscles around his bladder. The stink of urine filled the air, mixing with the iron-smell of blood and flesh. I let go. The Slovak shuffled back, wide-eyed with dread and anger. Blood rained over the three of us as the hunting knife was ripped out of Rahul's body. He met the ground with a thud, the resultant red puddle staining my shoes and trousers.

That left the imported thug. I lashed out with my left leg, feeling his arm break from the impact. His knife fell to the ground. I pivoted in the air, bringing my other leg up in a textbook martial arts flying kick to the side of his face. He staggered back. I bent down to pick up the knife he had dropped, ready to finish him off. But Moorthy spared me the dirty work. A short burst of gunfire and it was over, or almost.

Rahul's moans were eerily muted as he twitched and thrashed in his own blood. He would take some time to die, and it wouldn't be easy. I nodded to Moorthy, who put him out of his misery.

The respite was brief; there was a scream and then the sounds of a small scuffle. A distant part of my brain noted that Hari was trying to escape and that Maya was trying to stop him. Before Moorthy or I could respond to her warning call, Hari was gone, making his way down the passage by which we'd entered the cavern. Maya crumpled to the ground, her body heaving with quiet sobs. She would have to wait.

Willing energy and clarity back into me, I forced myself to move, first going over to Maya to pry the Vajra out of her clenched fist and then running ran back to where I had left Manohar.

'Moorthy!' I shouted to him, even as he followed me. 'Moorthy, help me! We need to get Manohar on to the altar.'

Moorthy grunted with the effort as we hoisted a wheezing, groaning Manohar on to the sacrificial altar, laying him out on the cold stone. 'What...what are you going to do?' he asked me.

I didn't know how to explain what I had to do, or why I had to do it. Vengeance meant little when those we avenged were gone; all it left was a dark, endless void within, a void that I no longer had the strength to carry. I didn't care whether it was science or faith that drove my actions, nor did I consider what would become of me if the power of the altar were unleashed. All I knew was that, for the first time, I feared death, but the death was not mine.

Holding the Vajra in one hand, I used the other to place the knife I had picked up against Manohar's throat. His eyes opened at its cold touch. He cast around, disoriented with the pain, before eventually focusing on me.

'Professor...n-no!' Manohar grabbed weakly at my arm. His eyes held every emotion I could have hoped to see, and it was reprieve and torment, both. 'Someday...' he whispered.

He could say no more, but he didn't need to. I understood what it was he wanted to tell me. It was what the spirits of my fellow scholars and kin waited for, having sacrificed me to keep the spark alive. It was what Nagarjuna held on to through the metaphor of his promised resurrection, having hidden what he'd discovered and then dying to keep that secret. *Someday...*

Someday, humanity would find immortality and it would be neither science nor sorcery but natural evolution to achieve our true potential. Someday we would all be immortal. Someday, we would all be one with light. *Till then...*

Till then, I'd be the only one.

I raised Manohar into a sitting position, holding him close with one arm, letting his blood coat me as my father's once had on a battlefield long ago. Manohar tried to speak, but the effort it took him set off a racking cough. Red sputum spewed from his mouth, the viscous blood of his lacerated chest and intestines. I let drop the knife and cradled his head.

He smiled; proud, devoted, content. Then, he closed his eyes.

I wanted to say many things, to tell him that I'd hoped that someday, at the edge of an eternity beyond his reach, when I was finally gone, he would light my pyre; that he was my soul's heir of this lifetime and the only one who could send me into my father Agni's embrace. But the language we used wasn't mine any more. The only tongue I knew was the one with which I had praised Rudra for as long as I had known. The only words I had were prayer.

Agni, my father, take this man's being. Rudra, accept this offering that I was to have made millennia ago. Let him be one with you, in that oneness that is not the end but the beginning of all things.

The pulse at Manohar's throat weakened. I held him till it was imperceptible. Then I let him go.

My fingers curled again around the knife; I stood up and strode, determined, to where Maya sat huddled on the floor. The man who had earlier grappled with her lay dead, a couple of metres away. The bruise on his neck evidenced a precisely placed kick to the carotid sinus – a feat that required as much skill as it did strength. In the given circumstances, I felt little joy that the tough Ms Jervois had, once again, shown herself to be more than a meek desk-agent. I had other things on my mind.

I slapped her hard, bringing her out of her daze. She met my accusatory glare with calm acceptance. That further infuriated me. My fingers weaved into her hair, but it was hardly a tender act. She cried out as I used my grip on her to bring her to her feet. I let her feel the flat of the blade, warm with Manohar's blood, my blood, the blood of our enemies, against the intimate flesh of her stomach. A medley of emotions flashed across her face – fear, sadness, regret. I didn't care.

'Do it, Professor,' Maya whispered. 'Do it quickly, and... and then you can set yourself free...' She teetered, unsteady and unable to finish.

I tightened my grasp on her, making her flinch again. Then, silently cursing every god I could think of, I let go of her and hurled my knife at the unyielding rock around us.

'It's over.' The statement came from Moorthy, but its tone was new. It held a sense of calm and lightness that was vaguely familiar, like a shadow of someone I had met before. He would have made his Ayya proud.

But there was no time for such superfluous words. I said, 'Not yet. You need to get out of here as quickly as you can. Use the Vajra.'

The two of them exchanged baffled looks. Before they could voice their confusion, I placed the stone medallion on Moorthy's palm, aligning it into position relative to the sacrificial altar. 'Follow the other half of the pattern. It's an exit map of the maze, a fail-safe device. No one can leave this place without taking something of it back into the world. This isn't a legend that will die easily. But its time has not yet come.'

'But...' The interjection came from Maya. She did not say more, and her gaze swept over the altar before coming to rest on me with sad comprehension.

I took a piece of paper from my pocket and, handing it to Maya, instructed, 'Take the guns; you'll need to kill those two goons outside. Then head back to the park and call this number. Tell whoever picks up that you need an immediate exit and give them your location. Someone will come for you. Leave with them. Don't wait for me.'

I quickly added, as Moorthy began to protest, 'Don't worry. I'll deal with Hari.'

He nodded, satisfied.

'Take care, Professor.' Maya's eyes held finality.

'Go now, both of you,' I repeated. 'Get yourselves out.'

With that, I turned to go after Hari.

38

I followed sound through darkness to find Hari in a circular, moss-lit chamber that we had not been in before, on his knees, wheezing and panting. He held up a hand as I came in, indicating that I wait. I did, without complaint. We both knew there was nowhere else to go, for the room was a dead end, one of the many labyrinthine traps Nagarjuna and his colleagues had left for us.

At length, Hari settled himself into a comfortable, cross-legged position, flashing me a grateful look. I shook my head in indulgent disapproval and lowered myself down to the floor with the telltale grunt of a man my age.

He began, as he had many a conversation, with, 'Do you remember that film we watched together, one drunken night? It was called… Oh, I forget what it was called, but it was some wham-bam action flick. We laughed about how, even with a dozen guns around, in the end it always came down to a fist fight. Of course, thinking back, it wasn't all that funny. Must have been the ganja in our veins…'

'Go on…' I prompted. Suddenly, I had all the time in the world.

'It's not dumb, you know. Guns are...unnatural. Once you're trained to use them, you might think of them as an extension of yourself, as you've said you do a sword, but to me, both are externalities. For years, I couldn't bear to pick up either one. Not even to put myself out of my misery. But a man like you doesn't think twice about killing, does he?'

'Indeed. A man with a destination cannot wander, Hari.'

Hari laughed; the sound echoed off the walls in an eerie shriek. 'Death is the ultimate destination, Asva, the ultimate purpose. Manohar died to protect the secret of eternal life. His blood will stain your fate, one more innocent man dead by your hand. I too shall die here, but I will go with the satisfaction that I've dared reach for the impossible – for what is the meaning of life but what we leave behind after our death? And I leave behind Maya... You let her go, didn't you? I knew it; I knew you wouldn't be able to kill her, you bastard. I played you once again! The final victory will still be mine! Live with that. Live with the regret. Live forever!' He began cackling like a man gone mad, beating the ground with his hands, kicking his feet in the air.

I watched Hari execute the display to his fill and finally settle down into quiet chuckles. I wanted to explain to him how he was wrong, how it was *I* who had manipulated him, fully aware that he would give up his own life to give Maya her chance at escape, out of ambition if not out of paternal love. Her chance was also my calculated gamble – if she were indeed the daughter Hari believed her to be then, sooner or later, she would lead me to any associates or other loose ends that he might have left behind.

But my actions had come of another wager, the kind that he hadn't expected me to make, the kind that was meant to be lost. And Hari, I knew, wouldn't understand. His world was a vindictive one, as mine had been for so long: A world where one either embraced power or forever ran from it, a world where darkness, as we saw it, had to be fought with light, as we believed it to be. The world I now saw was beyond such dualities, a world where death was not the antithesis to life. A world where humanity was defined by much more than impermanence. A world where death was sacrifice, and it was good.

Manohar had reminded me of that.

Out loud I said, 'I'm not immortal, Hari. I'm just a man blessed with a very, very long life so that someday I can watch and rejoice as humanity discovers its own divinity, the real immortality that it seeks. That is the only answer I have ever needed and, for whatever remains of my existence, it is enough. As for the immediate and practical matter of whether or not eternity lies hidden within these walls…'

I reached out to switch on the flashlight Hari carried but had feared to use, letting brightness flood through and beyond the space between us. He gasped as, around us, the muted glow of the moss changed colour, from green to red, to bright orange and blazing yellow before turning finally into the purest, brightest white. No stone, no walls, no sense of place or time. There was only brightness, and it pressed down, more terrifying than any darkness, suffocating, maddening. One could bear it, fight it, despair of it or surrender to it and, eventually, just when it seemed one couldn't take it any more, one would find, the brightness lay within. Such was the power of light.

I switched off the torch. Hari blinked. His face showed dismay but also sadness, as though he had touched the edge of the inconceivable but had been forced back into the gloaming before he could see it.

I stood up, dusted my hands on my pants and took the single step that lay between us. Hari gave me a sidelong glance that was curious, childlike. I cradled his head in both my hands and, leaning down, whispered the truth of Nagarjuna and his secret into his ear.

Hari's breath came in a sigh, and I felt his jaw move as though he wanted to speak. But he did not get the chance. I knew he meant to thank me, for he would feel no pain. Done right, his snapped vertebra would instantly sever his spinal cord, putting an end to all sensation and cognition that was deemed life. Perhaps it was more than he deserved, but I wouldn't deny him what I didn't have.

Someday...

His head ensconsed in my grip, I twisted.

They trust me because they trust their horses, and their horses trust me. Not everyone can earn the right to tame these wild, unfettered creatures, these free-spirited stallions with their powerful chests and proud haunches. But they let me ride them; they come at my call, nuzzling up to me as though I were an old friend. Animals, they say, have an instinct for men, for the sort of man one is. I don't claim to be a good man, but I am a man free of guilt, unbound by any human device, including judgement.

The tribe has been my home ever since they found me, wounded and mindless, on the barren slopes of these mountains. If they haven't treated me with the suspicion that strangers merit in these parts, it is because of the horses. The man whose hearth I have eaten at all these days – an old man named Elam – tells the story often of how the animals of the tribe milled around me, licking my face as I lay staring into the sun, conscious but insentient. I cannot remember any of that, and the fleeting memories I have of searching for a way out, day after day through endless darkness, are now ephemeral dreams. This forgetfulness is a cherished feeling.

To think that in my long and tiring past there are moments that I will never recall makes me feel grateful.

I work in the fields alongside the nomads of what is now *my* tribe, toiling harder than them all to repay what I can of the kindness they have shown me. They call me Aimal, which means 'friend', and I respond in my heavily accented Pashto. The rest of my time I spend with the horses, uncaring of borders, of disputes and money, drugs, wars and politics. Sometimes we hear trucks and gunfire, and the tribe retreats further into the mountains. The world as it is is far away from here.

The winter is long and harsh. The tribe stays put. Occasionally, we hunt. They don't ask me how I know to fire a gun or to track game. In fact, they've never asked me anything, not even Elam. When the thaw finally comes, it brings news of a Pir — a holy man with the power to cure all ills. The tribe moves as one towards where he was last seen. We meet others on the way, and they ask who I am. Elam only says, 'He is one of us.'

The Pir is a young man; his eyes are familiar, very familiar, and he holds my gaze for a long time. Later, Elam asks me what I was thinking of when I met the Pir. I tell him it is time for me to go home.

There are many dawns, many dusks, many days of nothing. I make my way eastward. Things such as passports and credit cards come to mind, but I have none. I work my way, with nothing to lose or gain, through Afghanistan, China, Nepal.

There are bar fights and landslides. I break my arm. It heals. I twist my ankle. That heals too. I carry on.

I spend many weeks in Tibet, helping out at an Australian Red Cross camp. I hear of a group that needs a French-speaking guide on their trek to the Annapurna Base Camp and make myself useful in return for a decent payment that I spend on books and woollen clothing for children of a neighbouring village. As the flow of adventurers and tourists dwindles, I know the summer is over. I cross into India through the mountains – taking up with saffron-clad mystics who are making their way down from their Himalayan retreat through the Garhwal range. I refuse to take alms though, and work my way as I can or starve. After all, hunger can hurt, but it can't kill.

No matter how many steps I take, it sometimes feels as though I remain in the same place, though in my heart I know that I need to keep walking. Moving ahead becomes like breathing and I go on, thoughtless. No man should ever have to outlive his children or his home, but that is what I have done, and will do yet.

I reach my goal without knowing it.

I am suddenly aware of time. I stand, as I once did, on the banks of the Ganga, in Kashi, mindful of the actual number of days, that have passed since I last stood here, ready to leave it all behind but for Manohar's phone call.

Fourteen months. I am back again, nameless.

I examine my reflection in the river: My sunken eyes and tattered clothes, my long, matted hair and dirt-flecked grey-black beard. I haven't a coin in my pocket, and my stomach is taut with a week's deprivation. Beginning all over again is far from difficult – money, clothes, a place to live – I have much of those in storage. But what needs to be done before I can live that illusory life again needs be done honestly.

One step at a time.

I spend the day at the ghats, working as a scavenger, clearing away the remains of burnt bodies and ash-coated offerings of flowers and cooked rice. I earn thirty rupees, the sum officially bringing me out of government-delineated poverty. It is enough for me to eat a humble meal, smoke a beedi, and pay a barber in the morning. I find a place for the night by the funeral pyres, next to an ash-smeared sadhu who is wearing a garland of bones carved into the shape of tiny human skulls. He takes a break from his meditation by a fresh pile of human ashes and is kind enough to share his chillum of ganja with me over an enthusiastic debate on the nature of afterlife, at the end of which he blesses me with the choicest of boons he has to offer – liberation without rebirth.

The last time I'd heard those words, it had been in my own voice. I accept the benediction humbly, before lying back against the damp step that is my bed for tonight. I wait for the memories, the recrimination and the guilt to come, but they don't. I am ready.

Come morning, I'd get myself a long overdue haircut and a shave from a barber whose place of work is the waterside. I bathe in the river, doing the best I can to clean up – enough to find a job as a daily labourer in a construction yard. I spend the next week breaking stones and carrying bags of cement up six flights of scaffolding for ten hours a day. But already I have climbed the social ladder, and by the sixth day, I save enough. I make my way to the ghats, wearing a cheap new dhoti and carrying the required offering of rice, clothing and money. A priest comes up to me; he seems familiar. Even before he begins to pitch his offer to perform the last rites for seven generations of my ancestors, I engage his services.

He sets us up on the lowermost steps that lead to the water, laying out all his paraphernalia next to the river. I step into the water, submerging myself in that green murkiness, and emerge purified. The priest gestures; I sit, cross-legged, and switch my brand-new sacred thread to my other shoulder. It is always to be worn in reverse when performing last rites.

I recite the initial mantras outlining my lineage, the names of three generations of ancestors, inviting them to partake of and witness this offering.

'For whom?' the priest asks.

The words are unexpectedly difficult. 'For my son. His name was Manohar.'

Five hours later, wearing a pair of fake Levi's jeans and a khadi kurta bought from a roadside stall, I board the first-class compartment of a train and leave Kashi behind. I had needed only two of those five hours to make sure that neither legacy nor trace remained of the man I'd known as Hari.

This city is called Bengaluru, a name inspired by the tale of a wandering king and the village chieftain who had offered him boiled peanuts to eat. The first time I'd come here, many millennia ago, it had borne no name but that of its people – a forest-dwelling tribe that lived around a hill, the foundations of which can be seen even today in the city's Lalbagh Botanical Gardens. If I had a day for every time I have heard the modern label of 'forest-dweller' and 'tribal' used as a synonym for 'uncivilized', I could live forever. I chuckle quietly, enjoying the private joke, and make my way into the cool interiors of a large Café Coffee Day that flanks Cubbon Park, the patch of greenery at the heart of the city.

Moorthy stands as soon as he sees me. He comes forward and takes my hand, pumping it vigorously as he says, 'I can't believe it! I really can't believe it! It's good to see you, Professor.'

'Likewise, Moorthy. Thanks for coming.'

'It's a pleasure, to say the least. When that phone rang, two days ago, I didn't even dream that it would be you.'

We sit down as a uniformed young woman comes to take our orders. The lack of conversation between us is comfortable, but I am aware that Moorthy has much to ask. He already knows, from our exchange on the phone, what had happened to me since he and Maya made their way out of that cavern, and I have heard from him that the two of them have, after a fashion, returned to their lives as they had been just over a year ago.

I ask him about the Vajra. He tells me it has been dismantled again into three. I do not ask what has become of the fragments, but he tells me, without being prompted, that he knows the location of only one piece, and that secret he intends to take with him to his Maker. We then speak about some of the logistics and loose ends, but the central mystery endures. I believe he deserves an answer.

Moorthy apparently feels so too, for about halfway though our coffees, he says, 'I didn't believe... I didn't believe in it all. Not till I grasped who you are.'

'Oh? Who am I?'

'I'm not sure I even want to try to put it into words, Professor. The past months have been the ultimate test of faith for me. I'm willing to take this part of it on exactly that – faith. But...'

'Hmm?'

'It sounds...well...ridiculous.'

I smile. 'Your Ayya saw me for who I am. You've seen it for yourself too and, someday, you'll come to terms with it. Perhaps, when you do, we shall meet again.'

'What do you mean, Professor?'

I take a sip of my coffee. 'Do you know the story of Ekalavya, from the Mahabharata?'

Moorthy nods. 'He was a forest-dwelling hunter and an excellent archer. It was his life's dream to train under Dronacharya. Drona, however, was afraid that this hunter boy might be a better archer than his best – and favourite – student Arjun. So he told Ekalavya that if the boy truly considered him a guru, then a fee was in order – *gurudakshina*. When Ekalavya acknowledged as much, Drona asked him for the thumb of his arrow hand. Ekalavya cut it off and gave it to Drona without demur.'

I say, 'This is one of those stories that is as true as it can get; one where fact is as strange as fable. Ekalavya did indeed sacrifice his thumb, but he went on to become one hell of an archer even without it. He earned a heroic name for himself before he died. But no grandmother ever tells that story.'

'I'm not surprised. History is always written by the victors. Ekalavya certainly wasn't on the winning side.'

'Neither was I. And that is how I know: There is no human element more precious than fallibility. Nor is there a greater curse. It is…an unfathomable pain, one that you might touch the fringes of when you see an immaculate piece of art or read a book that slams you in the gut with its honest beauty. Such frailty breeds envy, a most evil despondence as you realize that such beauty is not of your creation but is born of the brilliance of another. It brings anger at one's self, at the whole world, and rage at having been shown that things are so. It's the darkest depth of the human psyche, for it can turn what is good, even godly, into the worst of motivations. But sometimes that feeling is the most sublime of sensations because it holds safe in its own despair a kernel of happiness, of hope.'

'But…'

I ignore the interjection and close my eyes. 'When I saw that hunter boy standing there, I thought the envy, the sorrow, the hurt that I then felt would never stop. But it did. You see, Moorthy, it didn't matter that I'd never be the perfect warrior that he was. What mattered was that I would spend the rest of my life trying. And that makes life worth living.'

I emerge from my contemplation to see that Moorthy does not fully understand. He does not need to. 'I'm not a physicist, Moorthy,' I continue. 'I was once a philosopher of sorts, and now call myself a historian. But the essential nature of knowledge is that no matter what lens you use to look at it, it still makes sense. Whether I quote Niels Bohr or the Upanishads, the concept is the same: duality. A universe in balance. Light and dark. Death and life. But the mystery of immortality is that we do not know its antithesis. Endless life is implausible but comprehensible. But endless death? Can such a thing exist? Blinded by my own need, I was looking for the nullifier, the counter-force that could destroy immortality. It was my karma to not find it, for it has taken me this long to truly understand…duality isn't about opposites, it is about complements, things that give meaning to the other. If we think of immortality as the perpetual endurance of matter, then the source of balance or duality I sought wasn't the antimatter which neutralized it, but that which give meaning to it — energy.'

Moorthy disagrees. I expect him to; it is what I've done for ages. 'Professor, you know, I'm sure, that the concept of perpetual energy is contrary to Newton's third law. It has been deemed impossible in reality.'

'And that, my friend, is where Ekalavya comes in. You see, Ekalavya and I, we were contemporaries, enemies, rivals… two men who sought the same goal but knew only one of us could reach it, not unlike Isaac Newton and Robert Hooke.'

'So that's how you made the link to Cell Theory and to genetic mutation. Thinking about Newton and his law brought you to Hooke. But how does the notion of quantum duality get us past the evolution issue, Professor? The fact that rapid mutation causes genetic instability?'

'Consider the parallels: In reality, to borrow your words, only matter begets matter. Only a living cell can produce another living cell. Both are subject to natural laws of decay. A unicellular lifeform – a cell with neither death nor function – might lose energy only during the process of replication and so maintain a near-stable state for millennia...and appear to us to be immortal. But in complex organisms, unlimited cell replication is a disease – *unless* some source of perpetual energy keeps the cell in stable state, that is, fully capable of its original genetic function. Which is why, Newton was adamant that Hooke was wrong, not about Cell Theory, but about...'

'Light!'

I nod. 'Light. The eternal metaphor for knowledge. Newton refuted Hooke's theory that light was composed of energy waves. Instead he claimed it was made of tiny particles – a claim that would support the idea of perpetual energy... or perpetual motion, to use the proper term. Einstein resolved the dispute decades later by stating that light can also behave like particles of matter. Indeed, it is now established that all subatomic particles potentially are both energy and matter, but at any time, only one property can be observed – Bohr's Complementarity Principle. Hardly a few months ago, theoretical physicists put up the idea that photons – the elementary particle in light – can be manipulated to create matter from pure energy. What was once deemed impossible – the alchemical vision of turning energy into matter – now appears to be within reach, though I think our ancestors might have had their own breakthroughs on the topic.'

Moorthy frowns in concentration as he puts the pieces together. 'So, not only is light both matter and energy, it is also the key to conversion of energy into perpetual or self-renewing matter…?'

'Yes, but I don't know exactly how that is. I have no doubt we could've found out, but as a good man once told me, not all mysteries are meant to be solved.'

'Then… I can understand not letting a man like Hari control it, but surely, this is something that we ought to share with the world, with science? At the very least, *you* could have used it, Professor. Maybe you could have saved…'

He does not say the name, and I know he still feels the pain. But time heals all, and there are forces in the world greater than time. He too will heal.

I tell him, 'Look at you, Moorthy, at your own eagerness. You're not Hari. You have nothing but good intentions in you, yet your fervour isn't very different. Why? Because you see immortality, *my immortality*, as valuable, more precious than human frailty. But it is not. I've had all the time in the world to learn better, but even so, my actions in Nagarjuna's chamber weren't driven by reason but by rage and passion. It was Manohar who…'

I falter, then continue. 'I, the immortal, failed where the mortal succeeded. The antithesis to eternal existence is not that which has forever ceased to be, rather, it is that which is yet to come into existence – what the scholars of old called – the pure potential of primordial creation. "*There was neither non-existence nor existence...*" the Ṛg Veda tells us before asking, "*what stirred then?*" The question is somewhat rhetorical, since the particular hymn ends with the observation that "*perhaps the primordial creator knew the answers, or even he knew them not.*" Such are the answers we seek, Moorthy. Humanity was meant for more, and discovering the secret to so-called eternal life, to this limited, physical deathlessness will only get in the way. Manohar saw it, my own forebears saw it, and even Nagarjuna saw it. I must carry this burden alone. I must remain a myth, a symbol of failure and sin, a part of history that ought not to be written into record.'

Moorthy studies me, deliberating whether to delve further or let the matter go. He decides on the latter. 'What now, Professor?' he asks, as though I have left no questions, quotidian or otherwise, unanswered.

'Now, go back to your friends. I'm sure the Vajra wasn't your only duty. With Ayya gone, you must lead the Custodians. It's what he would have wanted. Men like you are rare in these times, Moorthy. I don't mean to sound melodramatic, but what you know is both a bridge to the past and a key to the future. You will find your purpose. Go.' I look into his eyes and smile. 'This time, the coffee's on me.'

He gets up, holds out his hand. I grip it and we exchange a firm shake. 'Take care of yourself, Professor.' He walks away without looking back.

I watch him through the window till he disappears down the road and then turn back to my coffee, draining what is left of it before glancing at my watch – a new model that looks much like, but is not, my old HMT. It's time to deal with the last loose end.

Finding Maya isn't easy, but it isn't overwhelmingly difficult either. Moorthy has told me that Maya is living with her grandmother in Bengaluru. That much I could have ascertained on my own. When I'd asked him for the address, he had refused. 'She made me promise on Ayya's memory not to give it to anyone, Professor. She wanted nothing to do with her stepfather or her past. I don't think she ever expected that you'd turn up asking about her; else she wouldn't have been so categorical about it. However, it's not for me to break this promise.'

I hadn't pressed him. He is better off not knowing what happens next.

I buy a gun, a locally modified old-model pistol fitted with a state-of-the-art silencer. I do not bother to haggle over the price. The dealer asks no questions and doesn't give me a second glance.

In these times of gang rapes and acid attacks, people are only too cautious of outsiders in their area, ferreting for information. I am uncharacteristically appalled at how easy it is to circumvent even these small security measures, as I have. I hire a property agent to find my non-existent family and me a place to live – a task that takes some dexterity since I refuse, as always, to tell a lie. But it is done, and before I know it, I have an excuse to hang around the neighbourhood all day, go from one place to another making casual enquiries about the availability of ground water, the possibility of elderly companionship for my relatives and, of course, who the neighbours next door and further down the street might be.

I narrow my search down to two of the oldest residential areas in Bangalore. Malleswaram draws a dead end in two days, but Jayanagar, with its quiet, tree-lined roads and the omnipresent smell of filter coffee in the air, holds more promise. There are fewer apartments here and more individual houses, most of them built with carefully saved and completely accounted for retirement funds to cover as much of the plot of land they rest on as possible.

Just when I begin to think that I might need to sponsor a gulab-jamun-making competition in the neighbourhood to find Maya's culinary expert of a grandmother, I see the two of them coming out of a small Ganesha temple at the junction of a residential side road and the main street. I stay where I am, out of sight, wondering how to ditch my property agent in the next thirty seconds so that I can follow them, but it turns out to be unnecessary: Instead of hailing an autorickshaw or getting into a waiting car, Maya and her grandmother start walking down the by-lane, turning left at the first crossroad.

When the agent shows me the next house, I tell him I love it, I'm travelling for the next three days and shall contact him upon return. As soon as he leaves, I throw away the

SIM card on my cellphone and make my way back to the area where I had seen the two women.

I park down the street, keep the near-illegal tinted windows rolled up and open out a newspaper for effect. The car is a temporarily borrowed one – the euphemism my own for a morally acceptable modus operandi of stealing a car with every intention of bringing it back. Sometimes I even fill the tank with petrol.

I don't have to idle for long; I see Maya emerge from a white and red cottage-style house about ten doors down. She is wearing her usual short kurta with a pair of cotton pants, and her hair is in a ponytail. I can't be sure from this distance, but I think I see small silver hoops in her ears. She goes into another house a couple of gates ahead and re-emerges with an excited Labrador on a leash. His antics draw a smile from her, but it does not last long. If anything, she seems sadder than before, as though always aware of what is lost. I've had enough for one day. I start the car and drive off, heading back to the office block I'd taken it from. I leave it exactly as I'd found it, so the owner wouldn't even know it had been gone, though he...or she...might think the fuel tank has a leak – I am too preoccupied today to return the favour for the use of the car.

I spend a sleepless night, trying to reason with an absent inner voice. I hear no advice, no objections and no cynical observations. I am acutely alone.

In the morning, I head out after a late and leisurely breakfast, stopping on the way first to acquire a new ride for the day, and then to buy the largest bouquet of flowers that I can find.

I discover Maya leaving her house as I drive up and follow her autorickshaw all the way to Blossoms, a bookstore in the city not too far away from where I borrowed today's car. I risk the unappealing green sedan being towed away by parking right in front of a gate and make my way into the store. The towering stacks of books, their pages crackling with dreams, hopes and fears, draw me in. I find Maya in between those ceiling-high stacks, and watch her from a distance as she takes her time, browsing through everything from poetry to history and the comics section. She lays a loving hand on a book and then, briefly, she comes to life. When that happens, I find myself becoming even more resolute as to what it is I must do. She deserves so much better than this tortured existence. She deserves so much more than to live this way.

Slipping out of the bookstore before she leaves, I head back to her house. I park my car a couple of streets away and make my way to the temple where I had first spotted her. As I expect, her grandmother heads there in the evening. By the indiscreet but efficient means of eavesdropping from behind a pillar as the old lady chit-chats with her neighbour of twenty years, I learn of her concern that Maya, since she turned up over a year ago, meets no one and does nothing but read, walk the neighbour's dog and spend her days in silence.

The neighbour suggests heartbreak. The grandmother sounds all the more forlorn for it. I listen with clenched teeth and decide it has been enough. I walk back to where I've left the car and bring it round to wait near Maya's front door.

The streetlights have come on by the time she arrives. I watch her get out of the autorickshaw, lugging three recycled paper bags, each one filled to the brim with books. As light from the open front door hits her, I can see the dark rings that frame her eyes. She doesn't sleep, I know, her waking dreams haunted by a potent combination of horror and regret. I ache to hold her close and tell her that she is safe, safe for as long as she lives, for I will watch over her. I want to run my hands over her tormented body, soothing away all fear, feeling her melt at my touch. I imagine trailing my fingers over every curve and secret crevice, making her writhe with need, till finally, I wrap them around her graceful neck and squeeze. I want to see the veins bulge in blue-green protest against her skin. As she stiffens, caught between fear and ecstasy, I want to whisper in her ear, as I would a passion-laced endearment: 'Traitor.' I flex my fingers in instinctive reaction, then lay them on my lap, palms upward, and wait.

Maya appears on the balcony. She has changed into a faded T-shirt and her hair is wet. I wonder if she has been crying in the shower, if she cries often, and how much longer it will be before she finds forgiveness for her betrayal. She glances at the parked car, but I know she can't see inside it. A few more minutes of looking around and then she heads back indoors.

She doesn't deserve to live this way. Nor do I. Mine is a world where we worship the sacred with our actions, a world where death is sacrifice, and it is good.

With that thought, I pick up the bouquet of wilting flowers that has been on the passenger seat all day. My gun lies beneath. I tuck the weapon into the waistband of my pants, under my shirt, the metal cold against my skin.

I walk up to the red and white house and ring the doorbell. The pleasantly rotund grandmother attends at once. Her face is kind, and she bears her aged beauty with grace. It strikes me that Maya might come to look like her as she grows older.

'Namaste,' I say, folding my hands together around the large bunch of flowers. 'I'm sorry to drop in this way, but I'd like to see Maya, please?'

I wait, taking in the smell that is a soothing blend of coffee powder and incense sticks, the light fragrance of the oil-wick lamp in front of what I expect would be a mini-pantheon of framed poster gods and silver and bronzed statuettes. The house is tastefully decorated, and I can see Maya's preference for cotton fabrics and tribal block prints in the cushions and the tablecloth. Books cover an entire wall of the living room and newspapers lie scattered on the coffee table in the imperfect way of a real home. Beyond, a kitchen beckons, with its whistling pressure cooker, the aroma of tamarind and the light crackling sounds of mustard and curry leaves being seasoned.

The grandmother is still evaluating me with a mix of uncertainty and hope. She looks again at the flowers and settles on hope. I suspect she thinks me the errant boyfriend come to make amends, and that in her mind she is already buying wedding sarees and naming great-grandchildren. I don't bother to deny the tinge of regret that hits me.

'I'm sorry,' she says eventually, flustered. She turns in the general direction of the stairs that lead to the upper floor and calls out, 'Maya! Maya, someone's here to see you.' Coming back to me, she asks, 'I didn't get your name?'

I hear Maya's tread on the wooden steps and smile in anticipation. 'Asvatthama. My name is Asvatthama,' I say.

Stepping inside, I shut the door behind me and ring the bolt home.

Acknowledgements

Counting my blessings, and the list continues to grow with each book.

Jai, the man who dislikes fantasy but loves his wife.

Shobana, for patiently reminding me for the thousandth time that it was 2 a.m. and even rakshasis were asleep.

Boozo, son who begot the mother; Zana, daughter of my soul; and Maya, who taught me to believe in eternity.

Poulomi Chatterjee, for putting up with me on many counts.

The team at Hachette India, especially Avanija Sundaramurti and Thomas Abraham for their faith in the book. A special thanks to Sohini Pal for her many inputs on the text and the really cool diagram, and Arushi Pareek for her work on the proofs.

Amish Raj Mulmi, for his suggestions, particularly the jellyfish.

Kunal Kundu, for the awesome cover illustration and his astounding levels of commitment, and Maithili Doshi Aphale, for the beautiful initial cover concepts and her patience.

Sukanya Venkatraghavan and Aravind N.V. for rescuing this book the many times it nearly drowned in despair. Please note that all death threats received by yours truly shall be redirected to your respective addresses.

Aravind and Siddharth Sekhar Barpanda, for beta-reading the science references and making sure I wasn't putting my (other) foot in my mouth (too).

Jayapriya Vasudevan, super-agent and friend – can't believe how far we've come.

My long-suffering family – Jaya and K.S. Krishnamurthy, thanks for your support. Chitra and N.S. Vembu, thank you for being proud of me.

Finally, all those individuals I know I'll remember as having missed thanking in the middle of some night one month after the book has gone to press. Please know that if your name is not here it is not because I lack gratitude.